No man s'

en,

A MOST
UNSUITABLE MAN

ALSO BY JO BEVERLEY

Winter Fire
Skylark
St. Raven
Dark Champion
Lord of My Heart
My Lady Notorious
Hazard
The Devil's Heiress
The Dragon's Bride
"The Demon's Mistress" in
In Praise of Younger Men
Devilish
Secrets of the Night
Forbidden Magic
Lord of Midnight
Something Wicked

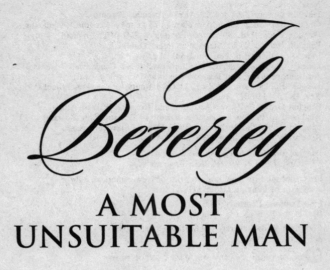

A MOST
UNSUITABLE MAN

A SIGNET BOOK

SIGNET
Published by New American Library, a division of
Penguin Group (USA) Inc., 375 Hudson Street,
New York, New York 10014, USA
Penguin Group (Canada), 10 Alcorn Avenue, Toronto,
Ontario M4V 3B2, Canada (a division of Pearson Penguin Canada Inc.)
Penguin Books Ltd., 80 Strand, London WC2R 0RL, England
Penguin Ireland, 25 St. Stephen's Green, Dublin 2,
Ireland (a division of Penguin Books Ltd.)
Penguin Group (Australia), 250 Camberwell Road, Camberwell, Victoria 3124,
Australia (a division of Pearson Australia Group Pty. Ltd.)
Penguin Books India Pvt. Ltd., 11 Community Centre, Panchsheel Park,
New Delhi - 110 017, India
Penguin Group (NZ), cnr Airborne and Rosedale Roads, Albany,
Auckland 1310, New Zealand (a division of Pearson New Zealand Ltd.)
Penguin Books (South Africa) (Pty.) Ltd., 24 Sturdee Avenue,
Rosebank, Johannesburg 2196, South Africa

Penguin Books Ltd., Registered Offices:
80 Strand, London WC2R 0RL, England

First published by Signet, an imprint of New American Library,
a division of Penguin Group (USA) Inc.

First Printing, February 2005
10 9 8 7 6 5 4 3 2 1

To the "Get Caught Reading at Sea" readers. You were all so much fun, especially in the "gaming hell."

Prologue

December 26, 1763
Rothgar Abbey, England

On this, the day after Christmas, the great hall of Rothgar Abbey was merry with holly, ivy, and mistletoe, all tied up with festive ribbons. The massive Yule log burned in the hearth, and spiced oranges scented the air.

The Marquess of Rothgar had invited many of his family to his home this Christmastide, and this chamber had been the heart of the celebrations. Now, however, the guests were drawn to a very different sort of entertainment.

Scandal.

The Dowager Marchioness of Ashart, short, plump, and ferocious, had just stormed into the house. She had brushed aside the welcome of one grandson, the Marquess of Rothgar, and commanded her other grandson, the Marquess of Ashart, to leave this hated roof immediately.

No one was surprised at that. The Trayce family, headed by Lord Ashart, had been at daggers drawn with the Mallorens, headed by Rothgar, for a generation. All of the guests had been astonished that Ashart had attended the gathering, and no one was surprised by the dowager's outrage. But how could he respond to being ordered around like a puppy? All eyes turned to the handsome, dark-haired young man who was notorious for his temper.

"Why not stay?" Ashart asked the dowager with remarkable mildness. "There are family matters to discuss."

"I wouldn't stay in this house if it were the last one in England!" she snapped.

He shrugged. "Then allow me to present to you the lady who is to be my bride—Miss Genova Smith."

Not a few of the guests gasped, while others began to compose in their minds letters to friends describing the shocking announcement. Ashart, to marry his great-aunts' companion!

"What?" screeched the dowager, turning red as a holly berry. Then she looked around with furious eyes. "I heard the Myddleton chit was here. Where is she?"

All eyes turned to a straight-shouldered young woman in a green striped gown whose cheeks suddenly flushed with red. The color didn't become her and she was no beauty to begin with. Her hair was an ordinary brown, her eyes blue, and her lips too thin for fashion. At the moment those lips were tight with anger.

Damaris Myddleton hated being the center of attention, but she'd been watching the scene in horrified fascination and growing fury. Ashart was *hers*.

When she'd discovered she was rich she'd determined on making a grand marriage. She'd had her trustees draw up a list of the neediest young, titled gentlemen in England. She'd studied it carefully and picked the Marquess of Ashart.

Since then, she'd visited his country seat and been approved by the dowager. Her trustees were even now negotiating with Ashart's lawyers, drawing up marriage settlements. It was all settled barring the formal

proposal and the signatures. He couldn't marry someone else! He needed her money, and he was her key
to her acceptance into the world of the aristocracy.

What should she do? Her instinct was to shrink
away from so many unfriendly eyes but she would not
be a coward. She stepped forward and curtsied to the
old lady. "I'm glad you've arrived, Lady Ashart. I
haven't known what to do. As you know, Ashart is
already promised to me."

Silence fell, and it was as if a chilly draft brushed
Damaris's neck—a faint warning that perhaps she'd
just made a terrible mistake. She glanced around,
painfully aware of being an outsider. She had no blood
connection to the Mallorens, and was here only because her guardian was Lord Henry Malloren. She
came from a simple family and she didn't know the
rules of this world. Had she broken an important one?

Part of her wanted to run away and hide. But she
would not—could not—let Genova Smith steal Ashart
from under her nose!

Beautiful, blond Miss Smith broke the tense silence.
"You must be mistaken, Miss Myddleton."

"Of course she is," Ash snapped.

That brought hot, angry blood to Damaris's face
and fire to her courage. "How could I be mistaken
about that?" She swung to the dowager. "Is it not
true?"

It seemed as if all the listeners held their breaths.

Lady Ashart fixed cold eyes on her grandson.
"Yes," she said. "It is."

Damaris swung triumphantly to the marquess, but
before she could demand an apology, Miss Smith
reacted.

"You rancid fish!" she yelled at him. "Scum on the
sewer of life!" Then she ran into the breakfast room
and returned to throw food at him.

Damaris watched, as aghast as everyone else, but

inclined to cheer Miss Smith on. She'd like to hurl some stewed fruit at the wretch herself.

But then Ashart went onto one knee, stained, messy, but still gorgeous. "Sweet Genni, forgiving Genni, redoubtable Genni. Marry me? I love you, Genni, I adore you—"

"*No!*" Damaris screamed, her voice clashing with the dowager's bellow of "*Ashart!*"

Damaris ran forward in a rage, but strong hands snared her from behind. "Don't," a man said softly in her ear. "You'll only make it worse."

Fitzroger. Ashart's friend, who'd pestered her over the past days, preventing her from staying as close to Ashart as she'd wished. And look what had come of it! She struggled but was relentlessly drawn back out of the crowd, farther away from Ashart.

Then she heard Genova Smith say, "Yes, Ash, beloved, I'll marry you."

"*No!*" Damaris screamed. "He's *mine!*"

A hand came over her mouth, and then another pressed at her neck.

Everything went black.

Damaris came to her swimming senses to realize that she was being carried upstairs. Carried by Fitzroger. She couldn't find the will to protest, for behind her she heard chatter and laughter.

Oh, God. She'd lost Ashart! But worse than that, everyone was laughing at her. She'd mortified herself in front of the people she'd tried so hard to impress, among whom she'd hoped to belong. Now they were laughing at that silly Miss Myddleton who thought her wealth could buy her a place among them. Miss Myddleton, daughter and heiress of a man who, after all, had been little better than a pirate.

She was placed on her bed and could hear her maid Maisie's anxious, questioning voice. She kept her eyes closed, as if that might change everything, make everything right. Someone raised her and put a glass to her lips. She recognized the smell. Laudanum. She hated opium and its lingering effects, but she swallowed it gratefully. She only wished it had the power to wipe away the past hour and let her react with more dignity.

The curtains were drawn around the bed. Voices became dim whispers. As she waited for the drug to take effect, Damaris's mind whirled around and around disaster.

She could not bear to face any of those people again.

Who was she, after all? For the first twenty years of her life she'd known no finer home than Birch House, Worksop. It was an adequate house for a gentleman physician like her grandfather, but nothing compared to Rothgar Abbey or even Ashart's decrepit seat, Cheynings.

Until a year ago, in fact, she'd lived in genteel poverty, for within months of marrying her mother, her father had gone adventuring and the little he'd sent home had not allowed for luxuries. Or so Damaris had been told. She and her mother had made all their own clothes and mended them again and again. Food had been of the simplest, much of it grown in their garden. They'd had servants, but clumsy young ones, because as soon as they were trained, they left for higher wages.

But upon her mother's death, Damaris had learned the truth. Her father had become extremely wealthy, and he'd left nearly all his fortune to her. He had even arranged for a remarkable guardian if both he and her mother died while she was young. That guardian was Lord Henry Malloren, the elderly uncle of the great Marquess of Rothgar.

That was why Damaris was at Rothgar Abbey. Lord Henry and his wife had wanted to attend and they'd had

no choice but to bring their unwelcome responsibility—
Damaris—with them.

Damaris had been delighted to escape Lord Henry's
dull home and to have an opportunity to learn more
about the glittering aristocratic world which would
soon be her own when she became Marchioness of
Ashart.

How had she ever thought to reach so high?

She should have known that a person didn't change
because of fine clothes and magnificent jewels. Covering a dung heap with silk, they called it in Worksop.

She didn't truly belong here, and she couldn't bear
to face their sniggering tomorrow. As darkness gathered in her mind, she knew she would have to leave.

Chapter 1

At crack of dawn the next day a coach sped away from Rothgar Abbey as fast as the overnight snow would allow. Inside, Damaris prayed that they'd not be caught in a drift. Briggs, her guardian's coachman, had dourly predicted that they'd not get far, and if they did it would snow again and stop the journey, but she'd poured out guineas until he agreed.

Being one of the richest women in England had to be useful for something.

What if she was pursued? The crunch of her coach wheels and the pounding of the horses' hooves blocked any sound of pursuit—or perhaps she was deafened by the pounding of her own frantic heart.

"It'll come to disaster; I know it will," Maisie prophesied, for perhaps the twentieth time. Twenty-five-year-old Maisie was plump, plain, and generally merry, but today every line of her round face curved downward. "How're we going to get all the way back home without being caught, miss?"

Damaris would have screamed at her except that Maisie could be the only friend she had left in the world. "I told you. We only need to reach the London road and buy tickets north. I'm twenty-one. The Mallorens can't drag me off a public stage."

Maisie's grim silence said, *I wish I were sure of that.*

Damaris felt the same doubt. The Mallorens seemed to be a law unto themselves, and her guardian, Lord Henry, was a tyrant.

Perhaps they wouldn't care. Perhaps they'd be glad to see the back of her.

The coach swayed as it turned out of the park of the abbey. It was probably irrational, but she felt relief at no longer being on Malloren property.

She began to look ahead. She would switch to a public coach at Farnham, then in London buy tickets north. Once back at Birch House . . . Her vision ended there. She had no idea what she'd do then. She'd probably be back in poverty, because her father's will allowed her guardian to withhold her money if she didn't live where he said and do as she was told. She would hate it, but she could survive with little. And it would be only until she was twenty-four—

Movement in the corner of her eye made her whirl to her right.

A rider thundered by her window. Fine horse. Fine rider. Wild blond hair flying in the wind.

Fitzroger?

No!

He cut off her coach. It shuddered to a halt and the coachman said, "Trouble, sir?"

The reply came in that crisp, cool voice that had tormented her for days. "I need a word with Miss Myddleton."

Maisie moaned. Damaris wanted to. Instead of a means of escape, the coach now felt like a trap.

Fitzroger rode to the window and looked in. He was always plainly dressed, but now he looked the very picture of a vagabond. His blond hair curled loose about his shoulders, his shirt lay open at the neck, and he wore no waistcoat beneath his plain blue jacket. He was as good as undressed!

His ice-blue eyes seemed . . . what? Exasperated? What right did Ashart's penniless friend have to be exasperated with her?

Damaris let down the window, but only to lean out and call, "Drive on, Briggs!" Cold air cut at her. Briggs, plague take him, didn't obey.

Fitzroger grasped the edge of the window frame with his bare hand. He couldn't hold back the coach by brute force, but that commanding hand unnerved her, preventing her from raising the glass between them.

Bare hand. Bare neck. Bare head.

She hoped he froze to death. "What do you want, sir?"

"But a moment of your time, Miss Myddleton."

He released the coach and swung off the horse, calling for the groom to come down and take the animal. That snapped Damaris back to action. She leaned out farther and yelled, "Drive on, you spine-less varlet!"

She could have saved her frozen breath. Despite the extortionate bribe she'd paid him, Briggs was abandoning her at the first challenge. If she knew how to drive, she'd climb up on the box and take the reins herself.

The wide-eyed young groom, in his frieze coat, gloves, and hat, appeared outside the window and took charge of the horse. Fitzroger opened the door, smiling—but at Maisie, not Damaris. "Return to the house behind the groom. I'll bring your mistress back shortly."

"No, he won't. Maisie, do not dare to obey him!"

Maisie, the traitor, scrambled toward the door. Damaris grabbed her skirt to stop her. Fitzroger chopped sharply at her hand, shocking it open, and pulled Maisie free.

Damaris gaped at him, her hand still tingling. "How *dare* you."

She reached for the door to slam it, but the man leaped into the coach and closed it himself. He took the seat opposite her and addressed the groom through the open window. "Take the maid up to the house, and keep quiet about this."

"Aye, sir."

Pure fury blazed through Damaris, and she reached for the holstered pistol by her seat. She knew nothing of guns, but surely one had only to point one and pull the trigger.

A strong hand closed over hers. He said nothing, but she was suddenly unable to move, frozen by his bare hand controlling hers and his cool, steady eyes.

She pulled free and sat back, tucking her hands back in her muff and directing her eyes to a spot behind his head. "Whatever you have to say, Mr. Fitzroger, say it and be gone."

He leaned out of the window. "Walk the horses, coachman, and you might as well turn them."

Back toward the house. She wouldn't return—she couldn't—but right now she didn't see how to prevent it. Tears choked her, but she swallowed them. It would be the final straw to cry.

He raised the window, cutting off the bitter winter air, but trapping her in this enclosed space with him. Their legs could hardly avoid contact, and she could almost feel his heat.

"You don't really want to run away, you know."

She responded to that with silence.

"I'm impressed that you persuaded Lord Henry's servants to carry you away. How did you manage that?"

"Guineas," she said flatly, "which I have in abundance, and you, sir, significantly lack."

"Whereas I have understanding of this world in abundance, which you, Miss Myddleton, significantly lack."

She fired a look at him. "Then you understand that I am ruined."

"No, but this mad flight might do it."

She looked away again, out at the bleak scene. "I won't be here to find out."

But how did she escape? Fitzroger looked impervious to reason or tears. Despite his obvious poverty, she didn't think he could be bribed.

"You have a fighting spirit," he said, "but a fighter needs to understand the terrain. Running away won't help, because you'll have to meet all those people again one day. Unless you intend to live like a hermit."

When in doubt, attack. "It's Ashart who should be ashamed. He was supposed to marry me. You know he was."

"He was supposed to marry your money."

It hurt to have the truth stated so bluntly, but Damaris met his eyes. "A fair bargain. My wealth for his title. He'll not survive without it."

"A penny saved is a penny earned."

She let out a bitter laugh. "He's planning economy? *Ashart?* He of the diamond buttons and the splendid horses?"

"A point, I grant you, but what's done is done. It is your future that matters now."

She suddenly wondered if she saw the reason for this interference. Fitzroger was a mystery to her, but he was clearly poor. He survived as unpaid companion to Ashart.

"I'll not trade my fortune for less, sir, if that is your plan."

If the truth hurt him, he hid it well. "I wouldn't aspire so far above my station. Think of me as Sir Galahad, Miss Myddleton, riding to the maiden's rescue from pure and noble motives."

"I don't *need* rescue. I need only to be allowed to go on my way."

He looked as if he might shake her, but then he relaxed, stretching out his long legs so they brushed her wide skirts. She almost shifted away but stopped herself in time.

"I embarrassed myself once," he said. "I was fifteen, a freshly minted ensign, proud of my uniform but certain that everyone knew I was a lad pretending to be a soldier. I was hurrying across the busy barracks square one day and stepped back to make way for one of the officers' wives. Alas, I hooked up the skirts of another with my sword. It tangled with some ribbon or some such and I couldn't pull it free, so I turned, which made matters worse. Her legs were exposed up beyond the knees, and she was shrieking at me to stop. I was sweating and desperate. I tried to back away. Something ripped. . . . I was certain that no one would ever forget it. I'd have taken ship to the Indies if I could. But after some teasing, it ceased to matter."

She could imagine all too well, and felt some sympathy, but said, "It's hardly the same."

"True. My misfortune was pure accident, whereas yours is to some extent willful. You wanted the prize you'd picked out, and if I hadn't stopped you yesterday—"

"Stopped me! I still have the bruises." But the whole horrible event rushed back to her as if it were happening right then. She leaned forward in desperation, pulling her hands from her muff to beg. "Please let me go. Please! I'm going to my old home. I'll be safe."

He took her hands. She tried to tug free, but

strength seemed to have deserted her, and her vision
was blurred by tears.

"Flee and your bad behavior will be fixed in people's minds. Return, seem in good spirits, and everyone will doubt their own memory of events."

She blinked, trying to read truth or error in his face.
"Every detail must be etched in their minds."

"Every detail is etched in yours, as my sword misad-
venture was etched in mine. In the minds of others, it's
merely part of a tumult of fascinating drama, and for
the most part you were the injured party. We can return
you to that, to the point where people sympathize."

She snatched her hands free. "With a pitiable creature, jilted because all her jewels and riches couldn't
compensate for a plain face, awkward manners, and
inferior birth."

She froze, unable to believe that she'd just exposed
her secret shame to this man; then she covered her
face with a hand.

He swung over to sit beside her and gently tugged
her hand down. "Begging for compliments, Miss
Myddleton?"

Damaris had to look at him, but she could hardly
think with his body suddenly so close in the confinement of the coach seat. She'd lived most of her life
in a world without men, without their effect at close
quarters. Now this man pressed against her at leg and
arm, and his strong, warm hand enfolded hers.

"You can't compete with Genova Smith in beauty,"
he said. "Few can. But plain, no. And I've seen nothing amiss with your manners except when strain over
Ashart rode you. Come back with me. I promise to
stand by you, to make sure everything turns out as
you would wish."

His tone as much as his words shivered along her
nerves, weakening her will. Was it possible?

"How can I? What will I have to do?"

"Face them and smile."

Damaris's mouth dried, but she recognized the second chance she'd prayed for in the night. She wasn't sure it was possible to regain her foothold here, but she had to take the opportunity if only to prove to herself that she wasn't a coward as well as a fool.

Logic didn't defeat fear, however, and she had to fight a tight throat to speak. "Very well, I'll return and put on a glad face. But I hold you to your promise. You will stand by me?"

His smile was remarkably sweet. "I will."

He had to have an eye on her fortune—no other reason explained his apparent kindness. "Before you go any further, Mr. Fitzroger, please understand that while I appreciate your help, I will never, ever offer you my hand and fortune."

"Damaris, not every man who does you a service will be after your money."

"Are you claiming to have no desire to marry riches? I cannot believe that."

He shrugged. "I'd take your fortune if you offered it, but you won't do anything so foolish, will you?"

"No."

"Then we know where we stand."

How could he tie her in knots by agreeing with her?

"Lord Henry is taking you to London for the winter season, isn't he? You'll have your pick of the titled blooms there. A duke, even. Think of it. As a duchess, you'll outrank Genova, Marchioness of Ashart."

He seemed to see right into her petty soul, but she couldn't deny the appeal of that. That list of the needy, titled gentlemen had included a duke—the Duke of Bridgewater. She'd passed over him because he'd sounded dull, but high rank had its charms.

"What are you plotting now?" he asked in lazy amusement. "You make me nervous."

"I wish that were true."

"Any sensible man gets nervous when confronted with an inexperienced lady weaving plots."

"Inexperienced?" she objected, but in truth she could hardly claim otherwise.

"Very. Are you experienced enough, for example, to choose your husband wisely?"

"Are you offering to guide me?"

At that moment, perhaps from some reaction of his, she recognized that she'd spoken flirtatiously. She would have said that she didn't know how to flirt, but she was doing so, and it shook her.

If she were going to flirt, it should never be with this man. If she'd asked her trustees to draw up a list of the *least* suitable men she might meet in polite society, Octavius Fitzroger would have been near the top of it.

Octavius was the name given to an eighth child, so he came from a large and probably impoverished family. He was without employment, seemed to enjoy idleness, and she'd heard rumors at Rothgar Abbey about some dark scandal in his past. She'd been too intent on pursuing Ashart to find out more, but she knew some of the guests were surprised, even shocked, that he'd been allowed in the house.

All the same, when he took her hand and raised it to his lips, when he murmured, "I could be your guide in many things . . ." Damaris's grasp on common sense faltered.

He's kissing your hand, nothing more, she told her misty mind, but it didn't help. Her heart pounded, and moisture gathered in her mouth, forcing her to swallow or drool. When he leaned closer she recovered enough to put a hand on his chest. "No, sir!"

"Are you sure?"

No. His body felt like fire beneath her palm, for only his shirt covered his hard chest. If she slid her hand higher, her fingers would touch naked skin at the base of his throat. . . .

"Practice," he murmured, "leads to perfection."

"Practice?" she squeaked. "At what?"

"Flirtation." He raised a hand and brushed his knuckles down her slack jaw. "If you're happily flirting with me, no one will be able to believe that you're still pining for Ashart, will they?"

"Why would I ever choose you over him?" The question was rude, but the desperate truth.

His eyes danced with wickedness. "For Christmastide amusement. You're a wealthy young woman who is soon going to London to marry well, but for the moment you amuse yourself with me."

They were fixed in place, he stroking her jaw, she holding him off. It created a strange illusion of being within a magical circle, one she didn't want to break.

"Very well," she said, but clung to reason. She pushed at his chest and said, "There's no need to embrace here."

Her push achieved nothing but to press her hand harder against his heat and make breathing more difficult.

"No kiss as a reward, fair lady?" His fingers brushed between the fur lining of her hood and the skin of her neck. "Chinchilla," he murmured, making the word sound like a whisper of sin.

Oh, he was wicked, and she should push harder, even scream for help, but she wanted his kiss. Her mouth tingled for it.

"Just a kiss," he said softly. "Nothing more, I promise."

He dislodged her hand that was still feebly trying to hold him off and took her into his arms. She couldn't remember ever being touched like this before, with such tender power.

Resist, resist!

He caught any protest in a kiss.

She was helpless, but his embrace felt not at all forceful, except as a force of nature. Thought evaporated, and Damaris let him tilt her head so he could deepen the kiss, then let him crush her to his strong, hard body, enfold her, protect her.

His lips freed hers. Damaris opened stunned eyes to look into his. Silver blue around endless dark. But he looked insufferably pleased with himself.

She gripped his hair. His eyes widened. *Good.* Before he could resist, she pushed him back against the side of the coach and kissed him as thoroughly as he'd kissed her. She'd never done such a thing before, but let instinct rule as she whirled with him back into the storm.

When she broke the kiss to pant for breath, she realized she was straddling him. Her breasts ached, and she pressed them against him, returning stinging lips to his again and again and again—

He twisted away. "Damaris, we have to stop!"

"No."

"Yes."

Then she heard what he'd heard.

Gravel. They were nearing the stables!

She was back at Rothgar Abbey, and tangled in disaster again.

What had she been thinking?

She'd not been thinking at all. She'd been overtaken by a force as fierce as the panic that had driven her into flight. Heaven alone knew what would have happened if they'd not had to stop. As the coach rattled into the stable yard of Rothgar Abbey she stole one quick glance at him.

Her look clashed with his. She instantly looked away again, trying to interpret his dark, blank expression.

Lord Henry Malloren wrenched open the carriage door. "Pox on you, you plaguey chit! What in the name of the devil are you up to now to shame us all?"

Chapter 2

Fitz stared at the sinewy, red-faced man, trying to think what to do for the best. When Lord Henry grabbed his ward's arm, however, instinct took over. He chopped at the man's hand as he'd chopped at Damaris's, but a great deal harder. Lord Henry cursed and backed away, but he flailed the riding crop in his other hand. The crop he'd intended to use on his ward?

"Devil take you, sir! I'll have you in court for abduction and assault!"

Fitz swung around Damaris and out of the coach, putting himself between her and danger. "Be quiet and have some sense, Lord Henry. Do you want to provide a show for the stable yard?"

Lord Henry was old, scrawny, and a head shorter, but he leaned forward. "She's already made herself a laughingstock. What's one more folly?"

Damaris appeared by Fitz's side, hissing, "Stop it!" but Fitz didn't take his eyes off his opponent.

"We can discuss this in the house—"

"We will discuss this nowhere, cockerel!" Though Lord Henry didn't take his eyes off Fitz, he addressed his ward. "Get back in the coach and stay there, girl. We're leaving within the hour now that you've embarrassed us so badly."

"Not unless she wishes to."

Lord Henry curled a lip. "Her wishes have nothing to do with it, cockerel. She's under my thumb until she's twenty-four or marries with my consent. So you've years to wait before she can fall into the clutches of a scandal-ridden fortune hunter like you."

"I have no intention—" Damaris cried.

But Lord Henry cut her off with a blistering, "Do as you're told!"

Fitz used all his strength to control himself. "Lord Henry, no one is traveling far today. It will soon snow again."

The man glared at the gray heavens as if they were a personal affront, then turned on Damaris. "Then you'll come with me and be locked in your room."

He reached for her, but Fitz moved between them again. "No."

He worried that Lord Henry would expire with rage, so deep a red he turned, but then the man snapped, "So be it. You know the consequences, girl." He turned and marched off toward the house.

Fitz watched him go. "What did that mean?"

"If I don't do as he says, he will withhold my money."

He turned to look at her. She was almost as white as the snow. "All of it?"

"Every last farthing. Until, as he said, I'm twenty-four or marry with his consent."

" 'Struth. Three years isn't a lifetime, but it's long enough without a penny. But wouldn't running away have had the same effect? How did you hope to survive?"

"In poverty," she said flatly. "But I'm no stranger to that. The Worksop house is mine. That was my mother's, so it isn't governed by my father's will. I have a home, and I'd sell the contents down to the pots and sheets if necessary."

"No need for such high drama, is there? The emeralds you wore on Christmas Day would support most people for a few lifetimes."

She turned stark eyes on him. "But they *do* come under my father's will, you see."

Lord above. One of the richest women in England might be reduced to selling household items to survive. Of course, it would never come to that, because she could not be allowed to live unprotected. It would be like leaving a gold nugget in the street and expecting no one to steal it.

There had to be a way around this, but Fitz needed more information, and he needed to get to a fire. His exposed skin was burning with cold. He'd been an idiot to rush out so inadequately dressed, but when he'd looked out of the window and glimpsed the coach, some instinct had told him whom it contained and why. He'd dashed to prevent her flight without a thought.

Now, after that kiss, his urgency was warning of a problem he definitely didn't need to add to his quota. He could not grow too close to Damaris Myddleton. At least he'd have her full cooperation in that. She intended to marry the highest title she could buy and would never consider a man like himself, as she'd made crisply clear.

He put an arm around her and urged her out of the stable yard. "We must return to the house. I'm cold, and even though you're in furs, in my experience ladies never wear warm enough shoes."

"You think we should wear boots?"

"Why not? A grand heiress can do anything she wants."

"Not obviously," she dryly pointed out.

It made him laugh. She was forthright and clever, and over the past days he'd often found himself delighted with her, even as he'd been exasperated by her unseemly pursuit of Ashart.

As they crunched through snow toward the house he laid out her situation. "Listen to me. Forget Worksop. You cannot live unprotected. Every fortune hunter in England is after you."

"I suppose you'd know."

"I am *not* a fortune hunter."

She flicked him a skeptical glance. "I don't see any problem, anyway. If I don't have my money, there's nothing for them to hunt."

"That shows your ignorance. Your husband could borrow against the expectations."

"Oh." She frowned, and Fitz thought he'd won that point, but then she looked up at him. "So *I* could borrow against my expectations."

He felt as if his hair must be standing on end. "No one would permit it."

"How could they prevent it?"

"They'd find a way. In truth, I'd find a way."

"It seems most unfair."

"And that surprises you?"

As he'd suspected, at heart she was practical. "No unfairness perpetrated on women surprises me. But it's a relief to know that if the worst happens, I need not beg in the streets."

The worst? She had no idea of the worst. She was a lamb in a forest thick with ravenous wolves. A lamb who thought she had sharp teeth.

She needed a strong protector, someone to guide her through this dangerous world and teach her how to survive. He certainly could be neither protector nor guide, even though he had the knowledge. His hold on a place in the highest social circles was by the fingernails, and besides, he planned to leave England as soon as he was able.

The snow hid the paths, so they were making a beeline for the house, but his booted foot suddenly sank deep. He held her back, found more stable footing, and helped her to it.

"Why is Lord Henry your guardian?" he asked as they went on, part of his mind trying to remember the layout of the grounds here. They were safely away from the ha-ha, at least, the deep trench that kept the deer from the gardens. "You have no connection to the Mallorens, have you?"

"None at all. It seems my father persuaded him."

"How?"

Her eyes smiled with a touch of real humor. They were slightly slanted—cat's eyes—and they fascinated him.

"With money," she said. "Lord Henry's a wealthy man, but he's the sort who always wants more. As I understand it, he became interested in an investment in one of my father's ships—or one was dangled before him. My father suggested that instead of laying out money, he simply promise to be my guardian if I were left an orphan. It must have seemed a safe gamble to Lord Henry. I was fourteen at the time. In ten years I'd be independent, and my parents were healthy people in their prime. Certainly my father lived a dangerous life, but my mother's was the epitome of safety. It was Lord Henry's misfortune that she died at forty-eight. If my father hadn't already died four years earlier, I'd suspect him of engineering it so that I might invade the highest levels of society as he failed to. Lord Henry would hate to admit it, but he was captured, by a pirate—lock, stock, and aristocratic connections."

Which could explain why Lord Henry was so vicious about it.

She was probably correct about her father. Fitz had seen the dossier Ash had been given on his prospective bride. Marcus Myddleton had been a black sheep of the Huntingdonshire Myddletons, who'd taken his wife's modest dowry and traveled to the Orient to make his fortune. He'd succeeded brilliantly, but been as much pirate as merchant.

It had probably amused Myddleton to gamble on the chance that his daughter would enter such elevated circles. But had he given a thought to his pawn in this game—his only child?

Fitz also wondered—had wondered for some time— why Damaris and her mother had lived so simply in Worksop before Mrs. Myddleton's death. He and Ash had assumed both mother and daughter preferred it that way. But her enjoyment of fashionable clothes and jewels—and her obvious desire for a brilliant marriage—suggested otherwise.

She stopped and looked up at the enormous house that now loomed over them. "Can Lord Henry forbid me entry?" she asked, a betraying quaver in her voice.

He'd not even considered that. He gently urged her toward a door. "No. It would be for Lord Rothgar to do, and I can't believe he would be so unjust."

"They do call him the Dark Marquess."

"Because of his position as power behind the throne, not because of his nature."

She stopped again. "He killed a man in a duel not long ago. Lord Henry crowed about it."

"You are in no danger from him. And besides, I'm your Galahad, remember, proof against all forces of darkness?"

She looked at him, clearly assessing the honesty of his words. Then she inhaled, turned, and marched resolutely toward the door.

His words had been light, but she'd accepted them as a vow, God help him.

He joined her at the door and stated the obvious. "The easiest way to escape Lord Henry is to choose a suitable man and marry quickly." When she flashed him a suspicious look, he raised a hand and added, "Not me. I'm the most *un*suitable."

It made her smile a little. "True. But I won't be hurried, especially after this debacle." She put her hand on the latch but paused again. "I don't know whether you've lured me back to hell or heaven, Mr. Fitzroger, but I do thank you for good intentions."

"The road to hell, they say, is paved with good intentions. But let us advance to paradise, which at the moment is the warmth of the kitchens."

He put his hand over hers and opened the door, then impelled her across the threshold. He felt her shudder. It might be relief at being inside, or fear of what lay ahead, or simply reaction to the warmth. His own hands had started to prickle as the warmth spilling from the nearby kitchen hit his icy fingers.

They were in a plain corridor lined with storage cupboards and pungent from the bundles of herbs and garlic hanging from the ceiling. Sounds and smells told of preparations for breakfast.

Ahead, Damaris's maid was slumped weeping against a wall, being comforted by another maid. She looked up, dabbing her streaming face with a sodden handkerchief. "Oh, Miss Damaris! He's ever so angry. He boxed my ears and has cast me off without a penny!"

Damaris ran to take her into her arms. "I'm so sorry, Maisie. But he can't dismiss you. You're my servant." The other maid slipped back to her duties, and Damaris glared at Fitz. "If you hadn't torn her from the coach, she wouldn't have had to face Lord Henry alone."

"True. Does he beat you?"

"No."

The maid said, "But—"

"Once. And I'd been very foolish."

"He slapped you that time, miss."

Having that revealed clearly embarrassed her, but it enraged him, no matter what she'd done.

"Hush, Maisie," she said. "Come along. We must return to my bedroom so I can prepare for . . . for whatever."

"So we're not leaving, miss? I thought it foolish to run away, but that were before. Now Lord Henry knows you tried to leave, there'll be the devil to pay."

"No, there won't. He's washed his hands of me."

The maid's eyes went round. "Lawks a mercy!"

Damaris turned to Fitz, and he saw the struggle before she asked for help. "What do I do?"

"I have a solution in mind, but we need to talk about it. I'll come with you to your bedchamber."

"What?"

"In the presence of your maid there's no scandal." When she hesitated, he added, "I'm not trying to compromise you, but this is not the place to talk of delicate matters."

As if to make his point, a manservant hurried out of the kitchen and down the corridor carrying a large covered bowl.

Her dazed eyes followed the servant for a moment, then returned to look at Fitz. "Very well."

Her maid looked as if she'd object, but with a sniff that might simply have been because of a runny nose, she turned and led them to the service stairs. After one shadowed look at him, Damaris followed.

She was wise to be suspicious, but illogically he wished she'd trust him.

They climbed the plain stairs and went through the door that was covered with green baize on one side and polished oak on the other, marking the transition from the servants' domain to the family's. They entered an opulent corridor lined with doors, and Fitz followed Damaris and her maid into a bedchamber.

Damaris turned to him, stripping off her gloves.

"Your solution, sir?" She was trying to hide her desperation, but failing.

Fitz went to the fire to warm his hands, making himself not go too close. He didn't need to add chilblains to his other problems. "What if you were to ask Lord Rothgar to replace Lord Henry as your guardian?"

She gaped at him. "What? Is it possible? Would he do it? I'm nothing to him. Wouldn't it be an imposition? A burden?" She clapped a hand over her mouth. "I'm babbling."

He couldn't stop a smile. She sounded as if she'd never babbled before.

"I suspect that becoming your guardian would be as much of a burden to Rothgar as an extra button on his coat. As head of the Malloren family, however, he's the logical choice to take over from his uncle."

"But wouldn't it seem like an insult to Lord Henry? And it's not necessary. He's given up the responsibility himself."

"No, he hasn't. If he had, he would have no power to keep you in poverty. Does he receive a handsome sum for the job?"

She caught his point immediately. "That he'd not want to give up? It's five hundred guineas a year on top of any actual costs, such as tutors, clothing, and travel. A substantial amount, but not to him." She stopped. "Why are you smiling like that?"

"Too many women think matters of money, even their own money, either beyond or beneath them."

"Lord Henry thought my interest unnatural."

"We will forget Lord Henry."

"Gladly, but he is my guardian. . . ."

"Unless you change that." He walked to her portable writing desk and opened the lid. "Request an appointment with Rothgar and put your petition."

She was rubbing her hands together now, but he

didn't think it was from cold. She glanced at the ticking clock on the mantelpiece. "It's not yet nine."

"The Dark Marquess, they say, never sleeps." He deliberately put command in his voice as he added, "Send the note."

She responded, coming over, sitting, then taking out a sheet of paper. He uncapped her inkwell and mended her quill. When he handed it to her she still seemed hesitant, but she shook herself, dipped the pen, and wrote a short message in a flowing but very even hand.

A week ago, Damaris Myddleton had been nothing more to Fitz than a name—the rich heiress Ash intended to marry. On arrival at Rothgar Abbey he'd found a persistent problem for his friend, whose heart was already lost to another. Though he'd privately thought Ash should marry Miss Myddleton's money, he'd done his best to draw her from the hunt. It had soon been as much for her sake as Ash's. She deserved better than marriage to a man who loved another.

She sanded the ink, then folded the paper, perfectly aligning the edges. Neat and efficient, but wild and willful.

A fascinating young woman.

He pulled back from perilous thoughts and tugged the bellpull, reminding himself that Damaris Myddleton could never be for him.

He'd served over ten years in the army and served well, achieving the rank of major. But Damaris Myddleton would have no interest in a mere major, even if his reputation was glorious and his name clear of scandal.

Neither was true.

Four years ago he'd made the mistake of saving the life of the king's uncle, the Duke of Cumberland. As reward, he'd been taken from his regimental duties and made a secret bodyguard. In order to be secret, he'd had to appear to be an idle equerry at various embassies and courts. Thus many had concluded that he was avoiding the battlefield.

That certainly hadn't done anything to restore his reputation, which had already been badly damaged by his affair with Orinda. When, four months ago, he'd sold his commission and returned to England for the first time in years, he'd hoped the old scandal would be dead. However, no one had forgotten the Fitzroger affair. Hardly surprising when his brother Hugh bellowed his outrage about it whenever he was drunk—which was most of the time.

He watched Damaris drip sealing wax onto the fold of the letter and press her signet into it. No, even if she showed interest in him he could never let it come to anything. He was only tolerated in the better circles for Ash's sake.

Not long after he'd arrived back in England he'd met Ash and discovered an instant friend. As Ash was currently out of favor at court—over a woman, of course—and weary of elegant society, Fitz's situation had presented little problem. Then Ash had impulsively decided to accept Rothgar's invitation to this Christmas celebration.

Fitz had approved, for he'd thought it time his friend responded to Rothgar's offers of peace, but he'd wondered how he would be received.

With Ash's friendship and Lord Rothgar's tacit acceptance, Fitz had not been cold-shouldered, but he'd been aware of how some people skillfully avoided more than passing conversation with him.

A knock announced a liveried footman. The maid, Maisie, carried the note to him and he left. It was done, and soon, God willing, Damaris would be in Rothgar's hands. Fitz would then be free to retreat to a safe distance.

She shot to her feet and paced the room. "This seems so bold. What if Lord Rothgar knows I tried to run away?"

He thought of lying, but she deserved better. "I'm sure he does. He has a reputation for omniscience."

"Oh, dear."

"Miss Damaris," said her hovering maid, "you need to change before visiting his lordship." A sharp glance from the maid's eye said that Fitz could leave now.

She was right, but Damaris was wound too tight. Fitz did what he'd do with a nervous subaltern before battle; he distracted.

"What sort of man was your father?"

Damaris shot him a puzzled glance. "My father? I met him precisely three times."

Fitz absorbed that. The dossier had mentioned that Marcus Myddleton had spent most of his last decades abroad, but not to that extent.

"How could that be?"

She shrugged. "He preferred to live abroad."

Something in her manner suggested she was keeping a detail back, but it was no business of his. "He seems to have been spectacularly successful at foreign trading, even though he died quite young. How old was he when he died?"

"Fifty-two."

"How did it happen?"

"On a ship attacked by pirates somewhere near Borneo."

"Do you know anything about his business affairs in Asia?"

She suddenly frowned at him. "Why?"

He chose honesty. "I'm distracting you."

Her blue eyes widened, but then she said, "Thank you. As for my father's affairs, you have to understand that until my mother's death I thought him a failed dreamer, all bluster and show."

"Good God, how could that be?"

"I knew only what my mother told me. We lived frugally, and she said it was because my father sent little money. That wasn't true. He was neglectful in other ways, but he sent generous amounts. She painted him as a monster in any way she could. How was I to know otherwise?"

"You discovered the truth upon his death?"

"Oh, no. Then, she said that even the small amount he'd sent had ended, so for four years we scrimped and saved, keeping on only Maisie as maid of all work." She smiled at the maid, who still seemed to glower at Fitzroger. "I think Maisie stayed on only from kindness to me."

"That I did, miss. Heaven knows where you'd have been without me. Are you not going to change, Miss Damaris, before speaking to his lordship?"

Damaris looked down at her brown woolen skirt and quilted jacket.

"It's not necessary," Fitz said.

"Your hair, then, miss. It's all messed up."

Damaris looked in the mirror and put her hand to her brown hair, blushing. Perhaps she remembered where it might have become disarranged—in the carriage, in those kisses.

She sat, and the maid began to pull out and reset hairpins to neaten the confection of plaits that held the hair close to her head. It was an unforgiving style, but Damaris's head was neatly shaped and her neck slender, so it suited her.

Fitz knew the maid thought he should leave, but he'd stay until he was sure everything was settled. "When did you find out you were rich?" he asked.

"After my mother's death," she replied, meeting his eyes in the mirror. The reflection made him more aware of her features. She wasn't a classic beauty, but she certainly wasn't plain. Her face was heart-shaped, but with a neat, square chin. Her lips were not full, but they were prettily curved.

"One of my trustees came to Birch House," she went on. "I didn't know I even had trustees. Dinwiddie and Fitch had always dealt with my mother because she was my guardian. I couldn't take in the vast amount Mr. Dinwiddie told me about, but I immediately ordered generous fires and a roast for dinner. Do you remember that sirloin, Maisie? Nothing since has been quite so delicious."

"That I do, Miss Damaris." The maid pushed in hairpins with obvious fondness. "And the cakes afterward."

"Cakes from the bakery," Damaris said, as if that were a wonder.

"And you hired a few extra servants."

"And bought new stockings rather than darning my old ones. And soft, perfumed soap. And chocolate." Her eyes closed and she smiled. "I'd never had chocolate to drink before."

"You shared it with me, miss, but I didn't care for it."

Damaris smiled at her maid. "That's because I like it with very little sugar, and you like everything sweet."

"I'll stick to good old English tea, miss. Strong and sweet."

Fitz managed not to laugh. "Good old English tea" came from India and China, and had probably been much of the basis of Marcus Myddleton's fortune. But he was touched by the obvious fondness between mistress and maid, and by this glimpse into Damaris's earlier life. What a strange upbringing she'd had.

"Then," Damaris said in a different tone, "Lord Henry arrived."

When silence fell, Fitz asked, "He was cruel?"

Damaris turned to him, her hair neat again. "No,

but he was a complete stranger, yet had command of my life, and he was brusque and cold. He moved me to his house in Sussex without a by-your-leave. I was happy to escape Birch House, but I had to fight to take Maisie. He wanted to hire what he called 'a proper lady's maid' for me. But I won, and thank heavens for that." She smiled back at the maid. "I don't know how I would have survived without you, Maisie. And you've become a lady's maid as I've become a lady."

The clock tinkled the hour of nine, startling her out of the past. She looked to the door as if begging the footman to return. Her hands worked, each fiddling with the rings on the other.

Back to distraction. "Are all your father's enterprises in the Orient?"

Her eyes flicked back to him. "You are perhaps overly interested in my fortune, for one who claims no interest at all."

"I'm fascinated," he said with truth. "For example, if your inheritance is abroad, who manages it?"

She still looked suspicious, but she said, "He left his trading companies, or houses as they call them, to the lieutenants who ran them for him. I merely receive part of the profits."

"And if they don't pay? It seems a perilous arrangement."

"Don't worry; I wouldn't starve. My father invested in properties here, and there's enough income from those to get by. I suspect he planned to return one day, a wealthy nabob."

She began to count on her fingers. "I own houses in London; five rural estates, including two with coal; an interest in a shipping company out of Bristol, plus docks there and in Liverpool; ten, I think, merchant ships; and a large part of the town called Manchester."

The "enough to get by" had clearly been ironic.

Fitz felt stunned. Perhaps her trustees had held back the full extent of her wealth, for he didn't remember such details in Ashart's dossier on her.

But this slender young woman with the sharp mind, bold spirit, and disastrous lack of worldly experience possessed extraordinary wealth. It was astonishing that she hadn't been snatched, seduced, or at least kidnapped for ransom.

And this morning, she'd tried to slip away.

He'd come up with the idea of Rothgar taking over her guardianship simply to remove her from Lord Henry's clutches. Now he realized it was essential. She must have the strongest and most powerful protector available.

A knock at the door at last. Maisie opened it and the footman announced, "The marquess will see you in his office at your convenience, Miss Myddleton."

That clearly meant now, for the man stood ready to escort her. Fitz saw her surreptitiously wipe sweating hands on her skirts, and he wanted to take her into his arms. He wanted to go with her, even speak for her. It wouldn't help—this she must do for herself—but he could escort her there.

He said so, adding, "In case Lord Henry tries to interfere."

She gave him a pale-faced, gallant smile and accepted the warm shawl the maid offered. Rothgar Abbey was luxuriously maintained, but no house could keep corridors warm in winter.

They left the room and followed the footman toward the center of the house.

"Thank heavens I didn't change my clothes," she said, breaking the silence. "I would hate to arrive at this appointment trembling."

He could kiss her for her brave spirit. "Didn't King Charles the First go to his execution in an extra layer of woolen underwear in case an uncontrolled shiver be mistaken for fear?"

She stared up at him. "Did he? I think I'd shiver if I were about to have my head cut off, no matter how warmly I was dressed."

"Especially considering how often the headsmen made a mess of it." Then he winced. "I'm sorry. Not a subject for a lady."

"Oh, I don't know. My mother delighted in reading stories about Christian martyrs. She even had books with illustrations."

They had arrived at the grand staircase that went down to the vast central hall. Festive garlands made it merry, but he knew the scene must remind Damaris that here, yesterday, she had mortified herself.

He gave her his arm down. At the bottom, the footman indicated that Damaris should follow him to the marquess's estate and business offices. Fitz knew he could go no farther.

"I'm sure this will go well," he said, "but I offer you good luck, for luck never comes amiss."

She dipped a curtsy. "I do thank you for your assistance, Mr. Fitzroger." Then she walked away, back straight, head high, even though he was sure she was quaking inside.

Chapter 3

Fitz wanted to hover until Damaris emerged from the interview, but he felt conspicuous. This early, most guests were still abed or breakfasting in their rooms, but two footmen stood in the hall, and voices told him some people were in the breakfast room. He'd rather not return to his bedchamber, however, because he was sharing one with Ash and had left him asleep.

When Ash had received Rothgar's invitation, he had declined to attend. To be precise, he'd thrown the invitation on the fire. Ash's patient secretary had written and sent the polite refusal.

Then Ash had encountered his great-aunts on their way here and changed his mind. His great-aunts' beautiful companion, Genova Smith, had been part of the reason, but Fitz suspected Ash had been glad of an excuse to take up the invitation. It certainly seemed now that the feud might be over.

Upon his arrival, a suitably grand bedchamber had had to be instantly found. Fitz had heard that Lord Henry had been asked to share a room with his unpleasant wife, which might explain some of his sour temper.

There'd been no question of finding a room for Fitz, so he was sharing with Ash. They'd done it often enough before, in inns and other crowded houses, but it meant that now he'd rather not disturb the sleeper.

Fitz crossed the hall to the enormous hearth where the massive Yule log still smoldered, as if seeking its warmth, though it couldn't do much for the vast chamber's chill. He had been impressed to notice that Rothgar provided his footmen with fur-lined jackets and warm gloves for duty such as waiting in the hall. Most employers were not so considerate.

Fitz wondered what Rothgar would make of his own part in Damaris's adventures. Would he, too, think him a fortune hunter? If so, what would he do?

He moved to the side of the hearth to consider the *presepe*, the Italian nativity scene that belonged to Genova Smith. It was as charming as she was. In fact, she was more than charming—she was clever, strong, and brave, and she'd make Ash an excellent wife in all respects if she were only rich.

The plan was that the Dowager Lady Ashhart had run the estates almost into ruin and Ash should marry a fortune to restore them.

The seeds of destruction had been sown in this house nearly forty years ago, when Ash's aunt, the Lady Augusta Trayce, had married the present Lord Rothgar's father. Within a year she had satisfactorily produced a son, but two years later she'd given birth to a daughter, fallen into a deep depression, and strangled the newborn babe.

Her horrific act had been kept out of the hands of the law, but she'd been confined here, where she'd died not long afterward, perhaps of guilt and grief. She'd been not yet twenty. Her mother, the present Dowager Marchioness of Ashart, had placed all the blame on the Mallorens. The Mallorens had destroyed her daughter, she claimed, so she would destroy them. Unfortunately, she'd been able to try, for her husband and two sons had been weak, indolent men willing to let her run their estates, and Ash had inherited as a child. She'd diverted every farthing into trying to destroy the Mallorens in politics, in society, and at court. Her efforts had generally been for naught, and in the past decades the Mallorens had grown rich and prospered under Rothgar's brilliant management.

"Ha! You, sir."

Fitz turned to find Lord Henry marching toward him. "Where is my ward, sir? Where is she, eh?"

"With Lord Rothgar, sir." After a moment's thought, he added, "Requesting that her guardianship be transferred to him."

"What?" The permanent red in Lord Henry's face deepened. "Impudent chit!" But then he added, "By gad, he might do it."

Fitz suddenly realized that Lord Henry had found his guardianship as unpleasant as Damaris had. It didn't excuse him, but presumably he wasn't going to fight for the right to continue it.

"Childless, you know," Lord Henry said. "Not used to young people around the house. Gives my wife the megrims. And she's a difficult young woman, sir. Very difficult. Willful. Unwomanly. Bold. Very bold. I don't hold with boldness in females. It always leads to trouble, as it has with her."

Fitz wondered exactly what she'd done to outrage the man, but he was also thinking that the qualities that upset Lord Henry were exactly the ones that appealed to him.

Lord Henry turned to look toward his nephew's office as if trying to see through the walls. But in the end, he grunted and marched off in the direction of the Tapestry Room, the more intimate of the Rothgar Abbey drawing rooms.

Well, Fitz thought. Everything was falling into place.

But then his idle glance caught one of the footmen sneering at him. The expression was instantly wiped away, but Fitz realized he was still in the state in which he'd ridden out after Damaris—in an open-necked shirt and with his hair loose.

The deuce! Hoping he wasn't blushing for it, he hurried away to repair his appearance. He entered the bedchamber quietly, but found Ash up and dressed, and being fluttered around by his valet, Henri.

"It must be love," Fitz commented dryly.

Ash threw the hairbrush at him. Fitz caught it, smiling. Despite the problems caused by Ash's betrothal, he delighted to see his friend facing a day brightly. Ash was not by nature dismal or violent, but he'd been raised under gloomy burdens and had moods as dark as his hair and eyes. Enter Genova Smith; enter light. *Long may it shine.*

"You're taking breakfast downstairs today?"

"Where Genova doubtless awaits." Ash rose, snatching the soft, lace-edged cravat from Henri and carelessly tying it himself. "Be done, Henri. I'm not going to court. By the way," he added to Fitz, "I'm leaving today with the dowager."

Fitz stared at him. "Zeus, why?"

"What choice do I have? Grandy won't stay here, and I can hardly wave her good-bye from the door after she made such a scene."

Grandy was Ash's name for the Dowager Lady Ashart. In Fitz's opinion the old woman was a viper, irretrievably warped by her daughter's tragedy, but Ash felt some fondness for her. His parents had been estranged within weeks of the wedding and had shown no interest in their child, so the dowager had raised him. Fitz couldn't imagine she'd ever been an ideal mother, but she'd done enough to create fondness. Remarkably, it seemed to have survived even yesterday.

Fitz glanced at the window. "I doubt anyone's leaving today, Ash. It's snowing again."

Ash turned to look. "Perdition. She'll have a fit."

"Look on the bright side. More time to bring about healing between her and the Mallorens."

Ash shook his head. "She's accepted that Aunt Augusta was unstable, but to exonerate the Mallorens she would have to take some blame on herself. She'll never do that." With wry understatement, he added, "She does not have a flexible nature. But I will be as kind to her as I can be. When she leaves, I will escort her home."

"What about Genova?" Ash hardly seemed able to bear to be apart from her.

"She comes with us, of course."

"To *Cheynings*? In winter?"

Cheynings, Ashart's principal house, was the most uncomfortable place Fitz had ever visited, leaving aside actual ruins. Damp and drafts seeped from every corner. The carpets would ripple with the wind if there were any. A vague smell of rot hung around the great house, and bits of plaster were inclined to drop from the ceilings or flake off at a touch.

"Genova's no delicate bloom," Ash said. "After living most of her life on navy ships, with her father, even Cheynings can't be intolerable."

"I suppose not. But I thought you intended perfect propriety from now on?"

Ash took the handkerchief on which Henri had been dropping perfume and shoved it in his pocket. "Grandy will be there."

"And keep to her own rooms, as always. Cunning. The appearance of propriety that allows you to do exactly as you wish."

Ash turned sharply to him. "If I could do exactly as I wish, I'd marry Genova today. As it is, she might as well see what she's taking on with me."

He left, and Henri darted into the separate dressing room, doubtless to fuss with Ash's garments even more. Fitz sat to pull off his riding boots, wondering if Cheynings might turn even Genova off the marriage.

No, of course not. Love had her in its jaws, and Ash was right about her experience. Her father had been a naval captain, and she and her mother had sailed the seas with him. She'd even been involved in a sea battle with Barbary corsairs, and, so the story went, won the day by shooting the corsair captain. If that were true, she was equal to Cheynings and the dowager.

Damaris Myddleton had led a less adventurous life, but she seemed to have much the same spirit. Fitz froze, one boot in hand, remembering his words to her.

"I promise to stand by you, to make sure everything turns out as you would wish."

He could tell himself that once Rothgar agreed to take care of her, his obligation wouldn't matter, but Fitz's word meant more to him than that. He'd implied that he'd keep an eye on her during the rest of this house party, and he was sure that was what she'd understood.

However, now he would have to leave with Ash. There were a number of reasons, but the most pressing was that he was Ash's bodyguard. Ash didn't know it—he didn't even know his life was in danger—but his safety must come first.

Three weeks ago, when he and Ash had been in London, Fitz had been astonished to be summoned to Malloren House. As the time specified was before noon, he'd harbored no illusion that the Marquess of Rothgar was extending a social invitation.

He'd gone to find out what was in hand, hoping if it might have something to do with healing the old wounds between the Trayces and Mallorens.

The truth had been completely unexpected.

Rothgar, all cool courtesy, had informed him that

Ash stood in danger of assassination. No, Fitz could not be told who wished Ashart dead, or for what reason. However, as someone of his talents happened to be part of Ashart's household, he was requested to put those talents to the king's service once more by keeping Ashart alive.

His talents as a bodyguard.

Rothgar had assured him that his services would not be required for long. By the opening of the winter season on January 18, the danger should be over and he would be free to do as he pleased. He would also be a thousand guineas the richer—assuming, of course, that Ash survived.

Fitz had searched the proposal for traps, but seen none. It had been a peculiar and frustrating proposition, however, for Rothgar clearly knew more than he would say. And, as they said, in knowledge lay power.

Rothgar had at least assured him that those who wanted Ash dead also wanted no hint of murder. Any attempt would be made to look like an accident. That ruled out the more obvious means of murder from dagger to most poisons. On the other hand, Ash enjoyed active adventures, and Fitz was forbidden to warn him of his danger.

He'd almost balked at that, but he'd known he probably was the best man for the job. Time and again he'd proved to be skilled at keeping people safe. He seemed to notice danger signals before others did—a footstep, a shift in a crowd, the expression on a face, even sometimes a stir in the air that raised the hair on his neck. Most of the time he was simply very, very thorough in prevention.

Whatever the explanation, he was good at protection. How could he entrust Ash's safety to someone else?

Thus far, the warning had turned out to be for nothing. In the past weeks before coming here Ash had ridden around the countryside, engaged in fencing matches, attended wild parties and hells, and had riotous evenings of drink and women. He'd not suffered so much as a scratch. Fitz was relieved, but not surprised. In the hothouse world of courts and politics, the smallest issues grew huge.

But even so, he couldn't let Ash head off to Cheynings without him. Which meant he had no choice but to abandon Damaris. He hated that, but he couldn't cut himself in two.

He remembered an old army joke about being bisected left and right or top and bottom. Which way would a wife want her husband split, and if top and bottom, which half would she want?

The least he could do was to attend Damaris for as long as possible. He tidied himself and returned to the hall.

Damaris had been taken to an elegant but businesslike room. A large carved and inlaid desk dominated the space, its surface lit by a reflecting lamp suspended from the raised hand of a bronze lady in classical robes. Shelves full of books, ledgers, and even scrolls lined the walls, and the air was pleasant with wood smoke and leather.

The marquess, in a simple suit of dark blue, had been working on some papers in the pool of light, but had risen as she entered. He directed her to one of two chairs on either side of the fire. Now she sat facing him, trying to find the right words.

He had the same dark coloring and heavy-lidded eyes as his cousin, Ashart, but seemed more formidable. And Ashart was formidable enough. Rothgar was older, of course, but in addition, the whole world knew he was the king's adviser. And she was going to ask him to take charge of her mundane affairs?

"How may I serve you, Miss Myddleton?" he prompted.

"My lord," she said through a constriction in her throat, "Lord Henry has done his best to take care of me, but . . ." Her prepared speech escaped her.

"But he has no idea what to do with a lively young woman. I had begun to suspect as much. I believe you are in his care until you reach twenty-four or marry with his approval?"

Omniscient, as Fitz had said. "Yes, my lord."

"And you are twenty-one now?"

"This past October, my lord."

"What is it you wish me to do, Miss Myddleton?"

The blunt question numbed her. "I was hoping . . . hoping that it might be possible for . . ." Courage failed. "For someone else to become my guardian." Then she became ashamed of yet more cowardice. "I humbly request that you take over this responsibility, my lord."

"But of course."

Just like that? Enormous relief was tinged by annoyance. Indeed, she meant no more to him than an extra button on his coat. But relief sang uppermost. It made her so light-headed she could hardly take in his next words.

". . . to take Miss Smith to London and present her at court before her marriage to Ashart. You shall be her companion in this."

His announcement acted like a spray of icy water.

"This doesn't please you?" he asked.

She struggled for words. "Yes, of course, my lord. It's just that I'm not sure I'm ready for court."

"You and Miss Smith will prepare together in London."

Damaris smiled, wondering if her expression looked like the grimace it felt. She wanted London and court, but she didn't want to make her entrée at the side of her victorious rival. Her stunningly beautiful victorious rival, beside whom she would look like a monkey. She had no choice, however.

"Thank you, my lord. I do need to go to court to choose a suitable husband."

"You are set on immediate marriage?"

She blinked at him. "I have never considered it a choice, my lord. Women who can, marry. Heiresses always marry. It's as if an heiress exists to gift some man with her fortune."

Now where did that tart comment come from?

His lips twitched. "Men certainly like to think so. As a wealthy woman, however, you have choice. Once you turn twenty-four you can, if you wish, live free of anyone's control."

Live free. The concept dazzled Damaris, but common sense broke through. "I suspect such a course would not be easy, my lord."

"Freedom is never easy, and the management of wealth brings heavy responsibility and hard work."

"I'm accustomed to hard work."

"But are you ready for challenge, risk, and danger?"

"Danger?" He had a way of springing new angles of conversation.

"Isolation is dangerous for anyone," he said, "but especially for a woman. I think you lack close family?"

"Yes, my lord."

"Your father's family?"

"Cast him off long before he married my mother."

"And your mother was an only child of only children."

How did he know these things? It unnerved her.

"Men of the world spend a great deal of time building alliances," he said, "using family as their bricks. A woman alone is cut off from this. You have, however, acquired a family."

"I have?"

"You are now within the circle of the Mallorens, if you choose to be."

If she wanted to be? She was hard-pressed not to laugh. During this past week she'd watched with wonder and wistfulness the careless warmth of Lord Rothgar and those of his brothers and sisters who were present. It was something she'd never experienced at Birch House or Thornfield Hall.

"Why?" The startled question popped out. "I've not behaved well."

"You've made mistakes, in part because you lack training for this world. That is easily corrected. You are also strong and willful, which is not a bad thing."

"My mother thought it a deadly sin."

"Perhaps that was key to her problems. If a woman has no will of her own, she must be ruled by the will of others."

"Is that not the way of the world, my lord?"

"Is it what you want?"

Damaris tried to think. "I don't know."

He smiled. "Consider it. As for your preparation for court, you lived quietly until recently?"

Damaris twitched her mind to follow this new direction. "Until arriving here, my lord."

"Did Lord Henry not entertain for you in Sussex?"

"I was in mourning, my lord, but there were some small gatherings of neighbors."

"Even mourning for a mother does not require such a quiet year. And before that, did you not enjoy the society of Worksop?"

She was tempted to laugh. "My mother did not care for such things."

"And your father?"

She felt an impulse to object to this inquisition, but Damaris fought down the tart response. *Be careful, careful.*

"My father lived in the Orient, my lord, as I'm sure

you know." That jab slipped out. "He visited us only three times that I remember, and briefly."

He nodded. "You had a governess?"

"My mother taught me."

"Dance? Deportment?"

"No. But in the past year Lord Henry arranged for lessons."

"And in music, I assume. You play well, and your voice is remarkable."

She blushed with pleasure at being praised for something. "Yes, my lord. My mother taught me the keyboard, but singing I learned by myself. And then, of course, Lord Henry provided a teacher."

"Then you will need to learn only the finer points of court etiquette. But as you and Genova will be presented at the queen's birthday ball, you have only three weeks of preparation."

That started a flutter of panic, especially in light of recent social disasters. But she could—she would—do it. "Thank you, my lord. For agreeing to act as my guardian, for the education, and the presentation."

He gestured away thanks. "We will not try to alter the legal arrangements. I understand that my uncle can approve anyone to act in his place."

It was as if he'd already investigated the possibility.

"Lord Henry will not object, my lord?"

His eyes smiled. "I pray this won't offend, my dear, but from comments he's let slip, I believe he will be relieved."

"Then I don't know why he clung to his power! I would have been happy to return to Worksop at any time this past year."

"Responsibility." The clipped word stung like the rap of her mother's stick across her knuckles. "Your father left you in my uncle's care. He had no choice but to take that seriously. I understand there was a fortune hunter?"

Alleyne. Lonely and unhappy at Thornfield Hall, Damaris had been easy prey for Captain Sam Alleyne. He'd been handsome and dashing and she'd let him kiss her. She'd thought he'd loved her and might have let him do more if Lord Henry hadn't caught her . . .

That had led to the whipping and a much tighter control on her movements. That hadn't been necessary. Lord Henry had told her that lists of heiresses were sold to fortune hunters and that she was at the top of them all. That had been when she'd decided on an arranged marriage. "I learned my lesson, my lord."

"Then you should understand that you could not and cannot live alone. The days of marriage by abduction are past, but a prize such as you present is still vulnerable in many ways. You tried to flee this morning."

Another stinging rap. "Yes, my lord. I apologize. It was folly."

"There will be no similar folly whilst you are under my care."

"No, my lord."

"You won't find my rule onerous. Unless, that is, you are inclined to be wild."

Perhaps exhaustion loosed her tongue. "What of free will, my lord?"

"That is for when you come into your independence." He rose, indicating that her time was over.

Damaris rose, too, wondering fuzzily if they'd covered the important points. The change of guardian. Freedom from Lord Henry and Thornfield Hall. Presentation in London, where she would select the perfect husband. Probably the Duke of Bridgewater . . .

Fitzroger. They hadn't spoken about Fitzroger. She turned at the door. "There is the matter of talk, my lord. About yesterday. Mr. Fitzroger and I devised a plan."

"Yes?" Did she hear displeasure?

"He suggested that we give the appearance of happy flirtation, so no one can think me broken-hearted over Ashart. But perhaps it's not necessary now?"

He seemed thoughtful. "You will look foolish to have chosen him over a marquess."

"Chosen?" she asked, trying to sound amused. "Mere Christmastide amusement, my lord. He is handsome enough for that."

"Indeed?"

She knew she was coloring. "I assure you, my lord, I have no lasting interest. He offers nothing that I require in a husband."

"Which is?"

"Title, position, and power."

"Lord Ferrers had title, position, and power. He abused his wife almost to death and was hanged for the murder of his servant."

The story was infamous. "He was insane, I believe, my lord. You would warn me away from a madman or cad, would you not?"

Too late, she realized she was being pert again, but he didn't react.

"Fitzroger is smirched by scandal, but that need not concern you, as you have no lasting interest."

For some reason that warning made Damaris feel hollow. She couldn't stop herself asking, "And if I did have a lasting interest in such a man?"

"As long as you are my ward, Damaris, you may marry any honorable man you choose. An honorable man will woo you and convince me that he is worthy. He will not use the weakness of the flesh to twist your judgment or to attempt to seal your fate."

Damaris instantly thought of the way she and Fitzroger had kissed in the coach. Fearing this man would read it on her face, she curtsied, thanked him again for his many kindnesses, and escaped.

Outside the door she paused, hand on chest, to breathe, to steady her heart. She still must face people here, but she clung to the main point. She'd won! If the rest of the plan worked, she had regained a future full of glorious possibilities.

And she owed it all to Octavius Fitzroger. He deserved a reward. He might be too proud to take money, but there were other ways to reward someone. She could purchase influence to get him a lucrative court or government position for instance. Or buy him his own regiment in the army. She need only discover what he wanted and grease the way.

She walked on, feeling as if the sun rose inside her. When she entered the hall smiling, she found Fitzroger waiting.

He wore the same clothes as when he'd stopped her coach—dark blue coat and breeches and white shirt—but with orderly additions. Shoes had replaced boots, and his wild hair was tamed by a ribbon. A plain cravat circled his neck, and he'd put on a waistcoat. Typically, it was a plain gray. It was as if he proclaimed his poverty to the world. Even in the evenings, when the guests here put on their finery, Fitzroger's clothing was subdued.

She wished she could dress him in silks and velvet, and yes, even in diamond buttons. With his blond hair he'd look splendid in the gold-embroidered, cream velvet suit Ashart had worn on Christmas Day.

My pale gold Galahad, she thought, but then pushed away that image.

"Well?" he asked.

For a moment she thought he was asking the result of her assessment, but of course he referred to her appointment. She went to him, smiling. "He agreed."

"Felicitations."

"And I'm going to London. To court, to choose a

fine husband. All is well, and I grant you the credit, sir."

He bowed. "Your security and happiness are thanks enough, Miss Myddleton."

Everything necessary was said, but Damaris regretted the formal tone, especially when contrasted with their behavior in the coach. Given that wild passion, however, their formality now was doubtless just as well. The memory still sizzled in her mind, and perhaps even sparked between them.

Oh, my. She dropped a curtsy and hurried up to the safety of her room.

Chapter 4

Fitz watched Damaris go. She had Rothgar's protection, but would soon move into a world full of hazards, and Rothgar couldn't hover by her side. There was Rothgar's wife, who would also be her guide. She was the Countess of Arradale, however, a peeress in her own right, and had almost as many demands on her time as her husband did. Damaris needed a guide with more time to spare. . . .

He turned away both physically and mentally. Damaris's affairs were settled, so now he was free to plan a safe journey tomorrow. He'd think better with a less hollow stomach, so he turned toward the breakfast room.

Just as he did so a voice said, "Sir!"

He turned to see a footman hurrying after him, bearing a note.

With a *what now?* feeling, Fitz unfolded the unsealed letter to find a blunt summons from Rothgar. *Damn the man.* Fitz was tempted to eat first, but when the Dark Marquess summoned, one hurried to obey. He followed the footman, entering the office to find Rothgar standing by the fire, looking inscrutably cool. Fitz's uneasiness elevated to watchfulness. Had Damaris told the marquess what had occurred in the coach?

Fitz bowed. "My lord."

Rothgar nodded and gestured toward a chair. When they were both seated he said, "Pray give me an account of this morning's events surrounding Miss Myddleton."

Trying to sense the mood, Fitz told the story, of course leaving out the kiss. He read nothing on the other man's face.

"You saw the coach leave. How?"

Fitz almost said, *By looking out of the window,* but controlled his tongue. "I rise early, my lord. When I rise, I look out to see the nature of the day. Thus I saw a coach leaving at dawn."

"Why suspect that it carried Miss Myddleton?"

"It was a possibility worth investigating."

"But your investigation left Ashart unprotected."

Fitz had years of experience at hiding irritation in front of superior officers. "We agreed that I would never be able to shadow his every move, my lord, without telling him why. I assumed he was safe abed, here in your house." But he saw escape and grabbed it. "But he is up and in the breakfast room. I should hasten to my duty."

"Please resume your seat, Fitzroger." Despite the courtesy, the words were a command. "Ashart is safe at the moment, and I will be informed of any change in his situation."

Fitz sat, aware that something had changed. This Christmas gathering had been a perfect confection of elegant but relaxed amusement, and as he'd said, he'd assumed that Ash was safe here. He'd still taken precautions and kept alert, but in a casual way.

"Yesterday's events may have increased Ashart's peril," Rothgar said.

Fitz desperately sought the aspect of yesterday he'd overlooked. Boxing Day was a holiday for the servants at Rothgar Abbey, so as much as possible, the guests fended for themselves.

Most of them, at least. The marquess's sister, Lady Walgrave, had recently given birth, so the nursery servants would have been needed, and he was sure Lady Ashart had not released her minions to feasting and dancing. The dowager's arrival and the resulting dramas had been exciting, but hardly dangerous.

"The dowager?" he asked. "You think she's a danger to Ash? I assure you, my lord, she dotes on him."

Rothgar's raised hand stopped him. "Of course she wouldn't harm him. Not by violence, at least. The disaster is his betrothal, especially the passionate nature of it."

"Undignified, my lord, I agree. But disastrous?"

"When we spoke in London, my cousin was on an unhurried progress toward union with Miss Myddleton's fortune. Now he's hurtling toward marriage with Miss Smith. I've bought time by persuading him to delay the wedding until after Genova is presented at court, but that gains only weeks."

Fitz's patience cracked. "Weeks before what?"

"Before the assassin becomes desperate. Ashart's intention to wed increases his danger. His intention to wed soon creates a crisis. His decision to leave here with our grandmother adds a certain extreme even to that."

"The journey does present challenges, my lord, but it can be completed in a day."

"Cheynings, however, will not be as secure as here."

He was right. "It's severely understaffed, that's true."

"I will send extra outriders with your party, and they can stay to assist with the later journey to London. I will also arrange for some suitable people to be in the area and under your command if needed. I recommend keeping Ashart indoors as much as possible."

"Not easy, but I will do my best, my lord. So after

the wedding, Ash will be safe? Then why not hold the wedding soon? I'm sure he could be persuaded."

Rothgar's expression was grim. "The wedding will be the ultimate disaster. We must hope that by then the problem is solved."

Frustrated, Fitz rose. "If there's no more information you can give me, my lord, I'll continue to do my best."

"You sound distressed."

The hint of humor was the final straw. "It's damn tiresome to fight shadows, my lord. When engaged in matters of life and death, I prefer solid ground and a clear day."

"All wise men do." Rothgar rose to escort him to the door. "I do apologize, but I'm under the strictest requirement to keep the details secret. It is to your benefit," he added. "Knowledge can be a dangerous possession."

At that, Fitz's mind both shivered and leaped into speculation. He'd assumed the amorphous threat arose from the usual sort of enemies. Men who envied Ash's way with women, or even his way of wearing a coat. Men who'd been on the receiving end of his temper, or even men who thought he'd cuckolded them.

Rothgar's words moved this into deeper, darker waters, into state affairs and secrets, things that Fitz thought he'd escaped. But what in such matters could affect Ash? He played less a part in politics than he should.

"Ignorance, too, can be dangerous," he pointed out.

"Choose your poison."

Fitz hesitated but said, "I choose knowledge."

Rothgar's slight smile might have been approving, but he said, "Then I regret that I cannot provide it. That is forbidden."

"By whom?" Fitz was aware that his tone was outrageous, but he was past caring.

"By the king."

Everything stopped. Fitz could have believed that the gilded clock ceased ticking and that the very flames in the hearth went still.

Rothgar had presented his original instructions as coming from the king, but many things were done in the name of the king that had little to do with His Majesty. If the king took a personal interest in this, then yes, Fitz wished to hell he knew nothing about it. Except that he might be the only one able to keep Ash alive. He was trained, experienced, and on the spot.

He pulled together his frazzled wits. "So, my lord, Ashart is threatened by important matters of state. I am to keep him safe, but without giving him a hint of his peril. His betrothal increases the danger, but you're not trying to prevent his leaving this house, where I assume he is safe."

"I see no way to make him stay. He's correct that he cannot let the distressed dowager return to Cheynings alone, and she will not stay here a moment longer than necessary. In any case, Ashart will soon move to London for Genova's presentation. How good is he with a sword?"

Fitz considered. "Good."

"Only good, or are you niggardly with praise?"

After further thought, Fitz repeated, "Good."

He understood what Rothgar was asking. A challenge to a duel had been used to murder a man before now.

Rothgar looked thoughtfully into the distance for a moment. "I would like to evaluate his ability myself. We'll have a fencing demonstration. Shortly before dinner. At two o'clock." He looked back at Fitz. "Short of a duel, how would you kill him?"

This conversation was like a rapid fencing bout itself.

"A slender dagger during a country dance. If slid in right, the victim feels only a blow at first, and there's little blood. Time to slip away. But no, it must appear to be an accident. Can you explain that aspect, my lord?"

"The king, as I said, takes a personal interest and has made it clear that Ashart's well-being is sacrosanct."

"I had the impression they disliked each other."

"No loyal subject dislikes his king," Rothgar gently chastised, "but yes, His Majesty is not fond of Ashart. It goes back to childhood rivalry."

Fitz's astonishment must have shown, for Rothgar smiled. "They're close in age, and the dowager saw an opportunity to establish Ashart at court. She arranged for them to play together. Ashart had many gifts from the cradle, but courtly tact came later."

"He won."

"At everything. Of course, His Majesty is above such petty grievances, but he cannot quite forget."

"Generous of him to be so protective, then."

"His Majesty is just. Thus those who see Ashart's death as desirable don't wish to be caught at it. So what types of apparently accidental death could you devise?"

"Bad food, bad horse, a minor wound that doesn't heal. A needle to the heart can go undetected. There are poisons that mimic heart failure, apoplexy, and fits. Would any assassin know the finer points of the trade?"

"Possibly, which is why you were recommended for defense."

Fitz had nothing more to say. The situation was bizarre, but he didn't for one moment doubt that Rothgar, and presumably the king, were truly concerned.

"As for the journey," Rothgar said, "Ashart has

two coaches here, the one that brought the great-aunts and the one the dowager arrived in. They might as well both return, along with two coaches for baggage and servants. My people will ride in the first of those, the one that will prepare the stops along the way for changes of horses or refreshments. They can be trusted to ensure the stops are safe."

Fitz supposed the Dark Marquess had to provide for his own safety at times. He considered the further logistics of the journey. "The dowager will insist on traveling in the best coach, my lord, so Genova can travel in the other. Unkind to put them together."

"Assuredly. But Genova will have a companion. Great-aunt Thalia has agreed to go with her."

Fitz hoped his eyes hadn't flashed the alarm. He was beginning to feel like the camel loaded with more and more straw. His priority was to keep Ash safe. In addition, he had to transport a furious dowager and the person she was most furious with—Genova. On top of that, he was now to take along the dowager's sister-in-law, Lady Thalia Trayce, and there was no love lost between the two elderly ladies. Lady Thalia was the sister of the dowager's long-dead husband, so Cheynings had once been her home. Rumor said that shortly after the wedding, however, the marquess's mother and his unmarried sisters had taken up residence in Tunbridge Wells and hardly returned to Cheynings since.

It perhaps wasn't surprising if Lady Thalia wanted to revisit her home, but she was eccentric, to put it kindly. She dressed in her seventies as if she were seventeen, chattered like a lunatic, and loved to meddle in other people's lives. She was also addicted to whist. Fitz was not particularly fond of the game, but he knew who'd have to make the fourth. The dowager certainly wouldn't.

"I suppose it's as well that blond hair doesn't show gray, my lord."

Rothgar smiled. "Especially as I intend to send Damaris Myddleton on this expedition, too."

Fitz rarely wondered if dreams were real, but perhaps he still slept, for surely he was now hallucinating. "She's the last person Ash and Genova would want along, and Cheynings is the last place she'd want to be."

"It will remove her from the attention of people here, thus giving me time to amend any impressions of yesterday. I also hope that she and Genova will learn to be cordial. When they join society, eyes will still be on them."

The manipulative marquess was weaving some plot, and Fitz wished he understood what lay behind it.

"You are sending Miss Myddleton into danger, my lord."

"This assassin knows his target and will not be careless."

"The easiest way to disguise a death is to make it one of many."

Rothgar frowned. "A point. However, Genova will insist on going, and Lady Thalia wishes to. I put my faith in you. And you must understand, it really will not serve to have Damaris remain here. She would be constantly on trial, and she is inclined to fight first and think later. Perhaps you can correct that while you're at Cheynings."

"I am to be her tutor?"

"In that, and in other things. I wish you to help her to understand that she is a desirable woman."

Perhaps Fitz's shock showed, for Rothgar added, "Merely through flirtation and flattery, I need not say. But she is a pirate's daughter and inclined to reach for what she wants. Better for her not to seize on the first court gallant to thrill her, don't you think?"

"Unlikely, my lord. She's determined to make a good bargain."

"I would want more for her than that."

"You are a romantic, my lord?"

Fitz meant it to be caustic, but Rothgar's brows rose. "I married for love not five months ago. What else could I be?"

Fitz didn't know what to say. Marital devotion was not fashionable.

"Shameful, I know," Rothgar said, amused, "but like most new converts, I'm a devotee. I wish love for all. Ashart has become a true believer. I wish the same for Damaris and, when the time is right, for you too, of course."

"Thank you, sir, but no."

"In my experience, love has a will of its own and is not easily rejected. Therefore, do not let flirtatious games get out of hand."

Fitz felt jumpy, as if moving through foggy territory, expecting ambush at any moment. "If you don't trust me, my lord, I wonder at your giving me the task."

"But apparently you and Damaris have already made such a plan. I merely elaborate on it. The fencing will be an excellent opportunity to show that Damaris cares not at all for Ashart and is happily amusing herself with you. If, that is, you fence?"

"Yes, my lord."

"Then you will escort her down, charming and pleasing her so that it is obvious that she does not nurse a broken heart. At the fencing, she will encounter Ashart and Genova without any hint of strife."

"Does Ashart know this?"

"I will inform him. Damaris and Genova will sit together as friends—"

"Friends!"

"Friends," Rothgar repeated.

The man was impossible.

"You don't fear any of the guests might use sword-play to attempt assassination?"

"No," Rothgar said, "but if one of them did, it would certainly clarify the situation, don't you think? But we will use foils," he added. "It is so very difficult to kill anyone with a foil. You approve this plan?"

Feeling beleaguered, manipulated, and at the end of his patience, Fitz asked, "Am I allowed to win?"

The heavy-lidded eyes widened slightly. "You think you can?"

Rothgar was said to be a brilliant swordsman, but Fitz said, "Yes."

Rothgar considered him in silence, then smiled. "The event becomes even more intriguing. Very well. After the fencing, we dine buoyed on harmony and merriment. In the evening there will be dancing, which will provide more opportunity for flirtation and for Damaris to be cheerful and heart-whole. Then, weather willing, she can leave tomorrow before the mask can slip."

"You will inform Miss Myddleton of all this, my lord?"

"No, you will. I'm sure you can find a way to persuade her to oblige."

Fitz wondered if this was his punishment for any sins he might have committed in bringing Damaris back to the house. "Is our discussion complete, my lord?" he asked, not caring anymore if Rothgar objected to his tone.

"Not quite. Can you afford a fashionable appearance?"

"No, so you will have to provide other protection for Ashart at court."

"Do you frequent gaming hells?"

Impossible to hope that Rothgar didn't know he'd used the hells when his pockets were too close to empty. "Occasionally."

"Do you know Sheba's in Carlyon Street?"

"I've heard of it. It's somewhat select for a hell."

Rothgar smiled. "A charming whimsy, a select hell. I'm sure some of our noblest sinners hope to at least end up in a select hell rather than burning beside the riffraff. In any case, play at Sheba's. You will win against the house, which will explain why you can afford finery."

It would seem Rothgar had his manicured fingers in some very peculiar pies. But Fitz didn't want to go to court or move in any elevated circles, even suitably dressed.

"A reasonable night's winnings won't equip me, my lord."

"Then I recommend Pargeter's, a discreet establishment where valets unburden themselves of gifts of clothing that are too grand for them to wear."

Fitz knew of such places, but Rothgar had to know he would be cold-shouldered at court and barred from many houses.

"And if I prefer not to move in court circles, my lord?"

"I would be disappointed. More to the point, Ashart would be less well protected."

"Despite your constant presence, my lord?"

Rothgar seemed truly amused. "My dear Fitzroger, when at court I'm engaged in duels with a dozen opponents, and a dance with sharks circling my feet. I have no time for distractions."

The simple honesty of the words was disarming, and Fitz found he couldn't persist. Perhaps Rothgar's and Ashart's patronage would avoid open embarrassment, but moving in those circles would be damned unpleasant. He prayed that the mess would be sorted out before it came to that.

"Very well, my lord." He executed one of his more flowery bows and retreated from the marquess's presence, seeing one bright side to the mess. He could now protect Ash without abandoning Damaris. If, that was, he could persuade her to fall in with the plan to go to Cheynings as Genova Smith's dear companion.

He couldn't face that on an empty stomach.

He went to the breakfast room, where he found Ash and Genova still side by side, looking as if they could live upon air as long as they were together. Lord Bryght Malloren, Rothgar's brother, was also at the table, but within minutes of Fitz's arrival he made his excuses and left.

Coincidence?

Or had Lord Bryght been temporary bodyguard, even here in Rothgar Abbey?

Chapter 5

When Damaris returned to her room, the desperate energy that had swept her through the morning drained away. Under the influence of laudanum she'd slept away most of yesterday. However, that and certainty of disaster had kept her sleepless through most of the night.

She was exhausted, and after giving Maisie the news, she took off her outer clothes, crawled into bed, and fell fast asleep. She was woken by Maisie shaking her. "It's quarter to one, miss. You have to get up."

Damaris rubbed her eyes. "Why? Dinner isn't until three."

"Yes, but that Fitzroger stopped by to say you're supposed to go down with him to a fencing match or some such at two. Part of your plan to appear not bothered about Lord Ashart, remember? Not that I think you ought to be having much to do with that one. He's a fortune hunter for sure."

"Lord Ashart?" Damaris asked, deliberately misunderstanding. "Of course he is. Or was."

"Fitzroger!" Maisie exclaimed. "And here's a note come from the Dowager Marchioness of Ashart, and her servant said as it was right urgent. He's waiting outside the door."

Damaris sat up, rubbing her eyes. "What could she want?"

She opened the folded paper to find a terse command to present herself immediately in the dowager's room. She considered refusing, but she wouldn't show fear of the old tyrant, so she climbed out of bed.

"I'll put my traveling clothes back on for now, but prepare something for when I return." She hurried into the heavy skirt and quilted jacket as she reviewed her wardrobe. "The Autumn Sunset."

Autumn Sunset was the mantua maker's flowery term for the russety-pink silk used to make that gown. Damaris hadn't worn it here yet, for while finding her feet in this strange new world she'd chosen more muted shades.

Today, however, called for boldness if anything did.

"Your hair's all over," Maisie said.

Damaris sat so she could tidy it. "Hurry. You can redress it properly later."

"Then you'd best not dally, miss."

"Don't worry. There will be no temptation to do that."

Damaris joined the footman and followed him on a winding route to a door, where he tapped. On command, he opened it.

The old lady was bolstered up in bed, not looking like the tyrant she was. Lady Ashart was short and plump, which gave a deceitful impression of softness, especially as she dressed in gentle colors trimmed with frills of lace. A true wolf in sheep's clothing.

Her nightcap, though quilted for warmth, was edged with a deep frill of blue-embroidered English lace, and tied with blue ribbons beneath her plump chins. Her silvery curls frothed out, matching a fluffy shawl of gray wool. There was no old-person smell here, either, only a delicate hint of lavender.

This had all been part of Damaris's undoing. When she'd visited Cheynings as Ashart's prospective bride, Lady Ashart had seemed kind—haughty, but gracious. There was no kindness in her now. She waved her middle-aged maid out of the room, then snapped, "I'm not pleased with you, Miss Myddleton."

Damaris wouldn't descend to squabbling. "I'm sorry for your disappointment, Lady Ashart."

"Disappointment! It's a disaster, girl, and it all lies at your doorstep."

"Hardly—"

"Ashart's being here was no plan of mine. But when it occurred, could you not take advantage of it instead of letting that hussy get her claws into him?"

Damaris counted to three. "Ashart arrived here with Miss Smith, my lady. I believe they were already attached—"

"Attached! *Attached!* The whole country is talking of them being caught attached on an inn bed!"

"Then it's necessary that they marry, is it not?"

"Ha! If Ashart married every woman he bedded, he'd need a harem."

"But he loves—"

"*Love!*" the dowager shrieked. "A pox on love. Springtime dewdrops that never last. I've seen more disasters from love matches, girl, than from sensible arrangements. I will not have it. Ashart must marry money. He must marry you."

Damaris stared at the impossible tyrant, then spoke flatly. "I would not have Lord Ashart now, my lady, on any terms."

"Are you such a fool? You'll do no better, girl, for all your pirated guineas."

"I'm sure she will."

Damaris whirled to find that Lord Ashart had entered the room. She'd never expected to be so happy to see him.

He strolled forward. "Stop belaboring Miss Myddleton, Grandy. None of this is her fault, and by entangling her we've done her a disfavor."

"If she embarrassed herself, it's because of you, you rascal, and it's for you to fix. You can charm any woman out of her fidgets—"

"I love Genova, Grandy. If you fight me over this, you will lose."

The marquess did not speak harshly, but despite the affectionate name, Damaris thought no one could miss the authority in his words. She was wrong.

"Puppy!" the old woman snapped.

Ashart didn't react. "As Miss Myddleton said, she has too much sense to take me now, even if I could be compelled to give up Genova, which I cannot. There comes a time, my lady, when anyone has to accept defeat."

Damaris winced at both *my lady* and *defeat*.

The dowager seemed to rear up on her bank of pillows, flares of red in her cheeks. "I will remove from Cheynings and never speak to you again!"

"So be it."

Caught midfire, Damaris edged toward the door. She jumped at a touch, but Ashart merely escorted her there. "My apologies, Miss Myddleton," he said as he guided her into the corridor.

The dowager's voice blasted out again—"Do not think . . ."—then was muffled by the door closing with Ashart still inside, brave man.

"Snatched from the jaws of the dragon by a fearless hero?"

Damaris started, hand to chest. "What? Are you Ashart's hound, sir, to be left waiting at the door?"

"Woof!" But Fitzroger smiled. "I came as squire to Saint George, but I don't seem to be needed except to escort the maiden to safety."

She glanced back at the door. "A dragon, indeed."

"Think what a lucky escape you've had."

"I assumed the dowager would leave Cheynings when Ashart married."

"Highly unlikely."

"She's threatening to leave if he marries Miss Smith."

"A delightful prospect, but still unlikely. She's lived there for sixty years, and ruled there for most of it. But speaking of Cheynings . . ."

"Yes?" she asked.

"Have you visited the library here?"

She saw no connection. "Briefly, when we were given a tour of the house."

"Come, then. It's nearby."

Damaris hesitated, aware of something strange in the air. But they wouldn't be compromised by being together in the library, and they were conspirators of a sort. Perhaps he needed to discuss their plan.

"I don't have long," she said, setting a brisk pace. "I have to dress for this fencing match. What's the purpose of that?"

"Merely amusement."

She looked at him, trying to see through his smooth facade. "How did you and Ashart come to save me?"

"Omniscience. Rothgar knew you'd been summoned and asked Ashart to intervene."

"Thank heavens the dowager will soon leave."

He opened the door and she walked into the magnificent room, not surprised to find it deserted. Despite its gilded carving and painted ceiling, the Rothgar Abbey library was a sober, even demanding room. It could certainly never be described as cozy.

No upholstered chairs sat by the crackling fire for the comfort of people wanting to read a newspaper or catch a nap. On the contrary, each window bay held a stern, medieval desk, and plain chairs were drawn up to the three tables running down the middle of the room, ready for those who wanted to consult a weighty tome.

Would the scholars and philosophers painted on the ceiling cry out in horror to see people enter with mere conversation in mind?

"Well?" Damaris asked, strolling toward one of the medieval desks as if fascinated by it, but really to put one of the long tables between herself and Fitzroger. He still had that stirring effect on her.

"I, too, had an interview with Lord Rothgar."

She turned to face him. "Was he very angry?"

"For bringing you back? Quite the opposite."

"I'm glad then. Perhaps he'll become your patron."

A strange expression flickered over his face. "Perhaps he will, but that requires that I oblige him."

"What does he want you to do?"

"Go to Cheynings with Ashart and Genova. Ashart wishes to escort his grandmother home, and of course his betrothed must go with him."

Damaris gave a short laugh. "Poor her. I visited in October and it was damp and frigid then." But then she realized. "You're abandoning me!"

"I regret the necessity, but I suffer from a conflict of obligations—"

"Is Ashart a child needing a nurse?"

"Are you?"

She jerked as if slapped and headed straight for the door. He intercepted her between two tables, blocking her way. "My apologies. I shouldn't have said that."

"Please don't distress yourself, sir. I release you from any obligation. Now that I have Lord Rothgar as my guardian, I don't need—"

A kiss stopped her words. She was too shocked to react, and it was brief, but still left her lips tingling.

"Of course you don't need me." His eyes seemed stormy, as if he felt as staggered as she. "That doesn't mean you have to be alone here."

"Then you won't go?"

"Alas, I must."

"Why?"

"Once Ashart leaves, I have no place in this Malloren nest. How and why could I stay?"

"To court me," she snapped. "Who'd be surprised if a penniless adventurer overstayed his welcome in order to pursue an heiress?"

"Damn you for a sharp-tongued virago."

She raised her chin. "Thank you. I've always wanted to be a virago."

"A shrew? A termagant?"

"A woman who behaves like a man. A woman who speaks her mind, challenges errors, makes her own decisions, and pursues what she wants with all reasonable force. As I will do!"

"You terrify me."

She pounced. "Good. Then you'll have to stay to guard me, won't you?"

"I can't."

She laughed with disgust and turned to escape around the table.

He caught her wrist. "Don't run away again."

Damaris froze, sparks shooting up her arm from that contact. "Leaving your pestilential presence, sir, is not running away."

"I suppose it isn't." He stepped closer and kissed the nape of her neck, nuzzled it, even. Shivers shot through her at this new sensation. "Of your kindness, sweet lady," he murmured there, "stay."

She tried to cling to her invigorating rage, but when he turned her to face him, both hands on her shoulders, she couldn't resist. His thumbs pressed through layers of cloth, circling in a way that sent her mind circling, too.

"I have to accompany Ashart to Cheynings, Damaris. That obligation takes precedence over my promise to you. I regret this, for my promises are sacred to me.''

"You'll have to explain better than that.''

"I can't.''

"What on earth are you talking about? State secrets?'' An expression flashed across his face that made her stare. "At *Cheynings?*''

"Don't.''

The soft warning silenced her but set her thoughts spinning. State secrets at Cheynings? It made no sense, but every instinct cried danger, and not the elemental danger of man and woman. It should have warned her off, but instead she thrilled at the idea.

"What is it? Spies? I wish I were going with you, then.''

"Then come. You could be a companion for Genova.''

"What?'' She pulled free of him. "I'm the last person she'd want, and I have no intention of being locked in with her and Ashart for a week or more.''

He closed the gap between them. "You'd be locked in with me, too.''

Sinful ripples ran up and down her core. "At Cheynings,'' she pointed out, retreating. "Musty, damp, niggardly, and icy.''

"We can find ways to stay warm.''

Her back hit shelves. "The place will be freezing. We'd catch pneumonia first.''

He put his hands on either side of her and leaned closer. "You're stronger than that, and you have those lovely, thick furs.'' He drawled out the last few words, turning her thoughts to mist.

Because of his height, she felt surrounded, but she didn't mind, especially when his soft, deep voice made her skin stir as if brushed by those furs.

"Come," he tempted. "It ensures victory. After today you'll have convinced everyone here that you're heart-whole, and you can leave with flags flying."

She loved the image of that. "Kiss me," she whispered, "and perhaps I will."

His lips pressed against hers and she relaxed into delight. She'd wanted this since their kiss in the coach. She reached her arms up around his neck and tilted her head to savor him the more, astonished at how a kiss, how lips to lips, could stir her whole body into pleasure.

She pushed away from the wall to be closer, and his arms came around her, molding her to him, exactly as she wished. She would fuse with him if she could. She'd never known such bliss, never known it existed. She turned her head, seeking to be closer, opening her mouth wider to explore him, the heat and taste of him, so special, so right. . . .

He eased them apart and she opened her eyes. "You look startled," she said, smiling. How could she help it?

"Terrified, more like. But you'll come to Cheynings? You set a kiss as your fee and I paid it."

She pushed him away, but he grabbed her arms. "I didn't mean it like that."

"You seem to say a great many things you don't mean!" she snapped.

"Only with you."

She ceased her struggles. "I think I like that."

"Virago," he said, but with warmth in his eyes. "It does make sense, Damaris. You don't want to stay on here."

"But Cheynings . . . ?"

"And me." He moved his hands to her waist and she put her own on his shoulders, playing her fingers there. "Cat," he said. "Keep your claws sheathed."

She knew her tilted eyes gave her the look of a cat.

Until now she'd thought that a bad thing. "Won't it be improper? Ashart and Miss Smith? You and me?"

"And the dowager. And Lady Thalia will be there, too. She is fond of Genova. And she wants to visit her childhood house." He began to drop kisses on her nose, her cheeks, her lips again. "You'll come?"

"Satan," she muttered, trying to think.

The bleak house. The dowager. Ashart and Miss Smith, sickeningly in love.

Fitzroger. Mysterious Fitzroger, whom she wanted to explore. More kisses . . .

With Ashart and Miss Smith sickeningly in love, and their chaperones two elderly ladies who would need naps, wouldn't there be considerable time alone with him? A wise woman would avoid that as if it were the plague, but how could she be wise when his lips played softly against hers?

There was so little time until she had to be sensible. Before London, and a suitable husband . . .

She shifted away, feeling her clothing brush against her sensitive skin. Temptation warred with sense, and sense did not entirely lose. She captured his face in her hands. "Will you promise not to seduce me there?"

His eyes widened, but then became steady on hers. "I promise not to seduce you anywhere, Damaris. Not because my baser nature wouldn't like to, but because my honor won't permit it. And also," he added ruefully, "I have a healthy instinct for self-preservation. My apologies if it seems paltry, but I would not care to make Rothgar my deadly enemy."

Damaris took a deep breath, feeling as if it were the first in a long time. "Then by all means, if Genova Smith can bear it, I will accompany you all to Cheynings."

He stepped back. "Good."

The library door opened, and they both turned as

Ashart strolled in. "Rejoice! I'm still in one piece. Does Miss Myddleton agree to come with us?"

Damaris stared at Fitzroger, shockingly hurt. He'd just kissed her into agreeing with an already established plan. Why couldn't he have simply told her? And why, now she came to think of it, was Ashart speaking as if she weren't even here?

"Miss Myddleton does," she snapped, which at least made Ashart look at her.

Warily, she noted with satisfaction. She wasn't proud of her recent behavior, and given the opportunity she'd wipe it out. But she liked the fact that the powerful Marquess of Ashart was nervous of her.

He bowed. "My apologies, Miss Myddleton. And apologies in advance for the discomforts of Cheynings."

"I have been there, my lord."

He frowned for a second before saying, "Ah, yes."

Damaris's teeth clenched. Did the pestilential man not even *remember?* He had been there, paying charming attentions to her. Or rather, to her money.

"It will be even more uncomfortable now," he said, and she realized he'd be pleased if she refused to go. Well, good. She'd enjoy being a constant thorn in both his and Miss Smith's consciences.

"I will survive, my lord. *I* was not raised in indulgence."

He shot her an unfriendly look, and Fitzroger intervened. "At the fencing, Ashart will be Genova's favored champion. Will you be mine?"

He picked up her shawl, which must have slid off during their kiss, and came toward her. Damaris snatched it and wrapped it tight around herself. She knew it would harm her cause to object to this latest plan, but she was furious with him.

"Very well," she said. "Does that mean you and Ashart will fight each other?"

"Probably."

"Then I hope you kill each other," she said sweetly, and left.

"Tiresome shrew," Ash said.

Fitz controlled a desire to pound his friend to a pulp, not least for interrupting and saying the wrong thing. "She's had a hard time of it, and you bear some of the blame."

"I never offered for her."

"The dowager made promises on your behalf, and you didn't object. Before you met Genova—after you met Genova!—you intended to marry Miss Myddleton's money."

Color flared in Ash's cheeks. "No longer—so why is she agreeing to tag along to Cheynings? Rothgar's her guardian now."

"You've clearly had an interview, too."

"A brief one. I was sent to rescue her and informed of the plan. I hoped she'd refuse."

"I had to talk her into it. She'll be better away from here. She's not part of the family and has no true friends here. And I don't want to abandon her."

Fitz wished he hadn't said that. A great many faculties seemed to be slipping out of his control.

Ash's brows rose. "Have you hopes? Good luck to you, but don't count any chickens. She's after the highest title she can buy. By the way, Rothgar has a strange request."

Fitz welcomed the change of subject. "What?"

"He asked if there were documents at Cheynings relating to Betty Crowley. You know—my great-great-grandmother?"

"One of Charles the Second's many mistresses, and thus source of the royal blood supposed to run in the Trayce veins? I believe the dowager might have mentioned her once or twice."

Ash laughed, for his grandmother made sure to

mention the "royal connection," as she called it, as often as possible, though heaven knew, descendants from the Merry Monarch's liaisons weren't rare.

"What's Rothgar's interest?" Fitz asked.

"He's Betty's great-great-grandson, too. Perhaps he's filling in his family tree. It seems an innocuous request, and I've decided that peace between us would be wise."

"Thank heavens. Are there any documents?"

"There must be. Though Betty married Randolph Prease, she bore only the one child, the royal one. He went by the name Charles Prease and later became Lord Vesey. His only surviving child was Grandy, so the title died with him and Storton House was sold. She was then Marchioness of Ashart, so the Prease papers were removed to Cheynings. I believe they were stored in the attics. I said I'd check while we're there."

"You," Fitz asked, "or me?"

Ash grinned. "You can't expect me to neglect Genova. Recruit Miss Myddleton to help you, and make love to her over the musty papers. Just make sure she doesn't harass Genova. I won't have her made unhappy."

"Genova can hold her own. And I'm sorry if this will dent your pride, but I doubt Miss Myddleton lusts after your title and grandeur anymore."

"She said as much to the dowager, and I liked her better for it."

"She is likable, Ash. She's no gentle, blushing maiden, but she has spirit."

"You are smitten! I thought you planned to make your future in Virginia."

"I do." Fitz walked toward the door, hoping to escape. "We should prepare for the fencing. How's it to be arranged?"

"You, I, Rothgar, and Lord Bryght, along with any

other gentleman who cares to take part. Each to fight the others."

"There's thirty or so men here. It could last all day."

"Given Rothgar's skill, I doubt many will try their blade. Lord Bryght's good, too. Should I have asked if you wanted to take part?"

Ash was clearly remembering that Fitz's performance at fencing had been unimpressive.

"Oh, I don't mind."

"Why are you looking wolfish?"

"I haven't exactly shown my full range of abilities. I'm hoping to beat Rothgar."

" 'Struth! You think you can?"

"I've never seen him fight, but yes, it's possible."

Ash laughed. "Why hide your light under a bushel?"

Fitz shrugged. "I've preferred not to draw attention, but this I cannot resist."

"Then I hope you do beat him. A blow for the Trayces."

"My apologies, but it will be a blow for the Fitzrogers."

"Perhaps it will win the heart of the heiress and make her forget the hunt for a coronet. I tell you, Fitz, I don't like the look of things in the colonies, and here you've a fortune ripe for the plucking."

"Zeus, Ash. I've no profession, no home, a scandal stuck to me like pitch, and a family I'd rather not bring into contact with anyone I cared for. If Damaris Myddleton offered herself to me on a plate, I'd have to refuse."

Ash looked as if he'd been hit on the head. "Do you want me to find you a position? As estate manager, perhaps? Or something in government?"

The offer was generous, but pointless. Employment had never been raised before, but at this point it was

the least of Fitz's problems. He ended the embarrassing moment by leaving the room.

Fitz went to the bedchamber to tidy himself for dinner, which would follow the fencing. He did so
quickly, preferring to avoid Ash for now, then whiled
away some time by wandering the corridors of the
great house making plans for a safe journey tomorrow.

At least, he tried to. His mind persisted in returning
to Damaris Myddleton.

Why had he not realized that flirting her into going
to Cheynings would be so dangerous? Fire blazed
when they touched. If he were free to do so he might
woo her, but he wasn't. He'd spoken the truth: He'd
bring no person he cared for into the mess of his life.

Temptation prickled all the same. Her fortune might
enable him to save his mother and sisters from his
brother, Hugh. He couldn't do anything directly about
Hugh, but with money he could afford to take Libby
and Sally with him to America and protect them there.

He pushed trepidation away. He doubted it would
work, and he'd not abuse any woman by marrying her
for a reason like that.

Chapter 6

At a quarter to two Fitz went to Damaris's room. He knocked and she opened the door herself, glowing in a gown the color of flames and indeed looking ready to run him through. He had to suppress a smile of pure pleasure at her straight shoulders, firm chin, and challenging eyes.

"Come in," she commanded.

He obeyed, noticing only when she shut the door that her maid was absent.

"You shouldn't have tried to trick me into agreeing to go to Cheynings," she stated. "You should simply have told me it was arranged, and why."

"But that wouldn't have been nearly so delightful."

He knew he shouldn't be doing this, shouldn't be teasing her, not when they were alone. He simply couldn't resist.

Her color almost matched her dress. "You will not do anything like that again."

"Kiss you like that?"

"Try to persuade me like that! And kiss me."

"Damaris, you asked me to kiss you."

"I admit it, but you used it."

"I also enjoyed it. I wanted to kiss you. As I do now. You look quite ravishing in that shade."

She frowned. "It's called Autumn Sunset. Idiotic,

for sunsets in autumn are no different in hue than in other seasons."

He took her hands. "No poetic temperament, I see."

"None."

"A poetic temperament isn't a weakness, you know. Poetry can combine with courage and power."

He shouldn't do it, but he kissed one long, elegant hand, fine and nimble from years at the keyboard. Hands that he could imagine touching him, even in intimate places. Her bed framed her. He wasn't insane enough to carry her there and do what he wanted to do, but he wasn't exactly sane, either.

"You have an example as proof?"

"What?" He had no idea what she was talking about.

"An example of a poet who is also brave and powerful."

He laughed softly and let her force him back to sense, if a nonsense conversation could do such a thing. They were due downstairs, and the bed was too tempting by far. He picked up a heavy silk shawl woven in browns, golds, and pinks and draped it around her shoulders.

"Let's see." He linked arms with her and led her to the door. "Many of last century's poets were forced into the civil war. Then we have Sir Philip Sidney, who died in battle in Tudor times."

"Was he a good soldier?" she asked as she pressed her hoops together to pass through the doorway. "Or a good poet?"

"Both, they say, but I confess, I cannot quote him."

"Having better things to do than to study the literary arts." She looked directly at him. "What is your real purpose here, Fitzroger?"

Her shrewdness caught his breath. "To enjoy Christmastide."

"And before that? You've been Ashart's boon companion for months, which can hardly be challenging."

"You'd be surprised," he said, but lightly, as if this were a game. "When I left the army, I decided to indulge in amusement for a while."

She made a thoughtful humming noise. "My life in Worksop was quiet, but that gave time for observation. People seek amusement that matches their natures. The idle amuse themselves in another type of idleness. The active are active in a different way. It even affects illness. The idle embrace bed rest too much, whilst the active fidget themselves out of bed and into trouble."

"And what trouble could I be fidgeting myself into here?"

"Me?"

The truth silenced him.

"What's more," she said, "you strike me as a hawk in a cage of singing birds."

Easy to laugh at that. "Do you truly see Rothgar, Ashart, Lord Bryght, and the rest as chirping canaries? You'll see your error soon."

"Perhaps it's just your army experience."

"What?"

"The glow around you."

"You see me as a saint now?"

"I didn't say halo, sir. It's as if you have a purpose when everyone else is idle."

'Struth. He must definitely be more on guard. He did feel more alive when involved in an important mission, and she was wickedly observant.

Two women emerged from a corridor just ahead. They turned to go downstairs, but not before giving Fitz and Damaris a speculative glance. He remembered their purpose here—to persuade everyone that Damaris was heart-whole.

"Perhaps the glowing effect comes from you," he murmured. "My pretty autumn sunset."

She stared at him. "Don't be foolish."

"I'm attempting brave poetic flirtation. *For effect.*"

He saw her remember. They were approaching the head of the great staircase where others milled. From below, the murmur of voices indicated people already gathered for the swordplay. A middle-aged couple approached from the opposite direction. The Knightsholmes were good-hearted people who hadn't cold-shouldered him, so they'd start their performance before them.

Fitz stepped back and declaimed: "Damaris steps in russet hue, which suits her as well as her cloak of blue. Her eyes so sharp affect my heart, and soon will pierce me through!"

People chuckled, and Damaris did, too. "I hope you fight better than you rhyme, sir."

He put a hand to his chest in pretend hurt. "I thought it clever for an impromptu, and it sprang sincerely from my broken heart."

"In badly broken verse, Fitzroger," drawled Lady Knightsholme, causing more chuckles. "You seem well recovered, Miss Myddleton."

Damaris paled, but Fitz raised her hand and kissed it, holding her eyes. "Join me in poetry, sweet lady. You and I together mend."

She stared, and he thought she couldn't do it, even with a simple rhyme, but then she said, "You will your steady presence lend?"

"Even if the heavens rend."

"Then I thank you, my dear friend."

Lady Knightsholme led applause, and Fitz linked arms with Damaris again and moved toward the stairs. The crush parted, so they led the way down, their audience following. He heard people comment on the clever exchange.

Had they been as surprised by her quick wit as he had? No, he'd not been exactly surprised, but impressed by its emergence despite panic. Damaris Myddleton was remarkably brave, and might be one of those people who achieved brilliance only when pushed to their limit. He wondered if God sometimes made mistakes. If she'd been born a boy, might she now be like her successful, piratical father?

As they reached the bottom of the stairs, he reminded her, "Smile and adore me."

"Only," she said, sweetly beaming, "temporarily."

Damaris hoped her smile didn't look as grotesque as she feared. This nonsense rhyming helped, but she still felt shaky to be facing the people who'd witnessed her behavior yesterday, so many of whom eyed her as if anticipating more of the same.

"Relax," he murmured into her ear as they mingled with the guests who were already in the hall. A circle of chairs awaited the audience, and some were already filled. Damaris felt as if they settled to observe her, not the swordplay.

She tried to act as if yesterday had never happened. A smile for middle-aged Miss Charlotte Malloren, uncertainly returned. A comment on the weather with Dr. Egan. An inquiry about Lady Walgrave's baby to Lady Bryght Malloren.

She turned to Fitzroger, trying to think of something witty to say, but nerves blanked her mind.

"There's nothing to fear. Nothing to hurt you here." Then he winced. "The deuce, I didn't intend that to rhyme."

It made her laugh, and she silently thanked him. "Do you think rhyming's addictive? If so, I've found the curative. What could rhyme with *addictive*?"

He raised a brow and she winced. "I didn't mean that, either. We're stuck in a rhyming trap!"

"Endlessly spouting pap."

"Forcing our tongues to flap—"

"Fitz."

They both turned, midlaugh. Ashart had come over with Genova Smith, her blond beauty enhanced by happiness, on his arm. Damaris held on to her smile. She had a part to act here, and what point in resenting Miss Smith's looks? As well curse the sky for being blue. Besides, the future Marchioness of Ashart was clearly as tense and wary as she.

"Fair friends," Fitzroger orated, "we greet you on this merry day, ready as always for most elegant play."

Ashart laughed, but in confusion. "What the devil . . . ?"

"Miss Myddleton and I are trapped in a rhyming curse."

Damaris's brain and tongue unlocked. "Than which, I assure you, nothing could be worse."

"I don't know," said Miss Smith. "We could all be stuck in a hearse." But then she frowned. "That's terrible."

Ashart kissed her hand. "Thank God. We're un-blighted."

"Except by love," Fitzroger said. "You are by Cupid benighted. Perhaps that's the key to protection."

"A magical antidote derived from affection?" Damaris offered. "Then we must seek devotion. Let's put it in motion!"

Ashart applauded, as did some people nearby. They were becoming a center of attention again, but creating the right impression.

"Your rhyming is skillful," Ashart remarked, "but you both scan atrociously. You could turn this curse to profit on the stage, however."

"A curse that leads to a fortune from bad verse?" Damaris asked.

Fitz grinned. "Such a fate could cause a man to expectorate."

"Internal rhymes now," Ashart said. " 'Tis bad, 'tis very bad."

"Sad, very sad," Fitzroger said.

And Damaris realized that she was thoroughly enjoying herself. She assembled a passage and turned to Fitzroger.

"Sir, before this curse grows worse we must both become very terse. No one can turn a single word to verse."

"Bravo!" cried Ashart, leading widespread applause. "Single words only from now on, Fitz. 'Tis my duty as your friend to keep you safe."

"Aye," said Fitzroger.

"Why?" asked Lady Arradale, newly arrived in the hall.

The whole place exploded with laughter. Ashart explained and their hostess laughed. "A duel of rhymes. We should try it again. But for now, everyone, please be seated for a duel of blades."

Damaris took her place beside Genova Smith, grateful for a moment to settle. She'd been swept up in the moment, but last time that had happened, she'd been swept to disaster. Most people's interest now seemed amused or even kindly, but she caught Lord Henry glaring at her. Doubtless he thought she was too bold. She almost glared back, but remembered she was free of him and inclined her head. He turned puce, which was a victory of sorts.

Rothgar stepped into the oval through the one-chair space left open. She was shocked to see him undressed down to stockings, breeches, and shirt. Would Fitzroger fight in a similar state?

"My friends, my cousin Ashart and I have long wanted to test each other's skill with the sword.

Hence, this tournament—merely for amusement, I assure you. No blood will be spilled."

A ripple of laughter stirred, because only days before a duel between the cousins might well have been to the death.

"A tournament with a small prize to lend excitement." Like a conjuror, Rothgar produced a spray of jewels on a golden chain. "A trinket, no more, but a pretty gift for a favored lady. At present the contestants are myself, Ashart, Lord Bryght, and Mr. Fitzroger, but any of you gentlemen are welcome to compete if you wish. We fence to first contact. A three-minute bout without contact will count as a draw. Sir Rolo has agreed to be timekeeper."

Sir Rolo Knightsholme grinned, holding up a large pocket watch.

"I would like to take part."

Lieutenant Osborne stepped forward, and Damaris suppressed a groan. He'd been a persistent suitor here, and she'd sometimes encouraged him to try to make Ashart jealous. She didn't want him to make a fool of himself over her, but she certainly didn't want him to win.

Another young gentleman, Mr. Stanton, rose, and he and Osborne left to take off confining layers of clothing. Lord Bryght joined his brother in the center of the oval, carrying two foils and also stripped down.

"Note well," Lord Bryght said to everyone, as he tossed his brother a foil, "that I have never claimed to be a better swordsman than Rothgar."

Even so, as soon as the match began he seemed brilliant to Damaris, who was shocked and gaping. She'd never seen men fence before and had imagined, especially in "play," some sort of delicate, tapping dance.

Instead, they hurtled backward and forward on

strong, supple legs, blind to all but each other and to seeking an opening for the delicate buttoned blades. She couldn't follow it, and could only react to the violent danger it pretended to be. Lord Rothgar's button touched his brother's chest, the blade flexing like a birch twig, and the bout ended.

Damaris breathed and put a hand to her chest. "Oh, my!"

"Indeed," said Miss Smith.

Damaris glanced sideways. "This is new to you, too?"

Miss Smith was flushed with excitement. "No, but I've never seen such speed. I doubt Rothgar need fear to give up his trinket."

"Ashart cannot compete?"

Miss Smith stiffened. "I'm sure he can."

Ashart entered the oval next, partnered with Mr. Stanton. It was soon obvious that Ashart *could* compete, and might even be as good as his cousin. When the bout about lasted the full time, Damaris suspected an act of kindness. Even so, laughing and breathing hard, Mr. Stanton bowed out of the contest.

Fitzroger and Osborne were next. Damaris was disappointed that neither showed the skill of the other fencers. Perhaps a soldier's life didn't leave space for ornamental fighting.

Nor, she remembered, was swordplay always ornamental. Not long ago Lord Rothgar had killed a man with this deadly art, and it almost seemed that Osborne would have liked to kill his opponent. He lost in the end, and shot her a thwarted, angry glance before stalking out of the circle to stand waiting for another contest.

The burden of her wealth weighed on her—that men might kill for it.

The air seemed full of tension now, and when Ash-

art returned to match Lord Bryght, she saw that both
men's shirts clung to their bodies. Even these short
bursts of violent power had summoned sweat.

Perhaps something of the feud between the Mallorens and the Trayces sparked to life, for Damaris
sensed an extra edge to Ashart's intensity, an extra
power to his drive. Lord Bryght was soon grinning,
clearly finding it great fun, but Damaris had her hands
clasped tight as she prayed that no one be hurt.

"Time!" called Sir Rolo, and both fencers stepped
back, sucking in breath.

Damaris, too, was breathing deeply, and part of it
was because of the beautiful contours hinted at by
damp, clinging lawn. She glanced at Miss Smith and
saw a similar reaction, but perhaps also a similar fear.
Why in heaven's name did men think this amusement?

Rothgar and Osborne fought next, and the young
man looked nervous before they started, which
showed some sense. Though Damaris knew nothing of
the art of the sword, she suspected that the three minutes that followed were an exhibition of mastery that
gave Osborne no chance of scoring while bringing the
bout to a courteous draw. It was, she assumed, a gentle suggestion that he bow out as Mr. Stanton had,
and he took it, though not without another thwarted
glance at her. It might have been flattering if she
thought he cared for anything but her fortune.

"So," said Miss Smith, perhaps to herself, "the main
four are left." She turned to Damaris. "Who do you
think will win?"

Damaris didn't want to be unkind, but she said,
"Rothgar."

Miss Smith nodded, frowning. "I hope Ashart
doesn't mind too much."

Murmurs around the room suggested others were
speculating. Two men slapped hands, which probably
indicated a wager. If she had the chance, would she

place money on Rothgar? She wanted to wager on Fitzroger, but when he came out with Lord Bryght, she anticipated only defeat.

But then everything changed. Perhaps Lord Bryght had intended to stage an entertaining bout before ending it, but in moments his relaxed good humor fled. His eyes became intent, and his movements increasingly desperate.

Damaris couldn't imagine how the quick wrists and supple legs kept both men out of danger, but the bout went the full three minutes. When Sir Rolo called, "Time!" both fencers bent to breathe, running sweat.

Men handed them cloths to wipe their faces, and they straightened to do so, chests still heaving. Fitzroger pulled the ribbon from his hair, which had mostly escaped to plaster around his face. His sudden grin at Lord Bryght, fully returned, hit Damaris, shocking as lightning on a pitch-dark night.

Joy. He'd enjoyed that. Why was she sure his life was short of such pure joy? How foolish to want to shower it upon him like sunlight, like diamonds. She realized she was applauding, that everyone was. There'd be money laid on Fitzroger now, and she felt fiercely proud of that.

Rothgar came out, smiling, even if there seemed something wolfish about it. "This becomes more interesting than I expected, I admit. So Bryght has completed his matches with a score of a loss and two draws."

"What did I tell you?" Lord Bryght said amiably. "I'll fight Fitzroger again for the pure pleasure of it, though."

"Another time," his brother said. "Ashart, myself, and Fitzroger have a win and a draw each. Ashart and I should match off next, being rested, but then Fitzroger would have two bouts in a row. Therefore if you agree, gentlemen, I will fight to retain the trinket. Against you first, Ashart?"

Ashart stepped forward, then halted. "That gives you two bouts in a row, cousin. If you will allow him a short rest, I designate Fitzroger my champion."

"By all means. As long as the champion receives the prize."

Ashart agreed, and Rothgar turned to Fitzroger, who was still mopping sweat. "I welcome an opportunity to test blades with you, sir. Where have you learned?" The two men fell into a discussion about fencing that Damaris couldn't hear, especially with chatter rising all around.

Ashart strolled over to Miss Smith. "I hope you don't regret the necklace, Genni. I'll buy you a better."

Damaris looked elsewhere, thinking, *So much for economy.* But she couldn't help overhearing the couple.

"Of course not," Miss Smith said. "A match between you might not have been wise."

"But interesting. Fitz against Rothgar will be equally so, I think."

Damaris looked at Fitzroger, who seemed recovered now except that his shirt still clung and his hair still rioted. He brushed some back from his face, and the movement emphasized his long, lean body. He was more lightly built than the other men, but there was clearly nothing weaker about him.

She felt as breathless as the fencers, and almost as hot. It was a strictly physical reaction, but something she'd never experienced before, not even during their quite astonishing kisses.

It was animal, she recognized. Base, but powerful, throbbing between her thighs and urging her to embarrass herself again here. To rise and go to him, touch him, wind herself around him . . .

She inhaled and tore her eyes away to see that she wasn't the only woman ogling him. She looked to Ashart, similarly undressed and damp, and so close she could smell his sweat. He had no special effect on her.

Fitzroger announced that he was ready. Ashart sat on the floor at Genova's feet. "Pray for victory, love."

"Can he win?" Miss Smith asked, putting a hand on his broad shoulder.

He covered it with his own. "There's a chance, at least, a better one than I would have had. You haven't seen either of them fence his best yet."

Rothgar could be more brilliant? Damaris's heart sank.

The bout began with surprising gentleness. Both men seemed to be tapping and trying, a secret dialogue that she couldn't understand. Little movements of the blade, countered in a certain way. The step back, the return. The new test. The response.

Then, abruptly, Fitzroger fired into action, driving Rothgar back in a flurry of attack almost into the watchers sitting at one end. But Rothgar evaded in a twist that clashed bodies for a moment, and the positions were reversed. It was the first physical contact of the day, and showed a different level of intent. This, she suspected, came closer to fighting to the death.

They fought fast and furiously now, but with moves, twists, and turns she'd not seen before. Sometimes she thought one or other attempted to flick the sword out of the other man's hand. She knew it mostly by the shared grin that followed.

Then Sir Rolo bellowed, "Time!"

Both men stepped back, breathing deeply, running with sweat. Both nodded, and plunged back into battle. Damaris put a hand over her mouth. Did they mean to kill each another?

She gasped when Fitzroger went down on one knee, but then his foil shot up toward the heart. Rothgar spun and knocked the blade aside, and almost skewered Fitzroger from above, but Fitzroger was already rolling to his feet in one action, lithe as a cat, his weapon flicking toward the exposed flank. It was parried and they were off again.

Damaris had to remind herself that the flexible, buttoned blades couldn't do much damage except to an eye, and these skillful men never let the blades get close to the face. All the same, her mouth was dry as paper, her heart pounded, and she wanted this over—over before someone was hurt.

And she wanted Fitzroger to win.

With burning ferocity, she wanted her hero to win!

It was stopped in the end by pure exhaustion. As if spoken and agreed, both men stepped back and bent over, fighting for breath. They were swarmed by excited men as they wiped their faces and necks, both grinning and radiating extreme delight.

Clearly, this bout would be talked about in manly circles for years to come. Looking around, Damaris could see that many women would remember it, too.

"Men!" Genova Smith said, and Damaris saw Ashart had joined the throng.

Damaris wasn't used to men and didn't understand their ways, but she knew exactly what Miss Smith meant. Mysterious, exasperating, but breathtakingly wonderful men. And she had just witnessed their true delight.

She recognized the spirit that had sent her father sailing the seas. Perhaps the fortunes won had been incidental to the thrill of the challenge. And her mother had expected him to settle in Worksop.

Fitzroger slipped out of the crowd and came toward her, the necklace in his hand. Her heart began to pound again, so hard that she feared she might faint.

He dropped to one knee, holding out the prize. "I believe I'm supposed to present this to my fair lady."

The casual tone could be offensive, but his eyes

were bright and his skin glowed, making him impossible to resist. Besides, they were watched by everyone.

She took the pretty piece in which tiny stones and pearls made a circlet of flowers on the chain. "I believe," she said in the same tone, "I'm supposed to say something like, 'My hero!' "

His eyes lit with amusement. "No, no, dear lady. You are supposed to reward me with a kiss."

People chuckled, but a kiss seemed too intimate, too dangerous here, where she could feel the heat of his body and smell his sweat—a smell, she realized, entirely different from Ashart's. Unique. Identifiable. Arousing in and of itself.

He took her hand and placed it on his shoulder, his hot, damp shoulder. His bright eyes challenged her. In response, she wanted to grab his hair as she had earlier and ravish him. But instead she leaned forward and placed a chaste kiss upon his lips. "My hero."

He rose with a subtle power that could slay her all on its own, managing somehow to draw her to her feet at the same time and to turn her. Then his hands were brushing her neck as he put the necklace around it, as he fastened the clasp.

His fingers stroked the nape of her neck for a moment, sending shivers down her spine. She could do nothing but try to stay calm when she wanted to turn and press herself to his body, to inhale, to encircle.

Then he was gone. When she did turn, he was leaving to dress.

"How pretty," Miss Smith said.

Damaris fingered the necklace, dazed.

Lady Bryght came over, petite, red-haired, and smiling. "Congratulations, Miss Myddleton."

"I did nothing for it."

"No, no!" Lady Bryght said, laughing. "Never think like that. A lady inspires a gentleman's greatest achievements and thus can take credit for them all."

Lady Arradale joined them. "That's why we delight in capturing the best specimens."

Lady Bryght eyed her. "Are we going to fight over who is best, Diana?"

"Only with pistols." Lady Arradale smiled at Damaris. "I'm an excellent shot. Do you know how to use a pistol, Miss Myddleton?"

"No." Damaris remembered her foolish attempt to take out the carriage pistol, and Fitzroger's strong hand over hers.

"You shall learn. I'm delighted you're to be an even closer part of our family as Rothgar's ward. I shall call you Damaris, and you must call me Diana."

"Thank you, my lady. Diana."

Damaris felt overwhelmed, but was relieved to talk to the ladies for a while rather than having to mingle. She suspected it was an intentional kindness.

Then Diana said, "May I presume upon you as I would with a sister, Damaris, and ask you to sing for us? The men need to change their clothes, I fear, to be suited to polite company. A song from you would pass the time delightfully."

Nerves tightened Damaris's throat, but she was confident in this one thing, at least. And when Lady Bryght said, "Oh, yes, please do!" she could not refuse.

Diana clapped her hands and announced the treat, and everyone settled to listen. Damaris collected herself, wondering what song would best suit the moment. A playful piece came to mind that seemed daring, but it should confirm her carefree disposition, and seemed relevant to the moment.

She smiled around to everyone and began.

> *What does any lady wish*
> *More than a handsome hero?*
> *What good roast meat upon her dish*

Without a handsome hero?
For oh, a lady cannot abide
Without a hero by her side,
By her side, a hero.

Some of the ladies applauded, and all were smiling.

A lady may have a fine circle of friends
All of the finest station,
Theater and balls she attends
But she's saddest in the nation.
For, oh, a lady cannot abide
Without a hero by her side,
By her side, a hero.

She responded to Sir Rolo's grin by walking closer and singing to him.

Will any man do to assuage her desire,
To have a hero by her?
No, he must be willing to leap through fire
And challenge dragons for her.
For, oh, a lady cannot abide
Without a hero by her side.
By her side, a hero.

Laughing, Sir Rolo backed away in pretended horror. She turned and saw Fitzroger coming downstairs, restored to careless elegance. She strolled toward him, enjoying the acoustics of the hall.

Be gone, ye men of timid hue,
A lady needs a hero.
Find a villain and run him through,
To prove that you're a hero!
For, oh, a lady cannot abide . . .

People began to join in, and she turned to encourage them.

> *Without a hero by her side.*
> *By her side, a hero.*

Fitzroger reached the bottom of the stairs and said to all, "Are jewels not enough for you ladies?"

"No!" some chorused.

Damaris turned back to him, laughing with the rest.

> *Prove yourself through fire and steel, sir,*
> *Prove that you're a hero.*
> *Then before you a lady might kneel, sir,*
> *Kneel before a hero!*

In danger of faltering because of her own daring, she put her hand on his sleeve.

> *For, oh, a lady longs to abide*
> *With a true hero by her side.*
> *By her side, a hero.*

She stepped back and curtsied deep to him, then turned and curtsied to the applauding hall.

"By gad, Miss Myddleton," Sir Rolo declared, "you could make a second fortune on the stage!"

"That's always comforting to know," she replied, smiling but shivering with awareness of the possessive hand Fitzroger had placed on her shoulder.

"You would kneel?" he asked softly.

She turned to him, slipping free of his touch. "Before a hero, yes."

"Don't you think a true hero should avoid exposing a lady to fire and steel?"

"No, I want adventure."

The challenge shivered in the air between them.

"I shall have to arrange it then. Anything," he said with a bow, "to be my lady's hero."

Damaris felt as if the floor were melting beneath her feet, but he took her hand and led her in to dinner.

The long table was set for the fifty or so guests, and gold and silver platters gleamed in the candlelight. Rothgar's personal musicians began to play out in the hall, sweet music drifting in to enhance another magical afternoon and evening.

As always, music was balm to Damaris. It soothed her nervous excitement and helped her pay attention to the plan. However, clearly everything was going well.

It certainly wasn't difficult to demonstrate that she had no interest in Lord Ashart and found Fitzroger attractive. She knew it must show in every smile and gesture.

As it was, people no longer watched her. At first talk was of fencing and heroes, and then some began to play the rhyming game. Damaris happily took part, for she found it easy.

She truly did come to feel she belonged, but all the same, she was relieved when Lady Arradale rose and led the ladies away to the drawing room for tea and conversation. Once there, Damaris went to the harpsichord and played. Music provided respite.

"You play so well, dear!"

Damaris looked up, still playing, to smile at Lady Thalia Trayce, extraordinarily dressed in a white gown shot with silver and trimmed with pink lace. Her fluffy white hair was crowned with a confection of lace and feathers.

She was somewhat crazed, but Damaris had heard it was because her betrothed had died in battle when she was young and she'd never recovered. She was harmless—quite sweet, in fact.

"Thank you, Lady Thalia."

"And your song earlier. So witty. I do agree about heroes, dear. And we are to be traveling companions! I'm sure that will be so delightful, even at Cheynings." She pulled a smiling face and shuddered. "The dowager has let it go sadly, I hear. But Fitzroger! Now there's a hero for you." She looked around. "Whist!" she declared, and headed for a table.

Her sister, Lady Calliope—an enormous lady in a wheeled chair—and an older couple joined her.

Damaris stared after her, wondering if the words *a hero for you* had been meant as they'd sounded. *Of course not.*

Damaris would like to learn whist, for she gathered it was the most popular game in society, but cards had been forbidden in Birch House. Her only experience had been playing cribbage with a bedridden old woman. She should have taken lessons while at Thornfield Hall, but she'd not thought of it. She would take lessons in London. She'd watched some games here and thought she understood the basic principles.

As usual at Rothgar Abbey, the gentlemen did not linger long over their port, and they soon joined the ladies. When dancing was announced, Fitzroger invited her to go to the ballroom with him, and Damaris was delighted to accept. As the evening unfolded, she never lacked a partner. She had to dance with Osborne, who put on a tragic air and called her cruel, but even that couldn't dampen her spirits.

When she eventually returned to her room, definitely ready for her bed, she rejoiced that Fitzroger had been right to make her return. She wrote herself a note as reminder: *Reward Fitzroger.* Smiling idiotically to be writing his name, she tucked the note into her trinket box. In doing so, however, she saw her mother's wedding ring.

On her deathbed, Abigail Myddleton had asked Damaris to take the ring off her finger, saying, "They call it a symbol of eternity, daughter, but remember, that can be an eternity of sorrow, an eternity of pain. I'll not go into eternity wearing that man's shackle."

She wouldn't be dissuaded, so Damaris had obeyed, then asked, "What shall I do with it?"

"Keep it. And remember, never trust a man."

Inside the ring, Damaris had found words engraved, presumably at her father's request: YOURS UNTIL DEATH.

And then he'd abandoned his wife.

She rolled up her note to herself and put the paper through the ring as another kind of reminder.

Never trust a man.

Chapter 7

The next day, Damaris took breakfast in her room and supervised the packing. At ten o'clock, she went down the hall, cloaked and muffed. They could have made an earlier start, but the Dowager Lady Ashart had refused. And now, at the appointed time, she was not there.

Ashart and Miss Smith were talking to Lady Arradale. Lady Thalia, in a mantle of flowery velvet, sat between Lord Rothgar and Fitzroger. Damaris wanted to join him, but she would not give in to temptation. Instead she wandered the hall, savoring memories of pleasant times here. Especially of the the sword fighting.

A tingle of heat started and she slid a look at Fitzroger. She caught him looking at her and looked hastily away. Where was the dowager?

How selfish and irritating she was. She seemed to think she was the queen. Given command of this journey, Damaris would leave without her.

"What about that prickly garland causes such a ferocious scowl?"

Damaris started and realized that she had been scowling at a holly branch adorning the mantelpiece. "I was thinking of a prickly old woman," she said to Fitzroger, praying she wasn't blushing.

"What an excellent thing that she didn't become

your grandmother-in-law, my sweet. The war would have been endless."

"I wish you wouldn't call me that."

"My sweet? I'm hinting you in a more honeyed direction."

"What am I now? Vinegar?"

"At times."

"Vinegar is a very useful liquid, sir. For cleaning, pickling, dressing wounds . . ."

"But not welcome if it's supposed to be wine."

Damaris fought a smile. She delighted in these verbal jousts. "It's hardly strange if I'm sour. We're going to Cheynings in winter, and I'm doomed to the constant company of a blinding beauty."

"You can hold your own."

"Tell me I, too, am a beauty, sir, and I'll know you for a lying scoundrel."

Despite her words she waited for flattering reassurance, primed to fire at him again.

Instead, he looked her over. "Plain as a pikestaff."

"What?"

He pretended surprise. "You don't want to be a sharp and dangerous weapon? Very well, Genova is a faceted diamond that catches every eye with obvious flame. You, my honey, are a blood-red cabochon ruby, a smooth surface beneath which seethes fire and mystery. Don't gape."

He gently closed her mouth, then dropped a light kiss on her lips. "I might try to convince you of your charms, but it would be much too dangerous."

"Why?" she breathed.

"It would be like training a loaded cannon on all the men of England."

"Lud, sir, I can't follow you. Pikes, rubies, cannons? And besides," she said with a grimace, "the men will line up to be shot with my moneybags. They won't care about me."

"They will, Damaris. I promise you, they will."

He sounded far too serious, so she turned her back. "Flattery again? I do wish you wouldn't."

"I care about you." She felt him step close behind her. "And it has nothing to do with your moneybags, as I have no hope of marrying them."

"So you say."

"Don't doubt my word."

She spun around. "Or?"

Something crackled in the air between them, and she realized that she'd love a fight as fierce as the sword fights yesterday.

But he stepped back, adjusting the simple frill at his cuff. "Unfair, my sweet. If any other woman implied I was a liar I'd remove myself from her presence for all time, but I'm sworn to dance attendance on you."

"I release you, then. I want no unwilling servant."

"I'm not your servant."

"Attendant, then. I have no need of you."

"Have you not? You need someone to prevent you from throwing yourself away on the wrong man."

She brushed it off with a laugh. "I promise you, I will marry no lower than a viscount. Does that suffice?"

"Title has little to do with it. I'll make sure you choose wisely."

"Whether I want you to or not?"

"Yes."

She inhaled a truly irritated breath. "You have no authority over me, sir, and I'll marry whomever I choose!"

"Even me?"

Damaris snapped, "Yes!" before seeing the trap. "But not until you're a viscount." She escaped to Lady Arradale's side, knowing she'd lost that skirmish.

Perish the man.

All the same, she had a hard time not smiling. She'd had no idea that arguing with a man could be so exciting. She sizzled from that exchange and hugged his blatant flattery to herself.

A smooth surface beneath which seethes fire and mystery. Oh, if only it were true. Her priceless ruby necklace, which she'd not yet worn in public, had at its center an enormous cabochon ruby. When might she have an opportunity to wear it where Fitzroger would see it? It was suitable for only the grandest occasion. Perhaps in London . . .

A flurry on the stairs announced the dowager, finally deigning to join them.

"Don't worry," Fitzroger said, re-joining her. "Rothgar would never permit it."

"What? Shooting the dowager?"

He grinned. "Marriage to me."

"Oh, that," she said, deliberately dismissive. "At least we can be on our way."

"About time, too. Normally we'd cover the forty miles to Cheynings in daylight, but though the snow is melting here, there's no knowing what the roads are like elsewhere."

"You worry too much," she teased, but he did seem concerned.

Damaris went outside with him to find that four coaches were lined up in front of the abbey, each with six strong horses in the shafts. The first and fourth were plain vehicles already loaded with servants and luggage. The second was a huge, gilded vehicle with a crest on the door and a coronet on each corner of the roof. The third was a plainer but still grand traveling carriage painted green and brown.

Paths had been swept to two of the carriages' doors, and Ashart and Miss Smith were already waiting beside the green-and-brown one, which Damaris would share with her rival. As she went down the steps to join them she waited for the familiar resentment to bite.

It didn't.

Genova Smith was welcome to the wasteful, rakish marquess, especially as marriage to him meant close association with his bleak home and his bitter grandmother. She only wished she'd realized that earlier.

The pristine snow made the landscape beautiful, but the air was bitterly cold, so Damaris entered the coach immediately. A servant deposited her carriage bag at her feet, then closed the door. The couple remained outside, talking as if each were the other's food and they in danger of starving.

Damaris rolled her eyes, slipped her hands out of her muff, and took off her gloves. She realized the coach was pleasantly warm, so she unfastened her cloak and set it back.

Genova Smith's cloak was quite like her own in color, but of cloth, not velvet. And lined with rabbit rather than rare chinchilla. It was horribly petty to be pleased about that, but Damaris wasn't yet above such thoughts. To help avoid them, she looked away from the couple to inspect the carriage. It was as warm and comfortable as a cozy parlor in the finest home.

She found the explanation of the warmth beneath the carpet on the floor—a layer of hot bricks.

The thickly upholstered seats were covered in red damask, and curtains of the same material were tied back at the windows. Candles sat ready in gilded sconces shielded behind glass. No, she certainly didn't understand the style in which the impoverished Marquess of Ashart lived.

She found shallow cupboards set into the walls of the coach containing a selection of drinks and amusements—cards; counters; boards and pieces for chess, drafts, and backgammon; a cribbage board; and a copy of Mr. Hoyle's rules for card games.

Every eventuality provided for, including ignorance.

She decided she might as well study whist on the journey and took out the book. She'd read only part of the introduction, however, before the door opened and Genova Smith climbed in. She gave Damaris a quick smile, but then turned back to the marquess, who stood outside, keeping the door open. Damaris was about to complain when he closed it and went to mount his horse.

Miss Smith remained entranced, watching him settle into the saddle and his groom adjust his heavy riding cloak over the horse's back end. Good thing he had a servant to do it for him, for his wits were clearly still on Miss Smith. Damaris hoped his horse knew its way home.

Vinegar and honey, she reminded herself and turned to look out of her own window, which faced the house. Lord Rothgar and Lady Arradale stood there, cloaked, gloved, their breath misting, waiting to see their guests on their way. Fitzroger sat a horse nearby, definitely not gazing in rapture at her.

As if he would.

And better that he have more sense.

This traveling party certainly need not fear highwaymen. In addition to Ashart and Fitzroger, four outriders were mounted and ready, and the men on the driving boxes would be armed, too. Perhaps she needn't have left her valuable jewelry here, but she wouldn't need rubies and emeralds at Cheynings, and when Lord Rothgar traveled to London, he would be equally well guarded.

The coachman cracked his whip, and Damaris waved good-bye to her new guardian. To think that yesterday she'd been fleeing this place, certain that her life was blighted.

House and owners passed out of sight, but Fitzroger kept pace just ahead of her window, as magnificent on horseback as with a sword. What a dashing hero he would make.

He glanced sideways, caught her eye, and smiled. She knew she shouldn't but she smiled back.

"How delightfully warm it is in here."

Damaris turned to see that Genova Smith had also put aside her muff, taken off her gloves, and put back her cloak.

"Quite luxurious," Damaris agreed.

"I traveled to Rothgar Abbey in the other coach, and I assure you it casts this one into the shade." Miss Smith's beautiful blue eyes twinkled. "Risqué nymphs painted on the ceiling, gilded carvings every-where, and padding on the seats as comfortable as pillows."

"I'm surprised Lord Ashart can afford it." Damaris winced, wishing she could take the comment back.

"His father commissioned it. Ashart never uses it. He prefers to ride. I prefer simple living, too."

Damaris managed not to say something sarcastic about Lord Ashart's version of simple living. "You could hardly prefer to be poor."

"Would you think me foolish if I admitted that I'd rather Ashart were a simple man?"

Damaris hesitated, but then spoke the truth. "Yes, for how could he be? I mean, you love him because of what and who he is. If he were a simple man he would be someone else."

"Goodness, I suppose that's true." Miss Smith seemed astonished. That Damaris Myddleton might have said something insightful? "In fact, I know it is. My mother warned me to never marry a man in hopes of changing him. Marry a man you like and admire on the day you say your vows, she would say."

"Whereas my mother was more cynical. Her advice

was never to believe a word a man said when he was trying to get me to the altar. Or into his bed."

"She must have been a wise woman," Miss Smith said.

"Hardly. She married my father."

"He was cruel to her?"

Damaris didn't want to talk about this, but she couldn't think how to avoid answering. "Only by being absent."

"Ah. I understand he spent a great deal of time in the East, making his fortune. How sad that your mother couldn't travel with him."

Damaris wasn't sure that choice had ever been offered, but she said, "She was attached to Worksop."

Miss Smith didn't say anything, but Damaris could hear what a dismal epitaph that made. *Attached to Worksop.* She had to say more.

"My father founded his fortune on my mother's modest dowry. In return, she expected him to return to her once he was rich. Instead, he made only the briefest visits. It broke her heart."

"That must have been a difficult situation for you."

Understanding caught Damaris on the raw. "Good training for being jilted."

"Ashart did not jilt you."

"He coldheartedly planned to marry me for my money."

"As you coldheartedly planned to marry him for his title."

Damaris inhaled a sharp breath.

But it was true. "Very well," she said, then let out a sigh. "I was as calculating as he, and we are both best out of it." She might as well get it all over with. "I owe you an apology, Miss Smith. I behaved badly at times over the past days."

Genova Smith blinked, then grasped one of Damaris's hands. "Oh, no, you were shamefully misled! I'm so sorry for it."

Damaris was unused to such warm contact with women, and unsure how to react. "Perhaps we can agree to a truce then."

Miss Smith squeezed her hand. "Please, in that spirit, will you call me Genova?"

"Of course. How kind." Damaris smiled and responded as she meant. "But only if you'll call me Damaris."

"With pleasure. Such a pretty name."

Damaris slid her hand free. "It's Greek for heifer." Immediately she regretted the sharp response. To escape, she turned to look out of her window.

"Ah," said Genova Smith. "You want Fitzroger."

Damaris whipped around. "Certainly not!"

"Why not? He's delicious. He only needs some occupation. He's the sort to do well at whatever he attempts."

Mention of occupation reminded Damaris that she must reward him. Perhaps once she did that she could get rid of the effect he had on her. Meanwhile, she realized Genova Smith might know more about him than she did, and this journey offered a wonderful opportunity to question her.

"He must have family who could help him establish himself," she probed.

"He seems to be estranged from them. But it's a respectable family. From Herefordshire, I think. And a title. Yes. Viscount Leyden."

A viscount! Damaris hoped her shock wasn't obvious. But she'd joked about marrying a viscount.

"His older brother holds it," Genova went on.

"Old*est*, I assume, Octavius meaning he's the eighth in the family."

Genova considered her. "Yes, he's unlikely to inherit. Is that such a huge obstacle?"

Damaris shrugged. "Folly to marry low when the world is full of higher prospects."

"Then Ashart is a fool. I have nothing."

"He clearly values your charm and beauty." Damaris didn't intend the comment to be vinegary, but she feared it was.

Genova cocked her head. "If a lord can marry for charm and beauty, why shouldn't a lady do the same? Especially when she's rich."

"Perhaps women are more sensible. Beauty and even charm will fade, but title and position last forever."

"And how much happiness has that brought the Dowager Lady Ashart?"

Genova's observation was sharp enough to make Damaris gasp. When she added this to Rothgar's comment about Earl Ferrers, all her plans threatened to crumble. She turned away, but that gave her once again an alluring picture of Fitzroger.

Hers for the buying. It was true. Hadn't he said as much?

"More to the point," she muttered, "why can't women do as men do and take a spouse for some things and lovers for the rest?"

"Damaris!"

She turned back, pleased to have shocked someone so worldly-wise as Genova. Someone who'd sailed the seven seas and, they said, fought pirates.

"We can't, though, can we? Just as we can't be naval heroes, or sail to the Orient to make our fortunes."

"You're dangerous." Genova was wide-eyed, but admiring, too.

"That would be nice, but I'm sure it would bring nothing but grief. Do you play cribbage?"

Genova accepted the change of subject, and they settled to a game. Their skills seemed equal, so it re-

quired concentration, and by the time they stopped
for the first change of horses, Damaris was even enjoying herself.

She admitted she was coming to like her companion.
Genova was pleasant and had a droll sense of humor.
And what benefit was there in clinging to her
resentments?

Most of the time the snow was no problem, but in places
it had drifted, making the going difficult. It also masked
dips and deep ruts. The principal carriages weren't incon-
venienced too much for the advance one, and the outriders warned of problems, but the going was slow.

With cleaner roads they could have hoped to make
Cheynings by two and eat dinner there, but instead
they stopped to dine at the King's Head in Persham.
All stood ready for them. Damaris used a screened
chamber pot in a bedchamber, and then went to the
private parlor, where their dinner was laid out. Only
the dowager and Lady Thalia were there. She could
guess why Ashart and Genova delayed, but where was
Fitzroger? Oh, no, she would not constantly be aware
of his presence or absence.

The two old ladies had begun their soup, so she
joined them.

"Where are those silly creatures?" Lady Thalia
asked. "Living on love, I suppose. Ah, I remember
those days!"

The dowager looked up. "Your love died."

Damaris saw poor Lady Thalia's stricken face and
barely suppressed a shocked protest. She plunged to
the rescue. "Oxtail soup is so rich, isn't it? And welcome after so many hours on the road."

Lady Thalia was not distracted. "My dearest Richard did not die of starvation, Sophia, but of a sword
wound." She pulled out a lacy handkerchief and
dabbed her eyes.

"Wouldn't a romantic like you believe that love should have kept him safe?"

"No, how could I?" Whether real or assumed, Lady Thalia's incomprehension was an excellent response. "Many loved ones die in war. Or otherwise. Four of your children have died, Sophia, and I'm sure you must have loved them just as much as I loved dear Richard."

The dowager went white. "A mother's love is a different matter, Thalia, which you will never know."

"No, alas, but so very many children die. So unfair of God to make mother love a *weaker* power, don't you think?"

Horrified, Damaris leaped in again. "The ways of God are beyond human understanding."

The dowager turned on her. "Keep your nose out of things that don't concern you, girl! You've washed your hands of my family. So be it."

Praise the Lord, Genova and Ashart came in then, Fitzroger close behind.

Ashart entered smiling, but seemed to read the atmosphere. "The soup smells delicious," he said, seating Genova, who shot Damaris a wide-eyed glance.

That started Lady Thalia chattering about soup, oxen, and, by some invisible connection, a dress she'd worn to court forty years before. She seemed all froth and silliness now, but that moment of naked blades had not been an illusion. There was more to Lady Thalia Trayce than Damaris had guessed.

That made her wonder how many people were not what they seemed. Fitzroger, for example. And even the dowager.

The poor woman had lost many, perhaps all of her children, so perhaps she had reason for her bitter nature. She resolved to try to be gentler with her.

Fitzroger sat beside her and served himself soup

from the tureen. "I hope you aren't finding the journey too slow."

"No. Genova and I are engaged in a battle royal at cribbage."

He smiled. "I'm glad it's only at cards."

She wished she could talk to him about the battle between the old ladies, for it distressed her, but the conversation had become general.

When they were ready to leave, Fitzroger assisted her with her cloak. "Another hour and a half, I think. We've sent ahead for an extra change."

It was already after three and the days were short in winter. "So we will travel into the dark," Damaris said.

"Yes." Something in his tone gave her words a weight she had never intended.

Chapter 8

When Damaris settled into the newly warm vehicle, Genova asked, "Is something amiss?"

Damaris could hardly pin down her mood. "Fitzroger seems concerned."

"I think it must be the effect of the dowager. What a blighting presence she can be."

"Yes."

Genova sounded concerned herself, and it wasn't surprising. Her future must include the Dowager Marchioness of Ashart, and as Fitzroger had said, the likelihood of her leaving Cheynings was remote. Ashart had a town house, of course, but he would have to spend part of his time on his estate, and children were best raised in country air.

Even the weather had turned sullen. The sky had clouded earlier in the day, and now that the sun was setting, the clouds were turning the color of a bruise. The cold seemed damper despite the fresh hot bricks, and the pretty white snow was gray.

The carriage lights had been lit to help the coachman see the way, and while they provided a warm glow, they also made everything around them seem darker. Fitzroger rode near the light on Damaris's side, still watchful, still alert.

Genova leaned against Damaris's shoulder to look

in the same direction. Damaris couldn't remember another woman touching her with such careless intimacy, but she liked it. It was as she imagined a sister would act.

"I have wondered what he's up to," Genova said thoughtfully.

Damaris turned her head. "You, too, think he has some extra purpose?"

"He's not made to be idle. But he's not long from war. That could be why he seems on edge."

"Do you know what battles he was involved in?"

"No. Ashart might. Men tend to think ladies don't want to hear about such things."

"I don't suppose I'd want to hear the details." Damaris turned completely and settled back in her seat. "You must have experienced battle."

"Yes, though not often. Whenever possible women and children were put onshore before action. I saw more of the lingering effects."

"You nursed the wounded?"

"Yes."

"So did I. The local wounded in Worksop. My grandfather was a physician, so when he died there was a natural connection to the doctor who replaced him. Dr. Telford was one of the few guests my mother welcomed. As I grew older I assisted him sometimes. In the apothecary, but also in nursing the wounded or elderly. Not the sick, for that might expose me to contagion. I would sit with them, too. Reading or playing cards. It gave me something to do."

Genova frowned. "Did you not have friends your own age? Go to school? In our wandering life a part of me longed for a settled home and lifelong friends."

"Whereas I often longed to travel. Even to join my father in the East. A folly, that, when he cared nothing for me."

Genova briefly squeezed her hand, and this time

Damaris welcomed it. But she didn't want to talk about her parents.

"So you think Fitzroger is simply an ex-officer?"

"It could be so. Military action requires a fire inside, for most men don't easily kill their fellows. In some it smolders on for a while."

"Smolders," Damaris echoed, liking the word for all the wrong reasons.

It must have shown, for Genova said, "Be careful. It can be . . . inflammatory."

Damaris searched her face. "I had begun to suspect that you and Ashart wanted to marry me off to him."

"Faith, no! What made you think that?"

"It would be logical."

"Hardly. I'm sure it would be lovely. For him. Perhaps for you." She laughed. "You've startled me out of my wits, but I assure you, we've never spoken of it. Everyone assumes you'll marry a grand title."

"As I will." As defense against insanity, she summoned a name. "The Duke of Bridgewater, perhaps."

"A duke! Is he young, handsome?"

"He's twenty-seven years old, and from the engraving that accompanied my trustees' report, he's as handsome as I am beautiful, which makes a fair match."

Genova's eyes widened. "You have a report on him?"

"And on nine others. Including," Damaris added with a grin, "Ashart."

"Oh, my. May I have it?"

"Of course. But in exchange I want every scrap you know about Fitzroger."

"Aha! You *are* tempted by him."

"I'm merely curious. He's a puzzle."

"Curiosity killed the cat," Genova warned, but frowned in thought. "Let me see. I don't know much. Ask me a question."

"Why did he arrive at Rothgar Abbey days after Ashart?"

"Ash sent him back to London to supervise the delivery of his wardrobe, extra horses, and such. He hadn't intended to stay at Rothgar Abbey."

"See? He *is* a servant."

"More an obliging friend. Another question."

"How old is he?"

"Twenty-eight."

"Does he have any plans for his future?"

"To go to America." Genova clearly knew Damaris wouldn't welcome this news. "He's at odds with his family and doesn't want to stay in England. His father, Lord Leyden, died a couple of years ago, but if Fitz hoped for reconciliation after that, it hasn't happened. In fact, the main strife seems to be with his brother, the new viscount. Have I earned the report?"

"That depends on whether there's more to tell. What caused the estrangement?"

"I truly don't know. Before visiting Rothgar Abbey, I didn't move in these circles, you see."

"But you're close friends with Lady Thalia."

"Yes, but that's the extent of it. When my mother died, my father retired. Then he married again and we moved to my stepmother's house in Tunbridge Wells. There I met Lady Thalia and we became friends. She and Lady Calliope invited me to accompany them to Rothgar Abbey only to rescue me from my stepmother."

"She's cruel?"

"Oh, no. She's very gracious, and she makes my father happy. We just don't get on." She smiled. "She's very conventional."

Damaris laughed. "I see. Pirate shooting is not admired."

"Oh, don't mention that. People make far too much

of it. As for scandal, Thalia will probably know. She loves gossip. I'll ask her if you wish."

Damaris was suddenly hesitant. If Fitzroger had done something terrible, did she want to know?

"Ash did mention that Fitz's brother threatens to shoot him on sight," Genova said. "But Lord Leyden seems a most unpleasant man. How did Ash describe him? 'A great, blustering, uncouth brute.' Apparently he created a scene at the coronation three years ago. Another peer jostled him in the crush and he flew into one of his rages and had to be hustled away."

"Lud, he sounds like a madman. Could that explain his threats?"

"It's possible."

"Poor Fitz. Yes, if Lady Thalia knows more, please do find out, but you've certainly earned your reward. Lord Henry is to send my belongings to London, so I'll give the report to you there. I warn you, Genova, it paints a poor picture of the Trayce fortunes."

"Oh, Ash has told me all. It needs only economy and good management."

Damaris wasn't sure if Genova's words reflected admirable resolution or insane optimism.

They settled to more cribbage, and the time flew until the next halt. The final one, thank heavens.

The horses were changed and their cooling bricks replaced with hot ones. A man with a taper lit the candles inside the carriage. They were ready to resume when a sudden crash was followed by a shriek and people rushing past the windows.

Damaris leaned over to Genova's window, which looked toward the inn. "What's happening? That sounds like the dowager screeching."

Genova let down the window and called the question.

"Someone threw a stone through the carriage window, miss," one of the outriders called.

The servants had left their coach to try to help, and people were pouring out of the inn to see what all the fuss was about. Add some barking dogs, and they had chaos.

At least the dowager had stopped shrieking her complaints.

"I'm getting out," Damaris said. She pulled on her cloak and leaped out of the coach without assistance, then hurried to the big, gilded coach. Yes, the right-hand window was only vicious shards.

The dowager and Lady Thalia were being escorted into the inn. Fitzroger was there, but instead of looking at the damage he was looking at the crowd. Looking for who'd done it, she realized.

She went to his side. "Is everyone all right?"

"Yes, but it'll mean a delay while the hole's covered." He glanced at her briefly, but then returned his intent attention to the noisy throng.

Damaris looked that way, too, but saw only gawkers, some chewing on food they'd carried out with them. "Someone threw a stone?" she asked. "Who?"

"No one saw him." He turned fully to her. "Why not go into the inn? It's cold out here."

Join the dowager and Lady Thalia again? No, thank you.

She pulled up her hood, regretting that she'd brought neither gloves nor muff. "I'm warm enough. This is quite exciting. Do you think it was someone with a grudge against the nobility?"

"That's possible." But then she thought he cursed under his breath.

She followed his look and saw two servants emerging from the inn, each carrying a tray of steaming flagons. Refreshments for the stranded travelers provided by an opportunistic innkeeper. A burly maid headed toward them.

Fitz stopped her, took two, and drank from one as

if thirsty. Then he said, "Mulled cider," and gave the other to Damaris.

She thought he was acting strangely, but she was glad of the warm pot between her hands. The spicy steam was delicious, but when she sipped she pulled a face. "It's very sweet."

"All the better for vinegar," he said, then walked over to talk to the men who were discussing how to cover the hole in the window.

Damaris thought his words had been intended as a tease, but they had come out curtly because he was on edge. Why? She didn't see how he could have prevented a chance bit of malice.

She looked around, wondering if any of the people standing around was the culprit. A fat man appeared sullen, and an old codger leaning on a stick looked as if he was enjoying their predicament, but she couldn't imagine either of them throwing a stone and not being noticed doing it.

Two young women were flirting with anyone willing to play, but Damaris didn't suppose they'd damage a coach for the chance. Well, she amended, they could well be whores, so they might, but it seemed unlikely.

Then she was startled to catch a man snarling at her as he bit into a chicken leg. She stared, then made herself look away, excitement bubbling. Had she found the villain? Fitzroger would be impressed.

She considered what she'd seen. The man was in his twenties, she thought, and of average build. In the uncertain evening light, brightened only by carriage lamps and the flambeaux outside the inn, she couldn't tell his hair color, but she thought it had been reddish.

Scots? Some Scots hadn't abandoned the rebellion of 1745, when they'd risen to try to restore the Stuarts to the throne of England.

But he hadn't looked like a rebel, and he certainly hadn't been in Scottish plaid. His clothes had been those of an ordinary Englishman, perhaps even a gentleman. He wore riding boots and breeches, and his three-cornered hat had been trimmed with braid.

She sneaked another look and caught him looking at her again. This time he smiled. Or she thought it was supposed to be a smile. It looked more like a leer, because his upper lip was distorted a little and his front teeth were crossed.

She looked away again, embarrassed to have thought ill of someone because of a facial impediment. *Poor man.* She remembered a child in Worksop whose mouth wouldn't close properly, so she looked like an idiot when she wasn't.

She saw Genova over near the inn and moved to join her, but then Ashart went to Genova's side, offering to share his flagon of cider. Love was absurd but not to be interrupted.

Instead Damaris wandered around, inhaling the steam from the pot in her hands, glad of a chance to stretch her legs on this long journey. The inn sign declared the place to be the Cock and Bull, which made her think with a smile of a "cock and bull" story, one that no one could believe.

This almost seemed like one. Who would expect a stone thrown at a marquess's carriage in a quiet English town? It had probably been a mischievous boy with a slingshot, causing much more trouble than he'd planned. He'd probably fled as fast as he could, praying no one had seen him.

The high street was busy and had a number of other inns along it, all with bright windows and flambeaux outside. Most of the shops were still open, their lit windows brightening the scene, especially when the light played on snow and ice. Damaris noticed that the day's thaw was freezing everywhere, and took care where she stepped.

Word of the strange event must be spreading, for

people were coming out of inns, shops, and houses to look down toward the Cock and Bull. Some pulled on shawls or cloaks and began to hurry in their direction. A whole family arrived, adults carrying tiny ones. She heard a child chatter about the "golden coach."

Damaris bit her lip at the thought of the dowager's reaction to becoming a sideshow. *Serves her right for traveling in a gilded monstrosity.* Vinegar again. She made herself take another sip of the drink, sickly as it was. She certainly didn't want to end up as sour as her mother, but a sip was all she could bear. She'd never liked sweets, her temperament aside. She glanced around and surreptitiously poured the rest out on the ground.

More people were pouring past now, and Damaris stepped back to avoid being jostled. She wished she had gone into the inn after all. She came up against a waist-high wall and heard trickling water. She turned to look over the wall and saw a pond below. There was a water mill nearby, she realized, and a stream had been blocked by a weir to provide the power. The weir was half-frozen, and quite beautiful where it caught the lights, while the falling water made a kind of musical accompaniment. Delighted, Damaris looked back, thinking to call Genova over, but she was still with Ashart.

Hammering told her work had started on the carriage, but she thought it would be a while yet before they could leave. The carriages were now surrounded by a crowd so there seemed no point in going back there. Instead, she turned back to the lacy ice of the weir and the music of the water, placing the empty pot on the wall so she could tuck her hands beneath her cloak. The scene soothed her, but it also made her think.

Her mother would have thought it foolish to stand in the cold looking at ice and listening to water. Abigail Myddleton had been ruthlessly practical, and yet she'd succumbed to the charms of a rascal. Even though Damaris's father had returned home so rarely, she had understood the nature of that charm. He'd been a big, robust man who glowed with life as if he had a lamp inside him, one constantly lit.

She remembered his last visit most clearly. She'd been fifteen, and he hadn't come to Worksop since she was eight.

She had to admit that she'd been entranced by him herself. She'd even dreamed of his rescuing her from Birch House and carrying her off to the Orient, where she'd see the wonders he told her of and live adventures at his side. She'd hated her mother for carping at him, for always complaining.

For those few, brief days she'd thought her father loved her. Then he'd left, and she'd seen no evidence that he'd given her a thought thereafter. She'd recognized that he'd wooed her simply to hurt her mother. When word of his death had reached them nearly two years later, she'd thought it served him right.

At that intolerant age, she hadn't thought kindly of her mother either. Why screech at a man who paid no attention and never would? Why endlessly complain about him? Why cling to some promise he'd made to return to her and live in Worksop as her faithful, decent husband?

How common was it to despise both one's parents? It was a depressing thought, when people generally turned out to be like their parents. Perhaps she was destined to be both sour and selfish.

The hammering stopped. That probably meant they could leave soon. Despite the beauty and the music, this place was doing her no good. Even the chattering crowd sounded threatening, and she eyed the people standing nearby with concern.

It was illogical to be afraid, but she wanted to get

back to her party, to Fitzroger. She shifted her position and almost slipped on the ice. She grabbed the wall to steady herself and sent the pot flying to splash down into the water below.

Instinctively she leaned to watch, as if following the pot's fate could prevent its destruction. Someone bumped up against her, obviously doing the same thing, but threatening to send her in the same direction.

She pushed back frantically, but her feet hit the same patch of ice and went out from under her entirely.

There was a shocking moment of loss of contact with the earth, and then she landed with a crash, flat on her back.

The moon's up early, she thought dazedly, staring at the sky. Then the moon disappeared.

"Are you all right, milady?"

"What happened?"

"Likely she's killed herself."

"Wicked icy, it is."

People were all around staring down at her. *Like birds of prey,* Damaris thought, the breath knocked out of her. *Help!* she tried to shout, but nothing came out.

"Damaris! Are you all right?"

Fitzroger. Thank God. He knelt by her side and took her hand. "Speak to me."

At last she could suck in a breath. "I slipped."

"Are you hurt?"

She assessed her body. "No, I don't think so."

He gently raised her to a sitting position. "Are you sure? No serious pain?"

She considered that. "No. Just shaken." She laughed to prove it. "It knocked the wind out of me, that's all. Help me up, please."

She hated being the center of a crowd again.

"What's amiss?" That was Ashart calling, probably coming over.

Oh, no. She didn't want a fuss. "I'm fine," she insisted to Fitzroger. "Truly. Help me up, please."

"All's well," Fitzroger called back. "Damaris fell, but it's not serious." To the onlookers he said, "The lady isn't injured. Thank you for your concern."

As they took the hint and moved away, he carefully raised her to her feet, keeping an arm around her. "Can you walk, or shall I carry you?"

"I can walk, I'm sure. Just give me a moment."

"Of course. What happened?"

"I slipped on some ice. Or began to, so I grabbed the wall. There's a wall there and a stream. A weir. Very pretty."

His hold tightened. "Calm down. It's probably better not to talk yet."

She inhaled and made herself settle down. "It's all right. But I knocked a pot into the stream. One of the inn's pots."

"A few pennies will cover it. I believe you can afford that."

The joke put everything in proportion. "I looked over to see what had happened to it and someone bumped against me. I panicked, stepped back, and fell."

"I knew this crowd was dangerous. Are you able to return to the coach now? We're ready to leave."

She saw that everyone was aboard and waiting for her. "Oh, I'm sorry. Of course."

She hurried toward her coach, still grateful for Fitzroger's arm around her.

"It's such a strange feeling to suddenly lose contact with the earth," she said. Then he'd rushed to her rescue and everything had been all right.

As they neared the coaches, she heard, "What's

causing this interminable delay? I want to leave this benighted place!"

Damaris hastily thanked Fitzroger and hurried to where a groom stood ready to open the carriage door for her. As she reached him, the burly maidservant rushed up and put another flagon of spiced cider into her hand. "You've had a shock, miss! The gentleman said to take this. The pot's paid for an' all."

Damaris thought of refusing, but everyone was impatient to set off. She climbed in, struggling not to spill the drink. The groom slammed the door as Genova asked, "What happened?"

"I slipped on some ice. Could you hold this a moment?"

Genova took the pot, which was as well, as the coach jerked into motion then, toppling Damaris into her seat.

"Did you not get any earlier?" Genova asked. "It's good."

Now that it was over, Damaris was appalled at what might have been. She could have fallen over into the cold water, banged her head, broken a bone. Even in that slip she could have hurt herself badly. She grabbed the flagon and drank, but then winced away.

"Ugh. It's even sweeter than before." She tried another sip but couldn't endure it.

"Do you not like sweet things?" Genova asked, sounding astonished.

Damaris thought about vinegar and sighed. "Not really. Would you like this?"

"If you're sure." Genova took it and drank with apparent relish. "I shared Ashart's, which is very romantic, I'm sure, but he drank most of it."

"You're most welcome to it. In fact, I'm going to have some brandy."

She took a silver flask from one of the concealed

cupboards and poured brandy into the cap. She'd only ever had it mixed with hot water and honey for medicinal purposes, but gentlemen seemed to enjoy it.

The first sip made her gasp, but soon she felt wonderfully warm. "Oh, that does make me feel better. Why not have some in the cider?"

"Why not, indeed?" Genova held out the pot. "This has cooled, so it's not as tasty. You slipped? Are you hurt?"

Damaris took another sip of brandy. "A bruise or two, I suppose. Strange, I still don't know the name of the place."

"Pickmanwell."

Damaris laughed. "Is that a message to me? To pick my man well?"

"A lesson to us all," Genova agreed, eyes twinkling above the rim of the flagon. She tilted it to drain it, then pulled a face and wiped bits from her lips. "That must have been the dregs of the bowl. Still, it was welcome. And we're almost there."

Damaris laughed dryly. "Amazing, to look forward to Cheynings." Then she realized that wasn't tactful and settled for silence and sipping brandy.

Perhaps it was the brandy that spun fanciful dreams. She saw herself carried off by a masked highwayman, seized by corsairs on the high seas, or war-painted Indians in the Canadian forests. In each situation Fitzroger swept to her rescue, swift and skilled, until he stood, one foot on a villain's chest, his blade at the man's throat, demanding of her what he should do.

Death or mercy . . .

"I do hope I'll be accepted by the servants at Cheynings."

Damaris started out of her fancies to look at Genova. "Of course you will. You'll soon be mistress there."

"Old retainers can be vicious and Ashart paints a

grim picture of the place. I think the poor man worries that I'll barely last a day before fleeing. But it can't be so bad as all that."

Damaris didn't know what to say, for it could indeed.

Simply maintaining a house like Cheynings required a fortune, which was doubtless why it was in poor repair and niggardly with comforts. Even candles for light and fuel for fires in such a house could amount to horrendous sums, never mind mending the roof and replacing rotten plaster and timbers.

For decades all the income from the Trayce estates had gone not to their care but for court and show, for gilded carriages, outriders, and diamond buttons. All in the dowager's determination that the Trayce family be the grandest in the land and most especially that they outshine and eventually crush the Mallorens.

She sought a pleasant truth. "It's a handsome house with pleasing proportions and details, and the servants seem to have been there forever."

"Therefore devoted to the dowager, since she's been there forever, too."

"As soon as you're married, you can hire and dismiss whomever you want."

"Oh, I couldn't do that."

Damaris frowned, wondering if Genova, despite her adventures, had steel cold enough to deal with the Dowager Lady Ashart. The woman had, after all, unblinkingly used Lady Thalia's dead beloved as a missile in a minor spat.

It seemed presumptuous to offer advice when she was younger and had led a more limited life, but she did it anyway. "If you could make the servants aware that soon you will be their mistress, with power over them—if you make it clear you'll use your authority—they might see the wisdom of switching their allegiance."

Genova looked startled, and Damaris thought she saw another *I couldn't do that* hover, but then Genova nodded. "My father's ships were always in good order because the crew knew he would act if necessary. Occasionally he had to do so, which served as a reminder."

Since that probably meant flogging, keelhauling, and even hanging, Genova might be a match for the dowager after all. She certainly now wore the fixed, serious look of a captain planning battle strategy.

Damaris let her brandied mind slide back into fantasies. Fitzroger riding to her rescue, hair flying in the wind. Leaping off his horse to fight the Indian, to duel the pirate, to shoot the highwayman.

For, oh, a lady cannot abide without a hero by her side. . . .

Deep in her mind, Genova's words had set a seed. If a lord could marry to suit his pleasure, why shouldn't a rich lady buy whatever man suited her?

Now her imagination created pictures of herself and Fitzroger, married. What sort of life would they have? With her money, it could be anything they pleased.

Master and mistress of a house like Rothgar Abbey.

No, too grand.

A country manor like Thornfield Hall?

Too remote.

A house in a town such as she'd grown up in? She shuddered, but told herself that Birch House could have been a comfortable home. She knew for sure that she'd never live there again by choice, but something similar—no, a little grander, in London. Mr. and Mrs. Fitzroger, at the heart of the glittering world.

But then, like a worm in an apple, she remembered that Fitzroger was surrounded by scandal. Even Rothgar had warned her of it. Before she even indulged further fantasies, she must find out what Fitzroger's secret was.

The coach began a careful turn between stone pillars. "At last," she said, glad to be rescued from her own tangled thoughts.

She pulled her cloak up around her shoulders and fastened it. Lady Thalia would probably know the truth, and Genova would ask her. Then Damaris would know where she stood. The fact that she might not want to know had nothing to do with it. She would not make a fool of herself again.

"Here we are," she said with determined cheer as she turned to Genova. But Genova had her hand to her chest and seemed to be gasping for breath.

"Don't worry," Damaris said, astonished. "Ashart will defend you from the dragon."

"I'm sure. I'm sorry. I've never felt like this before. Nerves of steel, my father says, and here I am . . . throwing a nervous fit. This will never do. Perhaps . . . brandy?"

Damaris quickly pulled out the silver flask and poured some. Genova reached for the cup, but her trembling hand couldn't hold on. Damaris steadied her and guided it to Genova's lips, but dribbles escaped to run down her chin.

"I'm s-sorry. Such a fool you must th-think me."

"No, of course not. The dowager's enough to shake Hercules." Damaris was becoming alarmed, however. "Try another sip."

She steadied both Genova's hand and head this time and got a little more down her, but then the other woman pushed her feebly away. "I d-don't think it's helping. Heart," she said, pressing her hand to her chest again. "Going so fast. Too fast."

Her whole body was shaking now as if the coach was running over ridges, and Damaris could hear her teeth chattering. She tugged the rabbit-fur cloak close around her friend. "It won't be long. The drive here's quite short."

Should she call out for help? But what could anyone do but get to the house, which was happening anyway? Genova wouldn't want her first appearance at Cheynings to be all alarm and illness.

"Try to breathe deeply," Damaris commanded.

"Can't. Can't! I . . ." Genova looked into Damaris's eyes in a silent, frantic plea.

Damaris noticed the brandy flask in her hand and took a swig. She choked, but it cleared her mind. She let down the window, praying the blast of cold air would help. They were almost at the house, thank God.

"Fitzroger!" she yelled.

"Just about there," he called back.

"Genova's ill!"

He angled his horse closer and bent to look in. "What is it? A fever?"

"I don't think so. I think it's panic."

"Genova?"

"Anyone can have an attack of nerves. She needs to get into the house and into a warm bed, but preferably without everyone being made aware."

"I'll tell Ash."

Chapter 9

As Fitz rode off, Damaris turned back to Genova and became really frightened. The other woman's breaths were high and fast, seeming too shallow to sustain life. She was limp, and her eyes were only half-open.

She looked pallid, and a touch on her forehead found sweat even though the coach was now quite cold. Damaris hastily shut the window.

The other door opened while the coach was still in motion, and Ashart swung in. Damaris scrambled over to the opposite seat as he commanded, "Fitz, send someone for a doctor!" He slammed the door and gathered Genova into his arms. "Genni, love, what is it?"

Genova stared at him, but managed only, "Sorry . . ."

"Plague take sorry. Come on, Genni." He began frantically kissing her face, stroking back her hair as if he'd cure her by touch and love.

Damaris looked away, feeling as if she'd found herself in a marriage bed. A hand grasped her arm, and she realized the coach had stopped and Fitzroger was urging her out. She went with alacrity, clutching her cloak around her but shivering anyway, whether from the cold or shock, or both.

"I don't think that's just nerves," she said.

"Nor do I. Did she eat or drink anything at Pickmanwell?"

"The mulled cider . . . But everyone had some. I did. You did."

"Yes." He pushed her toward the house. "Go in. I'll help Ash." He ran back toward the coach.

Damaris pulled up her hood, her own teeth chattering. Cheynings offered no welcome, looming over the arriving coaches as nothing but a dark mass. The porticoed door was illuminated by a single guttering flambeau.

The servants' carriages must have gone directly to the back of the house. The gilded coach stood in front of the steps. The dowager was out and marching toward the door without a backward glance, Lady Thalia tripping behind, chattering. Had she chattered all the way? Quite likely. The dowager looked pursued.

Clearly neither lady knew of Genova's problem yet.

Damaris turned back to see Fitzroger helping Ashart extricate Genova. She hurried over, but could do nothing. Genova breathed in short gasps and lay limp as the dead.

To Damaris this didn't look like panic. It looked like *poison*.

Every scrap of common sense fought that idea. How could it be poison if only Genova was affected?

Then she remembered the last flagon of cider. Could there have been a concentration of something settled to the bottom? Herbs could be powerful. Even nutmeg could give people fits if consumed in huge amounts. She knew about such things because in Worksop she'd often helped Dr. Telford in his apothecary.

Ashart strode by, Genova in his arms. Damaris hurried to help Fitzroger with their carriage bags—and to find the flagon.

"It has to have been that last pot of cider," she whispered as she grabbed the pot from the floor. She put in her hand and felt stuff at the bottom. She scooped some out on a gloved finger and tasted it.

Fitzroger knocked her hand away from her mouth. "Are you mad?"

"If there's anything wrong with it, it doesn't work like that. I'm suffering no effect and I sipped it before giving it to Genova."

His startled glance showed how that sounded.

"I didn't—"

"Don't talk about it here."

The coachman and groom stood nearby, muttering to each other, but Damaris wanted to vindicate herself.

"If it's poison, we need to know what," she whispered.

"Not here," he repeated, taking both carriage bags in one hand. "Come on."

As they hurried up the stone steps, he asked, "Where did you get that flagon of cider? You said the one I gave you fell in the stream."

"Yes. A servant gave me another just as I was entering the coach. She said a gentleman had sent it. I think I assumed it was you. I was still shaken."

"You didn't drink it?"

Stupidly, she hated to admit it. "It was too sweet."

"Ah, yes, I saw you pour the first one away."

She stared at him. "How?"

They'd arrived at the door. "I happened to be looking that way."

"So you wouldn't send me another."

"And I didn't have time," he pointed out.

"Someone tried to harm me?" she gasped.

But he said, "No. Don't be afraid. I assure you, you have no need to be."

He drew her through the door, and it was closed behind them with a solid thump. His words should have comforted her, but she had heard a slight emphasis on the *you*. She herself didn't have need to be afraid, but someone else did?

Genova?

Who would want to hurt Genova?

The dowager, still intent on her grandson marrying a fortune?

Or herself, out of jealous rage? Surely no one, least of all Fitzroger, could imagine that. Could they?

Damaris shivered, but only from the cold and shock. As for the cold, being inside Cheynings was hardly better than being outside. Four single candles stood waiting for use, but as only one was lit, they did little for the gloom and nothing for the chill. The great marble hearth held no fire, and the black-and-white-tiled floor only increased the chill. Here, no greenery or berries celebrated the season, and a smell of damp decay permeated the place.

Oh, yes, Damaris remembered this grim house. And when she'd visited before it had been a milder season, and some effort had been made to welcome her, to entice her fortune into the pit of need.

Ashart, Genova, the dowager, and Lady Thalia had all disappeared, but the sturdy, grim-faced housekeeper—a Mrs. Knightly, Damaris remembered—waited to attend to them. Behind her stood three slack-faced, weary-looking maidservants.

"Miss Smith has been taken upstairs?" Fitzroger asked.

"To his lordship's room," the housekeeper replied through pursed lips.

"That doubtless being the only one properly

warmed and aired. You had a day's warning, Mrs. Knightly."

"Which can't combat an age of disuse, sir. I gather the doctor's been sent for?"

"Yes. Is there anyone here with healing skills?"

"For ordinary matters, sir, but what's wrong with the lady? Drink, perhaps?"

"Absolutely not." Fitzroger's tone should have frozen the woman on the spot. "Show Miss Myddleton to her room." He passed the bags to the maids, lit one candle from the other, and ran up the stairs.

Damaris stared after him, but then abandoned polite behavior and raced after, trying to remember the layout of the house. Pursuing the glimmer of Fitzroger's candle, she plunged from the top of the stairs into the anteroom to the open space called the Royal Salon, then turned right through an arch into the east wing.

She followed him left down a short corridor and into a bleak anteroom, which she remembered was the first of a number of rooms that made up the marquess's suite. They were arranged in the old style to run from one to another, and this had once been a guardroom, meant to protect the private chambers of the mighty lord.

Fitzroger was already into the next room, but he was leaving doors open, either in urgency or because he knew she was following. She chased him into a drawing room called the Hunt Room because of hunting scenes hung on the walls. A modest fire burned in this hearth, so she shut the door behind her before running through and finding herself at last in the grand corner bedchamber.

She shut that door, too.

In the bleak house, the luxury of this room was shocking. A fire roared in the fireplace, and a thick carpet cushioned the floor. Three branches of candles shed light on window and bed hangings of heavy gold brocade, decorated with Ashart's coat of arms. The walls were covered with painted wallpaper from China.

Genova was tucked into the big bed, waxy pale and breathing in shallow gasps. Damaris didn't like the look of her at all. She wished Dr. Telford were here. She herself had no training, only random experience she'd gained from helping him.

Ashart was sitting on the bed, supporting Genova, still trying to gently, frantically bully her out of the fit. Lady Thalia hovered, wringing fragile hands, looking every day of her age. Her middle-aged French maid was working a rosary. Fitzroger stood at the end of the bed, expressionless as a stern statue.

Damaris was the uninvited outsider, but she couldn't hang back. "Have her stays been removed?" she ventured, discarding her cloak onto a chair and putting the flagon on a table.

"Cut." Ashart never looked away from Genova's face, as if he could keep her alive by will alone.

With nothing to go on, Damaris had no other practical suggestion, so she picked up the pot, turned her back on the others, and tasted the dregs again. She detected nutmeg, cinnamon, and cloves. Honey. Brandy.

And something else.

She inspected her finger and saw dark flecks. They could be an innocent herb—marjoram, hypericum, perhaps even feverfew. But what was it doing in mulled cider?

"Well?" Fitzroger had come to her side and spoke softly.

She shook her head. "Nothing I know how to counter."

He did as she had and tasted the residue, but then he, too, shook his head. Her lurking suspicions were confirmed. Whatever he was, Octavius Fitzroger was no idle hanger-on. He'd been keyed tight all day for danger, and no ordinary man would think he could detect noxious herbs.

What on earth was all this about?

She wished the doctor would arrive, but she had no idea how far he would have to come, even if the messenger found him at home. The clock showed that it was nearly five, so he could still be visiting patients.

Damaris looked back helplessly at Genova, and then saw poor Lady Thalia. This, at least, she could deal with. She guided the old lady to a chair near the fire. The maid hurried over.

"She needs a warm shawl, sweet tea, and brandy," Damaris suggested, not sure if the servant would obey a command from her.

"Henri," Fitzroger commanded, opening the chest at the foot of the bed, "assist Regeanne to get the tea."

Damaris hadn't noticed the other servant, a slim, alarmed man with powdered hair—Ashart's valet, she assumed.

"At once, milord." He and the maid disappeared through a corner door disguised by the paneling. There must be a staircase offering private service to the lord of Cheynings.

Fitzroger brought over a blanket and helped tuck it around the old lady.

"I'm all right, dears," Lady Thalia said, though she didn't look it. "Such a shock." She lowered her quavering voice. "Her mother was taken suddenly, you know. In the middle of the ocean. Some sort of internal rupture."

"I'm sure that's not the case," Damaris soothed. "There would be pain." She hoped that was true.

Fitzroger went back to the bed. "Genova, are you in pain?"

Damaris turned and saw a slight shake of Genova's head. Some consciousness, at least, and no pain. There was nothing else useful to be done for the old lady, and an idea had stirred. Sweet tea for shock. She gathered her courage and approached the bed again.

Ashart growled, "Go away."

"This is no work of mine!"

"Whose, then?"

"I don't know." Ignoring the guarding beast, she picked up Genova's limp wrist and checked the pulse. Thin and far too rapid. No pain, however.

"She needs bleeding," Ashart said. "Can you do that?"

"No." Damaris hesitated, fearing ridicule, but then said, "Sugar sometimes helps in cases of palpitations. . . ."

She'd witnessed this only once, when assisting Dr. Telford, but she couldn't stand by and do nothing.

"Sugar!" Ashart spat and turned back to Genova.

But Lady Thalia said, "I have some!" and fumbled out of her blanket. She dug in her pink drawstring bag and produced a small box.

"Apricot crisps!" she announced, opening it. "They are made with quite a lot of sugar, you know. I took them to the abbey for dear Rothgar, for he did so like them as a child, but I kept a few. . . ."

Damaris had already grabbed the metal comfit box and tasted one. It was sweet, but even better, a layer of fine sugar lined the bottom of the box. She picked out the slices of apricot, opened Genova's mouth, and tipped in some sugar. "Try to eat it."

Genova's jaw moved and then her tongue came out weakly to lick at her lips.

"More," Damaris said, tipping more powder into Genova's mouth.

Her own heart was pounding and her hands were

unsteady, because she didn't know if this would help. It might even do harm.

"Water," she ordered, and a moment later Fitzroger presented a glass of it. "Get her to drink some," Damaris told Ashart, all her attention on Genova, testing her pulse again. Was it steadier, or was that her imagination?

"Sugar," Ashart snarled, even as he put the glass to Genova's lips. "Where's the damn doctor? Come on, precious one, sip a little. Come on. . . ."

Genova parted her lips, and when he tipped in some water she swallowed. Damaris thought the action quite strong, which gave her hope. She poured the last of the powder into Genova's mouth, then, when she'd drunk more water, popped one of the apricot crisps between her lips. "Suck on that."

Remembering Lady Thalia, Damaris put the crisps back in the box and returned it to her. The old lady smiled. "You're a competent young lady, aren't you? But I think you need a little sweetness, too."

For a moment Damaris was hurt, thinking it a comment on her vinegary nature, but then she realized the offer was simply of sugar for the nerves. She took a sweetmeat and found it did help. Her mind steadied, but it was like coming out of a protective daze.

Had she helped or harmed?

"I think she's better," Ashart said. "Come and check."

It was a command, but Damaris obeyed. At least he couldn't think her a murderer after this. Yes, the pulse was slower. Then Genova's eyes opened a little.

"I am better," she said weakly but clearly. "Much better. Heart not so fast. I thought it would burst. . . ." She looked at Damaris. "Thank you, my friend."

Tears stung Damaris's eyes. "It was nothing. But what—"

A sharp squeeze of her hand cut her off, and she let Fitzroger draw her away to the fire. "This isn't the time to talk about whys and hows," he murmured.

Then when? Damaris wondered, but energy was leaching out of her. This on top of her fall was just too much.

"Ah, the tea!" Lady Thalia announced, and indeed the maid had entered, carrying a tea service on a large tray followed by the valet bearing a silver teakettle on its comfort stand and looking as if he considered it beneath his dignity.

Fitzroger steered Damaris to the chair opposite Lady Thalia's, and she sat with something of a thump. She couldn't believe she'd taken such a risk. Dr. Telford had always warned that even the most common herbs and medicines could be dangerous in the wrong situation. If Genova had not improved, if she'd died, they'd all have blamed her.

She saw the sugar bowl on the tray and looked over at Genova, but she seemed completely recovered now. Some sweet tea should complete the cure.

Perhaps it was relief that started the shakes. She gripped her hands to try to keep them still. If she'd known how to find her room, she might have excused herself and hidden there.

"Set it all here," Lady Thalia said, pointing to a table by her. "A pot prepared in the kitchen would have been quite sufficient, I'm sure, but I'll make it. Regeanne, as you see, the crisis is over, so you may find out where I am to sleep and make sure the bed is aired."

"In here," Ashart said, still fixed by the bed as if with glue. "With Genova. I'm sure this is the warmest room. Henri, Regeanne, you may go."

Lady Thalia opened the wooden tea caddy. Or

rather, she tried to. "Well, really. It's locked! Are we supposed to beg Sophia for the key?"

"Do something, Fitz," Ash said.

Damaris looked at Fitzroger and, with a whimsical smile, he said, "*Woof.*" But he produced what looked like a set of very thin blades, poked them into the lock, and in moments had the lid open. Lady Thalia went about making the tea as if this were nothing out of the ordinary, but Damaris stared.

"I'll know not to try to keep anything from you with lock and key, sir."

"And why would you want to keep anything from me, Miss Myddleton?"

Did he, too, sound suspicious?

"Because a lady must have her secrets!" Lady Thalia declared, scooping out some tea. She sniffed it. "This is not of the best quality, Ashart."

"I'm sure you're right. I'll sort everything out. For the moment the only important thing is that Genova seems to be safe."

It was true, but when Ashart looked around the room, perhaps for the first time, he still seemed suspicious of Damaris. She felt weepy over that, which was proof she wasn't herself.

Whatever the quality, hot tea would help. By the time Fitzroger passed her a cup her hands had stopped shaking, so she didn't embarrass herself. He'd added a shot of brandy, and that didn't hurt, either. After one cup her nerves steadied. After two she felt no tension at all.

Genova was sitting up on her own, drinking her tea, and talking to Ashart as if nothing had happened. But something most certainly had.

Now, panic over, it seemed more sensible to see the episode as an attack of nerves, which had responded to sugar, but Damaris couldn't get the idea of poison out of her mind. Fitzroger hadn't dismissed it, and there had been something strange in that flagon.

What herbs could have such an effect?

She couldn't think of one, but she was not an expert.

If there was any question of poison, why did Fitzroger not want to speak of it, even now? She hated to consider the possibility, but could he have been responsible?

No. As he'd said, he'd not had time. He'd been with her, taking care of her while a hypothetical villain had been putting something in the cider and instructing the maid to give it to her.

Someone should definitely talk to that maid.

And test the dregs in the pot. On a rat or mouse, for example. She was sure Cheynings had plenty to spare.

Had Fitzroger really implied that someone was in danger and he knew who? Which brought her back to the notion of someone wanting to harm Genova. It seemed impossible.

Barbary pirates, Damaris thought, knowing her brandied mind was spinning out of control. Genova had killed that pirate captain. His devoted followers had crossed the ocean to wreak their terrible revenge. . . .

She startled when gathered into someone's arms. Fitzroger's arms. "Oh, no. I'm all right." ·

"You fell asleep. I'm moving you to the bed."

Damaris felt she should protest again, but her eyes closed on their own. She managed to say something about it being too early for bed.

"You had a nasty shock on top of some stressful days, and then this. Your bed's having an extra warming pan run through it. It'll be ready soon. Genova's up and well now, so you can take her place in Ash's bed."

"How risqué," she murmured.

As he laid her down, she heard the smile in his voice. "Have naughty dreams, then."

Damaris felt she ought to insist on discussing poisons, but it was simply too much effort. She fell back into sleep even as the curtains rattled shut around the bed.

Once Damaris's bed in the west wing was ready, Fitz carried her there and left her to the care of her maid. Ash had indicated that he wanted to talk to him in the marquess's private study known as the Little Library, which connected to his bedchamber.

On the way back Fitz paused in the Royal Salon, icy cold as it was, to think. He was about to face some questions that would put him in a difficult situation. He wanted to tell Ash the truth, but he'd given his word to keep the assassination threat secret, and he wasn't sure he had cause to break his word yet.

No, he didn't. The incident with Genova could well have a simple explanation. Decision made, he completed his journey, entering the Little Library through the door opposite the bedchamber.

This room was supposed to be the marquess's private office, similar to the one Rothgar used for weighty matters. Four Marquesses of Ashart had taken little interest in their estates, however, so it was now a lounge dominated by comfortable seating. A desk still paid homage to the notion of business, but it sat in one corner, displaced in favor of an ornate card table.

Ash turned from contemplation of the fire. "If you don't mind, I'll take your bedchamber."

It wasn't a request. A bedchamber lay beyond this room, and on the two occasions Fitz had accompanied Ash here, he'd used it. Ash wanted to stay close to Genova, which Fitz understood.

"Of course. Where do I sleep?"

"Take the room prepared for Thalia. The corner one in the west wing."

"Close by Miss Myddleton's."

Ash's brow rose. "You fear for your virtue?"

"I'll keep a pistol under my pillow," Fitz said dryly. "But it won't matter tonight. I'm returning to Pickmanwell to check things out."

Ash had been simmering, and now he came to the boil. "What the devil's going on, Fitz? What caused that?"

"Nerves?" Fitz suggested, hating the necesity of beng evasive.

"Genova?"

"I've seen similar fits of blind panic, even in brave men."

Ash paced the room. "Merely over arrival at Cheynings?" He stopped and narrowed his eyes at Fitz. "I saw you and Miss Myddleton hovering over that pot. Was something wrong with the cider? We all drank it."

Something he could respond to honestly. "I don't know. That's why I'm going back to Pickmanwell. Perhaps there was one contaminated bowl and others have been afflicted."

"Contaminated with what? And if not, someone tried to poison Genova—and the most likely culprit is Damaris Myddleton."

"Don't be absurd. Why would she do such a thing?"

"Why expect reason from a woman like that?"

"A woman like what?"

"Devil take it, she pursued me like a pit bull!"

"The dowager served you up to her on a plate. Of course she wanted a bite." Fitz controlled his temper. "This is absurd. She just saved Genova's life."

"Perhaps that was her plan. Cause the alarm and be the heroine."

"Oh, for God's sake! Look, put this aside until I return with information."

Ash paced the room, then faced him again. "Very well, but if something was put into that flagon, who else had a better opportunity? Who else could have been sure that only Genova would drink it?"

Excellent questions. "The answers lie in Pickman-well, so I'm off."

Ash glanced at the clock. "It's gone six and bitter cold."

"There's a moon, and the sooner the better."

"You're leaping into action, my friend."

Fitz had been afraid that Ash might become suspicious. He knew all about Fitz's work as a bodyguard, just not that he was being guarded.

"I'm willing to put my skills to use," he said casually, and took a gambler's throw. "If you'd rather I didn't . . ."

"No, no. It's just strange to see the theoretical become real before my eyes. The old warhorse called back into battle."

"Old?" Fitz queried.

Ash laughed. "Very well, the young stallion. Will you return tonight?"

"The inquiries at Pickmanwell could take some time, so my aged bones might as well rest there. But I'll ride back at first light."

Ash put out his hand. "Thank you."

They were not in the habit of shaking hands. Fitz knew this was a peace gesture after their argument, and took it.

"I am sorry for it, though," Ash said. "Calling you back into action. I have the feeling you'd rather leave such things behind."

Fitz picked up the flagon. "I would. That sort of work makes a man see devils in every corner and never sleep with his eyes truly shut. Then there were the times when I worked to keep someone alive that I'd rather have seen dead. I've no problem with this task, however." He went to the door but paused and turned back. "Try not to suspect Damaris, Ash. She's not the villain here."

"Don't get attached there, Fitz. I wouldn't like to see you hurt, and she has her value calculated to the penny. She'll buy the highest rank she can."

"As she should, as long as the man's honorable and cares for her. Don't worry. I won't slit my throat over her."

"I'd like to see you happy. If we could do something about your brother . . ."

Fitz escaped. In twenty minutes he was back on the road, leaving one rat in the stables suffering similar symptoms to Genova's. So much for nerves.

Damn and blast it all, the threat was real. That broken window had been the means to halt the party so the poison could be delivered. He'd been alert for that, but he'd tested the cider and seen no other threat.

No excuses. Someone had almost died on his watch.

It had never happened before.

He'd thought carefully before leaving, but the inquiries needed to be made. He'd set two of Rothgar's servants to patrol near the house through the night. He didn't think the villain would try to invade Cheynings, but as he had no clear idea who the villain was, he was taking no chances.

But why try to kill Genova?

Because she was Ash's betrothed?

He rode cautiously because of the icy roads, which gave ample time to think things through.

According to Rothgar, the danger had intensified because of the betrothal, and the attack fit with that. The swiftest way to end a betrothal was to kill one of the couple.

But why was the betrothal such a problem? He wished he'd pressed Rothgar on that point. If Ash had an heir, that person might have a motive to try to kill him, and a strong one to stop his having a son. But he didn't. He was the last of his line.

Qui bono? Who would benefit?

Damn this secrecy. He'd been tempted to send one of Rothgar's servants to the abbey with news of the attack, but he'd send a message from Pickmanwell.

Then there was Damaris. He felt sure she had no part in it, but how could the assassin know that she wouldn't drink the cider herself? It had to be the sweetness. The assassin, too, must have seen her pour away most of her drink and gambled that she'd give it to Genova. A hell of a gamble, though.

Emotions were shattering his attempt to be logical, because Damaris could have drunk that cider even if she didn't care for it. Then she would have suffered the same effects. Since no one else had her knowledge and quick wits, she might have been dead now.

His reaction to that revealed the truth. He was falling in love with Damaris Myddleton.

When he'd carried her from Ash's bed to her own, the journey had seemed both too long and over too quickly. In the flickering light of the candle carried by her maid, her ordinary face had become unbearably beautiful to him. The smooth line of her cheek, the dark arch of her brows, her lips softly parted, exquisitely kissable.

Asleep, all defenses down, she'd looked younger and more vulnerable, and he'd longed to stay with her, to protect her, to lie with her. . . .

The most damnable thing was that she might be interested in him as well. He'd do anything rather than cause her pain.

If he'd expected this danger, he would have avoided the flirtatious games they'd played. Why hadn't he re-

membered how inexperienced she was? This fraught
situation was bound to make things worse. She might
come to fancy herself in love with him. What had
Rothgar astutely said?

*"She is a pirate's daughter and inclined to reach for
what she wants."*

He'd leave if he could. Keep on riding. Head for
Portsmouth instead of Pickmanwell and take ship.
Yesterday he might have done it, but now he couldn't.
Not after the first evidence that the plot against Ash-
art might have sharp and deadly teeth.

Chapter 10

Damaris drifted up from a dream of difficult travel. She opened her eyes to musty darkness, but the gloom was from closed bedcurtains. She sensed it was morning, but even in the tent of the bed the air was icy against her nose. And damp. Damp in the air, damp in the hangings, damp in the very walls.

Ah, Cheynings. She remembered it well.

She was huddled as deeply under the covers as she could be and still breathe, and felt the lack of a nightcap to keep her head warm. She wondered if someone had started the fire, but suspected not.

Something made her think this was the same room she'd stayed in during her last visit. Maisie had slept with her then, but Damaris was now alone in the bed. Perhaps Maisie had gone to get hot washing water and someone to light the fire. Damaris decided to stay where she was and hope.

She didn't even remember coming to bed. . . .

Then all yesterday's events returned, and she sat up. Cold bit, and she slid back under the heavy covers. But now she wanted to get up and find out if anything new had happened. If Genova was well. If Fitzroger had solved the mystery.

She emerged far enough to pull back the hangings on one side of the bed, getting a sprinkle of dust for her trouble. The window curtains were still down, but weak daylight shone around the edges.

"Maisie?" Damaris called. Then she yelled, "Maisie!" Silence.

She'd been correct about the bedchamber. It was called the Blue Room, but the walls were a dingy gray. On her last visit she'd moved one of the paintings and found a cornflower-blue patch behind. It had struck her then that Cheynings had died at some point. Perhaps it all tied in with the dowager's dead children.

Damaris wasn't fanciful by nature, but huddled under the covers she wondered if there might be a curse on the house of Trayce. Thank heavens she wasn't marrying into this family or this moldering building.

Finding out what was happening meant getting up. Her skin puckered at the thought of being exposed to the icy air, but she was no delicate blossom. She'd never had a fire in her bedroom at Birch House unless she'd been ill.

She saw her brown woolen robe hung over a rack in front of the dead fireplace. An expanse of uncarpeted floor stretched between it and the bed. She braced herself, slid her feet out of bed and into her slippers, and dashed across the room and into her robe.

It was new and of thick wool, but even wrapped in it, she shivered. She hurried to the washstand, but found only a thin layer of ice. When she raised the festoon curtains and pulled open the warped shutters, she faced windowpanes obscured by a layer of ice so thick her fingernail made no impression. It must be as cold in here as outdoors!

Aha! She flung open the armoire and laughed with giddy relief at the sight of her blue cloak. In moments she was huddled in its furry warmth, hood up. She tucked her hands into the muff, rubbing them together and feeling much better.

Cheynings would not defeat her.

But she could hardly go in search of others until she was properly dressed. That would not have been a problem in Birch House, but now her fashionable clothes required a lady's maid.

What time was it? She looked at the clock on the mantelpiece, but of course it had not been kept wound. She glared around the room in frustration and saw the wood box beside the fireplace. She opened it and grinned. Kindling and two logs.

In moments she had the ashes raked out of the hearth. She paused to rub warmth back into her fingers, then built the fire. She coaxed a flame from the tinderbox and set it to the kindling. By some miracle, the chimney drew without too much smoke.

She brushed her hands off and tucked them back inside the muff, almost purring with satisfaction. So much for Cheynings, marquesses, and the whole pampered, aristocratic world! She might be a rich heiress, but she could take care of herself.

Even in danger? she wondered, yesterday's events settling on her. She couldn't rid herself of the thought that someone had been threatened by that drink.

Oh, perhaps it had all been sorted out. The sooner she joined the others, especially Fitzroger, the better.

The door behind her opened, and she rose to see Maisie come in, huddled in two shawls. She was followed by another shrouded maid bearing a bucket full of wood.

"You shouldn't have bothered with the fire, Miss Damaris," Maisie said as if it were a sin. "This one'll do it."

The other maid scurried to the fireplace. Her skirt was kirtled up to her knees, revealing darned sagging stockings, and her hands were red and chapped. The poor woman filled the wood box, swept up the cinders, and crept away.

"Do you want your washing water now, then, miss?"

Damaris shuddered. "I'm not going to strip to wash until this room warms up. Breakfast, please, Maisie. And how is Miss Smith?"

"I think she's well, miss. A doctor attended last night, but she didn't need him. They say the dowager screeched about the expense."

"A true miser. I hope the servants' lives here are not too uncomfortable."

"I'll survive," Maisie said, but in a martyred tone.

When she returned shortly with a breakfast tray she exclaimed, "I almost dropped the lot. A mouse ran right over my foot down there. I can't abide mice!"

Damaris helped with the tray, but said, "You grew up on a farm, Maisie. You must be used to them."

"We had cats, miss. Excellent mousers. And look," she declared, pointing at a corner. "There's mouse droppings in here, too. I won't sleep for thinking of it."

As Maisie went right to sleep in any condition and slept soundly, Damaris doubted this, but she made soothing noises. "Why not share some of this food? It's simple fare, but there's more than enough."

"Thank you ever so much, Miss Damaris!" she said, grabbing some bread and cheese. "Barley bread and dripping. That's all they have down there, and they're stingy with the dripping. And ale so thin I swear it's watered."

"Oh, I'm sorry. You shall share my breakfast every day. And," Damaris added, inspired, "I insist that you spend as much time as possible in this room. With a decent fire, of course. I'm sure my wardrobe needs much mending and altering."

Maisie giggled, but she didn't protest.

Damaris was ready to dress, and though the room was warmer, she hurried into her clothes, choosing the traveling outfit. The heavy skirt and quilted jacket were her warmest, but even so she wasn't looking forward to crossing the big house.

She went to the window to see the weather. The room had warmed enough to thin the ice on the panes so she could scrape a clear spot. The park was a study in gray and white, and no sunshine brightened it. In fact, the place looked dead, but then a figure entered the frozen landscape—a man in a long cloak, saddlebags slung over his shoulder.

Fitzroger! The very man Damaris wanted to see, and here was an opportunity to speak with him privately and find out what he knew.

"My cloak, Maisie. Quickly!"

Maisie picked up the blue velvet, but then said, "It's all dirty at the back, miss. How did you do that?"

"I fell." Damaris thought quickly. "I'll wear the red pelerine."

Muttering about the work it would be to clean the velvet, Maisie found Damaris's hip-length red velvet cloak that was lined with mink, and the matching muff. Damaris put them on and hurried out.

She turned down the service stairs near her door and two floors down found a door to the outside. A rusty key sat in the lock, and though it turned stiffly, it did turn. Once she'd tugged the warped door open Damaris was outside.

The air was sharply cold, but after the musty house, it was refreshing. She puffed mist for amusement as she hurried in search of Fitzroger.

Turning the corner of the house, she saw him at the same moment that he saw her.

She walked forward. "Up early again, Mr. Fitzroger?" she teased.

"Running away again, Miss Myddleton?"

His tone was more biting than humorous, and she realized he looked as if he'd been on a long ride. What had he been up to? "Have you been away all night?" she asked.

He continued on past her toward the house. "If so, it's no business of yours."

She hurried after, firing off a question in a tone as blunt as his own. "Where have you been?"

"In search of a saucy wench."

For a moment she believed the implication, that he'd spent the night with a woman, but then she made the leap. "I think that's a cock-and-bull story, sir." She saw his lips twitch and grinned with triumph. "You went back to Pickmanwell! What did you discover? Was the maid who gave me that pot an inn servant or not?"

She thought he sighed. "Inn servant."

"And she said?"

He didn't look at her or slacken his brisk pace. "That a gentleman gave her a penny to take the pot to you."

"And the gentleman's appearance?"

"Medium height and build. Crossed teeth at the front."

"I saw him!"

That stopped him. He looked at her. "When?"

"Outside the inn. I thought he was sneering at me, but then I realized that the poor man only had a deformed mouth. Or I thought so. He sent me poison?"

He raised a brow. "You are given to dramatics, aren't you, Miss Myddleton? He probably knew he'd upset you and wanted to make reparation."

He turned and continued his long-legged walk toward the house. "There was no dire plot. Others suffered the same effect as Genova, though not as seriously. It appears something got into one bowl of cider by mistake, and it must have been concentrated in the bottom. The inn is suitably horrified and chastened."

She hurried to keep pace with him, breath shortening, feet freezing, feeling deflated. She should be glad that there was no scheme to hurt Genova, and she was. But it had been exciting to be part of an adventure for a while.

As if sensing her low spirits, he put an arm around her and urged her toward a nearby door. "Come on. You'll freeze."

"In all these furs?"

"I don't suppose you're wearing fur-lined shoes."

"I'm thinking of commissioning some."

Once inside he took her this way and that through dingy basement corridors, where Damaris saw the effect of the mice Maisie had complained of. She wasn't squeamish about the rodents, but all the same, droppings unswept on the floor and gnawed skirting boards made her shudder.

When they arrived in the kitchen they found the room in keeping with the rest, with grease and soot heavy on the walls and the fire in the huge hearth smoking. At least the long deal table used for food preparation looked well scrubbed and the morose cook looked clean. Damaris could imagine the struggle of trying to run this huge kitchen with an inadequate staff.

Fitzroger set to charming the woman into giving him food. Damaris waited, growing rather hot in her mink-lined cloak. He didn't seem uncomfortably hot, but then, his riding cloak was not fur lined. That didn't seem right when everyone else's cloaks were. Ashart's cloak was of wolf, and she wanted to give Fitzroger something similar. Something better, even. Russian sable, or—yes!—the fur of the white northern bear.

She imagined it lining a cloak of ivory leather. Impractical, but with his blond hair and silver-blue eyes, he would look like an ice warrior. She bit her lip. This must be how a rich man thought when he wanted to drape a woman in silks and jewels.

When he came over to her carrying a tray covered with a cloth, she said, "Everyone has a fur-lined cloak but you."

"This is a dense weave of wool. Adequate and waterproof. Have you breakfasted?"

She almost said yes, but then realized he probably hadn't. So she lied, hoping for a chance to share his meal, to spend more time in his company.

"There's ample here," he said, and led the way upstairs.

Damaris wondered if he intended to eat in his bedchamber. That would present a problem, but she had to suppress a grin at the thought of a wicked meal like that. However, he eventually ushered her into a luxurious parlor she remembered from her tour. They called it the Little Library, though it didn't hold many books. It was the marquess's private sanctum, and Ashart was there.

"What did you find out?" he demanded, but when he saw her, his expression became neutral. "Miss Myddleton?"

"We met outside." Fitzroger placed his tray on the card table. "I assume you've eaten, Ash?"

"Yes." Ashart looked at her again.

The message was clear, and Damaris had no choice. Pleading hunger wouldn't move the marquess.

She dropped a curtsy and left, pulling a face. She would have liked to hear Fitzroger's report. But then, he'd told her most of the story and there was no poison, no snaggletoothed villain, no adventure. Probably that whole business of "state secrets" had been her imagination.

She paused in the Royal Salon, breath puffing white.

She had to accept that Fitzroger was simply what he appeared to be—an impoverished ex-soldier who ran errands. But he also stirred her passions. Most of her reason for rushing out to meet him this morning had been to spend time alone with him. Merely being with him was like sunshine in her blood.

And yet, he was apparently tarnished by scandal. She had to find out about that before she sank deeper into folly, and Lady Thalia might know all. She wanted to rush to demand the information, but it was too early to disturb the other ladies. Seething with impatience, she paced the large room.

The Royal Salon was used as a portrait gallery, and on her previous visit she'd been shown around by the dowager herself. There was nothing new to see, but she paused in front of the magnificent full-length painting of Ashart in his peer's robes of scarlet and ermine. This image of dark, arrogant beauty hadn't helped her sanity the last time she'd been here, but nor had her realization that as his marchioness she would have similar robes to wear.

A duchess's were finer, she reminded herself.

She looked right and left at similar pictures, but of monarchs in their coronation robes. She remembered thinking the arrangement peculiar before, but she hadn't been willing to question it. Since then, she'd seen the Rothgar Abbey portrait gallery, which contained no monarchs at all. A loyal portrait of the present king hung in the Tapestry Room at the abbey, but nothing like this.

Here, Ashart was displayed in company with Charles I, his son Charles II, and Charles II's brother and heir, James II. Kings of the last century and Stuarts, to boot?

The Stuart line had failed, and their distant relatives from Hanover, Germany, had been invited to take the throne. Thus far, there'd been George I, George II, and George III, but none of them were represented here.

Suspicions stirred in Damaris's mind. There had been two serious attempts to return the Stuart line to the throne. The supporters of the Stuarts were called Jacobites after King James—Jacob in Latin.

Were the Trayces secret *Jacobites*? Not so secret, even, if they hung Stuart portraits on the walls! It defied belief, but made her even more glad not to be embroiled with them.

Despite furs she was growing chilled, so she returned to her room. She sent Maisie in search of Lady Thalia's maid to ask that she be told when the other ladies were ready for a guest.

"And find out the time!" she called after her, then set to winding the clock. While she was at it, she used a handkerchief to dust it and the mantelpiece it sat on. She stopped when she found mouse droppings again. This place truly was disgusting.

When Maisie returned with the news that it was half past nine and the other ladies were up and eager for her to join them, Damaris was happy to move to cleaner and more comfortable quarters. She was also ready to question the older lady about Fitzroger's past.

She found Genova and Lady Thalia dressed and taking breakfast in front of the fire, which burned so hot that they were both shielded by fire screens. Damaris instantly shed her cloak but was still too warm.

Genova, looking fully restored to beauty and health, rose to take Damaris's hands. "Thank you, thank you, my dear friend! You are so clever!"

"You feel fully recovered?"

"As if nothing happened. How embarrassing. I've never fallen into a panic like that before."

"But it wasn't," Damaris said. "Fitzroger went back to Pickmanwell to investigate. A number of people were affected. Something got into one bowl of cider."

"How awful. Is everyone else safe?" Genova asked.

"Apparently. He thinks your flagon was the last of the bowl and the noxious ingredient was concentrated there."

"Thank heavens no one was in danger. Now, come sit and breakfast with us. Regeanne, another chair."

"I've eaten," Damaris said, "and I'm too warmly dressed to sit close to the fire. I'll take the sofa."

Talk turned to plans for their stay here. Lady Thalia wanted to explore the house.

"But didn't you grow up here?" Damaris asked.

"Yes, but I left as a young woman—when my brother married Sophia Prease, you see. Her nature was little better then than now. I haven't been back here since"—she thought—"since Ashart's christening! His majority was celebrated in London."

Damaris wondered what she'd make of the state of the house beyond this room. "Then I recommend you imitate me and wear your furs, Lady Thalia. It's very cold at the moment."

"How clever, dear! Cold can be so treacherous. And afterward we will return to this warm room and play whist.

Damaris confessed. "I'm afraid I don't know how to play whist, Lady Thalia."

"Not know how to play whist! That will never do. We will teach you." She began to rattle off the rules, giving Damaris no chance to ask about Fitzroger's scandal.

A knock on the door interrupted the bewildering torrent of information. The maid Regeanne answered and brought the news that "You are invited to join the marquess, ma'ams."

They all went to the Little Library to find both Ashart and Fitzroger were there. Lady Thalia immediately declared her desire to tour the house.

Ashart looked taken aback, which was hardly surprising when the house was so cold and in poor repair. There was no stopping Lady Thalia Trayce, however, when she had her mind set on something.

"We'll just get our furs, dear," she said and hurried back into the bedchamber.

"Furs?" Ashart queried.

"Damaris reports that the house is so cold, they're needed," Genova said and followed.

Damaris went, too, certain that hadn't made Ashart any fonder of her. But he'd soon realized how sensible it was.

When they all came back, Ashart offered his great-aunt his arm. "Lead the way, Thalia. I look forward to your stories." He offered his other arm to Genova.

Which left Damaris to walk with Fitzroger. "You might want to wear gloves, at least," she told him as they left the room.

"You think me a delicate bloom?"

"No," she said. "Never that."

They went first into the Royal Salon, where Lady Thalia looked around, wrinkling her nose. "How sadly neglected. It used to be very grand. It was often used as a ballroom when I was young, and as a banquet hall when Queen Anne visited. That's where the name comes from. I see the family portraits are here now. Come, Genova, and be introduced."

She tripped over to the right-hand wall and began an illustrated family history, which they all meekly followed. But when they reached the picture of a lovely young lady in classical dress playing a stringed instrument, Lady Thalia fell silent.

"Poor Augusta." Lady Thalia sighed, then quickly moved on.

"Who?" Damaris whispered to Fitzroger.

"Rothgar's mother, and the dowager's youngest daughter. She is the link between the Trayce family and the Mallorens, and thus the cause of all the trouble. You know the story?"

"Yes." Lord Henry had told her about Rothgar's mother going mad and murdering her baby. She'd imagined some evil hag, however, not this very young beauty. "Perhaps it's not surprising that the dowager hates the Mallorens."

"Portraits don't always capture the truth," he said.

Before she could ask him what he meant by that, Lady Thalia said, "How very peculiar."

She'd come to the wall of monarchs and was considering it with a remarkably severe expression. "I don't approve, Ashart. Sophia may be proud to be the daughter of a royal bastard, but it's hardly wise to boast of a Stuart connection these days."

Damaris came fully alert. "The dowager's father was a royal bastard?" she asked Fitzroger. "Ashart has royal blood?"

"Mourning your loss?"

But Ashart had overheard. "It's not something I'm proud of. Besides, bastard lines from Charles the Second are two a penny."

"That's why they called him Old Rowley," Fitzroger said close to Damaris's ear. "After a very active dog in his kennels."

Damaris blushed and shot him a frown.

Lady Thalia had overheard. "No scurrilous talk, sir!" she said, but she added, "Not that it wasn't true."

She regarded the wall again, tut-tutting. "And even a portrait of poor Monmouth. Charles the Second's oldest son, dears," she said to Damaris and Genova. "I suppose he was Sophia's uncle in a way, but even so, a sad story and an arrant rebel."

Damaris knew her history. Monmouth had led a rebellion against James II in an attempt to seize his father's throne. He'd failed and been beheaded.

Was Lady Thalia thinking along the same lines as she had—that the Trayces were Jacobites? Or, at least, that the dowager was? It was a peculiar notion, but the Duke of Monmouth's presence here had to mean something.

This whole wall had to mean something. She thought Fitzroger, too, was studying it as if it were a puzzle.

State secrets.

In this context that was enough to give her cold shivers. The heads of the Scottish lords who'd led the last Jacobite rising still rotted on spikes in London.

"He was very handsome," Genova said, looking at Monmouth's picture.

"It's those flowing curls," Fitzroger said. "Perhaps we should bring back the fashion."

"He was a fool," Ashart said rather grimly. "He chose to believe that his father had married his mother, and thus led thousands to their deaths."

"Who was the royal mistress?" Genova asked, looking around. "Does her portrait hang here? She was . . . what? Your great-grandmother, Ash?"

"Great-great." Ashart looked as if he'd like to leave the room, which wasn't surprising, but he would not deny Genova. He indicated the next wall, and a portrait of a young blond beauty in a simple white gown, cradling a snowy lamb.

"Betty Crowley, who later became Betty Prease. Married off to one of the king's devoted supporters to provide a name for her child."

"My goodness," Genova said, "she doesn't look the part."

"Probably because it's a complete invention. Grandy had it painted long after the lady's death. No true portrait exists."

"Of a royal mistress? Isn't that strange?"

"She chose to live quietly and privately."

Damaris saw yet another puzzle. "And was lover to Charles the Second? Alongside bold wantons such as Barbara Castlemaine and Nell Gwyn?"

"That is strange, Ashart, you have to admit," said Lady Thalia. "I have always thought so."

He shrugged. "That's the story. Come along. You were right. It is cold. We need to keep moving."

And leave evidence of Jacobite treason behind? Damaris wondered.

They all walked toward the arch that led to the main staircase, but Damaris stopped, caught by a portrait at the end of the royal wall—a very young man who looked confident of a brilliant future.

"Who's this?" she asked Fitzroger, who was by her side. "Another rebel?"

"Not at all. Merely a tragic footnote to history. It's Prince Henry Stuart, Charles the Second's youngest brother."

"I didn't know there was another brother besides James."

"Nor did I before I came here and saw this."

Damaris studied the handsome young man in those long, lush curls. "Why tragic?"

"He was born in 1640 as the Civil War began, was nine when his father was beheaded, and lived with his mother in impoverished exile until he was twenty. When England begged his brother, Charles, to return and take up his throne, Henry returned to share the wealth and power. Not long afterward, however, he died of smallpox. A sharp lesson in the capriciousness of fate. Come along," he said, putting his hand on her back. "The others are already downstairs."

His touch sent sparkles through her, even when she was armored in corset, quilting, fur, and velvet. She wished she could linger here, to ponder the strangeness of the royal portraits or, more precisely, to try to understand why they hung here and what about them had made Fitzroger suddenly tense and alert.

Was it simply the possibility of Jacobitism? Her instincts said not. That was too obvious.

What had he seen that she had not?

Chapter 11

They joined the others at the bottom of the stairs in the icy tiled hall near the empty fireplace. Lady Thalia was explaining that it was a masterpiece of some sort by an Italian, but Damaris thought even her enthusiasm for this tour was diminishing.

"The library," the old lady announced, and headed off briskly. "My father's collection was famous."

This turned out to be a room Damaris had not seen before, and no wonder. It stank of rot, and so many bits of the ornate plaster ceiling had fallen that the room was dusted gray. The glass doors over the shelves were filmed with it, but she could still see that many shelves were half-empty.

"Oh, dear," Lady Thalia said, sounding close to tears. "This was Papa's pride and joy."

Ashart looked drawn, and Damaris wasn't surprised. This whole house was soaked with sorrow, deep in the walls, warped in the wood, sighing on cold drafts. No wonder it shed flakes of paint and plaster like tears.

Had he not known?

She'd gained the impression that he visited here rarely. Perhaps he'd fallen into the habit of going to his rooms and avoiding the rest of the house.

He put an arm around his great-aunt. "Grandmother must have been selling the more valuable books. I'll put a stop to it, and have something done about this."

He looked rather helpless, which wasn't surprising.

"If you're thinking of lighting a fire in here," Genova said in a calm voice, "you'd better have the chimney checked first."

Ashart smiled at her as if she were a port in a storm. "A practical wife is above rubies."

Was it, as it sounded, a clear declaration that he'd still not exchange her for the greatest fortune in the land, including the Myddleton rubies? Damaris wondered wistfully if she would ever be loved like that. Being married for her money became less appealing by the moment.

Fitzroger broke the heavy silence. "Where do you keep the family archives, Ash?"

Ashart gestured to the far side of the room. "The older records are in cupboards there, and more recent ones in the estate office. Are you looking for an inventory of what used to be here?"

"No. You said Rothgar asked about documents concerning Betty Prease."

Who? Then Damaris remembered—the royal mistress, the one portrayed as such a pure and innocent miss.

Fitzroger continued, "We could oblige him and amuse ourselves looking for information about Mistress Crowley's real nature and her relationship with the king."

Ashart didn't look enthusiastic, but Genova said, "That does sound fascinating."

Her whim, of course, was law. "I have little else to offer by way of amusement," Ashart said. "Very well, but no one is poking through records here. They'd freeze. Bring anything up to the Little Library, Fitz."

Damaris thought Fitzroger looked anything but

pleased with this suggestion. He had no choice, however. "Very well. You said the Prease papers might be in the attic?"

"I believe so. If not, Mrs. Knightly should know. Come along, ladies. Let's return to the warmth. You were right about the cold. I'm likely to lose my fingers soon."

Genova reacted as if he'd announced a mortal wound and pressed her fur-lined muff on him. "I can tuck my hands under my cloak, see?"

Ashart put his hands into the large blue muff and looked neither awkward nor ridiculous. Damaris thought of making the same offer to Fitzroger, but it seemed too bold in public.

"Come along!" Lady Thalia commanded, heading for the door. "While Fitz finds the papers, we four can play whist!"

Damaris groaned, wishing she could stay here. Investigating the Prease papers with Fitzroger was immensely more appealing. No one would permit it, however, if only because whist required four players.

She looked at him and he suddenly seemed alone, abandoned.

She couldn't help herself. She thrust her mink-lined muff into his hands before hurrying away.

Fitz stood bemused. When the others were out of sight, he raised the muff to his face. Even lacking intimate smells, there was something of Damaris about it. Perhaps a faint hint of jasmine that he'd noticed as her perfume. His hands were cold, so he pushed them into the silky warmth, but then pulled them out again. The sensation had seemed indecently erotic.

He put the tormenting object aside. He had to have his wits about him, which meant avoiding Damaris Myddleton.

He'd lied to her this morning because he didn't

want her plunging into some impulsive danger. Her boldness terrified him, particularly when matters were so dangerous.

There were no other victims at Pickmanwell. Someone had put poison into one flagon and sent it via Damaris to Genova.

He'd told the truth about the sender being a man with crooked teeth, but he'd been unable to find him. The snaggletoothed man was remembered—his appearance made that inevitable—and he'd given the name Fletcher, but the trail ended there. He'd been riding and he'd left shortly after they had. No one knew which direction he'd taken.

Fletcher. A false name, Fitz assumed, but a clever one. Not trite such as Smith or Brown, but common enough to be hard to track down, even with his having a distorted lip and crossed teeth.

Reluctantly, not yet having permission to be honest, he'd told Ash the same false tale. He'd seen an advantage to the lie. What Ash knew Genova would know, and it could then spread to Damaris. She'd be poking and prying again.

He put his cold fingers briefly to his head.

He had the house closely watched now, and as long as he could keep Ash and Genova inside, all should be well. But their tour might have accidentally revealed the cause of the danger, and his suspicions chilled his blood.

He returned to the Royal Salon and considered the portraits again. If only they could talk. Especially Betty Crowley—the contradictory royal mistress who so interested Rothgar.

The portrait would never speak, but her secrets might be in her papers, and could contain the key to Ash and Genova's survival. Therefore, he would find them.

* * *

In the marquess's rooms Lady Thalia busily arranged for whist. She declared the Little Library too gloomy and commanded Ashart to summon servants to move the card table into the spacious bedchamber.

Whilst they waited, Lady Thalia continued her lesson to Damaris.

Damaris had watched some games at Rothgar Abbey. That plus the introduction to the game given by Mr. Hoyle enabled her to understand most of what Lady Thalia rattled off. She hoped not to embarrass herself.

When eventually they all took their places, she partnered Lady Thalia, who smiled at her encouragingly as Ashart dealt. At the end of the hand, Lady Thalia said, "A good start, dear, but you must keep track of the cards played. You should have known that you held the last club."

That lost trick had cost them the game, and Lady Thalia wasn't pleased.

Damaris applied her mind. She found remembering the cards easy as long as she didn't let her mind slide to the subject of Fitzroger, wondering what he was doing. Had he found the papers? How could she get to search them with him? What was he really looking for?

"Your play, Damaris," Genova prompted.

Damaris pulled her wits together and followed suit. She managed until Fitzroger entered the room. Then all memory of the cards played blew out of her head. By heaven's mercy, the hand played out without needing an important decision from her.

She went with the others into the Little Library, excited simply to be in his company again.

Four polished wooden boxes with brass locks sat on the floor, each about two square feet. Fitzroger lifted one onto the desk. "Do you have the keys, Ash?"

"No. Quite possibly they're mislaid. If not, Grandy will have them."

Fitzroger produced his slender tools and performed his magic. When he opened the lid, they all pressed forward. Perhaps everyone had secretly hoped for the glint of gold, a portrait, or even a scrap of lace. Instead the box contained a jumble of yellowed papers.

Ashart lifted the top ones and flipped through them. "Accounts and such. Do you really want to dig through these, Genova?"

Genova looked disappointed, but she said, "We should all help. . . ."

"That's not necessary." Fitzroger spoke so quickly that Damaris knew he wanted to search the papers on his own.

"I certainly have no interest," Lady Thalia said. "Come back to cards, everyone."

Impelled simply by that, Damaris said, "I'll start on the papers. I've enjoyed the lesson, but I'm sure Mr. Fitzroger will give you a more challenging game."

Genova, Ashart, and Thalia left without arguing that point.

Only Fitzroger hesitated, remaining by the box, close to her. "There's no need," he said.

Her skin was tingling simply from proximity. "I'd rather. Really. I'm a novice at whist."

After a moment he moved away. "Very well. But search carefully."

She felt able to breathe properly and look directly at him. "So what are we looking for?"

"Anything about Betty Crowley Prease."

"No, what are we *really* looking for?"

"What else do you expect? Secret treasure?"

With that light, dismissive comment, he left, but he didn't close the door between the two rooms. She wasn't sure if that was because it might have seemed rude, or because he didn't trust her, but it left the card table in sight.

The empty seat there almost faced her, so he would be able to observe her with the slightest turn of his head. However, that also meant she could observe him, and even as she took the first few papers out of the box, she did so.

She watched him sit, flipping back the skirts of his plain coat, every movement fluid and strong. *He's sitting in a chair,* she told herself. *Have some sense.*

She turned her eyes to the papers in her hand, realizing too late that some were thin and her tight grip had torn one. She spread them carefully on the desk and did a quick first assessment.

As far as she could tell, there was nothing connected to Betty Prease, but she became fascinated all the same. Accounts, inventories and bills formed a patchwork picture of the past—one that was more like a crazy quilt. For all its shortcomings, Birch House had been neatly organized. She'd always known where things would be and when things should be done.

These papers looked to have been tossed into the box without care or system, and she simply couldn't bear it. Apart from this mysterious search, there could be important documents here. A lease, a contract—or a letter from a royal lover. No matter what Fitzroger really wanted to find, she'd be delighted by something like that.

She set to organization, creating piles for household accounts, receipts, letters from merchants and other businessmen, and family correspondence.

Despite every effort of will her eyes and mind kept turning from one investigation to another. From documents to man.

What was the truth about Octavius Fitzroger? He'd seemed tense in the portrait gallery but now looked gracefully at ease. Some people could do that—arrange themselves for beauty without thought. He was beautiful in that way—a lithe, masculine beauty that summoned memories of the fencing match. And turned her hot all over.

She hastily returned her attention on the papers. That was when she realized that the documents she'd sorted were all from the early part of the present century, which was forty years too late for anything to do with Betty and the king. She flipped through them again. Some went back as far as the 1690s, but nothing from the 1660s.

There had to be some older ones and some more intimate ones.

She glanced first at the cardplayers, then at the other boxes, then at the slender picks sticking out of the lock of the box in front of her. Everyone seemed involved in the game, and the untouched boxes were out of their sight.

She slid the fine blades free and slipped away to kneel in front of another box and probe. It would help if she had the slightest idea what she was doing.

"It's not so simple a skill."

She shot to her feet, awash with guilt. "Then teach me."

"Absolutely not." He took the picks from her hand and looked back at the desk. "You don't seem to have finished that box."

"It's all household accounts, and not a thing from the 1660s."

"Yet. There's no point in a search if it's not systematic."

"Since you won't say what the point is, how am I to tell?"

"The point is clear to everyone but you."

Damaris remembered that they had an audience and pulled back from an enjoyable conflagration.

"As we're looking for personal papers," she said, "wouldn't it be more efficient to find which box contains them? Failing that, which box contains the older documents?"

"Shall I take over this boring task?"

She quickly returned to her seat behind the desk. "No, thank you. Enjoy your game."

She didn't even watch as he left the room—taking his lock picks with him.

Knowing he'd be observing her, she focused on the paper in her hand—a copy of an order for exotic plants placed in 1715. The Earl of Vesey—the royal bastard himself—wanted some *Geranium africanum* and *Pelargonium peltatum*, neither of which meant anything to her.

He also wanted an *Amaryllis belladonna*. Belladonna was deadly nightshade, a poison. She immediately thought of the mulled cider, but then remembered that it had been an accident. Such things happened all the time. A whole family in Worksop had been killed when someone had put rat poison into the stew by mistake.

She moved on to such exciting records as a request for puppies from Lord Vesey's hunting dogs, questions from an estate manager in Cumberland about draining and marling a field, and a report on the progress of a set of chairs to be covered in red Morocco.

"I come to relieve you."

Damaris started. She hadn't even heard him reenter the room. The others were chattering between hands, but the game hadn't ended. Wasn't it dinnertime yet? She truly didn't want to play more whist. A glance at an ornate ormolu clock told her it was only one o'clock, and dinner here was set for two.

"I don't mind continuing. I found this." She showed him the letter about belladonna.

"Belladonna merely means beautiful lady. This plant need not be poisonous."

"I know. It's said to make a lady's eyes lustrous."

He looked at her. "I wouldn't recommend it."

She frowned at him. "A gallant gentleman would say I don't need it. But then, I forget, I'm plain as a pikestaff, aren't I?"

"Damaris, I meant that your eyes are beautiful enough."

"Oh." She didn't know how to respond, especially when the others might hear. She moved out from behind the desk. "Very well, I'll take your place at cards." Once at a safe distance, she hesitated. "I've been sorting the papers by date."

"A good idea."

"You'll say if you find any royal letters?"

"Of course."

Why should such a practical exchange feel like sunbeams?

She quickly left the room and washed her hands, saying to the others, "I'm not sure if the trivial accounts of an estate are tedious or fascinating. It's strange to think that these long-dead people were concerned about dogs and chair coverings."

Genova smiled. "And that one day people might think our accounts of lace purchased or books read of any interest at all."

A new hand was dealt, and Damaris was now supposed to play without help. She applied herself to it, refusing to sneak looks at Fitzroger. As a result, she and Lady Thalia won resoundingly.

"What an excellent player you have become, my dear!" Lady Thalia declared. "And all in a matter of hours."

"With an excellent teacher."

"How kind."

Damaris was wondering if she could demand to switch again with Fitzroger when Lady Thalia sighed. "This has been so delightful, and you are all very kind to indulge me. But I think I need a little nap."

Genova went to her. "Thalia, are you all right? You don't usually nap before dinner."

"It must be the travel, dear. I'll be fit as a fiddle in no time, but I want all my wits if we're to dine with Sophia."

An excellent point. They were all to join the dowager in her private dining room at two.

"Off you all go. Genova, dear, please find Regeanne."

Of course—they were in her bedchamber. Genova picked up her cloak and hurried out through one door while Damaris went with Ashart to the Little Library. She didn't think Lady Thalia looked particularly weary, and when she looked back and caught a twinkle in the old lady's eyes, she understood: She was giving Genova and Ashart some time together.

A most accommodating chaperon, but where would this leave herself and Fitzroger?

When they entered he looked up from the second box.

"Thalia wants a rest," Ashart said, strolling toward the desk. "Found anything?"

"Nothing relevant, but thus far the papers are too recent."

Ashart looked at the two locked boxes. "Why not check those to see if there are older ones?"

"You and Damaris have much in common."

Ashart gave her a questioning look.

"I made the same suggestion, and had my knuckles rapped for impatience."

"He can't rap my knuckles. They're my papers to do with as I wish. Open them, Fitz."

Fitzroger obeyed, then executed a sarcastically flourishing bow. "My lord!"

Ashart winked at Damaris. "A knuckle rap, indeed."

He was mellowing toward her now that there was

no question of marriage between them, and Damaris thought she might come to like him in a while. Almost as a brother, which was a truly extraordinary thought.

He went toward the boxes, but then Genova entered, and clearly everything else was of no importance. Before Damaris could prevent it, they left.

Her heart fluttered with panic. Or with something. She knew she ought to leave, to retreat to the safety of her room, but she didn't want to. She wanted to continue the hunt for Betty Crowley's secrets. And she wanted, despite sanity, to do so at Fitzroger's side.

She went to one of the newly opened boxes. Before she could touch it, Fitzroger lifted it onto the sofa. "You will find that more comfortable."

He lit a branch of candles and placed them close by her. He hesitated, and she held her breath, thinking that he might be about to touch her and wondering what she should do if he did. Instead he returned to his seat behind the desk.

He was going to behave correctly, so she would, too.

Despite the space between them, however, they worked in a silence that was both intimate and fraught. The rustle of papers in his hands whispered of intimate matters, and the sultry glow of logs in the fireplace looked like passion.

You are a rich heiress, she reminded herself, *who could soon be the Duchess of Bridgewater if you only keep your grip on sanity. You'd give up that to be Mrs. Fitzroger, wife of a man attached to a notorious scandal?* She still hadn't discovered the truth of that, and she suspected that part of the reason was because she didn't want to.

He finished his box, replaced it on the floor, and lifted the last one onto the desk. Then he went to the wood box and put another log on the fire. It crackled and flamed anew. He paused between her sofa and his desk.

"You've smudged dirt on your cheek."

Their eyes locked. She waited hopefully for him to come to wipe it off. When he didn't, she rubbed at both her cheeks. "Better?"

His eyes smiled. "Not unless gray rouge is in fashion."

He came to her then, pulling out a handkerchief, and tilted her head up to his. Yes, she was melting, her insides softening, her blood pooling, abandoning her brain. . . .

He rubbed at each cheek, but then said, "Not much improvement. Perhaps you should go to your room to wash."

Was he trying to get rid of her? "It's a long way through the cold house, and there are more papers to check."

After a moment, he stepped back and returned to the desk to raise the lid of the new box. "More of the same."

"Nothing of interest in the last one?" she asked, simply because she wanted them to talk.

"No." He sat back down behind the desk. "And nothing dating back to the 1660s."

"That truly is what we're looking for? Documents confirming Betty Crowley's affair with the king?"

He took out a paper and glanced at it. "Yes."

She had to believe him, but at the same time she was certain that more lay behind it.

"When did Betty Crowley die?" she asked.

"In 1718."

"So she could have been writing letters up to that date."

He looked up, startled. "True, and we've found nothing by her."

"Suspicious, wouldn't you say? This is no idle search, Fitzroger. I can see that." When he didn't respond, she said, "Tell me the truth. I want to help you."

He leaned back then, long fingers resting on the papers. "If you keep prying, Damaris, I shall have to avoid you."

"I don't see how you can avoid me, not here with so few warm rooms."

"I can endure cold."

Chapter 12

Without really understanding his words, Damaris recognized a precipice and hastily retreated. "I think the dowager will have any documents to do with the royal connection."

After a long moment, he said, "So do I."

"So, when are you going to search her rooms for them?"

Something moved his lips and eyes. It looked like impatience, but she thought she saw humor, too. "How could I?"

"The same way you open locks. I do wish you'd teach me."

"No." He picked another document out of the box, ending the discussion.

She wouldn't allow it. "I'm sure this would go better if we worked together."

He stared at her. "I beg your pardon?"

"Side by side." She rose and picked up a chair to carry it over to the desk. He took it from her. She allowed it, but said, "I'm not a weakling, you know. I've moved heavier furniture in my time."

Looking into his eyes, she could think of nothing but his lips on hers, his body pressed to hers. . . .

He put his hands on her shoulders, but only to sit her in her chair so firmly that her teeth jarred. He opened his mouth as if he might apologize, but then he sat. "What, precisely, is your brilliant plan?"

To sit in your lap and kiss you.

The only thing stopping her was the certainty that if she did anything so foolish he would leave the room, and perhaps the house. He had recognized what hummed between them, as she had, but he was determined to resist temptation. A strong will could be an irritating thing. . . .

"My mind wanders," she said. *My, how it wanders.* "I'm sure I'm not paying sufficient attention to the letters. If we work together . . ."

"My mind doesn't wander."

She met his eyes. "Doesn't it?"

Color touched his cheeks and he looked away. "Very well." He picked up the letter in front of him and unfolded it. "December sixth, 1697, from Sir Roger Midcall about the new St. Paul's Cathedral, and also recommending a concoction to get rid of fleas."

Damaris picked up the next paper, aware of their sharing an intimate closeness. "Undated. A most effective treatment for worms in children. Fenugreek, wormwood, and treacle. I've used much the same."

"You had worms?"

"In helping the poor, sir."

But he'd teased, which was something.

He took out the next one. "We seem to have hit a lode of recipes. Pills composed of Norway tar and elecampane root. Effective against scurvy."

"That one I don't know." She picked a paper that was folded in half and opened it. She looked at it for a moment then slowly read, " 'Mistress Betty's Violent Purge.' "

He leaned closer, taking an edge of the paper, but she said, "There's nothing of interest in it, and it might not be the same Betty."

"True, but if it is, we have her handwriting. Betty

Prease was said to be a quiet, gentle lady. What use would she have for a violent purge?"

"To rid the body of poisons." Then she looked at him. "Not that sort."

"I know, but one can't help making connections. The main ingredient seems to be diascordium. What's that?"

"A concoction, but mostly *Teucrium scordium*, better known as water germander."

"Better known to some," he remarked, with a true smile this time. He let go of the paper, however, breaking the link, and chose another out of the box.

They skimmed a series of remedies, then paused at the same neat handwriting as Mistress Betty's Violent Purge. Damaris put them side by side, but said, "Betty Prease wouldn't describe her recipe that way, would she?"

He sat back with a groan. "Of course not. What a dunce I am today."

Damaris pulled out another paper, a begging letter from a distant relative, wondering if his wits were wandering for the same reason hers were. She hoped so. She longed to lean toward him, to rest against him, to press close.

He put a hand on her arm, and she realized she *had* leaned. She looked up at him, so close now, lips so close. . . .

What harm in a kiss? her hungry body whispered. *Only a kiss . . .*

Simultaneously he pushed slightly to straighten her, and she moved to be straight. Half the box was left to investigate, and more than half of the one she'd abandoned, and she was playing with fire.

She rose, moving her shoulders. "I'm growing stiff." She walked around the room to lend credence to this, carefully not looking at him. She really should leave before control shattered.

"We need a known sample of Betty Prease's handwriting."

His crisp voice broke the spell, and she turned to face him, glad to seize the practical.

"The dowager will have one," she suggested.

"So she will. I suppose I'm to steal that, too?"

"Actually, I was thinking that someone could ask her for it at dinner."

His eyes became fixed, as if her words had shocked him.

"Why not?" she asked. "It's not as if we're doing anything wrong." Instinctively, she added, "Are we?"

His very blankness showed that her question was meaningful, but he said, "No. No, we're not. Ash can ask her. He's the only one of us she can tolerate at the moment."

"There you are, then. He can ask for any and all papers relating to her grandmother. How can she refuse?"

"We're talking of the Dowager Lady Ashart," he said dryly, "but perhaps she won't see any harm in it."

"*Is* there any harm in it?" Her frustration exploded. "Why won't you tell me what's going on? This is so silly!"

"No. It's important, and dangerous, and I don't want you involved."

Silence shot through the room like lightning without thunder.

He inhaled. She saw it in a movement of his chest before he stood and turned away. "I shouldn't have said that. Forget it. No, you can hardly do that. I ask you not repeat it to the others."

She moved closer to the desk, closer to him. "That business with Genova. It *was* an attack—"

"No." The quiet firmness in his voice silenced her. He turned to face her. "I'm doing my best to keep everyone safe. I believe that everyone is safe here at this moment."

"Everyone . . ."

"I can say no more. I shouldn't have said so much." His hands flexed for a moment before being controlled, before he regained that deceptive calm.

The awareness of truths was like singing, Damaris decided, like the times when the notes were perfect and glided on the melody like a bird on the wind. She knew truth now and could not keep silent.

"You need someone. Someone to talk to about all this. Let it be me."

"Don't be ridiculous."

His tone alone should have shriveled her, but she stepped forward to press against the desk that separated them. "I'll try not to ask too many questions, but I want to help. I need to help. Because it's important and dangerous, you see? If you wanted me to ignore all this, you shouldn't have told me that."

"Is it your intention to heap coals of fire upon my head?"

"I'm not sure what my intentions are. I'm bewildering myself. I don't know this land, this place of great houses and lives that weave with history. I don't know men. You mystify me, all of you. I'm sure I shouldn't be saying these things to you, but what can I do but be honest?"

"Damaris, Damaris, don't you know the world hunts down and slaughters the honest?" He came around the desk and took her hands, raising them to his lips, brushing a kiss across each, his eyes never leaving hers.

She wasn't honest then. If she had been she would have laughed, or cried, or done something disastrously revealing.

Against her fingers, he said, "I cannot tell my slippery secrets to an honest woman."

"I said honest, not indiscreet."

"But if you are questioned, can you lie?"

He was still holding her hands. She curled her fingers around his and didn't want to let go. "I will lie in your cause. Please share what secrets you can, Fitzroger."

"Call me Fitz."

It caught her unawares, and she pulled her hands free before knowing she was going to do it. "Why does that bother me?" She answered herself. "Because we cannot be more than friends. We cannot."

He seemed to feel no trace of her anguish. "My friends call me Fitz."

"And those who are more than friends?"

His lips twitched. "Fitz."

"No one calls you Octavius? No one at all? It has a certain dignity."

"It means eighth, and where's the dignity in that? Besides, it's too distant, wouldn't you say, for lovers?" He leaned his hips back against the desk. "What would you call me if we were lovers?"

She caught her breath, but if he wanted to carry this to wicked heights she'd soar with him. For a little while, at least.

"A short form?" she suggested. "Octi?"

He grinned. "No."

"Or it could be put into plain English—Number Eight. You're right. It is a ridiculous way of naming children. Perhaps it would work better in French, *Huit*." She cocked her head. "Wheat does suit your hair."

"Rough as hay?"

"No."

Their words summoned that kiss in the coach, when she'd gripped his hair, which wasn't silky, but wasn't coarse either. In her memory it seemed alive as he was alive in every bone, sinew, and muscle.

She wasn't sure who moved, how she came to be in his arms, but she recognized the inevitable crescendo of the duet they had been singing. She slid her fingers into that curly, wheat-colored hair and blended her mouth desperately with his. She pressed closer, or he pressed her closer with his strong arms, a hand between her shoulders, another commanding the small of her back.

Duchess of Bridgewater, she reminded herself, but it was, after all, only a kiss. . . .

Only a kiss, but able to wipe all thought from her mind, able to make her a creature of fierce physical passion. She twined her arms around him, needing to be closer, far closer than clothing allowed.

His mouth broke with hers to trail little kisses across her cheek and around her ear. She wanted more and turned her head, seeking his lips again.

"My nurse," he murmured, "called me Tottie."

She broke into giggles. "I couldn't possibly!"

"Not even in private?"

She shook her head against his shoulder.

"Not even," he asked softly, "in the secrecy of a curtained bed?"

Her legs weakened and she clung to him, but then she found the strength to push out of his arms. Away from the searing fire.

"I apologize," he said, letting her go, turning sober and thoughtful. In a moment she'd lose him, and that she could not bear.

"Don't! Apologize, I mean. I liked it. And I need practice. In flirting and such . . ." She needed to talk them out of this dangerous corner. "For court. Won't there be flirtation and kissing at court?"

"Lesson number one," he said tersely, "don't kiss anyone like that at court. Lesson number two—don't be alone with anyone like this at court. Lesson number three—avoid men like me at court."

"Oh, my!" she declared, hand to chest. "Court is full of men like you, sir?"

He didn't smile. "In the baser respects, yes."

"And in the higher ones, in sweet charms?"

She immediately wished the words back, but then a raised voice in the next room saved them. By silent agreement they returned to the desk and settled as if they'd spent all their time absorbed by papers.

Lady Thalia came in, beaming. "That's so much better! Oh, dear, have Genova and Ashart slipped away? Naughty, naughty, but they'll soon be wed, and I'm sure you two have been good. Damaris, dear, I do think you should change to dine. So inconvenient in this cold house, but I'm sure Sophia will expect some formality."

Damaris hesitated, hoping Fitzroger—Fitz—would offer to escort her across the house. When he didn't, she left alone.

In a house like this it was a convenience to find Maisie in the room, engaged in needlework. Damaris changed quickly into silk, choosing a subdued blue-and-white stripe because it really was time to be sensible. She even added a large gauze fichu to fill in the low bodice.

Demure modesty might soothe the dowager as well, so that she'd be more likely to surrender Betty Prease's documents. But what the point of obtaining those was, she still had no idea.

As she sat so that Maisie could tidy her hair, however, Damaris knew that Betty Prease was not the mystery she sought to unravel here. That was Fitz and herself. She had only a few days before they moved on to London, when everything would change. There she would be under Lady Arradale's eye. She would have little time with Fitz, and probably none alone. She'd enter society and be expected to choose her titled husband.

"Where's your mink muff, Miss Damaris?" Maisie asked.

Damaris blushed for no reason at all. "Left in the hall." It wasn't actually a lie. "I'll collect it when I go down."

A little while later, however, a maid brought it up. "With Mr. Fitzroger's compliments, miss."

Damaris couldn't help a thrill that he'd thought of it, even that he'd recently touched it, but Maisie was scowling and muttering something about "that man."

As she put on her red cloak and took the muff, Damaris asked, "Why are you so set against Mr. Fitzroger?"

Maisie reddened. "He's trying to marry you, that's why."

"No, he isn't. And if he were I wouldn't. But if I did, how does it concern you?"

"Because he'll break your heart for sure." But Maisie looked away and was fiddling with her skirt.

"There's more to it than that."

Maisie worked her mouth, but then burst out, "I want to be a ladyship's maid, miss! Down below, we take our rank from our employer. With you as a marchioness I'd have been one of the highest. It would have been ever so lovely. If you marry that one, I'll be no better off than I am now."

Damaris shook her head. "I had no idea. How extraordinary." She'd better not tell Maisie there was a chance of her becoming a duchess in the servants' hierarchy or there'd be no living with her. "I can't marry to suit you, Maisie. And besides, wouldn't you rather marry, yourself, than be even a duchess in the servant's hall?"

Maisie blushed. "I might, Miss Damaris. But only to the right man."

"Then we think alike on these things."

"Then you won't fall into trouble with that one?" Maisie asked.

"I intend to make the right decision," Damaris said, and left the room.

She found Fitzroger outside her door.

"I have a room here," he said, pointing to the next door. "It was to have been Lady Thalia's, but, of course, she's with Genova. My usual room is on the other side of the Little Library, but Ash wanted to be close, so I agreed to let him use it."

"Oh," Damaris said, fighting laughter. She'd never heard him rattle on before. Was he as flustered as she? And for the same reason?

He must be. He'd not have kissed her earlier if he'd been in control of himself. Her mind was a mess, and she felt half-mad, but at least he might be in the same state. He offered an arm and she linked hers with it, feeling as if bubbles floated in her brain, bubbles of wicked possibilities that made it impossible to make sensible decisions.

She'd read stories of people hurtling to disaster this way—Lancelot and Guinevere, Romeo and Juliet, Mary, Queen of Scots, and Bothwell—and never understood it. Now she did, and it was just as well that she had his arm as they went downstairs, for she could easily have missed a step in her distracted, light-headed state.

The dowager awaited them amid the faded elegance of a small dining room. She was frosty, but the room was warm. They all took their places—Ashart and Genova on one side of the table, Damaris and Fitzroger on the other, with the dowager and Lady Thalia at head and foot.

Lady Ashart rang a bell, and servants came in to place the first course of dishes on the table. The food was plain but tolerable. Damaris ate, trying to distract herself from Fitzroger by looking for ways to turn the conversation to Betty Prease. Instead it wandered from the weather to books to minor matters of public affairs.

By the time the second course was placed on the table, she was ready to raise the subject out of nowhere. But at last Ashart said, "We've been going through the old Prease papers, Grandy. I hope you don't mind."

"A bit late if I do," the dowager said, but without an increase in ice. "I can't imagine why."

"We thought it would be amusing to look for evidence of the liaison between Betty Crowley and the king."

Damaris ate pear tart but watched the dowager. She thought the plump face stilled, but it could be simple annoyance.

"I assure you," the dowager said, "royal blood does run in your veins, Ashart. It is written in your features, if nowhere else."

"I thought so, too," Genova said.

Lady Ashart ignored her.

Fitzroger said, "I thought the resemblance closer to Charles the First than to Charles the Second. And perhaps," he added, "to Prince Henry."

Damaris had automatically turned to him as he spoke, so when she looked back at the dowager any immediate reaction had passed. She sensed something in the air, however, and Lady Ashart seemed changed—lips tighter, eyes fixed.

Prince Henry?

The discussion seemed in danger of dying, so she asked at random, "What sort of woman was your famous ancestor, Lady Ashart? A fascinating beauty, I'm sure."

The dowager raised her double chins. "She was a

lady much admired by all who knew her, and for more than her appearance. A lady of quiet dignity and pious goodness, free of all interest in worldly pleasures."

Damaris stared, almost choking on the obvious question. How, then, did she become lover of Old Rowley, the most decadent king of England?

"I always supposed her virtues arose from penitence," said Lady Thalia.

"If she had anything to repent!" The dowager rose to her feet, managing to make it look majestic, even though the elevation from sitting to standing was not very great. "I'm sure you would all prefer to remove upstairs."

With that she marched out of the room and closed the door with an eloquent click.

Eyes met eyes around the table.

"Sharing the king's bed is a holy duty?" Ashart offered.

Damaris expected Fitzroger to make the suggestion, but when he didn't she said, "Or it never happened. It's all a tale."

"Oh, it happened," Lady Thalia said. "Everyone knew that Randolph Prease was quite incapable of . . . Well"—she waved a vague hand—"his war wounds, you know."

Damaris realized then that Lady Thalia might know a great deal about these events. She'd still been a girl at the turn of the century, but she must have known people who'd been part of King Charles's court. She might even have known men who fought in the Civil War.

Ashart drained the last of his wine. "Grandy can't have it both ways. Either Betty was the king's whore, or we don't have royal blood."

Again, no one said the obvious. "Or," said Damaris, "there was a secret marriage."

It created a startling ripple of silence.

Lady Thalia said, "How very intriguing."

"But impossible." Ashart rose and assisted Genova from her seat. "Betty conceived my great-grandfather in 1660 at the time of the Restoration. The newly restored king would wench with anyone, but he'd never have married a commoner. He needed money, power, and a bride who created royal alliances abroad. That's why he married Catherine of Braganza. Come. I'll order tea served upstairs."

Fitzroger assisted Lady Thalia, so Damaris managed for herself, thinking furiously.

When they left the room, Thalia had one of Fitzroger's arms, and Damaris should have taken his other. Instead she walked on Thalia's other side. "What do you think, Lady Thalia? Was Mistress Betty the king's mistress?"

"You're tempting me to be naughty," the old lady said with a twinkle, "but let us say her child was not fathered by Randolph Prease."

Damaris understood. Randolph Prease had been incapable of fathering a child because of his war wounds that had damaged that part of his body. That, however, was irrelevant. No one thought him the father. Charles II was accepted as the father of Betty's son, but now there were the conflicting details.

As Ashart said, King Charles would never have married a commoner. But the dowager insisted Betty Crowley was virtuous.

Fitzroger had introduced the name of Henry Stuart, the forgotten prince, the one who'd died tragically young, surely at about the time Betty Crowley was conceiving her child. Once thought of, it was fascinating, but with alarming implications.

When they entered the Hunt Room, Damaris was wondering what to say, what to ask, but Ashart spoke first. "Was Betty Prease pious and good all her life, Thalia? Or was she a fatal siren in her youth?"

Lady Thalia sat in a chair near the fire, putting her feet on a footstool. "I met her only twice, dear, and in her later years. Once was when I was staying in Cambridgeshire with the Wallboroughs. We all went to Storton House for a ball. That was where my brother met the dowager—Sophia Prease in those days—which might have been better avoided. Then she was at the wedding. In her widowhood she lived in a private suite of rooms at Storton and rarely emerged except to engage in good works. The area is plentifully provided with almshouses and charity hospitals."

"Not a bad thing," Genova said.

"But evidence of a guilty conscience," Ashart pointed out. "Conundrum solved. Betty Crowley let virtue slip as a girl, perhaps just once, and did penance all her days. I have royal blood in my veins, safely from a bastard line, but Grandy doesn't care to admit her grandmother's frailty."

Two maids came in bearing the tea trays. Thalia waved to Genova. "You tend to it all, dear. You'll soon be mistress here."

As Genova did so, Damaris thought that Lady Thalia was not one fraction as silly as she appeared. That had been a pointed reminder for the maids to take back to the servants' hall.

She had to admit that Ashart's summary made sense. She could feel in herself how easy it would be to let wisdom and virtue slip under the attraction of a certain sort of man. It didn't matter whether Betty had sinned with wicked, worldly King Charles, or with his youngest brother, who had been much closer to her age.

It mattered only if there had been a marriage.

Because if Prince Henry had fathered Charles Prease, and if he'd also married Betty Crowley, the line that came down to Ashart was *legitimate*. She didn't fully understand the royal succession, but she thought it might mean that Ashart had a claim to the throne of England.

Now *there* was a state secret to shrivel the skin.

There'd been so much bloodshed over the throne. First the Duke of Monmouth, then the uprising in 1715 to try to install James II's son instead of the Hanoverian, George I. Most recently the one in 1745 that had led to so many deaths, including the bloody slaughter at Culloden.

Damaris was too young to remember the events of 1745, but stories about it had been vivid during her childhood, for the rebel army had come close to Worksop during its march on London. For a little while it had seemed the Jacobites would make it there and succeed.

She looked to Fitzroger, who stood by a window, lost in thought. She'd give much more than a penny to read his mind.

Lady Thalia proposed an evening of whist.

Perhaps Fitz read her reaction, for he said, "Why don't we play games of another sort? After all, once she's at court we don't want Damaris to lose her fortune at loo or faro."

"As if I would!"

He looked at her. "A passion for gaming can be as unexpected and irresistible as any other sort."

She hoped she wasn't as pink as she was hot.

Lady Thalia wasn't thrilled at the idea, but even she probably realized that they couldn't play whist all the time.

As far as Damaris was concerned, the card games they played that evening were easier and more fun than whist. They all seemed a silly way to risk money, but as they played with counters in the form of pearl fish, she didn't mind.

The light died, and candlelight took over. As they explored from dangerous faro to frivolous speculation,

Damaris soon realized that Fitz's warning might have been valid. She thrilled to scoop up a theoretical fortune in guineas and when she lost, it inspired her to play again and try to win them back. She was always so sure her luck would turn. At one point Ashart ordered claret and biscuits, and the wine didn't improve her self-control.

She pointed that out, and Fitz said, "Another lesson. Card playing is generally accompanied by wine. Learn to keep a steady head. Or at least to know when it's wobbling."

It was good advice, applied to love as well as cards. If the passion for winning burned in her, so did passion of another sort. As evening became night this candlelit circle of five wove a dangerous charm, and for her, Fitz burned at the heart of it.

At first he had kept himself slightly apart, but in time the gaiety had caught him. He'd relaxed, and his quick wit and ready smile reached her, touched her, dazzled her. There was that glow again, and now it seemed to her to be the glow of honest joy, as with the fencing.

Why did he find it so hard to be joyful? What was the darkness that surrounded him? It had to be that scandal, and she should cease avoiding it and ask Lady Thalia. After all, money could work miracles. It might wipe the shadows away.

Tomorrow, she vowed. She would ask Lady Thalia tomorrow. She staked and won, praying she wouldn't uncover too dark a sin. She wanted to weave this magical circle tight and hold Fitz safe within it. Wind him in golden streamers of joy and keep him forever in the light.

Chapter 13

Late that night Fitz walked the grounds of Cheynings, his breath puffing silver, and icy remnants of
snow crunching beneath his boots. He needed to check
the area before he slept, but he also needed to escape
the too-close proximity to Damaris. He'd hoped the
winter night air would blow away the nonsense filling
his mind.

It wasn't working.

He'd been aware all day of her attention on him. He'd
tried to keep his distance, but she would not be warned
away. Not surprising when he kept responding, dammit.

Devil take it, he was thinking about her again, and
it was like opening a pot of jam near a wasps' nest.
Now there was nothing else in his mind but buzz. A
villain could probably creep up behind him and ga-
rotte him with ease.

He'd vastly overestimated his control. That kiss in
the Little Library should never have happened; nor
should he have invited her to call him Fitz. An evening of lighthearted gambling games had been disastrous. He was besotted with her and impassioned by
her—by her quick wits, her forthright manner, her idiotic courage, and her piratical determination to get
what she wanted.

If the world were different, he'd kneel at her feet

and beg to be hers, but the world was as it was. He was as he was, rightly burdened by his sin.

He looked up at the unhelpful moon in a sky full of mysterious stars. Ash was fascinated by the reality of the planets and stars—where they were, what they were. Fitz preferred them to be a mystery, up who knew how high, a constant reminder that there was indeed more in heaven and earth than the obvious.

They helped clear his mind. For his own sake and Damaris's, he must go far away. To be free to do that, he must first ensure Ash's safety, which meant finding any documents relating to Betty Crowley and her child.

All the clues pointed to there having been a secret marriage, and that spelled disaster. No wonder the king was distressed. No wonder some people wanted Ashart dead.

It would be impossible to prove that such a marriage hadn't happened, so the best solution would be to find the proof that it had. Once found, it could be destroyed, preferably in the king's presence. It was the only way to end all danger.

He thought Damaris might be putting together the pieces. What keen wits she had. . . .

He blocked that, but not before he remembered her pointing out that anything of importance would be in the dowager's keeping. She was right.

He smiled at the memory of her suggesting he steal the papers. Piracy must run in the blood.

He sucked in a breath. He mustn't think of her!

He walked a circuit of the house, making sure his guards were in place. He finally entered the house by a side door, which he locked after himself. The corridor he stood in was pitch-dark, but he knew the house well enough to make his way to the service stairs and back to his room. There he took out his lantern and assembled it.

It was a variation on a smuggler's lantern, designed to provide light when necessary, but to show little when closed. Fitz had ordered this one made half-size and hinged so that it collapsed flat when not in use. In a pinch, he could carry it in his pocket.

He quickly transformed the lantern into the familiar peaked-roof shape and opened the door to set a candle in place. Once it was lit, he closed the door so that only a hint of light showed through the smoke holes at the top.

Putting the lantern aside, he took off his boots, replacing them with soft leather slippers that were perfect for silence in the night. He substituted fine-grain leather gloves for the sturdier ones he'd worn outside. The house was cold, and he couldn't risk clumsiness. A muff, he thought with a wry smile, might be a useful accessory for a thief.

He made his way down to the hall with the help of only the thin moonlight. The air was cold enough to prickle his skin, but all was silent.

Too silent. He realized that the long-case clock on the wall had wound down. Cheynings often made him think of a mausoleum. Perhaps that was why he had a strange feeling of being watched. He sensed movement and glanced up the stairs, but nothing disturbed the moonlit shadows.

Ghosts. That was all Cheynings needed.

He shook his head. It was more likely mice. Cheynings needed cats, but the dowager detested them.

He turned to the left, where two doors led into her suite of five rooms. The right-hand door led to the dining room, and the left to the adjacent drawing room. There was a door from the drawing room into her bedchamber, with a dressing room beyond. That room had a door into a back corridor, but he shouldn't need it.

The most likely place for papers was the office,

which lay beyond the dining room, but it would be damnable to search. Moreover, he couldn't believe that the dowager would leave explosive documents there, even in a locked drawer. She'd want to keep such documents safe, but also treat them with reverence and be able to take them out in privacy to cherish.

That meant that the likeliest spot was the bedchamber, the most dangerous place to invade. He considered leaving the search until daytime, but that wouldn't help. Servants and the dowager herself could be in and out all day.

He had to do it now. She'd often boasted of sleeping well. A result of a virtuous life and hard work, she would say. Fitz had heard that a bit of opium helped. He hoped so.

He'd made note earlier that the dining room door was in good condition and opened silently, so he hoped the drawing room one would be the same. It was, and he was in without noise. The curtains were up, so faint moonlight allowed him to navigate to the bedchamber door.

It, too, opened without a squeak, allowing him into the pitch-dark room. He stepped inside, feeling thick carpet beneath his shoes. Good. He should be able to move around quietly.

A noise froze him. After a breathless moment he relaxed. It was a kind of snuffling snore. He waited, and after a count of three he heard it again. The noise was in front of him, so that must be where the bed was. A clock ticked to his right, probably on the mantelpiece. He closed the door with slow care. . . .

A tinkling noise almost made him jump out of his skin.

The clock had begun to chime midnight. When it finally settled to silence, Fitz listened, one hand still on the handle so he could make a lightning escape.

The light snore ruffled on. The dowager was too accustomed to her clock to be wakened by it, but that didn't mean she wouldn't be roused by an unusual noise. The mind was very clever in that way.

He waited several minutes to be sure she was asleep, then walked forward until he encountered the heavy curtains around the bed. He followed them around the three sides, confirming that the hangings were completely drawn. Only then did he open one door of the lantern.

His nerves were still jumping, which was strange, since this was considerably less dangerous than most other searches he'd made. He doubted the dowager kept a pistol beneath her pillow, and if she did she'd be unlikely to shoot him if she woke. She couldn't summon guards to haul him off to prison and torture. His discovery here couldn't cause a diplomatic disaster.

But it would be disastrous enough.

She'd order him from the house, and Ash would find it hard to prevent it. He might not want to unless Fitz could explain his behavior, which, by his promise of silence, he could not easily do.

If Ash stood by him, the situation would be worse. Ash would leave for London, which would be hazardous, and would also mean abandoning the most likely location of the papers.

Fitz steadied himself and began the search. The room was sparsely furnished, and his attention went immediately to a lady's writing desk, which was of a type that surprised him. The dowager's office desk was massive and plain, but this one was a delicate piece with slender legs, decorated panels, and carvings. A secret taste for frivolity? He doubted it. All the decoration would serve to hide secret compartments and catches, however. He surveyed it, keeping track of the regular soft snores.

The key was obligingly in the lock, so he turned it, making only the slightest click, and raised the top. Paper, ink, sand, sealing wax. Pigeonholes with folded letters. Secret papers would not be in the open, not even here.

He eyed the writing surface and the dimensions of the desk, seeing a number of places where there might be a little extra space. He put the lantern on the floor, took off his gloves, and ran his fingers beneath the carved front edge. He pressed, pulled, pushed, gently at first, then more firmly.

This time the click was loud and a snuffle broke off with a snort. "What . . ."

The voice behind the bedcurtains sounded half-asleep, but Fitz took no risks. He closed the desktop, picked up his lantern, and moved silently to hunch down at the foot of the bed, shutting the lantern door as he settled there. Whichever side of the hangings she opened, she wouldn't see him. If she climbed out of bed he could creep around to the opposite side.

But damn it all to Hades, in the blackness the tiny glimmer from the top of the lantern might give him away. He couldn't extinguish it without opening the thing, and if he squeezed out the flame, there was always a smell from the dying smoke. She'd cry for help, servants would come running, and he would be trapped here.

"Who's there!" the dowager demanded. Curtains rattled apart—to his right. "Jane? Is that you? What are you doing, you stupid woman?"

He was already easing left. Time to slip out through the drawing room door. Even if she heard him, she'd not see him. He was pushing to his feet when the curtains on the side closest to him rattled. He whipped back down at the foot.

"Who's there? Come out. Reveal yourself!"

Plague take the old dragon, though he had to admire her courage. Perhaps she did have a pistol under the pillow. Perhaps it was even now primed and pointed.

"Come out, I say!"

At any moment she was going to cry for help, and if servants hadn't already been disturbed they'd come then. And here he was, pinned like a ferret in a trap. All he could do was wait to see which way she went, and hope to dash out before she could identify him.

Just how many six-foot-tall men with blond hair were there in this house? After surviving years of this sort of thing against far more skillful foes, he was about to be done in by an old lady in a freezing, run-down house because of a damn stupid saga of royal sin and folly. . . .

A thump somewhere startled him.

Then a shriek.

Thump, thump, thump . . .

It sounded as if someone had fallen down stairs. He rose to help, then realized he couldn't.

Deathly silence.

Literally.

A chill swept over him. Had that scream sounded like Damaris?

The dowager was muttering and moving, and he could hardly concentrate enough to track what she was doing. Climbing out of bed on his left.

Move to the right.

Vague sounds of her finding and putting on a robe. His head was pounding with the need to dash out through the dressing room to see if that had been Damaris, and if she was safe.

A door slammed somewhere far away.

The drawing room door opened and stumping footsteps moved away. "What's going on?" the dowager demanded from a distance.

Fitz was already sprinting into the dressing room,

searching desperately for the service door that had to be there. *Open the lantern, you dolt! There.*

As he ran into the corridor he heard the dowager exclaim, "Lord save us!" All sense of direction fled his mind, and he ran the wrong way before correcting and catapulting into the hall.

"Servants! Ashart! Someone!" the dowager was bellowing. All around, Fitz heard slamming doors, hurrying feet, voices.

He raced to the body sprawled from the lowest step of the grand staircase to the checkered floor. White nightgown. Dark robe. Long dark hair in a plait.

Damaris!

He slid to his knees, checking for breath. "She's breathing. Thank God."

"Of course she's breathing," the dowager snapped. "I saw that. What's wrong with her?"

"Presumably she fell down the stairs." He was feeling for bumps on Damaris's small, delicate head.

"You are insolent, sir. I always thought so. And so is she. What's she doing wandering the house at night? I should never have had anything to do with such a creature. She was never worthy. . . ."

He ignored her ranting as he felt for damage, aware of other people gathering, exclaiming, and chattering. He knew now what Ash had felt like when Genova had seemed close to death. He wanted to gather Damaris into his arms and plead with her to talk to him, to come to her senses, to live. Wanted to shower her with healing kisses.

"Damaris," he said, stroking tendrils off her pale face. "Come on. Speak to me. Where does it hurt?"

She moaned and her eyelids fluttered. She looked up at him.

Her moan wasn't very convincing, and her eyes revealed hidden laughter.

He just managed to stifle a groan of his own. He was going to throttle her. For the moment he turned her face toward his chest. "Hush, I don't think there's any serious damage."

Genova was there then, kneeling by their side. "Can you move your arms and legs, Damaris?"

Damaris looked at her, her expression better controlled. "I think so," she whispered pathetically, flexing arms and legs. "Just a little sore."

Only when Genova rearranged the rumpled clothing did Fitz realize that he'd just watched the flexing of a lovely leg, a pale, slender, but smoothly muscled leg that was doing nothing to help him regain his wits.

The damned fool had thrown herself down the stairs to provide him with an escape. Had that sense he'd had earlier been awareness of her watching him?

Ash knelt beside Fitz. "You're sure she's all right?"

"As best I can tell."

"Oh, dear, oh, dear."

Here came Thalia fluttering down the stairs, adding another candle to a collection of them. The hall probably hadn't been this bright at nighttime in a generation. Most of the sparse household seemed to be here.

"Sleepwalking, were you, dear?" asked Thalia, in danger of falling herself with her collection of trailing shawls. Ash hurried to help her.

"I think so," Damaris said in a tone of weak confusion, but she shot Fitz another wicked glance. *Throttle. Definitely.*

"Be off with you!" the dowager barked to the gathering servants. "I'll not accept poor service tomorrow because of this folly. Be off, be off!"

As they melted away, she turned her guns on Damaris. "Sleepwalking, indeed. Sneaking about, more likely. I awoke thinking something amiss."

"Why would I be sneaking around?" Damaris demanded, perhaps a little too vigorously for her part. "Especially," she added, sitting up and wincing, "as this house is so cold and damp."

He wanted to applaud her spirit, but instead he shrugged out of his coat and put it around her shoulders.

"Now you'll freeze," she said with a sniff that he thought could well be real. Her feet were bare.

"Mr. Fitzroger," the dowager demanded, "why are you fully dressed at gone midnight?"

Oh, damnation. "I went for a walk, Lady Ashart."

"Outside?"

She made it sound like proof of insanity. "I like fresh air."

"What is that?" she asked, pointing.

He turned and saw his lantern lying on its side, the candle out. For the first time in years he felt close to panic, and the dowager was sniffing for a criminal like a terrier after a rat.

He picked up the lantern and opened one door. "My own design, Lady Ashart. Ideal for lighting the way along paths on a dark night."

She glared at him, gave a thwarted snort, and marched back into her own rooms.

"Good thing," Ash said, "she didn't notice that you went for your midnight walk in your slippers. Which are remarkably unaffected by the adventure."

Fitz glanced at the footwear. It was the final bloody straw. When had he last been caught in such an awkward situation and spun a tale so open to contradiction? And now Ash clearly had serious questions to ask.

"I need to stand up," Damaris said, holding out a hand to him. Deflecting the conversation? What did she know? What did she suspect? Why the devil hadn't she been virtuously asleep?

"Are you sure you're not hurt?" he asked.

"Nothing to signify."

"All the same, I'll carry you back to your bed." A touch of gold to come out of this debacle, he thought as he gathered her into his arms, every soft, slender, lissome, desirable inch of her.

"Very wise," said Thalia, turning to go back upstairs. "You'll probably be stiff tomorrow, dear. I took a tumble once and felt no injury at first, but oh, how I ached the next day! I have an effective liniment. Your maid can rub it into your legs and back."

Fitz stifled a groan at the image. The very weight of Damaris was arousing. Carrying a woman upstairs was no easy task, but he loved having her so close to him, so dependent on him. Trusting him.

Genova hurried to where Ash was already escorting Lady Thalia, trying to avoid another casualty.

Fitz took the opportunity to say, "I would like to beat you."

He'd like to do many other things, all a great deal more pleasant, but that could be part of the reason he felt so violently about this jape.

Her plait lay down her front, and he'd never guessed her hair was so long. It must hang past her waist when loose. He wanted to drown in that hair, to kiss down the arch and up the instep of her pale, elegant feet.

Yet her plait and simple clothing suggested schoolroom innocence. Devil take it, despite her twenty-one years, Damaris Myddleton could as well have been raised in a convent. He was a cad to be lusting after her.

"Why," she whispered, "are you glowering at me? I just saved you."

"By risking your life? I'm supposed to thank you?"

"As if I—"

"Damaris? Is something wrong?" Genova was coming back to them as Ash escorted Lady Thalia to bed.

Fitz wanted to protest that he could take care of Damaris, could put her to bed, then rub liniment over her injured body. . . .

"He's lecturing me about running into danger," Damaris complained. "A person can hardly help sleepwalking."

"Perhaps we should lock your door at night," he said.

"Don't you dare!"

"Damaris, Fitz," Genova soothed. "Everyone's nerves are on edge. Let's get you to bed. Unless you would prefer to sleep with Thalia tonight?"

"No, I'll be all right. Maisie shares my bed."

"But clearly sleeps too soundly to be a warden," Fitzroger muttered.

Genova was leading the way with her candle, and he followed, aggrieved that there would be no chance for even the slightest impropriety—even though he'd geld himself before he'd commit any.

At least he did get to put her to bed. He placed his burden on the sheets amid fussing from a wild-eyed Maisie in a mobcap and shawls. Damaris looked up at him, and it seemed strange that in the muted light from a dying fire and one candle he could see the dark line of her lashes and her smooth, pale skin so very, very clearly.

Her lips moved as if she might say something, but then she smiled in a rueful way before the maid shoved him out of the room and shut the door in his face.

Wise maid.

He definitely had to get away from here—because a girl didn't throw herself downstairs to help a man unless she thought she loved him. And despite all his will and good intentions, he wasn't sure he could resist if she threw herself into his arms.

*   *   *

He retreated to his room and took refuge in drink, which was very unwise, because half an hour later his door opened, and Damaris slipped in. She was swathed in silvery fur and put a finger to her lips, which was ridiculous, because he'd lost all faculty of speech.

She hurried toward him, showing no sign of her recent flirtation with death. "We need to try again."

"We?" he croaked from a dry mouth and tight throat.

Try what? He couldn't even find strength to stand up.

She was a foot away now, a frowning cat in a frame of gray fur. "Are you drunk?"

He closed his eyes. "Of course not. Three glasses of brandy is nothing."

He heard her hum in that skeptical way she had. "We'd better wait until tomorrow then, but we can plan. Tonight would have gone better if you'd confided in me."

His eyes opened on their own from astonishment. "Why the devil should I do that?"

It wasn't wise to look. She was standing almost knee-to-knee with him, her eyes steady and censorious, pushing back the hood of her cloak. Beneath it she would be wearing that plain robe over the pristine nightgown. Her hair was still in its plait, falling down her front. He could imagine all too well unweaving it so that it spread around her and down her, veiling her body.

Her pale, naked body.

In his bed.

"Why?" she echoed. "Because you need help. You know you do. You'd have been in a fine pickle if I hadn't watched you and created a distraction."

He needed to escape.

To escape he needed to stand.

Standing would put them in contact almost every-where.

He scrambled for a way around this, but in the end resorted to bluntness. "Go away," he said.

Her hurt expression stung, but he had to protect her and himself.

"You're not showing much gratitude."

"I didn't ask you to risk your neck."

"And I didn't. I let out a shriek, thumped on some stairs, then arranged myself tragically at the bottom."

"Showing your legs to the world!"

She leaned forward, brows almost meeting in the middle. "It would have looked rather suspicious, wouldn't it, if my clothes had arranged themselves in perfect decency? Just as suspicious as your clean, dry slippers, which gave you away."

Damned clever virago. He grabbed her plait and pulled her close.

She resisted, gripping his wrist. "Let me go!"

"You came here of your own free will, didn't you? What for, Damaris? What for?"

He saw sudden fear, but she needed to learn a lesson.

"So we could go back downstairs and find the papers," she protested, but he knew better.

She was flirting with fire and needed to be singed so she wouldn't do it again. He forced her closer, then captured her head with his other hand and forced a kiss on her. He meant it to be harsh, but if anyone was singed, it was him.

He tore free of her hot, sweet lips and erupted to his feet, pushing her out of his way so sharply that she staggered. She was staring at him, eyes shocked wide.

He turned away and dug his hands into his hair. "Now will you go?"

"Of course." Her voice sounded small and tearful. "If you're intent on being unkind."

Oh, God. He lowered his hands and turned. "Damaris, you know you shouldn't be here."

"No one will know. Maisie's snoring again, and besides, she wouldn't tell anyone."

"Servants always gossip."

"Not when the gossip might force a marriage the servant doesn't want to have happen. She wants me to marry a title."

"Wise Maisie. But if anyone else found you here, you could end up at the altar with me. And you, too, want to marry a title."

"Why would Ashart, Genova, or Lady Thalia come over from the other wing? But if they did, they wouldn't make me marry you. Everyone agrees that you're a completely unsuitable husband for me."

"In which case Ashart would probably call me out. As you're a guest in his house, he'd see you as under his protection. Do you want someone to die for your whims? Perhaps you knocked your head when you fell. That's the only explanation for this."

"I *didn't* fall," she protested, but his words seemed to have struck home. "I'm sorry, then. You're right. But there's no true danger—"

"No danger!"

He dragged her to him for another violent kiss.

He knew he shouldn't, knew he was plunging into the heart of the fire, but he couldn't stop himself. Desire overwhelmed every scrap of sense and control.

Thought fell away and he could only feel—feel pleasure and hunger for more. He swept her into his arms and carried her to his bed, where he flipped open the catch of her fur-lined cloak and spread it, framing her in silvery softness.

Her eyes were wide, her lips parted, but she showed neither dismay nor fear.

With unsteady hands he opened her robe, distantly

aware of clamorous warnings, but more pressingly aware of imminent ecstasy.

He looked to those lovely cat's eyes, perhaps hoping for something to rescue him, but they were dark with desire. She smiled, grabbed him, and dragged him down for more kisses, endless kisses, kisses more wonderful because of her body beneath his hands and the soft, warm scent of her.

Jasmine.

Ruin.

He couldn't care. Not now. Not when she was kneading his back with hungry hands, surging beneath him with passion, opening her legs so he was nestled between her thighs. His left hand found the wonderful softness of her breast, and he felt her instant gasping response.

He was probably the first to touch her like that.

He shouldn't touch her like that.

"Oh, yes!" she whispered, hooking a leg over him, locking him closer to her, arching against him. He pushed up her nightgown until he felt the silky heat of her thigh, then scrabbled for his buttons so close by.

And found a remnant of sense.

Her chest rose and fell, as did his. Her body vibrated with need, and she pressed harder against him, clutched tighter at his arms. Her eyes were shut, but he read the change in her expression.

She was beginning to think, too.

He kissed her lips the lightest possible way. "Damaris, look at me."

Resentfully, she did so.

Oh, God, how he loved her for this quick and glorious passion on top of all her other gifts. But she wasn't for him.

"Do you want to marry me?" he demanded.

"That's a very ungracious proposal."

"Answer me."

She looked away, but he waited, and in time, as he knew she would, she looked back at him. "Maybe."

"You want to be a duchess," he reminded her, unhooking her leg. "One of the grandest ladies in the land."

But she clung onto his shirt. "I'm not sure I want to be mistress of a grand establishment."

"Don't take Cheynings as your model."

"I'm not. I'm serious, Fitz. I want a home. A real home."

He tore free and left the bed. "You certainly won't get one from me."

She raised a hand to him, tears in her eyes, silently pleading. He took it, but used it to pull her up and off the bed.

"You want to marry a man of title and position, and you should." He tried to be harsh, but he had to wipe away one trickling tear from her cheek, and he wanted to take her back into his arms and comfort her. "Yes, there's passion between us, Damaris, but it's nothing important. If I let it trap you, you'd hate me all your days."

He began to refasten her robe, but she snatched free and did it herself. "I might not."

Dear Lord, had he done this? With hindsight, he realized he shouldn't have chased after her that first morning. She'd have been better off by far if caught later by Lord Henry. Even a beating wouldn't have ruined her life.

He retreated to the fireplace, where flames licked sullenly at the last of the dark logs. He knew what he had to do, even though it would feel like plunging a saber into his own belly. "It's time you knew the truth about me."

She looked at him with wide eyes that anticipated pain.

"I am not received in society," he said. "Ashart

and Rothgar are exceptions—Ashart from friendship, Rothgar for Ash's sake and because I am of use to him. Those who shun me are justified."

It took effort to meet her eyes, but he did it. "I had an affair with my brother's wife. It wounded everyone involved and tore apart my family. It caused a fight with my brother, during which he fell and hit his head. Ever since he's been prone to wild rages, which makes the situation of my mother and sisters even more difficult. His wife, my partner in sin, threw herself down the stairs shortly after the event and broke her neck."

Her eyes were dark with shock.

"The story is widely known," he continued, "and my brother still thirsts for my blood. I will not lay the burden on him of killing me, so I must leave the country as soon as I can. Now, go back to your bed and forget this ever happened."

She grabbed her cloak, perhaps with a sob, then just stood there, swallowing tears.

Unable to help himself, he took the fur and placed it around her shoulders. "I'm sorry, Damaris."

He couldn't begin to list all the things he was sorry for.

She looked up at him, wrinkling her face as she sniffed back tears. "But you're involved in something important here—keeping people safe. You can't deny that."

"The one doesn't affect the other."

"It should."

He didn't attempt a reply to that.

"Right, then," she said, chin firm and raised. "I said I'd help and I will. Tomorrow I'll find a way to keep the dowager occupied so you'll be able to search again."

She left, and Fitz suddenly turned to the wall, shaking with loss, with tears, and with the violent remains of unfulfilled passion.

Chapter 14

The next morning Genova and Lady Thalia fussed over Damaris, seemingly unable to believe that she was none the worse for her accident. Quite possibly the signs of her sleepless night and her anguish over what Fitz had told her accounted for that.

She was a realist. She didn't expect men, especially worldly men, to be pure. But what Fitzroger had done . . . The worst possible betrayal of a brother, which had gone on to leave the poor man injured and deranged and his wife dead.

No wonder his family wanted nothing to do with him—and neither did she. The pain of that thought was measure of her folly, and showed the blessing of her escape.

At the same time, she'd tasted ecstasy in his arms, and her body would not forget. She felt bruised and almost ill with it. The thin winter sunlight dazzled her eyes, and the cold air abraded her skin. The brush of her own furs made her shiver with remembered need. Her mind could not reconcile what he'd told her with what she knew of him in her heart.

The men were off somewhere, so she didn't have to face Fitz yet. She didn't know what would happen when she did. She had no idea how to treat him.

As Lady Thalia chattered, Damaris thought of ask-

ing her about Fitz's story, but she had no scrap of
doubt that he'd told her the truth. It had rung in every
stark word.

It didn't bear thinking about, but she couldn't stop.
Even if no one else in the world knew about it, she
could have nothing to do with him. As it was, she was
weak enough to mind that so many people did know.
Any wife would share his shame.

Wife. Yes, she had been thinking of buying him for
her pleasure.

No more. Her broken heart ached.

She had to stop this or go mad! Lady Thalia's story
about a youthful adventure suddenly reminded Damaris of other things. There was still the matter of
Ashart's royal blood. If her speculations about Prince
Henry were correct, it was important.

Last night she'd promised to help Fitz search the
dowager's rooms, but it would be better if it weren't
necessary. Lady Thalia had known Betty Prease in her
old age, and she might know something.

She could try again to question her, but she didn't
think Lady Thalia was keeping secrets. She might,
however, have forgotten something. If they checked
through the last of the Prease papers together, perhaps
one would trigger a forgotten memory.

It was better than sitting here moping.

She suggested it, and they all went into the library,
though Lady Thalia was not enthusiastic. She mostly
sat by while Genova and Damaris sorted papers, saying what they were.

The old lady did come up with some gossip, but
nothing that seemed important, and she soon yawned.
"Such dull old stuff," she declared. "I shall leave you
to this and read a book. *Candide*. So wickedly
amusing."

When the door shut after her, Genova put down a

laundry list, showing she had little interest either. "Do you know what Fitzroger was up to last night?"

"I'm not sure, but he truly does want to find out about Ashart's royal blood. And if there are any papers to do with that royal affair, the dowager probably has them."

"So he *was* searching her rooms. There'd have been explosions if he'd been caught." Then she stared at Damaris. "You threw yourself down the stairs to help him escape?"

Damaris rolled her eyes. "Why does everyone think I'm stupid? Of course not. I made all the right noises, then arranged myself in a tragic sprawl."

"How quick-thinking."

"I am quite proud of it, though with time to plan I might have done better. Fitzroger keeps things to himself too much."

"I suspect it's his way. With his history." She cast Damaris a worried glance. "I did ask Thalia for the details."

"Don't worry," Damaris said quickly. "I know all about it. He's a wicked, incestuous seducer, and I can't have anything to do with him."

Genova looked shocked at that blunt description, but she didn't argue.

"I'm surprised that Ashart and Rothgar allow him in their houses to endanger innocent ladies," Damaris snapped.

"There's a deep affection between Ashart and Fitzroger," Genova said gently. "Friendships can be like that sometimes. Almost like falling in love. In Ash's opinion, the scandal was so long ago it should be forgotten, but the world is not so obliging."

"But Lord Rothgar allowed me to come here with Fitz," Damaris said, relieved to be able to talk about these things with someone. "He instructed me to come here. He must have known I'd be thrown into Fitz's company."

Genova frowned. "Yes. That is strange."

"So it's not so bad?" *Ah, pathetic hope.*

"I don't think that's it. Perhaps Lord Rothgar takes it for granted that a woman under his protection is untouchable."

"Which deprives me of any choice!"

"Of any *wicked* choice," Genova corrected.

Damaris blushed. "I don't see why I shouldn't make my own decisions."

"In the eyes of the world, Rothgar is now responsible for your safety and well-being. Damaris, do be careful," she added with new urgency. "Think of Ashart. In sending you here, Rothgar has in a sense given his guardianship to Ashart. You wouldn't want a quarrel between Ashart and Fitz over you."

Damaris looked at the paper in her hand—a burial record for a stillborn child.

Genova took her hand and squeezed it. "Dear Damaris, things are so strange just now. In London it will be better. You'll meet other men. It could be that you've known so few, especially of the handsome, charming variety."

Damaris hated to cause such distress, and found a smile. "I'm sure you're right." She put the paper on the pile she thought of as birth, marriage, and death.

"Back to Betty Crowley and the king," she said briskly. "There's something important about it, so I think we should help Fitz to search the dowager's rooms. He can't try at night again, because I'm sure she'll take extra precautions. So it must be during the day, and we need to draw her out of the way."

Genova looked startled, then shook her head. "I'm sorry. I can't do anything like that without Ash's agreement. Not when we're talking about stealing from his grandmother."

"It's not exactly stealing."

Genova would not be moved.

"Then ask Ashart's approval."

"He'd never give it."

Damaris managed not to lose her temper. "Then please remind him to demand to see any papers she has at dinner today."

And when she refuses, Damaris thought, *he may be more willing to approve larceny.*

Fitz had dealt with Ash's inquisition by using the best weapon: the truth. Or most of it.

"I didn't think the dowager would give up any papers no matter how courteously you were to ask. So I thought it best to sneak in and get them."

They were in the nether regions of the basement in search of a spot where water was supposed to be seeping in during rain. Ash had wanted a ride today, but Fitz had managed to head him off with this problem.

"There'll be no more of that," Ash said, grimacing as he brushed aside thick cobwebs.

Fitz wasn't surprised that Ash was displeased. If their positions were reversed, he'd be furious. "As you will," he said, aware that he might have to break the implied promise. "It was a whim of the midnight moment."

"What of Damaris falling downstairs?"

" 'Struth, do you think I recruited her to provide a distraction? I assure you, I did not."

"Good. She's in my charge here, and no harm shall come to her."

That warning, Fitz thought, referred to more than adventures. But in that, he and his friend were in harmony. He'd hardly slept in the night, but there'd been a kind of peace in his soul. No matter what happened, Damaris was now safe from him.

They found the evidence, a white stain on the stone

wall. "What does one do about something like this?" Ash asked. "Not that it isn't exciting to plumb these depths. I keep expecting to find a skeleton."

"Probably of the last person down here. Do you know the way back?"

"We should have unrolled a ball of string, shouldn't we?" Ash looked up at the barrel-vaulted ceiling of rough stone. "This must be part of the previous house. Fascinating. I suppose I need to learn architecture. Or is it simple masonry?"

Fitz wasn't surprised that Ash found this more of a stimulating challenge than a crushing burden. He had an excellent brain and, apart from his astronomy, had done little with it.

He was poking at the stained wall with a stick he'd found, but turned to face Fitz. "I know. I should have paid more attention before, but Grandy's always taken care of things, and I knew it would be unpleasant to try to make changes. In truth, I wonder if she'll crumble into dust without her work running the estate. Plus it's damned hard work currying court favor, you know."

"Am I arguing?" Fitz asked.

Ash laughed. "I'm arguing with my own conscience. Onward. We can only ever look to the future."

Fitz followed, wishing that were true and wondering just how long he could keep Ash from an extensive inspection of his estates. This situation couldn't go on. In his message to Rothgar, Fitz had included a cryptic request that he be able to tell Ash about the threat. He'd give the marquess a day to reply.

They found Genova and Damaris in the Little Library, replacing documents in the boxes, each of which bore a neat account of the sort of document it contained.

"I've acquired an extra secretary as well as a wife," Ash observed.

"Not me, sir," Genova protested, pushing a lock of hair off her smudged face. "Damaris insisted on this."

Damaris looked defensive. "I like things neat and in their place."

"And I approve," Fitz said.

He hadn't seen her since last night, and every nerve in his body was aware of it, especially here. Yesterday, here, they had kissed. Perhaps forevermore the musty smell of old papers would be erotic for him.

Ash was wiping marks off Genova's face—as Fitz had so foolishly done with Damaris.

Damaris came to his side, almost as if nothing had changed, except for the new tilt of her chin and the shadow in her eyes.

"We found nothing related to Betty Crowley," she said. "Lady Thalia helped for a while, but she recalled nothing of interest."

The old lady came in then, brightly inquiring about whist.

Time to be blunt. "Lady Thalia," Fitz asked, "do you remember anything about Betty Crowley's youth? Any stories? Anything she might have said?"

Lady Thalia wrinkled her brow over it, but said, "I don't think so. I did ask her what the court of King Charles had been like, and she said she'd never been there."

"Never?" Genova echoed. "So where did she meet the king?"

"Kings in those days roamed the country," Ash said. "Enough of this. We've checked the papers and found nothing. Rothgar will have to be satisfied with that."

Ash's patience was running thin, but Fitz had to persist. "You were going to ask the dowager if she had anything."

"Very well, I'll do it at dinner."

*   *   *

To Damaris's pleased surprise, Ashart did ask for the papers, bluntly and quite early in the meal. "Grandy, I need to see any documents you have concerning Betty Prease."

The dowager didn't pause in spooning up soup. "I have none."

"None? Nothing at all concerning your grandmother?"

"Not so much as a letter," the dowager said, unblinking. What mythical monster did people refer to? A basilisk.

Lady Thalia plunged in. "How very strange, but I have known cases like that. Sometimes people destroy all their papers before death, fearing what people will discover. Or their relatives do it later for the same reason. Likely that was the case here. She would have some spicy memories!"

"Cease your foolish prattling," the dowager snapped. "She was a woman above reproach."

Damaris stared at a dish of potatoes so she wouldn't demand how this could possibly be. Or suggest how this could possibly be. She prayed Ashart would insist, but instead he asked about some problem with the foundations.

It certainly changed the mood. The dowager's only explanation was that it was not urgent. That led to other questions about the state of the house, and an atmosphere that grew both chilly and seething at the same time.

This was completely the wrong path, in Damaris's opinion, and, what was more, gave the dowager an excuse to retreat. As she anticipated, halfway through the second course Lady Ashart rose and stalked out of the room. Damaris would have rolled her eyes at Fitz except that she was sitting beside him.

Would Ashart now agree to Fitz's stealing the papers? They finished the meal quickly, returned upstairs, and tea was brought. Conversation was general. Damaris was burning to open the dangerous subject, but she would trust Fitz to choose the moment.

As soon as the servants left, he spoke. "She has something, Ash, and I'd like to search for it."

"No. She's a difficult old woman, but she's entitled to her privacy. We have no right to invade simply so you can win Rothgar's favor."

"You don't want to learn the truth about your heritage?"

"Why should I care? Lady Betty's bedmates make no difference now, whereas the fact that this place is falling around our ears does." He looked ruefully at Genova. "It's a mess, love. We have years of work to do."

She simply smiled at him. "A lifetime's work, I hope. I can think of nothing sweeter."

Damaris stared at Fitz until she caught his glance, then sent the message that she could still draw the dowager out. He looked away, but not before she saw the look in his eyes—one very similar to his expression last night before he'd told her about his scandal. She shivered, and it wasn't because of drafts. She almost rose out of her chair to go to him, but he spoke.

"It's time for me to explain what's going on," he said. "There may be a threat to Ash's life."

Ashart stared and said only, "Go on."

"Because I was already Ash's friend, I was asked by some people in the government to be alert for danger. As you know, Ash, my army work involved keeping eminent men safe."

"Why wasn't I told?" Ashart demanded, looking both annoyed and skeptical.

"My orders were strict and specific on that. I'm breaking those orders now, but before I go into details I must have a promise from each of you to keep what I tell you secret."

"You presumably gave such a promise."

At Ashart's icy tone, Damaris could almost see Fitz raise a protective shield between himself and the friend he might soon lose.

His voice was level as he answered: "And it wounds me to break it, but an officer in the field must have some powers of discretion. I ask no more of you all—simply that you not reveal the truth unless it's necessary for the greater good."

"What greater good?" Ashart demanded.

"The security of Crown and country."

Ah. Damaris knew her worst fears were being confirmed.

"I promise," Genova said with the sort of calm that was supposed to be oil on stormy waters.

"And I," Damaris quickly added.

Lady Thalia added her promise, and last, somewhat reluctantly, Ashart. But he said, "Was Genova's illness any part of this?"

Ah, lud! Damaris saw from Fitz's expression that he'd lied to her. That the mulled cider had been poisoned. He must have told Ashart the same cock-and-bull story, and the effect now would be explosive.

"I assume so," Fitz said. "There were no other victims."

Ashart surged to his feet. "Damn you—"

Whatever he might have done, Genova was on her feet and between him and Fitz. "You can't think Fitz would deliberately put me at risk, Ash. Hear him out!"

After a long moment the marquess exhaled, but without becoming one whit less dangerous. They sat again, but Genova took one of Ash's hands. Damaris thought it resembled someone taking a tiger's leash. She prayed the power of love was strong enough.

"I received my orders a month ago," Fitz said, "but until the journey here I saw no sign of trouble. I concluded that the danger was slight, or even imaginary. These court alarms often are. However, I was warned that your betrothal increased the danger. I was skeptical, but it proved to be true, if we assume the attempt to poison Genova was intended to prevent the marriage. And I can see no other reason for it."

Ashart frowned. "Why would my marriage matter to anyone? I don't even have an heir waiting in the wings."

"It matters to Sophia, dear," Lady Thalia pointed out.

Ash glared at her. "I will not believe that Grandy tried to kill Genova."

"The supposed threat," Fitz interrupted, "arises from your royal Stuart blood, which is why we need any documents the dowager might have that relate to Betty Crowley."

"Explain." Damaris had not known Ashart could be so furiously cold.

Fitz seemed impassive, but this had to be painful for him in so many ways. "My supposition that your ancestor, Charles Prease, should have been called Charles Stuart. That he was legitimate."

"Old Rowley's son? Preposterous!"

"Prince Henry Stuart's son, born posthumously after a secret wedding to Betty Crowley."

Damaris remembered to breathe. Silence showed that everyone else understood the implications as well.

But then Lady Thalia put a hand over her mouth. "Oh, how tragic. I thought her a cold woman, when her situation was so like my own. Except, of course, that I didn't need to keep my love and grief secret."

Genova hurried to offer comfort, for Lady Thalia's tears were flowing. That left Ashart unleashed. Damaris kept her attention on the two men, ready to do something, though heaven knew what, to prevent murder.

"I do beg your pardon!" Lady Thalia dabbed at her eyes. "Old sorrows. Old pains. Do go on, Fitz. This is a startling story."

"It's a preposterous one," Ashart snapped, "but get it over with."

"What more need be said? You understand."

Ashart rose to pace the room. "What? That Grandy should be Queen of England?"

Damaris gasped, for she'd not thought of that. The crown passed to females, so indeed, the dowager marchioness, Charles Prease's—or Charles Stuart's—only surviving child, was next in line.

"Have you forgotten the Succession Act?" Ashart demanded. "Any Stuart remnants were specifically ruled to have no claim on the throne. And what threat are we anyway? Am I supposed to lead an uprising in her cause? With what? An army of a dozen grooms?"

"France," Fitz said.

Ashart stilled, but then stated, "Neither she nor I would be a puppet of France."

"By definition, a puppet is controlled by the one who pulls the strings."

"Damnation—"

Damaris plunged in before fists flew. "Explain France," she demanded.

After a tense moment, Fitz turned to her. "France is our ancient enemy and has just crawled away from war with its tail between its legs. King Louis would love to cause disruption. Maybe not in England. Maybe not in Scotland, which hasn't recovered from the 'forty-five. But Ireland is always ripe for trouble, especially Catholic trouble."

"I'm Protestant!" Ash exclaimed.

"You have an aunt in a French convent."

"Oh, 'struth! Is that come back to haunt us? Aunt Henrietta chose that as a way to escape Grandy, that's all. But do you mean she's in danger, too?"

"Possibly. She's somewhere in the line of succession and could easily be in the French king's power. Ash, this is all folly, yes, but that doesn't negate the danger. There are some in England still restive under German rule."

"The king's as English as you and me."

"Hardly. My ancestors go back to the Conquest, as do yours. More to the point, neither of us rules a German electorate whose interests we sometimes put first. The king was booed in the theater over the Wilkes business."

"A temporary fidget."

"Probably, but if people around the king are nervous, it cannot surprise."

"It can surprise me. In heaven's name, what do these madmen want? To kill my whole family to eliminate this absurd threat?"

The answer was clearly yes. Damaris hadn't known silence could be so noisy. When no one else spoke, she said, "So if we find the right papers, all this is over?"

"How?" Ashart demanded. "If we find proof of a marriage that lights the fuse."

"But once found, a fuse can be extinguished."

Ashart stared at him grimly. "And if she has no such proof?"

"Then the chances are high that it doesn't exist and everyone can relax."

"Except that someone might decide to poison my dinner, just in case. Or Genova's. Or our children's. This is intolerable."

"True. It would be better to find the marriage lines and destroy them, and I'm increasingly optimistic that they exist."

Ash swung to face Lady Thalia. "Your commentary?"

She was unusually sober. "It must be true, I think. Betty Prease never fit her role as royal wanton. And having proof would explain Sophia's pride and ambition. Poor Sophia, burdened with an indolent husband and two sons unable to achieve even her modest aim of ruling Britain from behind the throne. You're better equipped for it, but I don't think it's in your nature. Rothgar's the one in whom the blood runs true. One can see the Stuart in him, especially that brilliant, charming pragmatist, Charles the Second."

Ashart and Genova spoke softly together, while the rest waited. Fitz looked thoughtfully into the flames.

Ashart turned to Fitz and spoke in a clipped voice. "If we search, how will it be done? How can anyone find a few sheets of paper?"

"A thorough check of a room for papers is little different from a search for hidden dangers, and I'm expert at that. I found a secret compartment in her bedchamber desk that seems most likely."

Ashart was still reluctant. "I dislike the thought of anyone searching my grandmother's rooms. Why don't we simply explain the situation? Then she will surrender what she has."

"You think she doesn't understand the situation?"

"She doesn't know of the active, immediate danger."

Damaris saw that thought startle Fitz, saw him weighing the choices. She herself didn't know what she thought it best to do.

"So it becomes a gamble," Fitz said at last. "Can she bear to see the precious proof destroyed? If so, all is well. If not, she'll promptly hide it somewhere where we'll never discover it."

Ash paled. "I can't believe she is so deranged, so uncaring. I have to try reason." After a long silence he added, "But you will go with me. If she refuses we will restrain her in some way. And you will take the papers."

Damaris wondered if she was the only one who had

difficulty imagining the two big men being able to bring themselves to overpower an elderly lady.

"I think we should all go," she said.

Ashart shot her a look that showed he thought her impertinent, but Genova supported the idea.

"It could be very difficult for you, love."

"What excuse do we make for invading?"

"None," Genova said calmly. "We just do it." She turned to Lady Thalia. "Do you wish to come, Thalia?"

Lady Thalia still looked pensively sorrowful, her brightness gone. "I think not, dear. But be as kind as you can. And if I'm needed afterward, I will be ready."

They crossed the Royal Salon in weighty silence. Damaris didn't think she was the only one to look at the pictures of Betty Crowley and Prince Henry as they passed, and think of the tragic lovers.

She could imagine it. A brief time of joyous love full of the magical awareness of having found a special person to share life with. The vows and then one or two nights of passion before Henry rode away to inform his brother of what he'd done, face his anger, and have it over with.

Betty would have waited, dreaming, planning, and then the news would have arrived. Perhaps by a friend. Perhaps by a messenger from the king.

Ashart tapped briefly, then led the way into the dowager's drawing room. It was overfurnished, as if she'd crammed in too much. On one table, Damaris saw a large, slender book bound entirely in silver. There was a crest on the front, and engraved beneath was *The Illustrious History of the Prease Family.*

Above the fireplace two small portraits hung. Damaris thought one was of the dowager's father, known as Charles Prease, Lord Vesey. The other showed a young woman with a round face, high color, and a stubborn mouth.

Sixty years older, but just as stubborn, the Dowager Marchioness of Ashart sat beneath her portrait, eating cake with a fork, a tea tray by her side. She stared at them. "Ashart? What is the meaning of this?"

"I have some things to discuss with you, Grandy."

"In company?"

Damaris thought the dowager's eyes narrowed, and perhaps even shifted for a moment toward her bed-chamber door. She wanted to move that way herself in an attempt to block the door, but that wasn't her role here, and she knew Fitz would have that part of the action in hand.

"Grandy," Ashart said, "in some way suspicion has stirred that your father was not a royal bastard—"

"What!"

"—that he was legitimate. The legitimate son of Prince Henry and Betty Crowley."

The furrowed lips tightened, but Damaris thought she saw a sudden gleam in the dowager's pouched eyes. Probably after all this time, it excited her to have the truth out in the open at last.

"If true," Ashart said, "this is a dangerous situation."

"How? It is long in the past."

The air changed.

She had not denied it.

Ashart stepped closer. "How? By giving you a blood claim to the throne."

"As if I care for anything like that." Lady Ashart forked another piece of cake into her mouth. "And of course," she said when she'd swallowed, "it is all nonsense."

A far-too-belated denial.

Deliberately so.

"I don't think so," Ashart said, playing the game patiently. "It seems that some people have decided the simplest way to deal with the problem is to eliminate the line, starting with me, preferably before I sire a new generation. Hence the attack on Genova."

The dowager frowned at him as if the game were no longer quite what she'd thought. She put aside her plate. "Attack? I understood that she was one of many who suffered from a bowl of contaminated cider."

"It was poison, and only she was affected."

"Poison?" The dowager's shock showed that at least that sin didn't lie at her door. Then she spat, "That German impostor's doing, I suppose!"

It was treason, and Ashart flinched, then went on one knee before her. "Grandy, don't. This has to end—now. You have proof of the marriage. Give it to me, and I will see it destroyed."

"*What?* Never!"

"You'd rather see me dead?"

She shook her head, making her cheeks wobble. "No, never that. But I realize it is time to make it public." She leaned toward Ashart, smiling fondly. "We won't seek the throne, of course, my dear boy, but we will demand our rights. To be treated as the royalty we are—as favored cousins of the king."

"Grandy—"

"Once all is known there will be no danger."

Ashart surged to his feet. "No danger! We'd be the focus of every malcontent, at home and abroad. And for what? To be ornamental, second-tier royalty?"

The dowager rose, too. "For money, boy! Money and power. Enough to crush the Mallorens once and for all."

Ashart closed his eyes for a moment in despair.

Out of the corner of her eye Damaris saw Fitz move toward the bedroom door.

The dowager started as if she'd forgotten his existence, forgotten all of them. Then she ran with remarkable speed toward the door. Fitz grabbed for her arm, but the old lady whirled, her cake fork in her hand.

She jabbed at him with it, and he hesitated.

Just as Damaris had expected.

She looked around and grabbed the silver-bound book. It was remarkably heavy, but as she'd said to Fitz, she was accustomed to moving things for herself.

Thus armed, she ran around the pair to stand guard in front of the door. The dowager whirled to glare at her and jabbed with the fork. It clanged against silver, and she let out a screech. It might has been because Damaris was in her way or because of the scratch on the treasured book.

Fitz grabbed the old lady's wrists from behind, but he was so tall and the dowager so short that the move was awkward. Damaris could see how hard he was trying not to hurt the old woman, but the dowager was struggling like a madwoman, trying to get free. Ashart was frozen.

Damaris stepped forward and hit the woman on the head with the book.

She was careful to make it no more than a tap, but the dowager wore a silver aigrette in her hair and it made a satisfying *ding!* that seemed to shock her into stillness. Fitz deftly removed the fork.

Then Ashart was there, kneeling before the dowager, taking her hands. "Grandy, you have to end this. It's madness."

"Calling me mad now, are you?" Tears were streaming down the sagging cheeks, but she spat her words. "I never thought you'd turn against me. Not you. No one has ever really loved me. God's hand has been against me. But to be betrayed by my last flesh and blood!"

"I'm not your last," he said wearily, "but I won't desert you. Come now, and sit down again so that we can talk."

But she snatched her hands free, looking around

wildly. "That man! That lecher! What is he doing? It was him in my room, I know it was. Searching! My papers!"

She ran to the door again, but Fitz was already emerging, a red, silken document pouch in hand. The dowager let out an almost animal howl and lunged for it, but he sidestepped her while putting out a hand to steady her. At the same time he tossed the pouch to Ashart.

It was a deft, swordsman's move, and despite everything Damaris's heart ached for the old woman who had no chance against him, and who had truly been overburdened with tragedy in her life.

The dowager clung to his hand for a moment to stop herself from falling. Then she recoiled, a hank of white hair flying loose from its pins.

"Ashart?" she said in a voice strangled somewhere between plea and command. "Don't. Don't destroy them."

Her maid burst in then from the bedchamber. Instantly the old woman assumed queenly dignity. "Attend me!" she snapped, then retreated, head high, into her room. With a wild glance at Ashart, the maid closed the door between them.

Damaris realized she was still holding the book and carefully replaced it on the table, rubbing pointlessly at the scratch the fork had made. Then she sat, her knees weak. Genova went to Ashart and took his hands.

Damaris thought they all needed to get out of the room, but she wasn't quite ready to try walking yet.

Then the door opened again.

The Dowager Lady Ashart could not be said to be recovered, but her hair was neat, her face dry, and her expression arrogantly firm. "I am removing to live with Henrietta."

It could be the first time the Marquess of Ashart had ever gaped. "She's in a convent. A Catholic convent. In France."

"A suitable place to pass my declining years, and she has always been the least trouble to me. I am leaving immediately."

"It's sunset—"

She overrode him. "Hockney will manage."

Hockney was Ashart's chief outrider who commanded such journeys.

"I will take the best coach, of course," she continued, "and use the London house while arrangements are being made. But I will try not to inconvenience you there any longer than necessary. Once I leave these shores, I fear we may not meet again, Ashart, but I'm sure you won't suffer over *that*. You and your lowborn bride."

She turned and left, and someone, presumably the maid, closed the door once more.

Ashart leaned his head back on the sofa. "Always the last word." Then he added, "Oh, dear, poor Aunt Henrietta. What sin has she managed to commit to deserve her fate?"

Chapter 15

They returned to the Little Library and related it all to Lady Thalia.

"My, my. Perhaps I'm sorry to have missed it. Very good, Damaris! And France. Sophia always was quite extraordinary. We can only hope she finds peace in a convent. And after all, nuns must be grateful for crosses to bear, mustn't they? Now, Ashart, tell us what you have there."

Ashart sat at the desk, opened the pouch, and pulled out the folded documents. He read each.

"A record of the marriage," he said. "In the house of one Arthur Cheviot, with a service performed by the prince's own chaplain. Illegal now, but not then. Three love letters, one sent from London, with the prince saying he is unwell and wishing he had his sweet wife to care for him. Added confirmation. And a drawing of the prince with a note written on the corner, reading, 'My beloved prince and husband, Henry.' "

"Oh, dear," Lady Thalia said. "How very sad it is."

"No picture of her?" Genova asked.

"No," Ashart said, refolding the papers and putting them back in the pouch. "She remains an enigma."

"But why keep the marriage secret?" Damaris asked.

Fitz said, "We may never know, but if Betty was the virtuous country lady she seems, she might not have wanted to be connected to the Restoration court. It was notably amoral."

"But she ruined her own reputation and deprived her son of the crown."

"In her older years she was a very resolute sort," Lady Thalia said. "I can see her making the decision as Fitz explained it. Besides, admitting the marriage would have meant losing charge of her son, you know. He would probably have been raised in the royal nurseries."

"And when she made the decision," Fitz said, "it would not occur to her that her child could one day rule. Charles was about to marry, and he was notably virile, and James had already sired two daughters. I can understand how she might have decided it was better to be thought a king's whore but live out her life in the country and raise her child on moral principles."

"I suppose you're right," Damaris said. "She was an unusual woman. I wish I'd met her."

Fitz turned to Ashart. "Those papers must go to London as soon as possible."

"Not today. It's late for travel anyway, and we'll let Grandy get on her way." He glanced out at the glowing sunset sky, obviously still concerned for her.

"Hockney will look after her," Fitz said, "and they'll probably only go as far as Leatherhead. She won't stay here now."

"I know." Ashart nodded. "First thing tomorrow, then, we'll leave for London. I'll send a message for Rothgar to meet us there. I'll be glad to be done with this."

"Ashart, dearest," Lady Thalia said, looking her years despite frills and ribbons, "would it be possible for me to visit Richard's grave? It's not far, and it is so long since I have." She sighed, looking into the past. "I do not believe our earthly remains are of importance. His picture means more to me," she said, touching the locket she always wore. "But thinking of poor Betty, I would like to go."

Ashart glanced at Fitz. "Is it safe?"

"I think so. There's not the slightest advantage to anyone in harming Lady Thalia. Where do you want to go?" he asked the old lady.

"St. Bartolph's churchyard. It's less than two miles. In Elmstead, right by Richard's old home."

"I'll arrange for a carriage," Fitz said, and left.

Lady Thalia went to wrap up warmly. Ashart and Genova spoke softly together. To give them privacy, Damaris went to the window to look out. She didn't think nature shaped itself to fit with human affairs, but it seemed fitting that today they had the first glorious sunset she'd seen in weeks.

They had the papers, so Ashart and Genova would soon be safe.

The dowager was leaving, so Genova wouldn't have to share this house with the bitter old woman.

And tomorrow they would leave here. She had bittersweet feelings about that, but she knew it was for the best. There could be no future for her with Fitzroger, but whenever he was close, reason seemed to dissolve.

It would be better in London. She'd be busy with final preparations for her presentation at court—some new clothes, including a splendid court gown, and probably some lessons in court behavior, though she thought she'd been well trained there. Lord Henry had been conscientious in some respects.

There would be Bridgewater, who might turn out to be charming and able to make her skin tingle with a look.

Buying him should be simple enough, but she'd insist on a courtship. He could work a little for the prize. And as she'd resolved before, she'd not count on anything until he had formally requested her hand and the marriage settlements were signed.

She would then have the life she had planned ever since she'd understood the extent of her fortune. She would be a duchess, one of the grandest ladies in the land. She would have robes and a coronet of golden strawberry leaves. She would be a patron of the arts, particularly music. She would also promote her special interest, medicine, both the development of better treatments and care for the poor.

She had already given Dr. Telford money for his dream—a charity clinic and hospital in Worksop. As Duchess of Bridgewater, she would do the same in other places. It was an excellent future—but the idea of it left her hollow.

She shook herself. It would be better when the duke was a real person rather than a picture and some information. As Genova had said, she had too little experience of men.

Fitz returned to report that Lady Thalia was on her way and that the coach was being readied for the dowager.

"I had a word with Hockney. He won't let her push on into danger, though with this clear weather they'll be able to travel into the dark without trouble."

"It is a very pretty sunset," Damaris said. "Could we perhaps go outside for a little to admire it?"

Everyone looked toward the window as if sunset were the Second Coming.

"Oh, yes!" said Genova. "I've not breathed fresh air since we arrived."

"It's not safe, love," Ashart said. "The assassin doesn't know yet that matters have changed."

Genova pulled a face, but she didn't argue.

However, Fitz said, "We can go outside if we keep

close to the house. There's no sign that our assassin is desperate enough to come so close. He took an opportunity at Pickmanwell—a hasty, slapdash one that put him in no danger—but he has to know we'll move to London sooner or later. A much more promising scenario, and you are no threat until you marry, Ash, for legitimacy is key to everything."

Ashart rose, but he looked at the pouch. "What am I to do with this? I wouldn't put it past Grandy to search for it before she leaves." He put it in his coat pocket, but then shook his head and passed it to Fitz. "You guard this and the ladies. I must stay inside." He looked at Genova. "She might want to speak to me."

"Is that really wise?" Genova asked. "Perhaps I should stay, too."

He smiled. "No, you deserve some fresh air and a pretty sky. Don't worry. I won't beg her to change her mind."

He would hear no argument, so Damaris, Genova, and Fitz dressed warmly and left the house by the main door. "It really is gorgeous," Damaris said, smiling at the extraordinary pinks and golds. "God provides splendors beyond human skill."

"Winter sunset," Fitz said, and she turned to smile at him. Despite everything, there were still bright strands between them, and she would enjoy them while she could. Like the sunset, they would soon be swallowed by the dark.

They went down the steps and strolled around the southwest side of the house. Even sunset gilding couldn't hide the sad state of the gardens. Roses trailed unpruned and weak, and statues choked in ivy.

Genova sighed. "And I know nothing of gardens."

"You will hire gardeners," Damaris said.

"Which requires money."

"I don't think Ashart is quite as penny-pinched as that. Especially if he sells his diamond buttons."

Genova smiled. "You have such a practical head."

Damaris picked her way along a rough path, trying not to soil her cloak. Fitz was walking behind them. True, the path was wide enough only for two, but Damaris was aware that he was putting himself between them and the park. Just in case.

They were passing between the house and an arrangement of bare trees interspersed with ivy-dressed statues. Her eye was caught, however, by an ugly extension to the house that seemed to be made of dusty gray squares. "Oh, it's a conservatory!"

"With very dirty glass," Genova said, "where the glass isn't missing entirely. But it could be lovely. It faces south."

She went toward it, and Fitz followed. Damaris stayed where she was, not caring for yet more grime and destruction. She considered the poor naked statues, wondering whimsically if they appreciated their leafy garments in the winter. She assumed their decrepit state was ancient rather than recent, but she didn't think she cared for them. If she had statues around her house, she'd have them made intact. After all, she assumed these Greek or Roman specimens had not been made missing arms, or in one case, a head.

Perhaps she didn't fit in this world. She didn't admire broken statues, and she didn't want an ancient, rambling place as her home. What was wrong with a modern house, full of light and free of drafts, and just big enough for elegant comfort? If she married someone like Fitz, she realized, someone without property, they could buy or build exactly the home they wanted.

These were wicked, dangerous thoughts, but Damaris couldn't resist. If there were decisions to be made, they must be made before she reached London. They must be made now.

She heard a noise and turned to see Fitz forcing the sagging door open so Genova could step inside the conservatory. Damaris turned back to the uncommunicative statues. For a second a trick of the flaming light made it appear that one moved.

She was going mad.

She was certainly irrational even to think of marrying Fitz. All the same, if it weren't for his past . . . She made herself be honest; the truth was, she'd marry him if his crime weren't *known*.

But it was.

Why did his scandal have such sharp teeth? It wasn't fair. Anyone could make one mistake.

But people hanged for one mistake.

She puffed out a white breath. When had it happened? Perhaps it would fade with time.

But hadn't he gone into the army because of it? She remembered his story about his new sword. Surely he'd said he'd been fifteen.

Fifteen? It was even more scandalous, she supposed, for a fifteen-year-old to be so precocious, and yet . . . how old had his brother's wife been? Everything was looking different now.

Fitz was the eighth child, and his brother, Lord Leyden, was probably the first. There could be twenty years between them, so unless his brother had married a very young wife . . .

She stared blindly at a laurel-wreathed hero, working through the implications. He'd said nothing about who'd seduced whom—

A blow to her chest staggered her backward, and she sat on the ground with a jarring thump. Pain blossomed in her chest, and she choked for breath. She looked down to where a feathered stick—an arrow!—protruded from between her breasts. She tried to clutch at the agony, but her hands didn't respond. A circle of black began to close in.

She tried to cling to consciousness, tried to call out, but darkness sucked her down.

Fitz heard a soft sound, turned, and saw Damaris collapse on her back. He raced to her crumpled body and fell to his knees. If this was another trick . . . Then he saw the arrow sticking out of her chest.

He felt as if his own heart stopped dead.

Genova knelt by his side. "My God!"

Damaris was unconscious, but his frantic hand found a pulse. No blood yet, but no one could survive such a wound. He grabbed one gloved hand tight, but she was going to die before his eyes.

Genova grasped the other. "It's all right. It's going to be all right."

He didn't know if she was talking to Damaris, him, or herself, but her stark pallor belied her words.

As if summoned, Damaris stirred, her lids fluttering. Her hand tried to move toward her chest. "Hurts . . . hurts . . ."

"I know, love," he said softly, blinking to clear his eyes. *Zeus, what to do?*

He remembered danger and swiveled to scan the area, letting go of her hand so he could shelter her with his body, though it was far too late. *Too late. Too late.*

He'd been guarding Genova and left Damaris to be killed.

Such a straight shot had to have come from what was called the Grecian Grove, where the wide tree trunks and life-size statues provided plenty of concealment. When the assassin tried to escape, Rothgar's people might catch him, but what good would that do? All the same, he went through the motions. He pulled the small pistol out of his pocket.

"You can handle this?" he said to Genova.

She nodded, so he gave it to her. "Go and get help.

Send for a doctor. If anyone comes at you, shoot him, but let him come close. It's hopeless at a distance."

She nodded, got to her feet, and ran.

Damaris was conscious but shaking, and her gloved hand fluttered near the shaft as if wanting to touch but fearing the agony of it. He grabbed her hand, holding it tight. She looked up at him, eyes dilated, mouth open to take tiny, pained breaths.

"We'll have help soon, love," he said, praying without hope for a miracle. Probably the kindest thing was to let her die quickly, but he couldn't surrender her without a struggle.

The arrow stuck out beneath a button of her quilted jacket. He couldn't see blood, but it must be soaking the clothes beneath. He had to see the damage—as if he might be able to do something. As long as he didn't add to her agony.

"I need both my hands for a moment, love," he said, tugging his right hand free of her clutch. Her eyes were a little less frantic—*brave sweetheart*—but her breathing was still shallow with pain.

"I'm going to cut off your clothing."

Something in those huge eyes suggested a humorous comment, but when she inhaled to speak she choked with pain, and her hand went again to the shaft. He stopped it.

"That won't help." He drew on every ounce of strength to speak calmly. "If there are any risqué remarks, they'll come from me." He should be watching for another attack, but what point now? The evil was done. "This sensible quilted jacket will have to go."

He dug out his folding knife and flicked it open, giving thanks that he still kept it razor sharp. He slid it behind the neckline and cut through the thickness there, then a straight slash down to the bottom, which again was tougher. He tried to keep the center part still, but even so he heard a little sound escape her.

Beneath, her corset was splattered with blood.

But then he realized the scarlet was only embroidered rosebuds. Faint irrational hope began to torment him.

"Now your corset, pretty one," he said, trying for the tone of a villain in a play. "This sturdy cage of purity must go."

The arrow pinned the stiffened, boned garment to her body, seeming to have gone right through the busk, the long piece of wood that reinforced the center front. He couldn't see how to cut any part free without hurting her. He tried slicing the heavy cloth between two bones, but she immediately cried, "Don't!"

Her voice was tight with pain, but she sounded remarkably well for someone suffering a mortal wound, and he'd seen plenty in that condition. Some people met death with stoical calm or even joy, but death could still be read in their features.

Heart pounding, hardly able to hope, he touched the shaft for the first time, watching Damaris's face. She simply looked up at him, more alert by the moment.

Holding his breath, he pushed the shaft to one side, aware through his fingers that it wasn't behaving as he'd expected. She flinched and made a noise, but surely her discomfort was closer to "ouch" than to deathly agony. Had the arrow broken at the entry point? Unlikely.

Gathering all his resolution, he took firm hold of the shaft and jerked it free.

"*Ow!*" But no scream, no blood, and no shattered end on the weapon.

What he held in his hand was a feathered dart about five inches long, with a fine, sharp, crumpled metal tip. Relief made him sway for a moment, and he almost burst into mad laughter.

"Saved by your stays," he managed to say. "It never

made it inside you, Damaris. It never got past the busk."

She moved to sit up and instantly cried out again and went pale.

"Gently," he said, holding her down. "The impact might have broken a bone. Let me see."

A tear in the rosebudded linen over the busk showed where the dart had been. Beneath the tear the busk clearly bent down into a vee. Now he understood.

"You ladies are armored better than many soldiers, but I fear some splinters are sticking into you." He suspected some were more like small daggers of wood. "Is that what it feels like?"

"Perhaps. And an ache," she whispered.

"From the blow." He prayed it hadn't shattered her breastbone. A crossbow could fire a shot of great force, but this small dart must have come from a miniature weapon. Cunning device, but that was for later.

"I want to get you into the house, but if I try to carry you now I could drive a splinter deeper. Better to cut your corset off."

"How dashing."

"More of that and I'll suspect you of arranging this in order to have your wicked way with me."

Her lips fluttered with tentative amusement.

He held the center as immobile as he could as he sliced through the corset and the shift beneath, but he still felt and heard her flinches. Like a surgeon performing an amputation, he went for speed, but when he raised the center part to reveal the damage, he went very slowly indeed.

Blood. Enough to be alarming if he weren't just back from the brink of terror. Fangs of wood stuck in her flesh.

She gripped his wrist. "Stop! It hurts."

"At least you can complain more loudly." He

leaned down to look beneath the stays, trying to block the fact that he was leaning on her breast. "Jagged edges from both sides are sticking into you, love, but none are very long." He straightened to look at her. "There's nothing for it other than to pull them free, or it'll hurt even more to move you."

"Do it, then."

He jerked the front of her stays from her body. She let out only a tight gasp, but she went white. Blood spread, freshly red, so he pulled up her skirts, slashed out a chunk of her shift, and made a pad to press to the wound. But she cried out again, grabbing his hands.

"Splinters," he said, frustrated that he couldn't save her from the lightest touch of pain. "I'm going to have to carry you in as you are. I'll try not to hurt you."

She nodded.

He pulled out his cravat pin and used it to draw the two sides of her shift together, to make her as decent as possible, to cover her exquisite breast, a pale, firm mound crested by a pretty pink nipple.

She wasn't for him.

She would live.

It was enough.

And whoever had done this would shortly burn in hell.

He gathered her into his arms and stood. He could see that she suffered, but she made no sound except to say, "Splinters. I feel so silly."

"Don't. You could be dead."

"But why? What happened? What was that weapon?"

He'd put the dart in his pocket for later examination, and as he carried her quickly toward the house and safety, he said, "A dart, probably fired from a small crossbow. I've seen such things. They're small enough to be concealed in the clothing but can be deadly all the same."

"But who would want to kill me?"

Fitz hadn't had time to think. As he entered the house, the identity of the killer seemed clear. Whoever stood to inherit Damaris's fortune.

Genova hurried to meet them. "I've sent for the doctor! Ash is with the dowager." Genova stared. "Damaris! You're all right?"

"The bolt hit her busk." Fitz halted. Now that they were safely inside, relief and safety threatened to crumple him. "By God's grace she escaped death, but only by His grace."

"Praise heaven! Praise heaven. I was sure—"

"She has splinters that need to come out," he said, summoning his strength and carrying Damaris upstairs.

Genova came with him, hurrying ahead to open doors. As he laid Damaris on her bed, Genova slipped Damaris's cloak off, then spread a blanket over her chest.

"How do you feel?" Fitz asked, wanting to brush stray hairs off her face but knowing his control held by only a thread.

"Safe. Because of you."

"I notably failed to keep you safe." When she stirred, he said, "Stay flat until the splinters are out."

He couldn't remain here for that operation, but hated to leave her. He knew she was in little danger in the house, but all the same he wanted to stay close.

"Why me?" she asked. "I had my hood down. No one could have mistaken me for Genova."

He hated to frighten her more, but truth was best. "I'm realizing too late that you may have been the target all along. For your money, I assume. Do you know who your heir is?"

Her eyes widened. "No. I never thought to ask. How stupid of me."

"I should have thought of it. I was obsessed with the danger to Ash."

Genova said, "You have to go, Fitz. We can't dig out splinters while you're here, and Ash should be told." When he hesitated, she added, "I'm sure we're all safe in the house, but just in case, I have your pistol."

"Nonsense, of course, but it's as well to take precautions." He still felt as if he wore leaden shoes, but he made himself move toward the door. He turned to find Damaris frowning at him.

"This seems so silly," she said.

"Sweet one, if only it were." With that, he left.

"He's madly in love with you," Genova said.

Damaris looked at her. "Truly?"

"He wept when he thought you were dying."

"Because he'd failed to protect me. It was shame, not love."

"He called you 'love.' I see all the reasons against your marrying him, but feelings of that intensity aren't something to brush aside."

Damaris pressed a hand to the place where her torn flesh throbbed. A place so close to her wounded heart. "I think he'd fight me hardest."

Maisie rushed in. "What've you been doing now, Miss Damaris? I dunno, I can't let you out of my sight!"

There was no way to conceal the truth, so Damaris told Maisie the story.

The maid grabbed the bedpost. "Someone *shot* at you, miss?"

"Yes, but you're not to tell anyone. We'll say I tripped and bruised myself."

"Bloody clothes?" Genova queried.

"And gashed myself on some glass. We'll take the evidence to London, anyway. We're going there tomorrow, Maisie."

"Heaven be praised! But what about whoever did this?"

Damaris met Genova's eyes grimly, but said, "That's all taken care of. Now please find the tweezers and desplinter me."

Maisie hurried to the chest of drawers, muttering, and some of it was "that Fitzroger . . ."

Genova pulled out the long cravat pin so she could part her ruined shift. Damaris noticed it was silver topped by a plain knob. Fitz should have something finer. Diamonds, she thought.

Perhaps because of her brush with death, she was certain now: She wanted him, scandal or no. He was her handsome hero par excellence.

"Who might your heir be?" Genova asked, bringing a damp cloth to wipe away blood.

Damaris realized she'd been trying to hide from that thought. "I don't know."

"Your father's family?"

"They cast him off, and he cared nothing for them."

"A friend, perhaps. Even someone from the East."

"That seems most likely. How strange to have a deadly enemy I've never met."

Maisie came over with Damaris's small medicine chest. "It's all his doing," she grumbled, taking the cloth from Genova. "Oh, you poor dear. You're all torn up and swelling. This is going to hurt."

"Just do it. Make sure to get all the bits out."

It did hurt, but it was the kind of pain that could be borne, especially with Genova holding her hand, especially when thinking of a man who had wept for loss of her. She knew she was in no state for clear thinking, but she wanted him. Forever. Life was too short and chancy for second-best.

"There, miss. I think that's all of it. How shall I dress it?"

Damaris asked for a mirror. Her wounds looked rather paltry for all the fuss and discomfort, but there was always the danger of infection.

"The green salve and then basilicum ointment. A clean cloth on top. I supposed I'll have to wear a long bandage wrapped around me to hold it in place. And then I'll need a fresh shift and my robe."

"You're never getting up, miss! You stay in bed after such a nasty shock."

"I'll go mad lying here. I want to be up, and I want sweet brandied tea. But not too sweet."

Maisie dressed the wound; then Genova helped Damaris sit up so the long bandage could be wrapped around her. It didn't hurt much, but her head swam. It was sinking in that someone had tried to *kill* her.

Twice.

She remembered the snaggletoothed man and knew he had poisoned the cider at Pickmanwell. She hadn't entirely misjudged his unpleasant expression. He'd intended the poison for her. Was he her heir? Or a hired killer?

She needed Genova's arm to walk to a chair by the fire. Maisie put a footstool beneath her feet and wrapped a woolen rug around her, and Damaris didn't object. The room wasn't cold, but she felt chilled to her bones.

Maisie hurried away, and Genova put another log on the fire. Then she went to the window, which was ice-free at this time of day. But the ice would return with the night.

"I assume there's no one skulking out there?" Damaris asked.

Genova turned. "Of course not. And I'm sure you're safe inside."

"How stupid not to know who my heir is. I should have demanded to see my father's will instead of letting my trustees explain the relevant parts in simple terms." She sighed. "I found reading my mother's will tedious, so when I discovered my father's will concerned me I was glad to be spared the effort. And thus sloth is punished."

"Don't be too hard on yourself. Who would imagine such wickedness?"

"As soon as we get to London I'm going to read every word." But first, she thought with a glance at the window, she'd have to get to London without being killed. A shot could be fired from anywhere.

Maisie returned with a pot of tea and two cups. Genova poured it and added milk. When she picked up a second lump of sugar, Damaris said, "Not too sweet, remember."

They shared a wry smile as Genova passed the cup.

As Damaris sipped, the chill melted. Her heart rate steadied, but she kept thinking back to that moment when she'd felt the hard blow and looked down to see the shaft sticking out of her chest.

It was as pointless as probing a sore tooth in the hope that this time it wouldn't hurt, but she couldn't help it. She could have died.

There was a knock on the door and Maisie answered it. Fitzroger asked permission to come in.

Damaris gave it, and he came over to her. "Is it very painful?"

She realized she'd been pressing her chest. "No. Hardly at all now that the splinters are all out."

"Are you well enough to be up?" he asked, concerned, but without obvious love or passion.

"Yes, truly."

"Will you be able to travel tomorrow, then?" he asked. "Those papers should be taken to the king and I'll be happier to see you in the safety of Rothgar's London house."

"Yes, I'm sure."

He frowned slightly. "Was there anything suspicious about that fall in Pickmanwell, Damaris?"

"I'd been thinking about that. Someone did bump me, but the street was busy. Then when I was lying on the ground, the moon disappeared. I thought I'd half fainted, but it might have been someone hovering over me. . . ."

"I wish you'd told me. I might have guessed what was afoot sooner. A fine bodyguard I've turned out to be."

Before she could respond to that, Ashart knocked and was admitted. "This is infuriating—that someone should shoot at a guest here! And how are we to take Damaris to London in safety?"

Fitz was calm again. "We'll give no hint of our plans until the last moment and travel with six outriders. I don't think our man will make a direct attack on a well-guarded party. If we don't stop for more than a change of horses along the way, we should be able to make it in under four hours."

"And I was never in danger after all," Ashart said.

"The threat was and still is real. Rothgar would not take action without being sure of that. Those who want you dead are simply less desperate."

"Desperate?" Damaris asked.

He turned to her. "The attacker acted rashly. He was almost caught by one of the people patrolling the estate. The guard wasn't yet aware that you'd been shot, so he didn't pursue what looked like a furtive poacher, just made sure he left the estate."

"But why desperate?" Damaris demanded. "If the killer is my heir, he must have been so for years. Why take such risks now?"

"We'll find out when we catch him. . . ."

Lady Thalia came in, bundled in furs. "I hear Damaris has taken a fall. Are you all right, dear?"

Genova led her to the empty chair and told the truth.

Lady Thalia put a hand over her mouth. "Oh, such

wickedness in the world! And over money. You must sleep in my room tonight, dear. Ashart's room, I mean. I'm sure it's much more secure."

"Oh, that's not necessary," Damaris said.

"In fact," Fitz said, "this wing is more easily guarded. The only access is from the service stairs and the arch from the Royal Salon. I'll secure both with alarm wires."

"Alarm wires?" Ashart asked, looking astonished.

"Tricks of the trade. If disturbed they trigger a small explosion. The mechanism's the same as the firing pan of a pistol."

"'Struth," Ashart said. "No sleepwalking tonight, Damaris."

"No, I promise."

Darkness had fallen, crushing the last traces of glorious red. No one mentioned danger from outside, but Fitz closed the shutters and let down the curtains. Somewhere outside a man might still lurk, intent on killing her for her fortune.

As if she'd spoken, Fitz said, "I have the house under close supervision. You're safe."

She believed him, but fear still beat like a drum in her pulse, and she had to keep stopping herself from touching the tender spot in the center of her chest. She could so easily be dead.

When Lady Thalia suggested a move to the grand bedchamber and a lighthearted game of loo, Damaris was first to agree. She needed distraction. She let Fitz carry her, however.

He was hers, though he didn't know it yet, and she delighted in his touch.

Ashart ordered extra candles, and rum punch to brighten their spirits. Damaris perhaps drank more than she should, for it did push back fear—fear of more than the assassin.

Fitz seemed abstracted.

She knew he was planning for tomorrow, trying to anticipate every danger and prevent it. She worried that he was also making other plans—about how to leave her, leave England, as soon as possible.

Chapter 16

Fitz struggled to keep his mind on the game, but a frantic beat in his head pounded out, *She could have died, she could have died.* . . .

He could argue that even by Damaris's side he'd not have been able to block the dart, but the thought was no comfort.

She could have died.

The game stopped at ten, as if the chiming clock commanded an end to play and the beginning of their last night at Cheynings. He reviewed security again. There could be no more mistakes. He'd already posted guards around the house, but with so many doors and windows it couldn't be made into a fortress. Therefore Damaris's bedchamber must be impregnable.

He and Ashart escorted her across the dark, chilly house. He would have carried her, but she refused.

"I'd feel like a fraud after enjoying the game. My chest doesn't even hurt much anymore. I've always healed well."

She was putting on a merry face, but as they crossed the cold, gloomy house, he knew her fear was returning.

Ashart left once Damaris was safe in her room. Fitz explained the alarms to her and her fretful maid.

"They'll ensure your safety, but don't try to go downstairs until I'm up tomorrow."

The maid dropped a curtsy. "That I won't, sir."

He wished Damaris a good night, and closed the door on candlelight, a merry fire, and her lace-frilled white nightgown that hung over a rack in front of it. It was the same as or similar to the one she'd worn when she'd invaded his room.

He cleared his mind and stretched thin wires across the two openings to this corridor—the arch out into the Royal Salon, and the entrance to the service stairs. He set them shin high, where they'd catch a man but not a rodent. Then he attached the trigger mechanism and cocked each. He was quixotically tempted to lie down at Damaris's threshold, but was stopped not just because he would appear ridiculous if caught, but because he, too, needed sleep if he was to have his wits about him the next day.

He went to his room, undressed, and washed, but he was too keyed up to sleep. He extinguished the candles, but sat by the fire in his banyan robe, sipping brandy, making himself think about the enemy, not the woman next door.

If Damaris's heir wanted to kill her, why not strike years ago? Presumably it would have been laughably easy when she'd been living in Worksop.

What had changed?

Damaris's mother had died a year ago last November, and Damaris had come of age in October. If that was important, why not act then? Had she been so closely guarded at Thornfield Hall that it had been impossible? He wished he'd thought to ask her.

There'd been no attack at Rothgar Abbey, but security there, though discreet, was tight. A villain wouldn't have risked it.

The attack on the way here suggested that the killer

had followed them, had perhaps been watching Rothgar Abbey for a chance. Patient and cautious.

Why, then, the attack today?

The door gave the slightest squeak to warn of its opening. He stilled, regretting that his knife was already under his pillow and his pistol out of reach, though he already knew with despair who it was.

"Fitz?" It was the slightest whisper, but even so, every part of his body instantly sizzled.

He rose and went to her. "What's amiss?"

She slipped in and closed the door behind her. "I had an idea."

"Damaris—"

"Shush. It's important."

"It's not safe."

She looked around. "Here?"

He let silence speak for him, and she cocked her head. "I don't think I'm going to be driven mad by lust—even though you do look splendid in that pale robe with your pale hair. Like a ghostly knight."

She walked over and sat in the chair opposite his. She was in her dark robe again, but it showed the high neck of her nightgown with its lacy frill, and the wider frill at her wrists. Her hair was not in a plait, but simply tied back with a ribbon that was already sliding loose. Silky hair, he thought breathlessly.

The chair put her back to him, and she turned, looking like a wide-eyed kitten. But she was much more dangerous than that.

"You don't seem to have considered that *I* might be driven mad with lust."

"I don't think you could be driven mad by anything."

"How little you know men," he remarked, but he crossed the room to her. "Brandy?"

"Yes, please. I've developed a taste for it."

"Lord save us all." But he poured some into a glass and passed it to her, then topped up his own before sitting.

She'd pulled her hair to the front, and the dark river of it flowed down, seeming to emphasize the breast it covered.

"I know I shouldn't be here, but after all," she added, mischief in her eyes, "your trip wires ensure that no one will interrupt us, don't they?"

He closed his eyes briefly. "Someone truly should throttle you. And I suppose your maid is deep in sleep. Very well. Your urgent idea?"

"My will. And fear. I couldn't sleep. I know you have me safe, but every creak of the house, every scuttle of mice . . ."

He absolutely mustn't take her in his arms. "What about your will?" he prompted.

"What? Oh"—her eyes steadied—"I don't have one. Once I make one, it will override my father's and there'll be no point in anyone killing me, will there?"

"Except whomever you leave your money to," he pointed out, but by Zeus, she was right. How dull his mind had become.

She dismissed his comment with a wave of her hand. "I can leave it to someone safe. Rothgar. You."

"Not me," he said sharply. "I might crumble under the temptation."

He might crumble under the temptation she presented now, lit with purpose and excitement, half schoolgirl, half siren, half fellow adventurer. It was in keeping with his insanity that the halves didn't add up.

He rose to pace the room, to think, to escape the necessity of looking at her. "It's a good plan, but with one weakness. The murderer, if it is your heir, won't know that things have changed."

"We can let it be known."

"How?" He had to face her again. He couldn't conduct a conversation with his back turned. "Throw handbills out of the coach all the way to London?"

She frowned in a way that made him want to kiss each furrow. "There has to be a way. Ah! We arrive in London, I summon my trustees, find out who my heir is, then I send a note informing him of his altered expectations."

"Or I kill him. But that assumes he's easy to find. What if it's one of your father's colleagues from abroad?"

She sipped her brandy. "That is likely, isn't it? It even explains why I wasn't threatened sooner. It might have taken time for him to get here. I'll put a notice in the papers, then."

"That would work." He put aside his glass. "Time for you to return to your room."

"No, wait. If I write my will, will it hold?"

"If witnessed, I believe so."

"Then I can write it now and you can witness it."

"I believe it needs two witnesses. Leave it until morning. In fact, leave it until we reach London and have it done in proper form."

He must get her out of here. He took the risk of pulling her up out of her chair. "Come on."

She didn't resist, but said, "No, it must be done before we leave. Don't you see? If anything goes wrong tomorrow, I refuse to let this villain gain by it. I *refuse*."

Her spirit and resolution dazzled him. "Ah, but you're magnificent."

"Am I?"

She was looking up at him, bright-eyed, and he knew he should deny his words, but he said, "You know you are."

"And so are you."

He shook his head. "I'm a low creature. By all means, write your will before we leave. But I promise you—if this miscreant manages to kill you, Damaris, I will hunt him down, and before he dies he'll wish he'd been caught, tried, and hanged by the legal system."

A shiver went through Damaris, but it wasn't fear. She stepped close to him, words coming to her tongue without thought and without hope of control. "I want you, Octavius Fitzroger."

He didn't move a muscle. "It's the punch. Let's get you back to bed."

He tried to steer her there, but she evaded him and blocked the door. "I can't sleep."

His stillness was frightening, but she would not be denied. This was their last night, her last chance.

"Hardly surprising when you're not in bed," he pointed out.

"Even in my bed I won't be able to sleep. Truly, Fitz. Can't I stay here until I tire?" She wasn't sure exactly what she wanted except to be with him. "I feel safe here with you," she said. "Perhaps we could talk."

"Talk." She heard a breath. It might have been a laugh. But then he said, "Of course."

Chapter 17

He put extra wood on the fire, every movement speaking to her of his wonderful body.

Temptation put her wickedness into words. *If we make love here tonight, he will never leave me. His honor will forbid it.*

Flames licked, then flared, brightening the room.

She returned to one chair; he took the other, leaning back, pale gold and burnished in the fire's light.

"Tell me about your life in Worksop," he said.

Damaris hid a smile at the skillful move. She'd meant that they should talk about him. All the same, she did talk about life at Birch House, dull though it was.

"My mother was a strange woman, an only child of elderly parents, and her mother died when she was three. She was raised by my grandfather, who was a distant man. He was a physician, but also a gentleman scholar. He died when I was ten, but I'd already realized that he'd have been happier if all his patients were statues. I mean without demanding emotions."

"Automatons, like those Rothgar so admires."

"Yes, exactly. Cogs and springs."

"It can't have been a pleasant home," he said.

He seemed relaxed, or at least resigned. Perhaps talking like this would be enough, for it was sweet.

But talking wouldn't bind him, and she wanted him bound. Against all laws of friendship, honor, and society, she wanted Octavius Fitzroger shackled to her without hope of escape.

"No," she said, "but I lacked comparison. There weren't even any close relatives. Grandfather had some family in the west country—Devon, I think—but he never traveled, and they didn't come to us. If there'd been contact with my grandmother's family, it ceased with her death before I was born. My father was estranged from his family."

"Did you have a governess?"

"My mother taught me. Because she said there was no money to hire anyone."

"You must have attended church, at least."

"Diligently, but we never lingered. I think perhaps my mother found my father's absence embarrassing. Even for a merchant engaged in foreign lands, it was strange."

"Did she love him, do you think?"

"Perhaps to begin with, but if so he killed it. By the time I had any powers of analysis, I'd say she believed she owned him. Her attitude to him always seethed with anger. At some point she learned that he kept a mistress in London, and that infuriated her, but I don't think she was hurt by it. Just furious. Because she thought she owned him. Because she'd bought him with her dowry."

Damaris realized that a similar rage of ownership had boiled in herself over Ashart. What a blessing it had come to nothing, for it had been no different except for the price.

"I wouldn't have thought that a mistress in London was much use to a man so much abroad," he remarked.

"True, but I doubt she was mistaken." It was peculiar to be talking about such things with a man, but

Damaris said, "I suppose he paid her to be available on the rare occasions he wanted her."

"Neatly efficient. Was she mentioned in his will?"

"I don't know. It's exactly the sort of thing my trustees wouldn't tell me."

His lips twitched. "I'm sure. But your mother was entitled to be bitter and angry if he took her money and left her in poverty, especially as he grew rich and squandered money on other women."

"But he didn't. I discovered that after her death. He always sent money, and the amounts grew over the years. In that, at least, he was honest. We could have lived in luxury, but she used as little as she could and pretended that was all he sent."

She shook her head and sighed. "It was a type of madness. Did she think it would force him to return? To abandon Sarawak, Moluccas, and Java for Birch House, Worksop, because she was depriving herself and me?"

"If she truly hated him, she could have hated his money."

"That's as good an explanation as any. But what of your family and early life?" she asked.

She intended to marry him despite the scandal, but she still hoped to find a way to erase it. Thus she needed to know more about his family. "You went into the army at fifteen?"

"Yes." He turned his head to look into the fire. "We weren't isolated, as you were. The Fitzrogers of Cleeve hold an important place in the county, having been there since the Conquest. Not far from my home there's a ruin of Carrisford Castle, built by one of my ancestors. Fitzroger of Cleeve was king's champion to Henry the First and became one of the great barons. There's a romantic story attached about his capture of an heiress. . . ."

He broke off then switched the subject. "So we

weren't isolated, but nor were we happy. My mother bore too many children, ten in all, and lost too many. My father blamed fate, not himself. My older sister, Sally, was simple from birth. She's thirty-one but thinks and acts like a child."

"How many brothers and sisters do you have?" she asked. "Living, I mean."

He faced her. "Hugh—he's the oldest. Lord Leyden now. There was another Hugh before him, but he died. Sally, Libella, and me."

Four out of ten, and one was simple, another a brute. His poor mother.

"Libella?" she asked.

He smiled. "The last and smallest, but with the most spirit. Libella means a tenth, or a little bit, but we always called her Libby. She's trapped there now, looking after Mother and Sally, and trying to prevent Hugh's cruelties. I'd free her if I could, but I can't." Some trick of the fire put flames in his eyes. "I am completely powerless over my life."

"Why?"

"You know why."

They had reached the crux of everything. Damaris breathed in and out twice. "Because you had an affair with your brother's wife. With Hugh's wife, I assume. How old was she?"

He frowned as if puzzled. "Twenty-five, I think."

"Ten years older than you."

"I was precocious." He stood and moved away from the firelight. "We shouldn't speak of such things."

"Why not? Apparently all the world does."

He faced her, but from the shadows by the bed. "Yes, all the world does. You don't want anything to do with me, Damaris."

"Isn't that for me to say?"

"No."

She shot to her feet. "You were only fifteen. It wasn't your fault!"

"What is fault? I was old enough to know right from wrong."

"And you knew it to be wrong?"

She thought he wasn't going to answer, but then he said, "It was half a lifetime ago. I no longer know what I knew or thought or felt or wanted. It is, however, like a thief's brand. It cannot be removed."

She moved toward him. "It's not a brand—it's ancient history. Remember what you told me about my embarrassment? It's etched in your mind, but not in the minds of others."

He gave a short laugh. "Oh, yes, it is. Understand that, Damaris. Hugh let the matter simmer as long as I stayed away, but I made the mistake of returning to England, and of going to Cleeve Court to see if my sisters and mother needed me. It threw pitch on old coals. Now he tells anyone who'll listen that he'll kill me on sight. He's even started a suit, charging me with responsibility for Orinda's death."

That was a sickening blow. "How can he claim that?"

"She killed herself not long after I left."

She gathered herself to fight on. "Do you believe she killed herself for loss of you?"

A touch of bleak humor flashed across his face. "Too self-glorious for you? No. She cared nothing for me beyond a physical hunger and hatred of Hugh. But I abandoned her, and she chose death."

"You were *fifteen*," she repeated intensely. "Why did you join the army?"

"I was dragged there by my father. It was that or starve."

Oh, poor lad. But she wouldn't weaken now.

"So," she demanded, deliberately harsh, "were you expected to take her with you as your mistress?"

"I was expected not to ruin her in the first place."

"Fitz, *she* ruined *you*."

He rocked back.

She gripped the front of his robe and shook him. "It wasn't your fault. She used you. You bear no blame for it."

He'd retreated before she'd grabbed him, but been stopped by the bed. "Which doesn't matter a damn." He gripped her wrists. "My name's dung, Damaris, and I'll not drag you into it."

"I don't care! We can fight this. We can fight it together. Why don't you challenge your brother? Kill him. I'm sure you're able."

He tore free. "Never! I hurt him once. Never again."

"Even though he hurts others? He drove Orinda to her death. What's he doing to your mother and sisters?"

"Damn you, Damaris. Stop this."

"No. I will fight for you, Octavius Fitzroger. For us. I want you," she said, grabbing his robe again. "I want you happy. I want you at ease, and in silk and diamonds. . . ."

She was unfastening the robe with trembling fingers, even though it became clear, button by button, that he wore nothing beneath. He pushed her away, but she held on and pushed harder, pushed him onto the bed, and fell over him.

"You're mine! Don't you understand? You're mine, so your brother is my enemy, and I have money as my weapon. Money can silence him. If he takes you to court, money will buy more and better lawyers—"

He kissed her.

She felt his control snap like a silent explosion, and it was too late then for caution on her part. Besides, this was what she wanted; this was what she'd come here for: the fire in her blood, the ecstasy of his touch, the heat that would fuse the shackles around both of them.

He rolled her, still kissing her, in a crazy tangle of limbs and clothing that made her laugh when her mouth was free, when he was kissing her breasts. . . .

Had he ripped her nightgown? She didn't care. She tore at his robe, feeling a button snap free. When she couldn't release more, she pulled it up, up, until her hands found his firm flesh.

He rolled away for a moment and stripped. She struggled out of her robe, eyes on him, feasting on him. Dear heaven, but was there anything more beautiful in the world? Her body felt like one strong, starving pulse—starving for him.

He had ripped her nightgown, tearing through the strong placket. She gripped the sides and ripped it further and further until she reached the hem, which she couldn't tear.

He did it for her, but his eyes were on her chest, on the bandage. "You're hurt."

She grasped his hair and pulled him down. "Not any longer. Love me. Love me."

The fierce joining of hot mouths blanked her mind of all but need for him, his strength, his smell, his delicious muscles moving beneath silky skin. She kneaded them, possessing them as he ravished her lips, then her breasts.

She arched high, crying out at that wild pleasure, spreading her legs wide because she knew where she needed him most. She would die if he didn't come inside her, fill her, assuage the burning need.

She felt pressure there—"Oh, yes!"—and pushed against it, wanting more, then realized it was his hand. But then what he was doing drove her beyond anything but bliss and need.

Her body throbbed, her head throbbed, her breasts were full of aching, hungry need. His fierce mouth summoned a miracle of pleasure that shot down to his hand, where that other pleasure was surely going to kill her, but she didn't care.

She gripped him tight, writhing in a wild demand for more and more and more, hearing her own gasping attempts to say just that. At the same time she felt almost as if there were something wrong with her, something blocked. Since she couldn't stop, didn't want him to stop, she'd die here, like this.

Then she shattered, or flew, or fell. All she knew was a pleasure beyond anything she'd ever imagined, a pleasure his now gentle touch drew on and on as his mouth sealed her gasps.

When she spun out of the maelstrom, she ravished him in turn, driven to claim, to capture, to straddle him, wanting more.

He looked as lost as she in the firelight, drugged and desperate. She licked his face, nibbled his jaw and then his ear. Despite all that wild pleasure she wanted more, and she knew what she wanted. Her body knew what it needed to be complete.

"Take me," she whispered, and nipped at his earlobe. "Take me now. Complete me. Please."

His hands clenched on her hips. She slid down to lick and nibble at his chest, running her hands over smooth muscles, tracing the arch of his ribs. She'd moved sideways to see him better, so she saw his phallus. So big—and yet a pulse began inside her still-sensitive body, a pulse of passionate recognition.

"Now," she said, putting her hand gently around him. He shuddered but didn't fight her, so she lay back, drawing him to her. She worried that she was doing this badly, even making a fool of herself, but she'd rather do that than lose him. Besides, it seemed natural and right to coax him like this, to look into his eyes and bring them together until he was pressed against her hot, hungry entrance as her heart pounded with need.

His eyes shut as if he struggled, or was in agony, but then suddenly he thrust into her. There was a moment of sharp pain, but she gritted back a cry and pushed hard up against him. This would not stop here. Could not. It was so eternally right.

His eyes opened and he looked at her, seeming almost lost but loving. Then he groaned her name and moved in strong, deep thrusts that she met even when they hurt because she wanted this more than anything in life.

Vaguely she noticed how he supported himself, how his torso never pressed where he might hurt her. Even in extremis he thought of her, and she loved him beyond bearing.

She didn't quite find that perfect pleasure again, but she loved the swirling madness of it and the signs of his ecstasy. His choked groan, his shudders, the pulsing deep inside her where they were securely, infinitely joined.

She ran her hands up and down his back from buttocks to shoulders again and again, drifting in sated wonder. She'd never known. It was wrong, she thought, to keep this secret. Everyone should know. Everyone should do this as much as possible.

Poor Betty Crowley, whose young husband died soon after the wedding, and whose second husband was incapable.

He stilled, resting his head beside hers, breathing deeply, even desperately. At that moment she sensed something terribly, terribly wrong.

He pushed back and rolled to collapse on his back. "I had better have killed you."

She reached for him. "Don't be silly—"

But he rolled back over her. "Damn it all to Hades, Damaris, I just ruined you!"

"Ouch!"

He jerked off her. "Zeus, I'm sorry." But then he looked at her and, teeth gritted, put a hand around her throat. "I really should throttle you."

She swallowed, aware of how easily he could do it and that he was truly furious.

"My chest did hurt," she whispered, tears stinging in her eyes. "A little. And you didn't ruin me, because I want to marry you."

"Then you ruined me. Rothgar will kill me."

"You can defeat him."

He practically levitated off her. "You think I would kill a man over this? When I'm in the wrong?"

She sat up, swallowing tears. No, she didn't want him to kill anyone, especially not a man who'd been kind to her, but this was a battle—a battle for the treasure she wanted more than anything else in the world.

"I love you, Fitz. You love me. Deny it if you can."

"I deny it."

"And I call you a liar!"

She remembered what he'd once said—that he'd walk away from any woman who doubted his word.

He turned away, dragging in a deep breath, sitting on the edge of the bed, head thrown back. She should have her mind on higher things, but truly he was a most beautiful man.

"I can marry whom I wish," she said in the calmest voice she could find, "and I wish to marry you. Rothgar has nothing to say about it. I'm of age. He can withhold my money, but a fig for that."

"And how do you intend to survive?"

"With you, and by borrowing from the money-lenders."

He dropped his head into his hands, his elbows braced on his knees, and his desperation finally silenced her. He really did see his actions as dire and dishonorable.

And she understood.

Too late, she understood what she'd done.

When he was fifteen a woman called Orinda had stolen his honor, carelessly, in lust and to spite her husband. Over the years, against bitter odds, he'd painstakingly re-created it as best he could, even with fate constantly stepping in his way.

Tonight she, in seizing what she wanted, had stolen it again. He didn't believe they should marry, but she'd forced this upon him, where he should marry her or be dishonorable.

It didn't even matter if anyone ever knew what they'd done here. He knew, and honor was more than reputation. It lived in a person's soul.

How like her selfish, piratical father she was.

All words seemed shallow. She longed to soothe him, to apologize, and yet still to find a way to possess him. She reached out to touch him but then pulled her hand back. Quite likely he'd throw her off, which would hurt her and slay him.

He coiled off the bed, picking up his robe and covering his long, lean body. Then he faced her from a distance of about eight feet.

"This is what we shall do. If you prove to be with child, I will marry you, if you still wish it. In the meantime you will tell no one about this. It will be as if it never happened. We go to London tomorrow, and there we'll find your heir and eliminate the danger. You'll follow Rothgar's plan and enter society. You'll meet eligible men, many of them far finer fellows than I. The Duke of Bridgewater may be exactly to your taste."

"How can I marry another man now?"

"It's possible to conceal the lack of maidenhead

from most men. And besides, given your financial attributes, your husband will probably put aside any suspicions."

"Don't," she whispered. "Please don't be cruel."

She struggled off the bed, dragging her own clothes together, feeling soiled for the first time. She hurt between her legs, and in her chest, where she'd been wounded twice—one above the heart and once deep inside it.

"It wasn't cruelly meant. You will do as I say?"

She stood with her back to that soulless voice, fumbling with buttons in the dim light. "What choice do I have?"

"You can tell Rothgar what happened here. Or Ashart, for that matter. It might result in my death, or I might be forced to marry you. Are you a gambler?"

She turned to look at him through blurred eyes. "Forced? It would be so bad as that?"

"I'm the worst possible husband for you, Damaris. I'm trying to protect you."

"Whether I want to be or not?"

"Whether you want to be or not."

The fire showed only the slightest, surly glow, and drafts nibbled at her bare toes.

"You'll thank me one day," he said. "I hope you'll thank me—"

A shriek cut off his words.

"Maisie!" Damaris gasped, rushing to the door.

He grabbed her. "You can't be caught leaving here like that."

Her loose hair, her torn nightgown, which was probably stained with blood.

Maisie let out another yelp, then shouted, "Miss Damaris? Miss Damaris! Save us all, she's been stolen away!" A moment later an explosion rocked the air, and Maisie really screamed, on and on and on.

Fitz's hand had tightened, but now he pushed Damaris away. "Stay here. I'll see to her. Then you slip back into your room." He looked her over, then shook his head. "Do the best you can."

Then, desperately, he kissed her, and it seemed to her that fate fought against their parting.

He pulled away and opened the door—to walk into a flood of light. Ashart stood in the archway, the flaring candle in his hand almost blinding Damaris to Maisie, hands over her mouth, behind him.

Silence crackled around them like thin ice. Ashart turned to Maisie. "Go back to your room and keep your mouth shut."

Maisie nodded fiercely and scurried away.

"Ash? Damaris? Fitz?" Genova appeared with another candle.

All in all, Damaris would rather have had less light than more.

Genova understood all at a glance and stepped close to Ashart, close to her tiger. Damaris wanted to faint. As Genova had said, Ashart considered himself her protector, Rothgar's substitute here in his house. And to him she had been violated.

Perhaps he'd insist on a wedding? The look in his eyes spoke of death.

He walked forward, and Damaris and Fitz retreated until they were all in the room.

"I should kill you," Ashart said.

"He didn't force me," Damaris protested. "I came here—"

"And he took advantage of it. I've ignored his reputation, which was obviously foolish."

"He was fifteen when—"

Fitz grabbed her arm. "Don't." He met Ashart's frigid gaze. "Yes, I'm in the wrong. But whatever you decide, it would be better if I accompanied you all to London tomorrow to ensure Damaris's safety."

Ashart's free hand was fisted, but he was otherwise

in perfect control of himself. Damaris found it more terrifying than open rage.

"Very well. Rothgar can deal with you, as you're his man anyway, I suspect. If I have your word that you won't flee before hearing his judgment?"

"No!" Damaris protested.

But Fitz overrode her. "You have it."

Ashart turned his eyes on her. "You will return to your room and stay there."

The icy authority almost had her bobbing a servile curtsy. She'd never known he could be so terrifying.

Genova urged her out of the room. Damaris didn't want to leave the two men together, but Genova gathered in Ashart on the way so that the three of them ended up on the other side of the closed door.

"It was my fault," Damaris insisted. She licked her lips, then bared her shame. "I wanted him, and thought this the best way to break his will."

Ashart's dark eyes seared her. "Then spend the night on your knees praying you haven't killed a good man in your greed."

He grasped her arm and marched her to her room, pushed her in, and closed the door. Damaris leaned back against it, tears streaming down her face, with an ocean more aching in her chest.

She thrust a hand to her mouth to stifle cries, and Maisie rushed over and took her into her arms. "Oh, I'm that sorry, Miss Damaris! I never guessed. But how could you? Oh, that terrible man. I warned you. I warned you. . . ."

Damaris burst into racking sobs in her arms.

Chapter 18

Damaris slept because Maisie insisted that she take laudanum. She woke when the shutters were opened, dulled by opium, remembering waking from another drugged sleep. Again she didn't want to face the day or the people who knew her shame, but there was no question this time of running away. She couldn't abandon Fitz.

Surely she'd be able to convince Rothgar that she'd brought about her own ruin, wouldn't she? Even if he barred them from marrying, he couldn't *kill* Fitz for being seduced by her.

But she knew enough of men now to know that he might do it. The challenge would be trumped up over something else to spare her name, but it would happen, and Fitz would die. He wouldn't defend himself when he thought himself in the wrong.

It was all her fault. How could she not have thought, not have known what being seduced by a woman he should not touch would mean to him? He who'd been seduced when young by his sister-in-law.

Her throat ached again, but she wouldn't cry anymore. Crying achieved nothing—unless it might sway Rothgar to mercy. Yes, she'd store up her tears for that.

"Up you get, miss," Maisie said, with a painful attempt at cheerfulness. "We're off within the hour. I'm mostly packed, and you need to eat breakfast. Your hot water's here. Oh, do come on, miss," she cried. "You *have* to."

Maisie had explained last night that a mouse had woken her by scuttling right by her face. Of course she'd screamed. Then she'd realized Damaris was missing and rushed out crying for help. And that nasty gun thing had gone off. She'd apologized long and often for it, in between berating Damaris for folly and predicting disasters of every sort. All of them Fitz's fault.

All of them possible, Damaris accepted as she climbed out of bed, but all that mattered was that Fitz be safe. She walked to the washstand, aware of changes in her body and soreness, but only longing to be with Fitz again.

She stripped, washed, and put on the shift that waited in front of the fire.

"How's your wound, miss?" Maisie asked.

Damaris had forgotten it, and she touched the spot. "Healing." Unlike the imaginary, bleeding one beneath.

"Sit and eat, miss. There's your chocolate just as you like it, and bread that was fresh yesterday. . . ."

Damaris's stomach rebelled, but she needed her strength. She drank some chocolate and ate a little bread, staring into the flames, trying to see a way out of this circle of fire.

She would run to the ends of the earth with Fitz, but even if they could escape Ashart and Rothgar, she knew he'd never agree. He would escort her to London and then submit to judgment.

And he probably hated her.

"Miss Damaris, come on! They'll be knocking for the luggage any moment now."

Damaris hurried into a warm blue gown. Maisie

pushed her into a seat and replaited her hair, then coiled it at the back and stuck pins in to hold it in place. If only life could be coiled back into order as simply. Then she remembered the trigger for last night, the excuse. Her will.

"Where's my writing desk?"

"In the big trunk, miss." Maisie put a three-cornered hat on top of Damaris's head and thrust another pin in to keep it in place. "You never want it now?"

Damaris pushed up and hurried over to the locked trunk. "I need paper. The key!"

Maisie dug it out of her pocket, complaining, but unlocked the padlock and threw back the lid. She pulled the wooden desk from under a top layer of clothes. Damaris took it to the table, opened it, pulled out a sheet of paper, and uncapped the small inkwell. She dipped the pen without trimming it, then paused, remembering Fitz trimming a pen for her with his very sharp knife that first morning, when he'd persuaded her to return to Rothgar Abbey.

The knife he'd used to cut off her clothing yesterday.

She'd dripped a blob of ink on the paper. She began to toss the sheet away, but what did an inkblot matter? She scribbled, trying to follow the form she remembered from her mother's will. She should have kept it simple, but she found herself listing the bequests she wanted to make, as if it might happen. As if she might die today.

She heard footsteps approaching.

"Here come the men for the luggage, miss. This is no time to be writing a letter!"

Someone knocked at the door. Damaris nodded, and Maisie went to open it. Two men came in, bobbing bows and going toward the trunk.

"Can either of you read and write?" Damaris asked.

The men had politely avoided looking at her, but now they did. One, a sturdy, grizzled man with bright blue eyes, said, "I can, miss."

"Your name?"

"Silas Brown, miss."

"Come here if you please, Mr. Brown. This is my will, which I've just written. I am about to sign it, then I want you to sign as witness."

The man nodded.

Damaris signed, then dipped the pen and passed it to him. He signed his name in a steady, strong script.

"Thank you. Maisie, you shall witness it, too."

Maisie looked alarmed, but she could read and write. She wiped her hands on her skirt, took the pen, and carefully wrote her full name, Maisie Duncott, below Silas Brown's.

Damaris let out a breath and even smiled. "Thank you both. Maisie, put away the desk again, please."

She gave the groom a crown for his service. As soon as the trunk was locked again, the men carried it away. The ink on the will was dry, so Damaris folded it, considering what to do with it. She didn't want to carry it herself in case something happened to her that could lose or destroy it.

She'd like to give it to Fitz, but they'd probably not let her close to him. It would have to be Ashart, which made her shudder.

"Are you ready now, then, miss?"

Damaris attempted a smile. "Yes, of course. Don't worry. I'm not turning mad. Once we're in London we can get this all straightened out."

"Aye, miss." But Maisie's expression was as doubtful as Damaris's thoughts. She helped Damaris into her cloak and handed her dark brown gloves. Damaris was as ready as she would ever be to face this day, so she left the room. At the sight of Fitz outside her door she stopped dead.

"Escort," he said impassively. "An attack between here and the coach is unlikely, but we'll take no chances."

She wanted to say many things, but it was as if he'd encased himself in ice. She'd expected it, but now it hurt like a bolt to the heart.

"Thank you." She held out the folded paper. "Please carry this."

He took it. "Your will?"

"Yes."

"Witnessed?"

"By Maisie and one of the grooms."

"Which one?"

"Silas Brown."

"One of Rothgar's men. He'll do." He put the paper in his jacket pocket and gestured for her to precede him through the arch.

Damaris hesitated, searching for something to say, something that might help. A raging fight might melt the ice, but she wondered if it wasn't the ice that was holding him together. She turned and walked the gauntlet of Trayce, Prease, and Stuart portraits, then down the stairs to where the others waited. When she joined them, Fitz stayed apart.

Damaris wondered if Lady Thalia knew. She must. She would have heard the trip wire go off.

A maid came in and curtsied. "All's ready, milord."

"We're leaving by the side door on the east," Ashart said. He seemed as calm as Fitz, and yet Damaris sensed fire beneath. Hot fury. She recognized that he felt responsible for her ruin, and there was nothing she could say that would ease things. "The coach can draw up closely there, and it's less exposed than the front."

They went quickly to where the coach waited. Six horses stood in the traces, stamping, breath white in the cold morning air. Damaris, Genova, and Lady

Thalia hurried inside their coach under Ashart's escort. Fitz kept his distance, but Damaris thought that now it was not so much ostracism as that he was alert for any sign of attack.

She would have taken the backward-facing seat, but Genova insisted. Fitz and Ashart mounted their horses, joining four other outriders, and they were off. Damaris wanted to get to London, where answers lay that could keep her safe, but she dreaded it, too.

What would her guardian, the Dark Marquess, do?

She wished she could talk it over with Genova, but Lady Thalia might not know everything. And anyway, she wasn't sure words existed for the pain and fear consuming her. She couldn't even watch Fitz. He rode on the opposite side of the coach and ahead, out of sight. On purpose, she knew.

She glanced at Lady Thalia, who had loved and lost. The old lady looked back, her eyes steady and in some way strengthening. But then those eyes widened and brightened. "Three-handed whist, dears?"

Damaris agreed. Anything to help this journey pass.

They stopped often for new horses, but never delayed. Just over three hours had passed, by Genova's heavy pocket watch, when rural hamlets came closer together, and much of the land beside the road was kitchen gardens. These provided vegetables for the crowded city.

Soon the road became busier, and even the groom's horn couldn't clear a way through packhorses, pedestrians, carts, and other vehicles. Damaris shrank back, seeing how easy it would be for someone to approach the coach and fire into it. Probably for that reason Ashart rode close on one side, Fitz on the other. She could see him at last, her hero, her lover, her despair.

Houses became larger and closer together, and then their horses' hooves clattered on cobbled streets past ranks of new, tall houses. The name of one, set in black bricks in paler stone, made her start: Rosemary Terrace.

That row was part of her inheritance. She'd never actually seen one of her properties before. It was such a peculiar notion that she stared, forgetting to be cautious.

"Do you know someone there?" Genova asked.

"No," Damaris said, sitting back. What good was enormous wealth if it wouldn't buy her what she wanted?

Not long after, they turned into a grand square. It was built around a railed garden with a pond. A woman and two children were throwing bread to noisily enthusiastic ducks by the water. Most of the houses around the square were in short terraces, but some were mansions. The carriage turned into a courtyard in front of the largest one.

They'd arrived at Malloren House, where Rothgar must be faced.

Damaris's knees weakened as she climbed out of the coach and went with the others into a wood-paneled hall. How unlike Cheynings. Here a fire blazed in the hearth and light shone in through a large fanlight over the door. Somewhere, potpourri carried memories of summer. On a table a bowl held crocuses, forced into early bloom. A promise of spring.

In what state would her life be by springtime?

A smiling housekeeper and cheery-looking maids and footmen stood ready, but Damaris was strung tight with apprehension, praying for a little time before she need face her guardian.

But then he emerged from the back of the house. "Welcome to Malloren House. Lady Arradale remains at the abbey to conclude our party there, but I came ahead to deal with these developments. Thank you for alerting me, Ashart. Ladies, you will want your rooms?"

For a moment Damaris thought Ashart had sent news of her disgrace, but she realized it would have been news of the documents. If Rothgar caught any hint of other disasters, he showed no sign of it. Damaris wanted to escape him, but she also wanted to take position by Fitz's side and defend him from all harm. She'd have done it if she didn't think it would make everything worse.

Cowardice or sense—she couldn't decide which— sent her upstairs with Genova and Lady Thalia. At the top of the stairs she looked back at Fitz, standing at elegant ease between two powerful men who could destroy him with a word.

He met her eyes and smiled. If he meant to reassure her, he failed.

Fitz permitted himself to watch Damaris until she disappeared. No point in discretion now. The omniscient one had to be skilled at reading expressions, and Ash was a walking growl. When she disappeared, Fritz turned back to the other two men, aware with detached numbness that he might never see her again. The most he could pray for was that his ability to protect people would buy him a few days' grace.

Rothgar indicated a corridor. "If you would come to my office?"

In the businesslike room, he said, "You have the papers, Ashart? May I see them?"

Ash gave him the pouch.

"Please be seated," Rothgar said, and settled behind his desk to read.

Ash flashed Fitz a searing glance, then sat, though he looked as if he'd rather pace the room. Perhaps the glance was a command that Fitz not dare to make himself at ease, but he preferred to stand anyway. It gave an illusion of being in control of his fate.

"So," Rothgar said, looking up, "there was a marriage." He folded the papers. "Lamentable."

"But of little importance, given the Act of Succession." Ash's voice was expressionless.

"Any element of doubt will distress His Majesty, and there's something in his nature that suffers from distress."

Fitz wondered what was coming.

"I think," Rothgar said, "that Prince Henry went through a sentimental form of wedding with Betty Crowley, but without witnesses. I could have such a document created, identical to these marriage lines, but with that small change." He looked at Ash. "It is for you to say, cousin."

Ash gave a sharp laugh. "You're a conniving devil. Oh, by all means. Whatever gets rid of this mess."

"Once that's arranged, the documents must be presented to the king, who will then reassure those who are anxious. It is yours to do."

"Thus showing that I willingly give over any claim."

"And ensuring His Majesty's kindness." He glanced at the clock. "I've requested a private audience with the king for four o'clock, if that is convenient."

"Better to get it over with," Ash said, rising. "I'd best go and alert Henri. He'll be in despair. A mere four hours. Hardly time to powder my hair." He hesitated. "There are other matters. . . ."

"About Damaris."

For a moment Fitz thought that Rothgar truly was omniscient; then he realized he spoke only of her safety.

"I should have anticipated her danger," Rothgar went on. "You did the right thing to bring her here. Ashart, I know you might prefer your own home, but the presence of you and Fitzroger here would add to Damaris's protection."

"I welcome the invitation. It's just possible that our grandmother is in residence." He briefly related the dowager's plans.

Rothgar's lips might have twitched. "Our gift to France," he murmured. But he added, "It might serve. She may well be happier away from her ghosts. As for Damaris, someone will arrive shortly with her father's will, which will reveal the enemy, who can then be dealt with."

"I will assist in any way I can." Ash hesitated, and Fitz braced himself. But then Ash flashed him a dark, complex look and left.

A reprieve, but a reprieve only. The loss of his friend's trust was an extra penance to endure.

"Your report," Rothgar demanded, and Fitz explained the events involving the papers.

"You appear to have broken your promise of secrecy. Into many fragments."

Fitz had forgotten that sin, and felt little patience with it now. "I needed Ashart's cooperation."

"But Lady Thalia?"

"I judge her more discreet than she might seem."

After a moment Rothgar nodded. "And if gossip starts now it will be harmless without proof." He flicked open an ivory-and-gold snuffbox and offered it to Fitz, who declined.

"So Ashart is safe now, my lord?"

"As soon as the king informs the others that he's no danger."

"Can you tell me now who wanted Ashart dead?"

Rothgar inhaled a pinch of snuff, considering him. "As long as you don't intend revenge. Bute and Cumberland."

The Earl of Bute, who'd been the king's mentor for years. And the Duke of Cumberland, the king's military uncle, the ruthless "Butcher" of Culloden and Fitz's unwanted patron.

Rothgar closed his snuffbox. "Cumberland proposed you as assassin."

The shock was a pain almost as deep as the loss of Damaris. "He thought I would do that?"

"He's not a man of subtle understanding. Now, your pay."

"I did nothing. Ashart was never attacked."

"Perhaps because you were on guard. Cumberland, at least, knows your talents." Rothgar unlocked a drawer and took out a piece of paper. "Is a bank draft convenient? I can give coin if you prefer."

Fitz glanced at the draft for a thousand guineas. This had once been his goal, his means of leaving England. Now it meant nothing. "Thank you, my lord."

"I hope you'll continue in my service for a little longer, for Damaris's sake."

"Of course, my lord. But I require no pay for that."

"You will work for love?"

Fitz glanced at the man, but risked no reply.

"She must keep to the house for now," Rothgar went on. "You will be her protection, inside and out. But you'll have to leave at some point to increase your wardrobe. She could be commanded to court at any moment, and you must accompany her."

Fitz had hoped to avoid this subject. "I doubt I'd be admitted."

"My dear Fitzroger, if the king barred any whom scandal touched, he'd have a thin court."

"It's rather more than a touch, my lord."

"His Majesty has a high opinion of you from Cumberland, which is why you were chosen to protect Ashart. We can use this to your advantage. Given your part in retrieving these documents, he may be persuaded to let some details of your service over the years be made public. I will present you at the first levee, unless Ashart wishes to. You are at odds?"

The shocking notion of being presented at court—key to social acceptability—made Fitz unable to deal with the abrupt question. Pointless to say no, but if he said yes, how could he explain?

Rothgar seemed to accept silence, or to learn from it what he wanted. He took a leather pouch out of the drawer. "We will bypass the subtleties of Sheba's," he said, tossing it to Fitz. "That's for expenses, not pay, but I still recommend Pargeter's for instant results."

Fitz caught the money, his brain still numb. He didn't want to go to court. He didn't want to mix in society at all, even if he was tolerated. Behind the tolerance lay snubs, and at all costs he must avoid Hugh.

"I'd rather set about catching the villain, my lord."

"Until we know who the heir is, we must wait, and even then he may not be easily found."

Fitz remembered the paper in his pocket. "Damaris made a will this morning, so the heir has nothing to gain now."

Rothgar's brows rose. "Your idea?"

"Entirely her own." How irritating to be a clever woman and have people always assume a man thought for her.

"Who, then, is her new heir?"

"She didn't say." Fitz wasn't going to give the document to Rothgar to read without Damaris's permission. "Her chief urgency was to ensure that if the assassin succeeded, he wouldn't gain by it."

"A remarkable young woman. I'm unsure whether to hustle her into the safety of marriage as soon as possible, or dissuade her in order to see what she can become as a woman alone. Do you have any opinion?"

"I, my lord?" Fitz was instantly on guard.

"You've been in close confinement with her for days," Rothgar said, watching him.

Fitz knew he was being played with, but he fought back as well as he could. "I have a high regard for Miss Myddleton. She has courage and intelligence, but she lacks worldly knowledge as yet."

Except what she'd gained in his bed.

"Given her upbringing, she's a marvel. So should she marry?"

"Why not?"

"The right husband is essential."

"She has the Duke of Bridgewater in her eye."

Rothgar's brows rose. "A suitable choice. Your brother is in town."

The switch of topic was a type of attack, and this was bad news. "I'd hoped he would stay in the country for the winter."

"He's been here over Christmastide, making his violent intentions toward you clear. As you'll accompany Damaris on any excursions, I hope you can avoid embarrassing incidents."

"I always do my best, my lord."

"And I always expect perfection."

"I'm not your servant." Fitz hadn't meant to issue the flat challenge, but it was done now.

"I expect perfection of my protégés as well."

Fitz stepped back before he could help himself. "Protégé, my lord?"

"You are a man of many and excellent talents—"

"For God's sake! If you review my recent career you'll see a catalog of disasters. Genova would have died without Damaris's skills, and only the hand of God saved Damaris herself from that crossbow. Add to that, I missed an attack on her in Pickmanwell."

Had anyone ever shouted in this room before? Perhaps, Fitz thought, he was begging for a speedy execution.

Rothgar seemed hardly to notice. "You are hard on yourself, which I hold to be a sign of character. I find you admirable in many respects, Fitzroger. More to the point, you could be of use to me, and thus to England. I understand that you plan to go to the colonies. I think that inadvisable for many reasons."

Fitz was breathing deeply and found it hard to speak. "Nevertheless, my lord, that is my intention. I will leave as soon as Miss Myddleton is safe."

His throat ached with another wild grief. First Ash, and now Rothgar offered him opportunities he'd once have bled for. With Ash it would be the building of a marquisate. With Rothgar it could be the building of a nation.

But if he stayed, even if his reputation could be made at least tolerable, Hugh would hound him to the gates of hell, and one of them would have to kill the other.

"Think on it," Rothgar said, as if unaware of his distress. At a tap on the door he said, "Enter."

A footman stepped in. "Miss Myddleton's legal gentleman is here, milord."

Rothgar walked to the door. "Accompany me, Fitzroger."

Fitz wanted time in a quiet place to recover, but he tucked the pouch of money in his pocket and obeyed.

A middle-aged gentleman awaited them in one of the reception rooms. Mr. Dinwiddie looked awed by the company in which he found himself. His sober brown suit was proper, but Fitz guessed he'd paid careful attention to his snowy stockings, well-polished shoes, and powdered wig. The lawyer bowed almost in half, but Rothgar soon had him seated and talking of impersonal legal matters.

Fitz elected to stand, in part because he could take a position behind Rothgar. He had himself in hand, but he'd lay no bets on being able to hide all reaction when Damaris entered.

He was right. When she walked into the room the

air turned thinner, his heart pounded, and he was sure his longing marked his face even though he looked away after the slightest bow.

One glance was enough. She was in pale blue again, which made her look cold and severe. Her gown was elegant, however, with skirts spread wide over hoops and a bodice cut low in the neck. Precious lace foamed at her elbows and frilled over the swelling tops of her breasts.

Her lovely breasts . . .

At least she had a sensible warm shawl draped around her shoulders, the golden russety one that brought out the creamy tones of her skin.

He realized he was staring at her after all, and that Rothgar had risen, so might have seen his expression. But Rothgar almost certainly knew how he felt.

As she sat, Damaris looked a question at him. *What? Ah, yes.* Had Ash told Rothgar? He shook his head slightly.

She smiled and said, "My will, Fitzroger?"

He gave it to her. She thanked him and turned to her trustee.

"If you wish to talk to Mr. Dinwiddie alone," Rothgar said, "it shall be so."

"No, of course not, my lord."

"Fitzroger came here to ensure your safety, but I'm sure he'll now agree that Mr. Dinwiddie offers no serious threat."

The lawyer chuckled as if at a grand joke, but Fitz knew it hadn't been. Rothgar was taking no risks.

"As you say, my lord." He bowed and left.

Chapter 19

Damaris managed not to turn and watch Fitz leave, but she would much rather have had him stay. Dangerous and distracting though he was, she felt she could do anything when he was by her side.

So Ashart hadn't yet told his cousin what had happened? She wondered if he'd changed his mind. It would be a blessing, but seemed unlikely.

Mr. Dinwiddie cleared his throat. "May I say what a pleasure it is to meet you again, Miss Myddleton, and to see you in such fine appearance."

"Thank you, Mr. Dinwiddie."

"And in such excellent care," the man went on, with an unctuous bow at the marquess. Damaris realized that she'd changed in that way, too. She respected and to some extent feared the Marquess of Rothgar, but she no longer saw him as a godly being.

"The marquess is all that is kind," she said. "Now, Mr. Dinwiddie, I have some questions for you."

He beamed. "I will be delighted to serve you in any way." He produced a pouch of papers. "I have your father's will here. What is it that you wish to know, my dear?"

Damaris kept her smile. "I wish to read the document for myself."

"I assure you, my dear, that we have conveyed in

simple language all that significantly affects you. However, if you would be so good as to say what other parts stir your curiosity, I will be honored to explain them."

Damaris was tempted to appeal to Rothgar, but instead she held out her hand. "Thank you, sir, but I wish to read it for myself."

Dinwiddie did appeal to the marquess. "My lord, it is a somewhat challenging document for a lady."

"All the same," Damaris said, before Rothgar could intervene, "I wish to attempt it."

The lawyer looked to Rothgar again for help, but then reluctantly rose and gave her the pouch. What, did he expect her to shred it for amusement?

Damaris took out the thick bundle of papers, determined now to read every word. She skimmed through the usual preambles, then paused over the precise wording of the division of her father's empire in the East. There'd been no names in the simplified version sent to her .

After glancing it over, she read aloud: " 'To my faithful lieutenants Johan Bose in Canton, Pierre Malashe in Cambaye, Joshua Hind in Mocha, and Amal Smith in Cochinchina, I leave the merchant houses they have managed for me, free and entire with all goods, chattels, and cash in hand, on condition that one-fifth of the quarterly profit, honestly accounted, be sent speedily to England for the benefit of my daughter, Damaris, of Birch House, Worksop, as long as she may live. Upon her death, this obligation ends. It may not be transferred by her to another by any will or contract.' "

She almost drew attention to the possible villains, but realized her trustee didn't know of the attacks. Instead she glanced meaningfully at Rothgar, and he nodded. "Read on."

She skimmed the next section, commenting, "Sums

to various people in England, presumably men who
managed Father's affairs here. I don't think he could
have had close friends when he returned so rarely."

She'd glanced at Mr. Dinwiddie out of courtesy, but
he cleared his throat. "More than rarely, Miss
Myddleton."

"Only three times that I remember."

He glanced between her and Rothgar anxiously.
"I . . . er, fear that he did not always visit Worksop."

Damaris looked down at her father's will. No wonder her mother had been vitriolic. Not only had Marcus Myddleton abandoned her within months of
marriage, but he hadn't bothered to visit her and his
daughter during most of his visits to England. Doubtless he'd preferred his London mistress, the swine.

She silently read the next two pages that outlined
her inheritance, wondering why he'd left her anything
at all. Guilty conscience? She didn't believe it. If she
ever did discover his reasons, she was sure she'd find
them unpleasant.

Ah, the succession. At last.

She read it aloud. " 'If my principal heir, my daughter, Damaris, dies before she comes of age, or
intestate"—she skimmed some legal flourishes—"her
inheritance by this will passes to my son, Marcus
Aaron Butler. . . .' " She looked at the lawyer. "His
son?"

Mr. Dinwiddie colored a little. "A youthful indiscre-
tion, Miss Myddleton."

She supposed it was surprising that there was only
one bastard, but then the word *youthful* sank home.
"How old is he?"

"Around twenty-five, I believe."

So at least he'd been born years before her parents'
marriage. Her mother had been spared that. But how
strange to have a brother she knew nothing of. Except,
she realized, that he might be trying to kill her.

She looked back to the paper and found her place.

" '. . . to my son, Marcus Aaron Butler, sometimes called Mark Myddleton, son of Rosemary Butler, born in Oxted, Surrey, sometimes called Rose Myddleton."

Rosemary! And he'd owned Rosemary Terrace.

Rothgar said, "Miss Myddleton wishes to know more about her heir."

But before the lawyer could respond, Damaris said, "This Marcus Butler was left nothing? How could my father be so heartless?"

"No, no," Mr. Dinwiddie said. "Separate provision was made both for his mother and for him before your father's demise. Annuities and trusts. What's more, the annuity his mother enjoyed in her lifetime passed to him upon her death not long ago. He is a very comfortably situated young man."

"When did his mother die?" Rothgar demanded.

If the lawyer had dog's ears, they would have pricked. "Late November, I believe, my lord. It is of importance?"

"Does the gentleman know he is Miss Myddleton's heir?"

"I don't know, my lord, but a will, once probated, is a public document." He had clearly come to some conclusions, for he added, "May I suggest, Miss Myddleton, that you make a will of your own as soon as possible?"

She showed him the paper in her hand. "I have already done so, sir, but now, if you have time, I would like to prepare a more formal one."

"Of course." He came over to take the document, then sat to read it, his bushy brows flicking up and down a few times. She prayed he wouldn't read it aloud. She wasn't ashamed of what she'd done, but she needed no extra problems now.

"Brief and not quite in correct form, but it would serve before the courts; indeed it would."

Rothgar rose. "I will begin a search for Mr. Butler Myddleton."

Damaris looked up at him. "You should start with a row of houses called Rosemary Terrace, my lord. I own it. We passed it on the way here."

"Indeed."

"And is there a way for news that I have made my will to be rapidly spread, my lord?"

He looked thoughtful, then smiled. "There is a broadsheet published every afternoon to spread the day's gossip about society. Which, of course, makes it popular in all quarters. The *Town Crier* will print anything for pay, but the item will attract more attention if it startles. Would you have any objection to giving some startlingly large amounts to charities that are also beneficiaries of your will?"

"None at all," she said, smiling back at him. "To hospitals. I assume my trustees will approve."

Mr. Dinwiddie looked a little distressed by rash expenditures, but he nodded. "Of course, Miss Myddleton."

"I will arrange all," Rothgar said. "Summon me if you require assistance or advice, Damaris."

When he'd left, Mr. Dinwiddie looked at her hastily drawn will again. "Fifty thousand guineas to Mr. Fitzroger, my dear?"

Damaris tried not to blush. "If I'd died on the way here, why shouldn't he have some money?"

"I gather that he is in some way responsible for your safety. If you'd died on the way here, therefore, he would hardly deserve such high reward. Another fifty thousand to Miss Genova Smith?"

"A friend."

"An annuity of a hundred pounds a year to your maid, Maisie Duncott. A handsome amount."

"A teaspoonful out of the whole. Please don't quibble, Mr. Dinwiddie. It is, after all, my will."

"The remainder to the Marquess of Rothgar to be used for charitable works? Ah, well, I suppose his shoulders are broad enough."

A footman entered then with a portable desk, and Mr. Dinwiddie gestured Damaris to a chair by the table. "Let us design the document you wish."

Damaris suddenly had no patience for it. She wanted to talk to Fitz, to find out what Ashart was going to do. She wanted to talk to him about this brother, and her father, and the mysterious Rosemary, who must be the mistress who had so enraged her mother. She simply wanted to talk to Fitz, and it seemed that for now no one would prevent it.

"Please put that will into better legal form, sir. I intend to marry soon, so it will all have to be done again. Send for me when it's ready."

She left expecting to have to hunt down Fitz, but he was in the hall. Of course. On guard. And looking distant.

"Woof," she said in an attempt at humor, and was rewarded by the flicker of a wry smile. Where could they talk? A footman stood nearby. "Will you help me with a task?" she asked.

"What task?"

The stark question stung, but she persisted. "We can take Maisie if you want a chaperon. When my mother died, I found a locked chest under her bed. A rough sea chest, but with no sign of a key. I was hurried off to Thornfield Hall before I could decide what to do about it, and I didn't know it traveled there with me. Lord Henry must have stored it away. Now he's sent all my possessions here, including that. I feel I should open it, but it frightens me."

He came alert. "You suspect some trap?"

"Nothing physical." She glanced meaningfully at the footman. "Come into the reception room for a moment."

She headed across the hall, praying that he would follow.

He did, but he stayed by the open door. She walked over and shut it. "This is private. I have a half brother, and he's my heir."

"I know. Rothgar told me a moment ago."

She searched his face. "He still trusts you? Ashart didn't tell him?"

"Ashart didn't tell him. I suspect because he didn't want to deprive you of my protection. Not that I've been of much use."

She put a hand on his sleeve. "Yes, you have."

He gently detached himself and began to open the door.

"Don't! I'll be good."

He didn't release the handle, but he didn't push it down.

"I have so many problems swirling in my head!" she said. "I don't want the villain to be my brother."

"Who else?"

"Those foreign heirs who have to send me a fifth of their profit every year."

"That burden's lain on them for years. Why the sudden action? This Marcus Butler's mother died only weeks ago. It's possible he didn't know the full story till then."

She turned away, pulling her shawl closer. The fire was small and only took the chill off the room. "But he's my brother. My only relative."

"Brothers aren't always a blessing. For God's sake, Damaris, what do you want me to do? Leave him to kill you?"

She turned back. "No. But Rothgar's spreading the news about my will. Once my brother knows my death will gain him nothing, there's an end of it, isn't it? I can't bring about a brother's death, Fitz—any more than you can."

"I'd kill Hugh if he threatened you." He looked at her, fire in his eyes. "Need I remind you that this precious brother of yours could have achieved his purpose but for a freakish chance? You could be *dead*, Damaris. He has to die."

"I wish you'd stop talking about killing as if it's nothing to you!"

"It's not nothing, but I've killed and I see its purposes."

"Revenge? That's base."

"Extermination."

She put a hand to her throat. "Dear God. May I forbid it?"

He inhaled, eyes closed for a moment. "You know you may command and forbid me anything."

It was like an opened door, one she longed to rush through so she could command him to flee with her to safety, but she couldn't. He'd opened it trusting that she wouldn't take that sort of advantage.

"Then I forbid killing or significantly hurting my brother unless he attacks me again."

He bowed. "It shall be as you wish. Now, the chest?"

He turned again to the door.

"Wait! I need to say something else. It is important in this context, Fitz."

He turned back, but leaned against the door, almost as if his legs had weakened.

"Oh, love, let's go." She walked toward him.

"No. Say what you need to say."

"It's nothing after all. Merely . . . I thought my father returned to England only three times in my lifetime, but apparently he returned on other occasions and didn't bother to visit his wife and child."

"You can't have harbored the illusion that he was fond."

"I must have, to feel like this."

"Then perhaps he was."

She shook her head. "He made a fuss of me when he visited, but he didn't truly care. I see that now. He simply tormented my mother by stealing my affections. Then as soon as he left, he forgot about me."

He straightened. "Damaris, we spoke of imagining ourselves the center of every situation. Your father was a man with a business empire that must have demanded every waking moment. I'm sure he did neglect you, but I doubt he had time for such a petty war."

She shook her head. "No, I know him. I know him with the tainted blood that runs through my veins. He would do that. He'd use any weapon to hand to win the war, and it was war. I don't understand it, but it was."

She paced away from him and back again. "I'm afraid of my heritage, Fitz. I think he and my mother were closer in their natures than it appeared. He had little time to spend on obsessive dislike, and she had time for nothing else. I know why she hated him, but why did he hate her? He won. He had everything. I dread what's in that chest."

"Then leave it to me. I'll check through it and let you know."

"No, I need to do it."

"Very well." He opened the door and stood back for her to go through.

As she came close, she asked, "Shall I summon Maisie?"

"I believe we are strong enough. Where is it?"

His words put a bond on her, as if she'd made a promise. If perfect behavior was the price of his company, she'd pay it.

"It's in a box room," she said, and walked past him.

But he said, "Damaris."

She paused.

"Consider that you may have the best of your parents rather than the worst. Any quality can be both good and bad."

"Obsession?"

"The ability to focus on a target."

"As I did with Ashart," she said. *As I am now with you.* "What of spite?"

He shook his head. "As best I know, your father was brave, inventive, hardworking, and able to attract excellent, willing service. Your mother I know little of, and she probably was warped by his callous treatment, but I suspect that somewhere you'd find a practical, resourceful woman."

"Then why couldn't she put aside her mistake and make a new life from the fragments?"

He smiled. "There speaks your father, but your mother had a more passionate, less pragmatic heart." Softly he added, "As do you."

She smiled sadly. "It's a perilous gift."

She led the way up to the small room where the plain wooden chest sat amongst other boxes and trunks. Damaris wrinkled her nose. "I recognize that smell. My mother's bedroom smelled like that."

"Because she kept the chest under her bed." Fitz put the branch of candles he'd brought on a pile of boxes, then opened the small window. "At least the stink doesn't suggest a corpse."

"Lud! Don't even suggest it."

"General rot, I'd say, with an overlay of spices and perfume. Let's see these wonders of the Orient. Do you have the key?"

"No. I'm not sure where it is."

He knelt and applied his lock picks. Damaris leaned against the closed door, allowing herself to admire his graceful movements and steady concentration. She was on her way to solving the problem of her safety, but what use was life without him?

He unlocked it, then rose. "Do you want the honor?"

She walked forward. "This little courage I believe I have."

She tugged, but the lid was stuck. He lent his hand to her, perhaps before he thought that touch was unwise. As soon as the lid jerked up, he stepped back. At the smell, she retreated, too.

"What a mess!" She moved closer again to gingerly pick up embroidered white silk that was hopelessly stained by a lump of gray stuff sticking to it. She let go of the silk and brought her fingers to her nose to sniff. "Ambergris. From the belly of a whale and used to make perfumes. Precious in small amounts, but vile in excess."

"Like some people I know."

It was a joke, and she looked up at him in startled pleasure. It didn't change anything, but it was wondrous.

"Perhaps we should do this outdoors," she said.

"Too dangerous. Don't wipe your fingers on your skirts." He passed her his handkerchief. "Why put ambergris on precious silk? Your mother was so careless?"

"She was the antithesis of careless. No, I suspect this chest is a careful testament to hate." She pulled the silk out of the way to reveal shattered, once-lovely vials and a wash of colored stains.

A thin wooden box poked up at one side. She pulled it out and realized it was a portfolio. When she untied silk cords, she found Oriental drawings, each ripped into quarters.

"And then she carefully put them away." Damaris dropped the portfolio back into the trunk. "She was mad, and she was my mother."

He put an arm around her and drew her close. She felt in his body the moment when he realized he shouldn't do it, but he didn't push her away.

"She was deeply hurt," he said, rubbing her back.

"Anyone can become overwrought when deeply hurt."

Was he thinking of his brother?

She drew in strength from his tenderness, strength enough to draw back, to separate. "He sent these things to hurt her. As an insult, a reminder that his world was the Orient, not Worksop. She hit back by destroying them. But why keep them? Why live with the stink?"

She answered herself. "Dear heaven, so she would remember. So she would never heal. And perhaps because she hoped that one day he'd know what she'd done with them! She must have expected to die first, for she went wild when we received news of his death. I couldn't understand why. I assumed she must have loved him after all. But it was because he'd escaped her one last, absolute time. She was mad, mad!"

He cradled her face. "Don't, love. They worked out their spite on each other. Let it die with them." She thought he might kiss her, and prayed for it, but he stepped away and closed the chest. "Let me get rid of it."

His suggestion was sensible, but she rebelled. "No. Perhaps there's something that can be rescued."

His look was skeptical, but he opened the chest again.

She leaned forward and pulled up another layer of cloth—a stiff and rich garment of some kind, stained and stinking—but all she found beneath was a mess of crushed scrolls, shattered figurines, and more broken vials. "And it can only be worse below."

She straightened and pulled on a golden cord that trailed out at one side. A gilded leather pouch came free. The leather was stained, but when she opened it the contents seemed unspoiled.

"Documents." She stepped back to empty the papers onto a flat surface. She unfolded one and read it.

"A copy of a letter she sent him. The same old complaints of abandonment and cruelty. What was the point?"

"She couldn't let go of a bone, no matter how bitter it tasted."

She looked at him. "As I was with Ashart."

"He's hardly bitter to any woman's taste."

"He's not to my taste anymore." She didn't want to distress him, so she opened another letter. "More of the same. Why?"

He took it from her. "Dwelling on these things is another sort of poison. Sometimes people's actions make no sense, and fretting over them is destructive. Let me check through this chest for you."

"Thank you," she said, but she gathered the papers back into the pouch.

"You should let me dispose of those, too. If you preserve them, you'll preserve what they represent."

"I won't. But I feel I should at least glance at them before burning them."

They emerged from the room to almost collide with a footman.

"Your lawyer asks for you, Miss Myddleton."

"Thank you." When the man left, Damaris turned to Fitz. "Am I presentable?"

He smiled. "Not for court, perhaps, but adequate for lawyers."

Another little joke. She returned his handkerchief, unable to stop herself from saying something she shouldn't. "I love you, Fitz. Whatever becomes of all this, I do. That is a treasure of itself, and I'll not let it spoil."

"But precious oil can ruin silk. Some combinations aren't meant to be." He touched her cheek. "Hearts don't truly break, Damaris. They crack a little, but in time they heal. Like chilblains."

She groaned at that descent to the mundane and

hurried away. Despite humor there was no joy in her cracked heart. She could fight everyone else in the world, but how could she fight him, the strongest person she'd ever known?

As she approached the reception room she realized she still clutched the bag, and it carried the curdled aroma of ambergris and spices. She gave it to a statuelike footman to take to her bedchamber.

In the room she found her will ready to sign. Rothgar was there, along with two men who looked like upper servants. She read through the document and signed it; then the men witnessed her signature. In theory she was now safe, but that depended upon her half brother's hearing about the will.

And being sane enough to accept that he'd lost.

When Mr. Dinwiddie and the witnesses left, she asked Rothgar, "Is there any word yet about my brother?"

"You were correct that his mother and he lived in Rosemary Terrace. Under the name Myddleton. He left there after her death, however, and sold the house. I haven't yet discovered his new home. When we do, I doubt he'll be conveniently waiting for us."

"How could he hope to get away with this?"

"If your death had looked accidental, all would have been well. The crossbow attack is more curious. I suspect he'll have an alibi."

"Meaning only that he has someone else do the work. The drink in Pickmanwell was probably the work of a man with crooked teeth. Do we know if my brother looks like that?"

"No. He's stocky, robust, and dark, with straight, even teeth."

"That sounds like my father, which is only natural." She looked up at the marquess. "Fitzroger wants to kill him."

"A natural instinct. As it stands, alas, it would be

murder. There are ways of dealing with such people short of that."

She shivered. "It may not really be his fault. It's my father's blood running in us. What we want, we grasp, no matter what or who stands in the way."

"Yet I don't believe that you'd kill for gold, especially if you already possessed enough for comfort."

"No."

"To do so is evil, Damaris. Life is not sacred. If it were we would not execute criminals or wage war. But a life is worth more than gold. It is always worth more than gold." He considered her. "You've left Fitzroger a substantial sum."

The sudden switch of subject was a trick of his, but she was learning. "I don't think I gave you permission to read my will, Lord Rothgar."

"True, but it seemed important to know whom to watch next."

"Not Fitz." His brow rose slightly, but she didn't fluster over the nickname. "And not Maisie or Genova, either. Should I watch you, my lord?"

He smiled. "Always, but I won't slip poison into your wine to gain a burden like that."

She lost patience with subtleties and fencing. "My lord, is Fitzroger's scandal as dire as he thinks?"

He studied her. "He was caught in flagrante delicto with his brother's wife. In a subsequent brawl, his brother received a blow to the head that left him subject to unpredictable rages."

"He was fifteen, and she must have been much older."

"Twenty-five, I believe."

"Doesn't that exonerate him somewhat?"

"My dear, we hang fifteen-year-olds for stealing bread. Many think it wise to cut off such poisonous shoots young."

"Fitz's army career argues that he's no poisonous shoot."

"To many he remains a dubious plant."

Did the fact that he was discussing this mean he didn't dismiss the possibility of a marriage? Or that it was unthinkable?

"Why is he still dubious?" she asked. "He's clearly highly trusted in some quarters."

He led her to a chair, and when they were both seated he said, "Five years ago he was taken away from his regiment to serve as flunky to generals and diplomats. Few know that he was a talented bodyguard who saved many lives. Sometimes diplomacy requires that defense and even attacks be kept secret. The effect, however, was that some thought he had contrived a life of ease away from the battlefield."

"That's horribly unfair."

"Undoubtedly. Do you want him?"

She'd expected the question sooner or later, but it still stole her breath.

"Yes," she said eventually. "But he thinks he's unworthy of me because of that scandal. No, I think it's more because of the injury to his brother. The headaches, the insane rages. How do I solve all this?"

"So wrens make play where eagles dare not perch," he said. "Facts cannot be changed."

"No?" She suspected he changed them whenever it suited him.

Perhaps his lips twitched. "His brother reannounces them at every opportunity, and Fitzroger has never denied them."

"What's the truth of his sister-in-law's death?"

"In her guilt and shame she threw herself down a stairwell."

"Or was pushed."

"Or was pushed. But Lady Leyden told the world

that her son was asleep at the time, drugged to deal with one of his violent headaches, which of course are a consequence of Fitzroger's brutality."

"Oh, sweet heaven." She remembered what Fitz had said. "She lost too many children and feared to lose another. Even though he's a monster."

"Does a mother ever recognize a monstrous child?"

"Don't mothers usually dote on the youngest?" Damaris protested, but then she sighed. "The poor woman endured so many years of birth and loss. Perhaps she lost the ability to grow fond of them, but clung to the one who seemed strong and likely to survive." She looked directly at him. "Why did you send me to Cheynings with Fitzroger?"

"It served a purpose," he said, but then smiled a little. "You're correct. I was playing with your lives. An addiction of mine. I wished to see what would happen between you because I see possibilities."

"You *wish* us to marry, my lord?"

"Only if it is for the best." He rose. "Once you're safe, we'll consider the matter further."

She shot to her feet, intensely frustrated. "But as soon as I'm safe, he'll leave."

Or, she remembered, Ashart would reveal their sin. Might that change Rothgar's mind?

He'd once condemned seduction, and she suspected that no matter what she confessed, he'd be like Ashart. He'd hold Fitz responsible. He'd wash his hands of him. Or worse.

"I love Fitzroger," she said directly, giving Fitz the only protection she could think of. "I intend to marry him no matter what you say. Thus I must keep him safe."

"Regrettably, my dear, none of us has perfect powers of protection."

A sweet bell sounded out in the hall.

"We are summoned to dinner," he said, opening

the door and offering her his hand. Anticipating her objection, he said, "It is wise to eat when we need to be strong."

The meal was made bearable by Lady Thalia's chatter and Genova's gallant assistance. Damaris managed to force down some of the delicious food and even to join in the conversation now and then. Ashart was thoughtful, and Fitz so distant it was as if he were pretending he wasn't there at all.

After the meal, Rothgar and Ashart went to prepare for court while the ladies took tea. Fitzroger didn't join them.

The two marquesses came to the drawing room before leaving, and Damaris couldn't help but be impressed. She'd seen both men in grandeur for Christmas Day at Rothgar Abbey when Ashart had worn his pale gold suit with the diamond buttons. Now, for a private audience, their appearance was less ostentatious, but no less potent.

Ashart's hair had already been powdered at dinner, but Rothgar's hadn't. He had to be wearing a wig, but it was skillfully made. His suit was of dark gray, richly embroidered in black and silver with touches of gold to catch the light. There might be tiny diamonds, too. He shimmered and an order glittered on his chest.

Ashart wore deep brown worked with red and gold. Rubies flared in the lace at his throat and in his ear, where he always wore an earring, but rarely a jewel.

Both men wore dress swords, and these, too, were jeweled works of art. Damaris suspected they were no less deadly for that, but their coming battle would not be fought with steel.

Everyone assumed that the king would be grateful, but history told her that kings were temperamental and unpredictable. For Genova's sake, Damaris prayed that all would go as planned.

Chapter 20

When Ashart and Rothgar left, Fitz disappeared as well. The three ladies played casino, hiding their tension with wild choices and discards, but revealing it with constant glances at the clock.

Over two hours passed, but then the courtiers returned.

Ashart was inclined to make light of their enterprise, but all had gone well. The king was delighted to have the mystery solved, and to his liking. He was clearly disposed to welcome Ashart back at court and even shower him with favors.

A relieved and joyful mood took over, and Damaris wished Fitz were here to celebrate with them.

But then Rothgar said, "There is one challenging development. The king wishes to inspect Ashart's bride. You are commanded to attend the drawing room tomorrow, Genova."

Genova went pale and clutched Ashart's hand. "I'm not ready!" Then, like someone seeing salvation, she added, "I don't have a court dress yet, so I can't go."

Rothgar dismissed that. "There are court gowns here belonging to my sister Elf and to Chastity, my brother Cyn's wife. Both ladies are close in size to you. Seamstresses can make alterations and even retrim them if you wish."

"Overnight?"

"But of course." He gestured as if it were nothing. "I will arrange to have them displayed for your selection."

"But I don't know what's suitable!"

Ashart kissed her hand. "I delight to see you flustered, Genni. If you will allow me to advise you?"

"Oh, indeed I will."

Rothgar turned to Damaris. "You, too, need a gown, and you should wear your rubies."

She started. "I? Why? This is nothing to do with me."

"You are a center of attention yourself. London already buzzes of the great heiress who has so much money that she not only makes hospitals the beneficiaries of her will but she gives money immediately to set up three more. That plus a rumor of your singing means that you, too, are to attend. You are to perform."

"But I haven't been able to practice properly in an age."

"I'm sure your voice will please. Where's Fitzroger?" Rothgar rang a bell. When a footman entered, he sent the man to find Fitz.

But the footman said, "He's close by, milord," and Fitz came in. He'd been outside on guard, and now, though he almost appeared bored, Damaris saw that he was braced for disaster.

"Make haste to equip yourself, Fitzroger," Rothgar said. "You are to attend court, too."

Damaris saw a flicker of something that might be panic. "Why, my lord?"

"To protect Damaris, of course. Her half brother may not hear the news in time."

"I doubt he has the entrée," Fitz said.

"Any suitably dressed gentleman has the entrée."

"Pargeter's will be closed."

It was like another fencing match, and Fitz was on the defensive.

"I'm sure you know how to open such doors."

For a moment Damaris thought Rothgar spoke of lock picks, but then she realized he meant money. He must have given some to Fitz.

If Fitz preferred not to go, however, he shouldn't.

"Surely I will be safe, my lord," she said.

"There is never certainty. And the king wishes Fitzroger to attend."

A coup de grâce that ended the bout.

Damaris went to Fitz's side, hoping to ease his tension. "What is Pargeter's?"

"A secondhand clothing shop of the grander sort."

Secondhand. She hated that, but she couldn't object. Yet . . . "I wish I could come. You'll buy something plain."

He smiled wryly. "I know the ways of court, Damaris. I assure you, I will glitter."

She watched him leave, then waited with Genova and Lady Thalia for Ashart to change out of his finery and for the gowns to be brought out from wherever they were stored. Soon the group was all taken to an unused bedchamber, where four absurdly elaborate and completely gorgeous confections stood on stands almost as if a headless lady were still inside each.

Lady Thalia sat to observe, Ashart standing by her side. Damaris and Genova circled them all—a cream trimmed with pale pink; a dull yellow with gold; a pale green; and a beige rioting with embroidered flowers. Damaris thought the last one breathtakingly beautiful, but she gave Genova first choice. She had to pick that one. All the others were terrible colors for her.

Genova looked to Ashart. "I don't know. You choose."

"The cream," he said, just as a seamstress arrived in a rush along with three assistants.

Damaris almost gasped a protest. He should know best, but pink and cream would make Genova look like garish pottery.

"Rip off the pink and replace it with blue," he told the seamstress. "Not a pale blue. Summer-sky blue. Ribbons and stitchery in shades of blue. White blossoms and pearls. Some silver thread to catch the candlelight."

He went, without apparent embarrassment, to inspect underlayers and accessories that were spread on the bed. He picked up a shift. "This one. Very pretty lace. And these silk stockings." He added a pair embroidered with flowers.

"I have my own stockings," Genova protested.

"Plain, I'm sure, but if you wish." He tossed them back. "There'll be no flashing an ankle at this event." He turned to Damaris. "Do you want advice, too?"

He was cool, but his anger had either faded or was very well cloaked.

"I admire the embroidered one. Will it do?"

He considered it. "With rubies? Yes. Certainly the other two are impossible. I'll leave you to your fittings, ladies. Tomorrow you'll need to practice maneuvering with court hoops."

He went to the door. Damaris had to know. She followed him and quietly asked, "Are you going to tell Rothgar?"

His look was somber. "I don't know."

After an hour of fitting, Damaris and Genova were set to court practice by Lady Thalia. Endlessly, it seemed, they sank into the deep court curtsy and practiced backing away from the royal presence without tripping over their own skirts.

Damaris had been trained in these things at Thornfield Hall, but that left her time to fret about having to sing and about why Fitz had been commanded to attend.

Lady Thalia soon agreed that Damaris would pass, so she was allowed to leave. She found the music room and settled to vocal exercises. All the same, her mind would not calm.

Was the king's summoning of Fitz good news or bad?

In a just world the king would be grateful to him, but the world was frequently unfair. She worried he'd be shunned by the court. If the king acknowledged him, however, then it might help. No matter how they felt, people would hesitate to be openly rude.

She emerged from her practice looking forward to a peaceful evening, but discovered that Rothgar had invited a small company for cards, music, and supper.

When she tried to excuse herself, Rothgar insisted she attend. "It will create allies for you. People you'll meet tomorrow at the drawing room. Allies for you and Fitzroger."

That persuaded her, so she dressed in finery and joined her first London gathering. Fitzroger was there, dressed in a dusky-blue satin suit that seemed neatly placed between his usual plainness and the glitter all around.

She thought he looked wonderful, but she still wanted to see him in brilliance.

She was introduced to so many people that her head was whirling, but all seemed to be going well when the Duke of Bridgewater was announced. She flashed a look at Rothgar. Coincidence? She doubted it.

Had she misjudged everything? Was he going to pressure her to marry the duke instead of Fitz?

She studied Bridgewater across the room. He seemed amiable, and was dressed appropriately, but as if clothes were unimportant to him. She liked that. He was a little short and slight in build, and she knew he'd once been considered of frail health. Whatever the truth of that, she thought he'd live a long life.

But not with her.

When introduced to him, Damaris curtsied. "I admire what I've heard of your canals, your grace."

His eyes lit. "Yes? It's going well, you know. Many doubted, but now they see. Soon there'll be canals all over England, speeding progress, making for pleasant travel. Far better to glide down a canal, Miss Myddleton, than to bump along a road."

"Wouldn't it be slow, your grace?"

"Why rush about? Enjoy the journey, I say. I still need money, however. I understand you're an heiress."

Damaris almost laughed at this blunt approach, but she also found his honesty endearing. He was like Dr. Telford on the subject of a promising new treatment— nothing else mattered.

"Are you seeking more investors?" she asked, with a slight emphasis on the last word.

"Always, dear lady, always. But if you're interested in a closer involvement, I wouldn't be averse."

He nodded and moved on. Damaris looked at Fitz and caught him looking at her. He instantly turned his attention back to one of the two overpainted women who sat on either side of him, both with something predatory in the angle of their bodies and the look in their eyes.

Feeling a growl in her throat, Damaris strolled over, wafting her fan and wishing she could hit both harpies with it. Fitz introduced Lady Tresham and Mrs. Fayne, who both had heavily painted faces, perhaps to disguise the fact that thirty was long past.

"What a delight to meet the canal duke," Damaris said. "So fascinating."

Lady Tresham raised a bored brow. "He talks of

nothing but waterways. That amuses you, Miss Myddleton?''

Fitz excused himself and moved away.

Damaris was glad to have given him a chance to escape.

"A duke is always interesting, don't you think?" she said.

"Especially an unmarried one," sneered Mrs. Fayne.

"You know Fitzroger well?" Lady Tresham asked, with pointed surprise. "Such a handsome man, but rather wicked for a mere girl." Lady Tresham actually licked her scarlet lips. "Wickedness is more fascinating than rank, however, isn't it, Miss Myddleton?"

"Wickedness?" Damaris asked, pretending ignorance.

"You haven't been warned?" Mrs. Fayne raised brows that were far too dark to be natural. "Very wicked. Too wicked for innocent ears. Really, it's astonishing that Rothgar permits Fitzroger to join his company."

"But a delightful treat for us, Susannah."

"He's staying here," Damaris said, trying not to sound as acidic as she felt. To protect Fitz, she plunged into exaggeration. "The marquess expects great things of him."

"Then it's to be hoped Rothgar's cloak of protection can prevent Leyden from acting on his gruesome threats," said Mrs. Fayne, shivering theatrically. "Such an unpleasant man."

"But all a result of his wound," Lady Tresham reminded her. "Suffered," she added with a sly look at Damaris, "during a most interesting situation."

Damaris prayed for an air of worldly ennui. "When he caught Fitzroger in bed with his wife? All the world knows."

The two women stared.

"Quite," Lady Tresham said at last. "It makes Fitzroger such delicious forbidden fruit."

All men other than your husband should be forbidden fruit, Damaris thought, but she kept her smile, seeing an opportunity to create a crack in the disgrace that imprisoned Fitz.

Dared she?

How could she not?

"He must have been very young," she mused.

Mrs. Fayne let out a piercing laugh. "My dear! You've led a sheltered life if you don't know the wickedness beardless youths are capable of."

Damaris put on confused naïveté. "I did, actually—lead a sheltered life, ma'am. My father was in the Orient making his fortune, and my mother preferred to live quietly in his absence." She lowered her voice. "You think it could have happened as portrayed?"

She took the excuse to look at Fitz, which unfortunately showed her the way many were subtly avoiding him. He'd warned her. She'd not entirely believed him. Instead of making her uncertain about her actions, it made them imperative. She was sure these two women were gossips of the first order.

"How else?" Mrs. Fayne asked. "Poor Orinda Fitzroger killed herself for shame not long afterward."

"But Fitzroger's brother was much older, so probably twice his size. It all seems so unlikely. But"—she sighed—"as you say, I know little of the world."

Lady Tresham's eyes narrowed. "You take great interest, Miss Myddleton."

Damaris parried. "Fitzroger did me a service, so I would like to think well of him. At a halt at a coaching inn some miscreant tried to attack me. Fitzroger was quick to save me."

"Doubtless hoping to curry favor. I'm sure you're too wise, my dear, to be so easily snared."

"Snared?" Damaris asked with a laugh. "Oh, he's positively cool to me. But in matters of protection I'm told he can be relied on. He spent years protecting

the lives and safety of some of the greatest men of
our age, you know."

Obviously they didn't. Too late—always too late
when the fire burned in her—Damaris wondered if
that was secret. Well, it was out of the box now. The
two gossips were fixed on her.

"Really?" Mrs. Fayne purred.

"Oh, yes." In for a penny, in for a guinea, as they
said. "Even royalty. You won't say anything, I
know"—the two women leaned closer to her—"but I
have the impression that the king intends to reward
him tomorrow. Perhaps even with a knighthood. Perhaps one of the lives he saved was His Majesty's own."

They were only perhapses, she told herself. She
wasn't directly lying.

"He's not received at court," Lady Tresham protested, but she was almost quivering with eagerness to
be the first with this news.

Damaris thanked heaven for a piece of firm ground.
"I think you'll find he is. That will prove that old story
to be nonsense, won't it?" She gave them both a
bright and, she hoped, guileless smile. "Perhaps his
brother invented it all, being somewhat deranged."

"I do remember," Mrs. Fayne said, "that Leyden—
plain Mr. Fitzroger then—was given to foul rages before the incident." She raised a quizzing glass and
stared at Fitzroger. "He's never denied it, however."

Damaris almost said that perhaps no one had asked
him, but then one of these women might do it, and
he'd confirm every word.

Her only option was risky.

"Then it's probably true. Even if he was young, it
was a terrible sin. But then," she added, looking between them in confusion, "why does Lord Rothgar
show him such favor? Why will the king? I put it to
you, dear ladies, for I cannot fathom it."

"Leyden always was a boor, Susannah," Lady Tresham said. "With the king's approval . . ."

"And Rothgar's," Mrs. Fayne concurred.

"He will attend the drawing room tomorrow?" Lady Tresham asked Damaris.

"I believe so," she said as hesitantly as she could manage, especially with triumphant glee building. "But perhaps I've gained the wrong impression. I just heard . . . But no, I must not spread speculation and gossip. Please excuse me."

She hurried away as if escaping, fighting a grin.

"What are you up to?"

Fitz had come to her side. *Blast him.* For them to be seen on good terms would undermine anything she'd achieved.

"Private matters," she said curtly, and swept past him.

She saw Lady Thalia alone for a moment and joined her.

"Did Bella Tresham and Susannah Fayne distress you, dear? Rothgar must have invited them for their influence—that means they're gossips—but such a dangerous ploy. They pay no heed to whether they do good or harm in their rush to be the first with the news."

Damaris hoped so. She'd planted seeds, and if the king did show Fitz some favor at the drawing room, they should blossom into doubt about that old story. She shouldn't have hinted at a knighthood, however. As usual, she'd rushed to extremes.

"Don't fret about Fitzroger, dear," Lady Thalia said. "I'm sure all will be well."

"But I can see how people avoid him."

"These things can turn in a moment."

Either way, Damaris thought.

When the guests left, Damaris went wearily up to

bed, but even when she was in her nightgown and
Maisie had gone to her own room, a restless energy
made it impossible to settle. So many things hung in
the balance and would be decided tomorrow.

She was tempted to go to Ashart's room to beg him
to keep the secret, but she knew that would be
disastrous.

She was tempted to go to Fitz, especially after re-
buffing him. He might think she'd changed her mind
and now favored Bridgewater. She couldn't do that
either. Not here in Malloren House.

She knew which room he had, however.

She'd made sure to find out.

It was only two doors down on the right.

Two doors. Damaris looked that way as if she might
see through walls, but she wouldn't go. She could explain everything in the morning.

Her restless eye saw the stained pouch on a side
table; the one with her mother's letters. She was too
agitated to sleep, so she moved a chair and the cande-
labra and sat to read them, tossing each bitter rant on
the fire afterward. What sort of person kept copies of
such things? Then she came to a letter that changed
everything.

> *Oh, caitiff! Oh, cruel deceiver. Foul enough to
> snare me with sweet lies and then abandon me,
> but you are a deeper dung heap than ever I
> imagined.*

Damaris stared at this opening, hardly able to imagine her cold, tight mother spewing such vitriol. And
why? She tried to read quickly to get to the meat, but
it was so high-flown and full of invective that she had
to go slowly, picking out splinters of fact.

When she had the pieces, the paper fell from her

hands. *By the stars.* So much was explained. So much was changed. And it might affect tomorrow.

She was at the door without thought, and thought didn't halt her. She had to discuss this with Fitz. And yes, she still wanted to explain. And yes, not to be with him was a physical void almost past bearing.

She'd heard people nearby not long ago, but now the corridor was deserted, the house silent. She didn't knock at the door for fear that someone else would hear, but opened it and slipped through, quickly closing it again.

Fitz turned, stark naked in the glow of a single candle. He snatched a pillow from the bed and held it in front of himself, which struck her as so funny she had to crush laughter under her hand.

He flung it aside, grabbed his robe, and put it on, but not before she'd seen his magnificent nakedness and a rising erection. He fastened only two buttons before grabbing her and shaking her.

"What madness possesses you? What are you doing here?"

He reached for the door handle.

"I'll scream."

He turned such a blistering look on her that she flinched. "I won't. I promise I won't!"

She went on urgently but softly. "I had to talk to you— No! Listen. Truly. I discovered something. And I couldn't sleep without explaining that I didn't mean to be cold earlier. That I'm not interested in Bridgewater."

He let her go and stepped away. "Then you're a fool."

"A fool for loving you?"

"Go, Damaris. Please."

The plea broke her will. "I will. In a moment."

Here, now, she could almost believe that he was

right. That it could never be. The darkness whispered it, echoed in his guarded eyes.

"But listen, love." She couldn't help but call him that. "I spoke coolly to you because I'd just convinced Lady Tresham and Mrs. Fayne that I cared nothing for you."

"That, at least, was wise."

"It was necessary in order for them to believe the seeds of doubt I sowed. About you and your brother's wife."

He ran a hand through his loose hair. "That's pointless, Damaris, because it's all true. I don't want you entangled with it. You must have seen how people treated me."

"I saw how Lady Tresham and Mrs. Fayne treated you."

It was an attempt at a tease, but he said, "You think I should be flattered to be weighed as bed amusement by bored wives?"

She swallowed tears but persisted. "We may not have an opportunity for private speech before the drawing room, so listen. I cast doubt on the story and buttressed it with Rothgar's approval and the fact that the king will accept you at court tomorrow. If challenged, do not undermine it with the truth."

"You expect me to lie?"

"Not outright, no. But don't drive truth through the questioner's heart."

He shook his head. "There's no hope for us, Damaris. Accept that and marry Bridgewater."

"And if I'm carrying your child? I won't foist a child on another man."

"You know in that case, I will have to marry you."

She hated that way of putting it, but seized on his words. "So you won't leave England before I know?"

His jaw tensed, but in the end he said, "I won't leave England before you know."

She hated to think of forcing him to the altar that way, but if he had to stay for a couple of months, surely she could find some solution.

"There's more," she said. "On a different subject. Those letters, the copies of the ones my mother sent? My father was a bigamist."

He stared at her. "What?"

She felt the relief of an almost impersonal subject. "Five years before he married my mother, he married Rosemary Butler, mother of my half brother."

"And Rosemary didn't die?"

"Not before he married my mother. Not until last year, in fact."

"The deuce. But I don't think it affects your inheritance, unless the will says 'legitimate daughter.'"

"No, I don't think it does, either, but that's not the point. My brother is the legitimate one! Don't you think he might have discovered this upon his mother's death and acted out of outrage?"

"Don't be softhearted. He fired that crossbow. He intended to kill you because then he would inherit your money."

"And he should have done."

"The money was your father's to do with as he wished."

"So he left it to me, knowing it would gall my mother to death."

"I doubt he ever expected it to come to that. Like most of us, he doubtless expected to live to an old age. This was all in a letter?"

"More or less. Marcus Myddleton was a monster. I don't understand why my mother or this Rosemary didn't kill him once they found out."

"They didn't have Myddleton blood," he said dryly, then added, "And, of course, they'd have been killing the golden goose."

"My mother cared nothing for money. She probably

kept quiet because of her reputation. Bad enough to
have a husband who rarely showed his face. She'd
rather have slit her own throat than let it be known
that she was his bigamous second wife. But his first
wife was the wronged one, and knew it. It's clear from
the letter that she approached my mother with a plan
of demanding more money as the price of their silence. Of course, my mother rejected the idea, but she
thought she had a weapon. She wrote to my father,
threatening to reveal all if he didn't return to Worksop
to live as her decent husband. Can you imagine?"

He shook his head. "I'm sure he shook in his
shoes."

"Quite. He'd have known it was a bluff, but no
wonder his last visit to us was so vitriolic. And I
panted around him like an adoring puppy."

He took her hands. "There's no blame to you in
that. You were young."

She looked wryly at him. "I was fifteen."

His hands tightened on hers. "I've made that step,
at least. I'm beginning to accept that I wasn't the author of that wickedness. Orinda seduced me, and a
lad that age in the hands of an experienced woman is
a lamb to the slaughter. Or a ram, at least. It doesn't
change the way the world views it, but my soul is more
at ease. As for your father's bigamy, it doesn't change
anything. Ignore it."

"But Marcus Butler—Mark Myddleton—has some
justice on his side."

"Not for attempted murder. But I've promised you
I won't kill him if I can avoid it."

"There's Rothgar, too. He's involved now."

"I have enough trouble in that area myself."

"I don't think Ash will tell him. I asked him not to."

His eyes flashed in the candlelight. "Damaris!"

"I'm sorry, but if you expect me not to be an in-
terfering, managing wife—"

"You will be no wife."

"Not to anyone?"

He dragged her toward the door. "Back to your room."

She didn't resist until they reached the door. "I have this terrible foreboding about tomorrow, Fitz."

"Don't worry. I'll keep you safe."

"But who will keep you safe? What if your brother is at court?"

"It's unlikely."

She could see, however, that it weighed on him. "Shouldn't he be confined?"

"Not by me."

"You can carry guilt too far. I don't think his rages come from a bump on the head."

"Don't, Damaris."

She managed to hold back more protests. Time enough for all that later. "What will you do if he does appear at the drawing room?"

"Avoid him."

"Not by leaving. Not before the king shows his favor."

"If the king's inclined to smile on me, Damaris, he'll do it another day."

She grabbed his arm. "You mustn't leave before being presented, Fitz. You mustn't." She didn't want to tell him, but she did. "I planted seeds in the minds of those two gossips, Lady Tresham and Mrs. Fayne. That you'll be at the drawing room, which is true. That the king is expected to show you some sign of favor. Which is probably true . . ."

"And?" His direct look demanded the truth.

"I made the point that the king's favor will prove the old story to be an exaggeration. Or a figment of your brother's demented mind."

"Damaris—"

"It will work," she insisted. "But only if they see the king accept you tomorrow." When his face set in resistance, she added, "You said I could command you."

"And you'll exploit that to the death."

"Till death do us part," she agreed. "I do wish you weren't always looking exasperated with me."

"It's likely to become a fixed expression." But there was a hint of loving humor there.

It created a blessed smile in her. "An eternal one. So I command you: Avoid your brother if you can, but even if he attends court, even if he tries to make trouble, do not leave before you're presented."

"I reserve the right to disobey in the field of action." When she tried to protest, he said, "No. You've reached the limit of your authority. If I come face-to-face with Hugh, I will follow my conscience and my honor."

She sighed and slid her hands down to his. "I don't suppose I'd love you if you could do anything less." She glanced at his bed. "I wish we could make love, because I'm afraid. But it's irrational panic, that's all. And it would hurt you, my love, to take me to bed again tonight, wouldn't it?"

He raised her hands and kissed each palm. "It would be wrong. I have no premonitions about tomorrow, but I do feel somewhat like a knight of old on the eve of battle. That I should be sober, chaste, and prayerful."

The touch of his lips on her palms made her want to curl in her fingers to hold the kiss like a jewel. "Were they? Sober, chaste, and prayerful before battle?"

His lips quirked. "I doubt it."

He kissed her hands again and then her forehead, then led her to the door. "I'll try to obey your commands, my lady fair."

"About my brother, too?"

"If we can find him before he tries any new mischief."

He opened the door and checked the corridor. As she left, he stopped her with a hand on her cheek and kissed her once again, chastely on her lips, before pushing her gently into the corridor. When she looked back from her own door he still watched.

On guard. Her golden Galahad.

She sent him all her love in a smile before entering and closing her own door.

Chapter 21

Damaris woke to sunshine through open curtains and hoped it was a good omen. Here in Malloren House, her room was lightly perfumed with potpourri, and a lively fire made it comfortable.

Maisie brought her washing water, and gave her a searching look. Searching for sin, no doubt. She said nothing other than, "Shall I get your breakfast now, miss?"

"No, I want to breakfast downstairs." Where she might have a chance of being with Fitz.

Damaris got out of bed and put on her slippers and robe. She hurried to her desk and wrote a note. "Take this to Fitzroger. There's no use in pouting," she added. "I intend to marry him. If you want to be maid to a duchess, you'll have to seek other employment."

Maisie pouted anyway.

Damaris gave her a hug. "On the day I marry Fitz-roger, I'll give you a handsome dowry. You'll be able to return home and pick any man you choose for a husband."

Maisie's eyes widened and she straightened. "Right, then!"

The note had been a request that Fitz escort her down to breakfast, which he could hardly refuse to do. She was only just dressed when he knocked. She'd chosen simple clothes because later she'd have to change into court finery.

They went downstairs talking of the weather, and lightly of the drawing room. Like ordinary people on an ordinary day.

"You've never attended court in England?" she asked as they approached the breakfast room.

"Until recently I was hardly ever in England."

Because he'd avoided his brother.

They found Rothgar at breakfast, which wasn't what Damaris would have chosen. He rang a bell, which brought a servant to take their orders. At least she saw no sign that Ashart had revealed their sin.

Conversation was of impersonal matters, which suited her perfectly. This was the lull before battle, and perhaps at such times soldiers spoke of incidental things. In a little while Rothgar excused himself and left them alone. They shared a look.

"A sign of approval?" Damaris asked.

"Of trust, at least. Have you decided what to sing?"

"Rothgar approved 'The Pleasures of Spring.' There's nothing in daffodils and singing birds to offend anyone, and it's a simple piece. I only hope my voice doesn't desert me because of strain. I should soon go and practice again."

They were interrupted by a footman. "Sir, a lady asks for you. She says she is your sister."

"Your sister?" Damaris queried. "Libella?"

Fitz frowned, but rose. "It has to be. Will you stay here while I see what she wants?"

"Of course, but I'd like to meet her."

His lips twisted. "It might not be a suitable moment."

Damaris watched from the door as he crossed the hall to enter one of the reception rooms. Why was his sister here? Not for anything good, she was sure, but she couldn't intrude. She paced the breakfast room, praying this didn't represent a new burden for Fitz.

She'd left the door ajar. When she heard voices, she went to it again and saw Fitz with a petite woman with similar blond hair who was fastening a simple red cloak. The day was milder, but that wasn't an adequate winter garment.

Fitz turned and saw Damaris. With a word to his sister he came over. "Libby came to warn me that Hugh's picked up some wild story of the king's knighting me today. It's pushed him beyond all reason. He's even threatening the king."

"No," she whispered, putting a hand to her mouth. This was all her doing! And not many years before, a raving madman had been horribly tortured and killed for attempting to kill the king of France.

"I need to escort Libby to her inn and see if we can persuade our mother to move to safety. She seems to feel that Hugh would never hurt her."

Damaris thought new lines were etched into his face, and longed with all her heart to ease him.

"Mother refuses to consider any kind of confinement for him," Fitz said. "I have to go." He took her hand. "I'll alert Rothgar. You'll be safe here. But don't go out. For any reason."

"Of course not." She hesitated, but asked, "Won't you introduce me to your sister?"

"I don't want you involved."

"I am, Fitz, whether you want it or not."

He shook his head, but said, "Come."

Libella Fitzroger was so short and slight that she looked like a child, but when close Damaris could see extra years on her too-thin face. Her smile was perfunctory, as if she couldn't imagine why they were wasting time on social niceties.

Fitz excused himself to speak to Rothgar, so Damaris kept up the conversation, but she didn't feel able to talk about Lord Leyden, or herself and Fitz, so was limited to the weather and the bustle of London.

Thank heaven Fitz soon returned—wearing a sword, she noticed. No doubt there was a pistol somewhere, too. Damaris had hoped to gain sisters through marriage, but this drawn woman wasn't very promising.

Fitz had ordered a sedan chair, and it was announced to be waiting outside. He and his sister left the house. Damaris went to the window in the reception room to watch as he handed his sister into it. The chairmen picked up the poles, and he took his place beside as they crossed the courtyard toward the street.

She was enjoying the way he moved when she saw a man charge into the courtyard and heard the blast of a gun.

Fitz and the chairmen fell to the ground—but before a cry could escape her lips she saw that they were unhurt. The chairmen were huddling behind the tall box, and Fitz was already helping his sister out.

The maroon-faced, hatless man in the flapping cloak and rumpled clothes had to be Lord Leyden. He was lurching across the open space, bellowing something while fighting his cloak to draw his sword. The task seemed to be too much for him, which was a blessing, for it gave Fitz time to make his sister as safe as possible before running out with his own sword already drawn.

She heard him cry, "Hugh! Stop! Think!"

She supposed he had to try, but she pressed her knuckles to her mouth. It was pointless. The man's eyes were almost rolling with madness, and spittle flew from his lips. The horrible thing was that he was a caricature of Fitz, more heavily built and distorted by mad rage, but in other ways so similar, even to the wild hair flying free of a ribbon.

Swords clashed so hard that sparks flew. She couldn't just stand here. She had to do something!

She dashed into the hall to see Rothgar and a half dozen footmen pouring out of the house. She ran after them, wondering why the fight was still going on when Fitz had to be able to defeat his brother in a moment.

Rothgar had his own sword out, and his men held bludgeons and pistols. One chairman held a pistol and was peering around the chair box pointing it.

But everyone watched.

To run in on such a mad frenzy risked death, but it also risked distracting Fitz. Rothgar must know better than she that Fitz could already have killed his brother. But still Fitz parried and dodged, talking, talking, talking.

But then, as Lord Leyden began to stagger and flail with his sword, she understood: Fitz still could not harm his brother, or allow his brother to kill him. Perhaps he hoped to touch reason, but mainly he was tiring his brother out. Now Leyden lurched and one leg gave way, so he tumbled with a grunt to one knee. But still he slashed at his brother like a maddened beast.

"Disarm him," Damaris said under her breath, but Fitz wouldn't even do that. He stepped back, sword lowered, still talking.

His brother heaved for breath, pouring sweat, glaring with hate. "I'll kill you," he choked out. "Come back here, you bastard, so I can kill you!" He pushed, swaying, to his feet again and lurched toward Fitz, finding breath to bellow, "I'll kill you and the king who thinks to honor you! Rotten, sausage-eating German . . ."

Outright treason. Damaris had to do something, so she used her most powerful weapon—her voice. She screamed long and loud to drown out his words.

She was too late. At the edge of the courtyard a growing crowd gawked and listened.

At least Leyden had stopped yelling. But then he

pulled another pistol from his belt and aimed it at her. She threw herself down even as she saw Fitz lunge to skewer his brother's right arm. The shot thundered, and she hunched down lower, praying it hadn't hit anyone.

Her throat hurt, and she was gasping with panic, but she peered out. Fitz was standing, obviously not hurt. Rothgar's men were swarming all over the still-raging madman.

Libella Fitzroger ran forward then, but to Fitz, not Hugh.

That might be a blessing.

Strength failing her, Damaris turned and sat on the ground. She feared her world had just become much darker.

The crowd had to have heard Leyden's bellowed treason. In moments the story would be flying around London from mouth to mouth. Within hours there might even be broadsheets about it, even though this was Sunday.

Fitz's brother could die for those words, and a traitor's family was ruined along with him. Fitz wouldn't be able to attend court today, or perhaps ever. And it had happened because of the story she'd impulsively spread that the king might knight his hated brother.

Then Fitz ran to her, looking frantic. "Are you hurt?"

She'd have to confess to him what she'd done. But not now.

When she said, "No," he helped her to her feet. She gladly leaned against him, but she also offered comfort. She knew what it must have cost him to hurt his brother again, and then there was the treason.

"Oh, my love, I'm so sorry."

"I'm not."

The sharp voice belonged to Libella Fitzroger, small and tight-lipped. "Hugh's been a monster all his life."

Fitz began to protest, but she overrode him. "Mother claimed his cruelty was all your fault, but it wasn't. Oh, the headaches, perhaps, but not the violence. Orinda seduced you because Hugh was so foul to her. Stupid, of course, but she was stupid. Even at ten I knew that."

"Hush," Fritz said, trying to soothe her. "Come back inside, Libby."

He put an arm around both of them and hurried them into the house. Damaris remembered the threat to herself. She'd been out in the courtyard when her enemy had that crossbow.

She relaxed only when they were inside.

Libella immediately tore free and faced her brother. "You are not to blame for Hugh, Tavvy."

So, another family name for him. Damaris still preferred Fitz.

"Do you know why Sally is as she is?" Libella demanded. "It didn't happen at birth. Hugh threw her against a wall when she was a toddler because she pestered him. He was only six years older, but he was a foul bully even then!"

Damaris heard Fitz inhale. "Why didn't you tell me?"

"When? I didn't know about Sal until a few years ago, and you never came back to England."

"You could have written."

Libella's lips worked and she bit them. "If I had, you'd have come back to try to help, and I didn't want you to. Hugh would hunt you down, and you'd let him kill you. I knew that. Until today." She flashed a glance at Damaris, suspicious and unfriendly.

"You should have told me," Fitz insisted.

"To what purpose?" Libella snapped. "You were always such an idealist, but this isn't some story of King Arthur and his knights! No one would believe the story about Sal, and you know Mother would deny it. I think she denies it to herself. There was nothing you could do."

"You should have had more faith."

Libella laughed bitterly. "In what? I saw you today." She flung out her arm, pointing into the court-yard. "You couldn't bring yourself to harm him, even when he was roaring treason. It was only when he threatened someone else . . ." She put her gloved hand over her mouth. "And what's to become of us all now, I don't know."

Fitz put his arm around her and drew her close. "It'll be all right, Libby. We'll have him declared mad and cite his treason as part of the proof."

She frowned up at him. "Is that possible?"

"I believe so. I have, as you see, powerful allies."

Libella looked around as if seeing the inside of Malloren House for the first time. The marquess entered then, supervising his men, who struggled with the burden of a trussed-up but still fighting Lord Leyden. He was puce and his eyes bulged. Damaris feared he'd die on the spot. But then, perhaps that would be good.

"Lord Leyden will be accommodated in a bedchamber," Rothgar said, "until decisions are made, Fitz-roger."

The implications were clear. He must be confined.

"I suspect the others are wondering at the noises. Please"—he gestured elegantly toward the right-hand reception room—"speak in private with your sister."

It was a gentle command to remove their business from the hall and the hearing of servants. They obeyed. Fitz escorted his sister to the sofa. Damaris stayed standing, not sure what her role was here but determined to be a part of it. To show that she was part of this family—heaven save her.

This was not the family she'd hoped to gain through marriage, but it was Fitz's family, so already it was hers.

Libella drooped, as if cold air had been the only thing holding her up. "Mother will fight his being confined. She always has. It's as if she's blanked her mind of all her children but one. She'll hear nothing against him, deny him nothing. She lives for his visits to Cleeve Court, and between them she prepares for the next."

She sighed. "I'm sorry about your money, Tavvy. I was so giddy about it I let something slip to Sal, and she told Mother. Mother demanded it and gave it all to Hugh, like an offering to a god."

Damaris thought her question was silent, but Fitz glanced at her. "I sent Libby the money I received from the sale of my commission." He sat beside his sister and took her hand. "I should have realized how bad things were. I should have done something."

Libella shook her head. "Galahad," she said, but fondly.

Damaris must have started, for Libella looked up at her. "We used to play King Arthur. Or rather, Tavvy and his friends, Jack Marchant and Harry Fowles, did. They let me be Guinevere sometimes. Tavvy would never be Arthur or Lancelot. He always wanted to be Galahad."

That glimpse into childhood was enough to break Damaris's heart. Unlike her, and despite his family's problems, Fitz had once had a normal childhood with friends and games. She could imagine him running wild in the countryside, riding a pony probably as he and his friends staged jousts and dragon slayings.

So when his life had shattered, he'd had so much more to lose.

Libella suddenly spoke again. "I've been waiting for Hugh to die," she said. "That's why I didn't ask you for help, Tavvy. The doctor says he soon must. He's ruined his heart and his liver and who knows what else with excesses, and he's diseased from his whores as well. But he keeps on living—and *I wish him in hell*."

She broke into tears, and Fitz took her into his arms.

Damaris heard voices and slipped into the hall. Genova, Ashart, and Lady Thalia were there, astonished. They'd each been woken by the gunshot and had to dress.

Rothgar appeared and directed everyone into the reception room.

As soon as the door was shut, he said to Fitz, "I've sent for Dr. Erasmus. He runs a private asylum on the most advanced principles. Leyden can be kept there until you decide on permanent arrangements."

Fitz had risen. "Can we save him from the gallows? For my mother's sake, at least. I keep thinking of Damiens."

"Oh, no," Damaris said and went to his side.

She heard sounds from the others as well. Six years before, a man called Damiens had tried to assassinate the king of France and been horribly punished.

"We are not France," Rothgar said. "We do not torture madmen and tear them apart in a public square, not even for an attempt on the king's life. And mercifully, Leyden never came close to action. It was unfortunate that so many heard, but even there, Damaris's excellent vocal cords helped."

"It was all I could think to do," she said.

"I hope it didn't damage your voice. You still have to sing at court."

"Still? After this?"

"The king expects you. There are hours yet. Time enough to prepare. Time enough," Rothgar added, "for the king to hear of Leyden's words."

"You want to delay my presentation?" Fitz asked. "I have no objection. My family needs me."

Damaris kicked his ankle.

After a moment and a glance at her, he said, "But I would prefer to proceed, if possible."

"So be it. I will make some adjustments."

With that cryptic statement, Rothgar left. Ashart, Genova, and Lady Thalia started asking questions, but Fitz turned to Damaris. "I still must take Libby back and attempt to explain this to our mother. If she'll even acknowledge my existence. Ash, you'll take care of Damaris?"

"Of course. I regret the complications, Fitz, but I'm glad you've been forced to deal with your brother."

After hasty thought, Damaris decided to share some of what Libella had said, even though Fitz probably wouldn't like it.

"And Fitz isn't responsible for Lord Leyden's wild nature. Apparently he's been like that all his life."

Fitz cast her a sharp look. "I'm sure finding me in bed with his wife didn't help."

"But you no longer need to leave the country," Ash said. "In fact, you'll have to stay to look after your family's affairs. I can't dislike that."

"There are estate managers and trustees," Fitz said curtly. "And my actions may depend on other matters."

On Rothgar's reaction to their fornication. Damaris saw the look between Ashart and Fitz, and realized that Ashart had just spoken out of friendship.

"I'll do nothing to drive you away," Ashart said directly.

Damaris almost swayed with relief, though she knew she'd still have to battle for her happiness. Unless she was with child, Fitz wouldn't marry her as long as his reputation remained tainted, and having a traitorous brother could hardly improve it.

But at least one threat was removed.

Fitz turned to her and kissed her hand, but used that to murmur a command. "Don't spill any more of my family's secrets."

"I'm sorry. I won't."

"Unless you decide it's best."

She had no reply for that.

His lips twitched. "I'll return as soon as possible. Behave and be safe."

He left with his sister. Damaris couldn't bear chatter and questions, so she retreated to her bedchamber. Her beautiful court gown was spread on the bed, and soon she'd have to put it on and play a part. And sing.

She tried a scale and found to her relief that her scream didn't seem to have damaged her voice. The soreness she'd felt before must simply have been tension. It had gone.

Even the prospect of singing before the king couldn't outweigh the real challenge. What happened to Fitz today at court could change her life. Frustratingly, she couldn't see anything to do to shape events.

So she prayed.

She wasn't a person accustomed to prayer beyond the routine of Sunday service, but now she directly addressed God. She didn't ask anything for herself; only that things become right for Fitz, that he find the honor and joy he deserved.

A knock at the door disturbed her. A footman carried a request from Rothgar that she visit his study.

As soon as she entered, Rothgar said, "We've found your brother." He was dressed for riding and holding leather gauntlets. "He's staying at the Swan in Church Lane."

"Openly? Doesn't that prove his innocence?"

"Who else has reason to kill you? But I go to find out."

"I want to come." When he stared at her, she said, "He's my brother. I made Fitzroger promise not to harm him, short of dire necessity. Will you pledge the same?"

He tapped the leather gloves against his palm, then said, "No. Do you think to be able to stop me?"

She met his eyes. "I would do my best."

He smiled. "Very well, I travel with force to this and can keep you safe. You will do exactly as I say."

She didn't argue that point, but hurried off to dress warmly, pausing for a moment in thought as she put on her cloak. Fitz wouldn't like this, and he'd know sooner or later.

She left him a note. How to end it? Smiling, she wrote, *With all my heart, Damaris.*

He'd be exasperated again to hear she'd left the house, but if she wasn't safe with Rothgar and his force, where would she be?

When she went down to the hall, she found that Rothgar was taking her safety seriously. A sedan chair had been brought into the house so she could enter it there. As soon as the door was closed a phalanx of armed footmen surrounded it. Thus guarded, she was carried out into the courtyard, where Rothgar mounted, joining three other armed horsemen.

Such a small army attracted a great deal of attention on the way to the Swan Inn.

Chapter 22

The Swan was a cozy-looking establishment with two bow windows, sitting in a row of shops on a narrow road that ran between two busier ones. A coach could pass down Church Lane, but only just, which was probably why none seemed to. The only traffic other than pedestrians was sedan chairs and the occasional handcart. There weren't even any riders until Rothgar's party rode in, hooves noisy on the cobblestones.

Damaris detected no hint of danger or dark deeds here. In fact, most of the people seemed to be making their way to the church whose spire could be seen ahead. Damaris felt certain there must be some mistake, but she was carried into the inn and allowed out only when the door shut on the outside and her guards were in position around her. She emerged feeling ridiculous.

She heard Rothgar asking for Mr. Myddleton and pushed her way through her wall of protection to go to his side. He was talking to a comely lady of middle years who was clearly mistress of her domain. She looked both alarmed and cross at this invasion, but wasn't about to offend a man like Rothgar.

"If you'll come this way, my lord."

They followed her down a short corridor until she

stopped in front of a door. "I've just served Mr. Myddleton's dinner, my lord. I hope there'll be no trouble."

Damaris had to fight laughter at that non sequitur, but it was hardly surprising if the woman was nervous. Her establishment had been invaded by men primed for violence. The very air hummed with tension.

When the innkeeper raised her hand, Rothgar put her aside and knocked himself. Damaris's heart was thundering now. She was about to meet her one and only brother—and maybe lose him to violence.

The door opened without caution and she saw a stocky young man in a fashionable suit of dark red cloth, a table napkin in his hand. He did look very much like her father, especially about the square jaw, the bright eyes, and the brows that grew too close in the middle. His look of polite inquiry turned to wariness, but there was no hint of guilt. If he was her would-be murderer, he was a brilliant actor.

"Mr. Butler-Myddleton? I am Lord Rothgar, and this is your sister, Miss Damaris Myddleton. We would like to speak to you."

Mark Myddleton gaped slightly, but fell back and bowed them into a decent parlor, kept warm by a generous fire. It had to be the best parlor, for it had one of the bow windows that looked out into the lane. A table stood there and held his meal. It looked as if he'd been halfway through his soup.

He waved a vague, bewildered offer of seating. Rothgar assisted Damaris off with her cloak and guided her to a chair, but remained standing himself. She noticed that two footmen had entered with them to station themselves by the door.

She looked from her brother to Rothgar with no idea what to say.

"Are you aware, Myddleton, that someone has twice tried to kill your half sister?"

Mark looked at her, shocked. "Gads, no. I'm

pleased you're safe, sister. I had thought sometime soon to seek your acquaintance."

Damaris almost said something warm and friendly, but stopped herself. If this was not her assassin, who was?

"Have you ever been to Pickmanwell?" Rothgar asked.

Mark looked honestly confused. "I don't think so. Where is it, my lord?" Then he became defensive and stood tall. "What's the meaning of all this? You can't suspect *me*?"

"You were, until recently, your sister's heir."

"And that is cause enough to invade an honest man's lodging?"

"How did you know?" Rothgar asked.

"Know what?"

"That you were your sister's heir."

Mark's features set as if he wouldn't answer, but then he said, "My father told me. He probably hoped I'd throw a jealous fit. Mama obliged instead."

"Oh, you, too," Damaris exclaimed. "What an awful man he was! But surely, sir, you must feel some resentment over my receiving most of his money."

She tried to read his expression but could see no evasion, no hint of dishonesty.

"I do, of course. Especially as I'm his legitimate son, and he treated my mother foully." Then he colored. "You do know about that?"

"Yes, but not the full story. Perhaps you can explain more. . . ."

But then the door opened and Fitz walked in, fending off one footman with a thrust that staggered the man. "Of all the foolish starts!"

Rothgar produced a quizzing glass and looked at him through it. "Are you accusing me of folly, Fitzroger?"

Damaris suspected that Fitz wanted to snap, "Yes!"

but instead he turned a deadly look on Mark. "So this is the brother."

"And probably innocent," Damaris said, leaping to her feet and putting herself between them.

Fitz grabbed her arm and dragged her to his side. "For pity's sake. Who else?"

Rothgar fingered the long stem of his glass. "An excellent question, Myddleton. There seems no reason to attack your sister other than to acquire her money, so who else could that attacker be?"

Mark Myddleton did suddenly look shifty, glancing away as if in search of an answer. Damaris's heart fell. Fitz had been right.

But then Mark sighed. "I fear it might be my brother, my lord."

"'Struth!" Fitz exploded. "Do you take us for fools?"

"Join me in folly, Fitzroger," Rothgar murmured. The tone was almost amused, but Damaris felt the presence of the Dark Marquess and all his faculties.

Her brother paced the room for a moment, then faced them.

"I'm sure my mother would have been true to a better man, or even one more present. But as it was, she bore two children who were not my father's. My little sister died at three, but William survived. He's five years younger than I. Father didn't seem to mind the infidelity, but forbade Mama to spend on Will money intended for me. There was no reason for such a command, but he was like that, as I'm sure you know, sister."

Was it folly to support him? Damaris couldn't help it. "Yes, though I think you saw more of him than I. He made only three visits to Worksop."

"Then I congratulate you on your good fortune."

"My mother didn't see it so."

"She wanted more of him? Mama would have been

happy to see nothing but his money. She was terrified of him, but terrified of losing the money more." He hesitated again, then said, "She started life as an innkeeper's daughter, you see, and dreaded above all things losing the trappings of a lady. He tossed luxuries to her like a person tossing bread to ducks, and she quacked."

"He tossed luxuries to my mother, too, but she tried to bite back."

They shared a look of complete understanding. How strange this was. Fitz grasped her arm, as if he expected her to do something foolish. That seemed to bring her brother back to the point.

"Mama always carried out his orders, even when he was far away. He had us watched."

Damaris wondered if he'd had Birch House watched, too, and decided he probably had. How amused he must have been by the reports.

"So Will shared our home and food," her brother continued, "but he wore only my cast-off clothes. I received fine birthday gifts and Will received what Mother thought she could excuse. When I went to Westminster School, he went to a lesser place. As I became a gentleman, he was apprenticed to an apothecary."

An apothecary. That could explain the tainted drink—if this William existed at all. Damaris posed that question. "How can we be sure this person exists?"

Her brother looked bewildered, but Rothgar answered, "He does. A William Butler lived with your brother and his mother in Rosemary Terrace, though people there thought him a poor cousin. However, in recent years he has lived like a fine young gentleman. Myddleton?"

Her brother's cheeks flushed again, and Damaris wondered if he had their father's temper. He answered, however. "When my father died I came into control of a trust fund, so I helped Will along. In fact," he said with a shrug, "I shared everything. Why not? There was plenty, and Will was my brother and friend. We had fine times, but alas, it was never enough for him. I came to realize that when Mother died."

He turned to Damaris. "I always thought myself illegitimate, and that Mama's existence as Mrs. Myddleton was pretense. Even so, when Father died, I asked Mama where his money had been left. She said to his Myddleton family. I accepted that. As I said, I had enough and she had enough. We were comfortable.

"On her deathbed, however, she told me the truth, that it had gone to you. She wept about the unfairness of it and tried to get me to promise to blackmail you with the scandal of bigamy so that you'd give me half. And that half of that would go to Will. I refused. I was shocked by the story, but I couldn't stoop to blackmail."

He was not, Damaris thought, like their father after all.

"I did check my father's will in case my legitimacy would matter there, but the money was legally yours, so that was that. But Will couldn't see it that way. You and the money became his obsession—the money that he saw as rightfully ours. He talked endlessly of what we'd do when we had it—where we'd travel, the grand houses we'd own.

"Eventually I couldn't bear it anymore. I decided to sell the house, and part of the reason was that I didn't want to live with him. I gave him half the proceeds—a goodly amount—and he went off on his own. I admit, I wondered if he'd try to carry out Mama's plan, but I didn't want to know."

He looked around at them. "But he wouldn't do

more than that. I can't believe that he'd do more than that."

Despite his words, he was close to weeping. He did think his brother could be driven to murder by greed.

"Does he own a small crossbow?" she asked gently.

He staggered back into a chair, all his florid color ebbing. "Oh, no, no."

"Well?" Fitz demanded.

Mark turned to him. "He's always been interested in weapons. Likes to fence, but unusual weapons, too. Slingshots, crossbows . . . Says they're as deadly as a pistol—he hates pistols—and easier to take care of and carry around. But he wouldn't!"

"Someone did," Fitz said. "Where is he now?"

Mark ran a chunky hand over his face. "I don't know! I haven't seen him for weeks. He said he would spend Christmastide with friends in the country." He looked between them. "I had no idea. What should I do?"

Fitz turned on Rothgar. "You brought Damaris out into this."

"An error, I confess. I failed to imagine such a convoluted tale. Quite extraordinary." He turned to Mark. "Your sister has made a new will. You are no longer her heir."

"I read about it in the *Town Crier* yesterday. I think I was relieved."

"Then your brother may have heard, too," Fitz said. "Will he still try to harm her?"

Mark shook his head. "I'd have said not, sir, but now I'm not sure. He's come to see all that money as ours. To hear so much has been thrown away on charity hospitals—that's how he'd see it . . . it might enrage him."

"Is he your heir?" Fitz asked. "Because if so, I'd be very careful."

Mark went white. "We are brothers, sir!"

"Believe me, that's no guarantee of kindness."

Mark pushed out of his chair and went to the table by the window to pour himself wine with an unsteady hand.

Fitz said, "We have to get Damaris back to safety."

But then he turned sharply toward the window and strode forward to dash the glass out of Mark's hand.

"What the devil!"

Fitz picked up the decanter and sniffed at it, then tasted a drop. "Believe me, sir, this wouldn't have agreed with you."

Damaris was staring at them, but something beyond the window caught her eye. A movement. When she focused, she saw the snaggletoothed man glaring in at them.

"There he is!" she cried. "That has to be Will Butler!"

Fitz was already out the door at a run—the sight of the man must have been what alerted him. But outside Will Butler was pushing through the crowd down the busy lane. Damaris moved to follow Fitz but had stopped herself before Rothgar did so. He ordered his footmen to the chase, and Damaris hurried to the window, but carefully. She remembered the crossbow only too well.

When she peered around the curtain, she saw Will Butler fighting his way down the crowded lane in the direction of the church like a ship struggling against tide and winds. No one was cooperating, and ahead of him a laden handcart almost entirely blocked his way.

Fitz ran into the narrow street and yelled, "Stop, thief! Ten guineas to anyone who takes the man with the crooked teeth!"

That changed everything. Everyone stopped and looked around for the thief. The man with the handcart grabbed for Butler's sleeve.

Butler whipped out a dagger and the man fell back.

Everyone nearby shrank away from him, but the narrow lane was too crowded for a way to become clear.

Damaris covered her mouth with her hand. As well as his dagger, Butler wore a sword, and he probably had that crossbow somewhere. There were women and children out there.

"Someone's going to get hurt," she said.

Mark flung open one of the casements and leaned out. "Will, Will! Have sense, man. Give over."

Butler glared up, showing those crooked teeth. Then his crossbow was in his hand and firing before anyone could move. Mark cried out, staggering back to collapse into a chair, clutching the place where the horrid bolt stuck out of his jacket high on his shoulder.

"He shot me! Will. He *shot* me."

Damaris ran to him. "Yes. Stay calm. I don't think it's too bad." She could hear shouting in the lane and longed to be back at the window. What was happening? Was Fitz safe?

She ran to the door and flung it open. Two of Rothgar's men stood there, looking uncertain. "Get a doctor," she ordered one. "You, come in and attend to a wounded man."

Then she ran back to Rothgar's side, where he watched from the window.

Butler was hopelessly blocked now. People close to him would have given him space if they could, all the space in the world, but the hubbub was drawing more and more people into the lane from both ends.

Fitz moved forward, drawing his sword, and people shrank back, creating a narrow passage between the two men.

"You want to fight?" he said.

Butler swayed from foot to foot, glancing around, then back at Fitz. Damaris could see that he was panicked, unable to decide what to do, perhaps sure there still had to be a way out.

"I'm no thief," he protested to all around. "I've done nothing. Stolen nothing. This man's a bully-boy for a man with a grudge, that's all. Let me away."

"You just shot an innocent man," Fitz pointed out, advancing almost casually, but preceded by his sword. "And not for the first time. You shot an innocent young woman in the country, didn't you?"

Butler dragged out his own sword, but said, "Not me, sir. I'd not do that. Why would I do that?"

"How many dainty crossbows are there in England, I wonder? Strange coincidence."

"I don't know what you're talking about! Let me go and there'll be no trouble. Otherwise, all these good people stand witness to what happens here. It'll be murder. You'll hang!"

"Where would you go? Your brother won't help you anymore; you just shot him. And the money he gave you isn't enough, is it? You'll have to turn to apothecary work again, won't you, and live on your wages?"

Enraged, Butler rushed at him, slashing his sword furiously. With screams and cries, people backed toward the walls.

Along the street householders began to open doors to let people in. Some were even pulling up children through upstairs windows.

Fitz parried Butler's slashes, but that was all. But the sound was deadly. These weapons weren't foils.

Damaris's mouth had turned painfully dry. "If Fitz kills him, he'll hang?" she asked.

"For killing a would-be murderer?" Rothgar sounded distant but calm. "A score of witnesses just saw Butler shoot his brother."

"Then why doesn't he *do* it?"

"What a bloodthirsty wench you are. It's no easy matter to kill a man."

A clatter behind made them both turn. A doctor came in, knelt by his patient, and went to work. Mark looked at her piteously, perhaps more agonized by his brother's betrayal than by his wound. What tortuous bonds blood made.

"I saw you fight, my flimsy."

Damaris whipped back to see that Butler was taunting Fitz now, and looking much more confident. What was he talking about?

"At milord Rothgar's house against that madman," he sneered. "I watched you. He was flailing around like a child and you couldn't touch him. So I'll prove my honor on you. That's the way it's done, isn't it? All these good people are my witnesses. When I kill you, it'll prove my innocence."

"By all means," said Fitz.

As some of the crowd escaped, the crush was easing a little, giving the two men more space.

"Have at you!" Butler yelled, and moved forward at speed, showing some skill. The blades clashed, and Damaris clutched something—Rothgar's sleeve. Mark had said his brother liked to fence. Was he good enough . . . ?

"Peace, child. There's no true contest here."

Fitz was proving that now, driving Butler down the widening space with masterful moves. He suffered one disadvantage, however: He was being careful of the crowd and Butler wasn't. There were still many people trapped in the lane, and they pushed and squirmed in all directions to avoid the fight. A child began to howl.

"Can't someone shoot him?" Damaris demanded.

"Too dangerous in a crowded space," Rothgar said, though he had a sleek pistol in his hand.

Butler had realized that he'd misjudged Fitz's ability. He was backing away now, running with sweat and glancing side to side, seeking escape like a rat in a trap. Soon he backed up against the handcart. People were stuck there, and they pressed away harder, while others cried out that they were being crushed.

Fitz retreated to give Butler space. Butler took one step, but then grabbed a young girl from where she clutched her mother's skirts. A hostage!

The woman, a baby in her arms, wailed and begged.

Butler threw aside his sword and pulled out his dagger. "Now let me through!"

Rothgar raised his pistol.

Fitz stepped to one side as if to give way, then spun and skewered Will Butler from the side.

Everyone watched in silence as Butler, looking astonished, crumpled to his knees, and the child tumbled from his arms. A man grabbed the screaming girl and gave her to the mother. Butler toppled to the ground and died, blood gushing from his mouth, eyes going blank.

Damaris clung to Rothgar. It was the first time she'd seen violent death, and her stomach heaved. The crowd was silent, too. A few had covered children's eyes, but most, of all ages, simply stared.

Then they came to life, turning to chatter about the extraordinary events. The man with the handcart started relating how the dead man had tried to kill him. Others pointed to the window of the Swan, where the villain had shot someone.

Fitz stood still, looking down at the body.

Damaris scrambled out through the window, hearing one of her cane hoops crack, and ran to take him into her arms. He said nothing, but clung, his heart pounding against her. But then he moved back slightly, and there was the hint of a smile in his strained eyes. "Do I qualify as a hero yet?"

She laughed, but with tears. "I'd kneel, except the ground is very messy."

He looked down and shuddered. Someone had flung

a sheet over the body, but it was bloodstained, and little rivulets of blood trickled between cobblestones. He turned her away and they went toward the window, where Rothgar watched.

Damaris felt twisted around and wrung out, but she was realizing that she was free to walk the streets again. And she had a brother who hadn't tried to kill her.

Best of all, she had her hero. No force on earth could separate them now. She was resolved on it.

Rothgar said, "Come along. We cannot be late for court."

Damaris stared at him. "We can't possibly! Not after this."

"She's right," Fitz said. "The king disapproves of dueling, and this was closer to a street brawl."

"There is some risk," Rothgar agreed. "Do you wish to delay?"

Not long before, Damaris had insisted that Fitz must attend, but now she didn't know. Then the drawing room had held promise of restoring Fitz's reputation. Now he'd been involved in two violent events, and his brother had screamed treason.

She looked up at him, and he gave her a wry smile. "We've built such expectations. By all means, let us continue this drama to its end."

Chapter 23

When they arrived back at Malloren House, Damaris knew she should rush to the elaborate preparations for court, but she had to have a little time alone with Fitz. Without explanation or apology, she took him to the reception room. There she drew him to the sofa, keeping hold of his hand. She wasn't sure what to say, only that they needed to be together now.

"How is your mother?" she asked.

His hand tightened on hers. "She wouldn't see me. I had to leave Libby to break the news. I don't love her," he said with a frown. "I can't, even though it isn't really her fault. She'd given up loving her babies before I was born. But she'll never be other than she is."

She realized that he was apologizing to her for his family. "No, but your sisters can be rescued."

"But Sally—"

"Both your sisters. Do you want us to live at Cleeve Court?"

"Damaris—"

"Whatever happens at the drawing room, we will marry, Fitz. Accept that. So do you want to live at Cleeve Court?"

Half-exasperated, half-amused, he said, "No, not particularly."

"Then why don't we turn it into an asylum for your

brother and others like him? If your mother dotes, as you say, she can live there in a comfortable apartment and not be too distressed by change."

"You're terrifying."

"I'm a virago, remember? And one with the money to carry through my plans."

He looked down for a moment in serious thought, then met her eyes again. "If all goes well today, will you honor me far beyond my deserts by becoming my wife, my sweet virago?"

She smiled through tears. "Of course. But I'll marry you if all goes badly, too. I'm a pirate, sir, and I've captured you, so surrender to your fate."

He gathered her in for a kiss that might have progressed to more if Lady Thalia hadn't bustled in. "Oh, la! I approve of young love, my dears—oh, absolutely— but you both *must* prepare for court *now*!"

After a laughing final kiss, Damaris hurried upstairs, and under Lady Thalia's stern supervision whirled through the absurd painting and powdering. Within the hour she stood before the mirror looking, in her opinion, like a porcelain doll.

Lady Thalia's French maid had arranged her hair in complex plaits and curls that had then been powdered snow white. A silver comb held a short veil that hung down and ostrich feathers that stuck up. Her skin was white, too, with pink on the cheeks and lips.

"Magnificent!" Lady Thalia declared. "It needs only rubies. I'll go along to Rothgar's room now and tell him you'll soon be there for them."

She hurried out. Damaris picked up her golden fan and smiled at Maisie. "Wish me good fortune."

"Oh, indeed I do, Miss Damaris. You look so beautiful. Like a princess, you are!" She dabbed her eyes with her handkerchief. "And I do wish you well with Mr. Fitzroger, miss. Such a dashing hero! Better than a duke any day."

Damaris gave her a careful hug, then left to find Fitz waiting outside the door.

Oh, yes, he was better than a duke, any day.

For once, his hair was neatly arranged and powdered. His suit was of cut velvet in shades of pale gold, braided in dark gold down the front and along the cuffs and pockets. His long brocade waistcoat repeated the gold shades and was fastened with golden buttons that looked to be centered with pale sapphires. Glass, she was sure, but the surprising touch of color matched his eyes. Similar stones winked on the buckles of his shoes.

She sank into a curtsy. "Sir, you render me breathless."

He bowed, then raised her. "You do look rather bloodless."

"You're paler than usual, too," she pointed out. He was lightly painted.

"We do what we must."

He looked easier in his manner than she'd seen him in days, but she guessed the effort it took. It had been an extraordinary day, and everything could still go wrong.

All she could do was play her part. They proceeded down the corridor, almost filling the width because of her skirts.

When they entered Rothgar's private sitting room, he was there with Lady Thalia. She saw the marquess assess her. He seemed to approve. He was in dense black velvet today, which seemed ominous, even when it was embroidered with flowers in rainbow colors. He opened a large flat box on the table.

She went to where the rubies gleamed on black velvet. "I've hardly seen them myself," she said, touching the necklace. "When my mother died, our solicitor revealed that he had various jewels in his care. Lord

Henry took charge and locked them away at Thornfield Hall. They made him nervous."

"Understandably. They represent a fortune in themselves. May I assist you?"

She nodded and let Rothgar put the necklace around her throat, feeling the cool weight settle there. It was composed of a circle of rubies, each of large size, set in gold, with diamonds on each link between. The staggering element, however, was the smooth teardrop ruby that hung in the center.

A bloodred cabochon ruby, she remembered. *A smooth surface beneath which seethes fire and mystery.* She glanced at Fitz. Had he known when he'd said that? How could he? She'd not then worn these jewels.

Lady Thalia clapped her hands. "Magnificent!"

Fitz seemed suddenly somber, however, probably because of such evidence of her wealth. He'd simply have to get used to it.

She put in earrings that each held a miniature of the teardrop jewel, and a bracelet composed of three bands of rubies. There was also a brooch, which she put over the clasp at her waist.

She heard voices just before Genova and Ashart arrived.

Genova said, "You look terrifyingly grand, Damaris."

"I don't feel it. You look lovely."

The soft-cream-and-bright-blue gown was pretty and cheerful. It gave Damaris a pang. Why couldn't she be pretty and cheerful? It had nothing to do with looks, however. She was a pirate's daughter, inheritor of his bloody loot, and there was no purpose in fighting it.

Genova was wearing the pearls she'd worn at Christmas. Apparently they had been a gift from Lady Thalia, not a loan. Her only other ornaments were pearl earrings.

Damaris turned to Lord Rothgar. "I have a sapphire pin I want to give to Genova."

She thought that as her guardian he might object to her giving away her property, and braced for battle, but he left and returned with all her jewelry boxes. She quickly found the brooch and gave it to her friend. "A belated birthday gift."

Genova blushed but didn't protest. "Thank you," she said, pinning it to her bodice between her breasts. "It's lovely. And it matches my ring."

She showed the lovely sapphire she wore on her third finger.

Damaris hadn't noticed it, but it was perfect—a round sapphire of exactly the right size. Not hugely flamboyant, but certainly not modest. The clear, strong blue said something about Genova's clear and honest heart.

What ring would Fitz give her? An idea stirred, and as the others talked of the upcoming event she went to close her jewelry boxes, and to take something out.

Then she turned to find Genova practicing her court curtsy again and wobbling every time she started to rise. Everyone was on edge, perhaps all for different reasons.

Rothgar took away the jewelry boxes. When he returned he said, "The chairs are ready. It is time for our grand entrance."

"Don't you mean exit, my lord?" Damaris asked.

"Not at all. Beyond the front door lies the world, and thus our stage."

Ashart took Genova's hand and led her out. Fitz offered his to Damaris. She curled her fingers around his fingers.

Rothgar and Thalia came behind. She hoped they couldn't hear when she said, "I have a gift for you."

He raised a brow.

She opened her other hand to reveal a ring—a man's ring of heavy gold that held an oval cameo of buff and cream. Tiny diamonds circled it, so small they merely formed a glittering border.

"I can't accept a ring from you, Damaris. Not yet."

"The carving's of a rapier with ribbons and flowers entwined. As soon as I remembered it, I knew it was meant for you. It's a talisman for today. For strength and peace."

"If I put it on, Rothgar will notice. He probably saw you take it."

"This is mine to give or not, as I wish." As they navigated the turn at the top of the stairs, she pressed the ring into his hand.

"This was part of your father's loot?" he asked as they began the descent.

"Probably."

"Somewhat embarrassing if I meet the true owner."

But when they arrived in the hall and servants came forward with cloaks and muffs, she saw him slide it onto the middle finger of his right hand. It didn't quite fit. Looking at her, he put it on the fourth finger. It was his right hand, but she knew that in some countries women wore a betrothal ring on that finger.

Damaris loved that thought and tried to hide it by looking down at her own rings, all of her own providing. Or rather, her father's. She could understand now why her mother had rejected every gift, even with fury. She, however, would wear them all, and make friends with her brother, and hope Marcus Myddleton was gnashing his teeth in hell.

Six gilded sedan chairs were carried into the hall, and they entered them, ladies first. Fitz helped Damaris fit her hoops and skirts inside while avoiding knocking the plumes off her head.

"This is ridiculous," she muttered.

"This is court." He closed the chair's door. Damaris tucked her hands into her fur muff, the chairmen picked up the poles, and they were off.

As Rothgar had predicted, a small crowd waited to see them leave. If they were disappointed that the nobles were already packed away in boxes, they didn't show it. They even applauded. No wonder Rothgar described this as a stage.

Ahead, she glimpsed Rothgar's running footman, carrying his golden-knobbed staff, clearing the way and silently announcing the approach of the great. She'd prefer to be slipping through back streets.

When they entered the narrower streets around St. James's Palace they became part of a stream of chairs and carriages. Here the crowd stood three or more deep, and children were hoisted on adult shoulders so they could see. They'd be taken to hangings, too, Damaris thought wildly. It was all the same to the mob.

Would the king have heard about Fitz's brother?

Would he have heard about Will Butler?

What would he do?

Should she have urged Fitz not to come?

Then they passed beneath an arch into a crowded courtyard. Fitz opened the door and assisted her out. He seemed completely at ease, but he had that ability. She didn't. Her heart was starting to pound in a way that threatened a fainting fit. She inhaled cold air as they joined their party to file up to the royal presence.

All around, people chattered and laughed, showing how familiar this all was to them. One man was even reading a book. Many bowed or curtsied to Rothgar, Ashart, and Lady Thalia. She caught curious eyes sliding away from her, and could imagine the whispers about the heiress.

She was more concerned by the less pleasant stares at Fitz. She was sure there was gossip concealed by hands or fans. She knew it couldn't all be about him, but some would be, especially if this world knew about his brother and about William Butler's death. A man in military uniform bowed to Fitz, who returned the salutation. A good sign, but she wished the officer hadn't looked as if he were performing a daring act.

She prayed that her two gossips had done their work, and that the king would smile.

They entered the guardroom, where their outer clothing was taken. Damaris remembered thinking about King Charles I's extra woolen underwear. She certainly lacked that.

At least the crowd here warmed the air. Before she could object, Damaris found herself separated from Fitz and between Rothgar and Lady Thalia. She twisted to try to be sure Fitz wasn't slipping away, but Rothgar quietly said, "Behave."

As they moved slowly onward, Rothgar remarked, "A gift of a ring?"

"He's served me well," she responded, working on posture and calm, suddenly remembering that she was soon going to have to sing before all these people. She'd tried to prepare, but events had swept that away. Compared to everything else, however, it didn't matter if she croaked.

They entered the crowded room where their majesties sat on red-upholstered chairs that looked like thrones. Their ladies- and gentlemen-in-waiting stood stiffly to hand, and at the queen's side an elaborate cradle was attended by two nurses. A toddler wriggled on her silken lap.

This was the very image of a happy, healthy family, and Damaris saw that as a good omen.

Queen Charlotte was not pretty. Her face was sallow and long, but that didn't mean she couldn't be a loved and loving wife. The king was fresh-faced, with rather bulging eyes, but he appeared amiable enough, with a word for each person who bowed or curtsied.

Surely he couldn't refuse to recognize Fitz, but would he show him particular favor? Damaris spotted Mrs. Fayne standing hawk-eyed nearby.

Then it was their turn, and as Lady Thalia introduced her, she sank into her deepest curtsy. When she rose, the king spoke first to Lady Thalia, then turned to Damaris to stare at her rubies. *Lud!* What did she do if he demanded them? He gestured her closer and took out a quizzing glass to inspect the central jewel. "Remarkable, remarkable, wouldn't you say, Rothgar?"

Rothgar agreed that indeed, it was a remarkable stone.

The blue eyes turned to Damaris's face. "And we're told you have a remarkable voice, Miss Myddleton. You shall sing for us shortly."

He nodded, and she could make her careful backward retreat to allow space for Ashart and Lady Thalia to present Genova.

Once out of the immediate royal presence, she could move about normally, but relaxation was impossible. She watched Genova, and everything went smoothly, though Ashart had to give her a little assistance in retreat. Where was Fitz? Still over near the door. Apart. Ignored other than by sliding looks.

Some people made their curtsies and left, but most stayed, and the room was becoming uncomfortably full. She might end up fainting from lack of air. Then she realized that she'd done her work too well. People were waiting to see what would happen with Fitz. Across the room she saw Lady Tresham head-to-head with a dapper man.

"Who's that?" she asked Lady Thalia.

"Walpole. The greatest gossip ever."

Rothgar was to present Fitz, but he was talking to someone. She thought it was the Prime Minister, Grenville. Had he changed his mind? Then Rothgar was at Fitz's side, moving him toward the king.

Damaris's mouth dried, and she vaguely thought how disastrous that would be for singing, but all her attention was fixed on Fitz and the king. He must show favor. He must.

Fitz's deep bow was every bit as elegant as Rothgar's. The entire room hushed.

"Ah, yes," said the king. "Leyden's brother, what?"

Damaris almost moaned. He'd heard.

"Yes, Your Majesty." Fitz showed not a trace of tension.

"We hear some rumor of his being indisposed."

"Severely, sir. I fear he must be confined in an asylum for his own safety. And for that of others."

The silence in the room was like a smothering blanket.

"Unfortunate, but he has long been disturbed, what?"

That "what?" was a peculiarity of the king's conversation, but it threatened to make Damaris giggle.

"Yes, sir," Fitz said.

"From childhood, we understand."

Was the king deliberately creating doubts about the common story? Surely that was a good sign.

"Given to irrational fears and suppositions, what?" Before Fitz could answer that tricky question, the king went on, "My uncle speaks highly of you, Fitzroger. Saved his life, Cumberland says."

A sibilant murmur ran around the room. Damaris was keyed so tight her head was pounding. This was the longest the king had spoken with anyone.

"I was honored to be of some small service, sir," Fitz said, bowing again.

"Small?" repeated the king. "Wouldn't call saving *our* life small, would you?"

Fitz was silenced for a moment. But then he said, "Emphatically not, sir. It must be any man's greatest honor."

"Preserving the peace and stability of our realm is any man's greatest honor, sir!" The stern correction sounded like a reproof, but then the king said, "We hear you dealt with a person disturbing our peace, today, here in London. Good man. Good man. You have a long record of service. We're minded to reward you."

For a breath-stopping moment Damaris wondered if the king would indeed knight Fitz, but then he said, "We appoint you a gentleman of our privy chamber," and held out his hand.

Damaris wasn't sure what that meant, but it sounded like a position of great trust. As Fitz expressed his gratitude and bowed over the king's hand, the room began to buzz.

Damaris was hard put not to beam like an idiot, or even laugh with pure delight. How had Rothgar persuaded the king to play such a part? However he'd done it, it had worked. Fitz's past was smothered by his recent achievements, and he was high in royal favor. Let anyone dare turn their back now!

She flicked open her fan and hid her smile behind it as she watched reactions. Some looked thunderstruck. Others seemed delightfully intrigued. Across the room she saw Lady Tresham give a smug *I told you so* to Mr. Walpole, who looked as if he couldn't wait to spread the story.

Fitz was stopped on his way to her by a number of people wishing to bow or curtsy, and the uniformed officer slapped his back, grinning.

Damaris bit her lip and fought tears of happiness, but she made herself look away and tried to look bored. All might yet be spoiled if the gossips realized how she felt about him. They'd know when they married. So that couldn't be too soon, alas. . . .

"Miss Myddleton?"

She started at the king's voice, and hurried over to curtsy.

"You may sing now. Without accompaniment, I understand?"

Oh, Lord! She ran her tongue around her mouth to moisten it. "Yes, Your Majesty."

He waved to a space nearby and turned to the next people in line.

Damaris backed into position, praying that her voice would not be affected by the turmoil inside her. Perhaps she did start awkwardly, but then the familiar joy in music caught her, and she surrendered to it. The paean to spring seemed entirely appropriate to the joy in her heart and the promise of the future. She was careful not to look at Fitz, but he was in her mind and heart right to the last note.

The king led applause, looking truly pleased, and declared that they would hear more of her. But then they were free to leave. It was no easy matter, however, for now that the excitement was over, half the room wanted to exit.

Because she shouldn't be at Fitz's side, Damaris walked with Rothgar. "I may marry him now?"

"Not precisely now, but yes. I would be disappointed to learn that you would be deterred by my opinion, but I will approve, and thus you will have your fortune."

She frowned up at him. "When did you decide he was a suitable husband?"

"I would not have sent you to Cheynings with him if I had not thought it possible. Love is hard to conceal."

"I didn't love him then."

"Did you not? It often happens in a day, in a moment, and he is a man worthy of that gift."

Their servants came forward with their outer clothing, and then they were outside, their chairs awaiting them.

Damaris inhaled fresh air and worked hard at not looking at Fitz. As he handed her into her chair, however, she softly sang, " 'What does any lady want, more than a handsome hero?' Rothgar gives us his blessing."

Softly, helplessly, he laughed. It was pure joy.

Once back at Malloren House, she emerged from her chair into the entrance hall caroling, " 'For, oh, a lady cannot abide without a hero by her side. By her side, a hero!' " She grabbed Fitz's hands. "What does being a gentleman of the privy chamber mean?"

"About five hundred a year, for a start," said Rothgar. "At the cost of occasional attendance at court. Enough at a pinch to support a wife."

Fitz turned to Damaris, a deep yet still unsteady joy in his eyes. He raised her hands and kissed them. "Marry me, Damaris?"

A number of saucy, piratical things came to mind, but instead she simply said, "It will be my deepest honor, sir."

Epilogue

February 14, 1764

Damaris might have preferred a quiet wedding, but a grand one was deemed part of the steady restoration of Fitz in society. The king and queen would attend, along with everyone of importance.

She tried to persuade Genova to share the ceremony, but her friend had shaken her head. "Oh, no, this will be your glorious day. I've no mind to be cast into the shade."

After six weeks of the winter season, Damaris and Genova were fast friends. One of the many joys ahead would be sharing their married lives, for Ash had agreed to sell Damaris and Fitz an unentailed house on the edge of the Cheynings estate. He was glad of hard cash and welcome neighbors, and Coldmoore House suited their needs perfectly—with a name change, they all agreed.

As with everything at Cheynings, the place was in need of repair, but it was a mellow, golden stone house with just enough land to suit them. Neither Damaris nor Fitz was interested in farming. Fitz intended to add a seat in Parliament to his royal duties, so they would purchase a town house as well—a neat, modern one that was easily kept warm—and divide their time between the two.

In the end they settled on a name from the story in Fitz's ancestry about the king's champion who had won an heiress as his bride. Coldmoore House became simply Carrisford.

Both houses would provide enough space for Fitz's sisters to live with them, even when there were children. Once the dowager marchioness had set off for France, Ashart and Fitz had moved to Ashart's London house, and Ashart had welcomed Fitz's sisters there, too. Of course, Genova and Damaris spent a great deal of time there, so Damaris was coming to know Libby and Sally.

Sally was nervous of new things, but easily pleased. Damaris had insisted on providing money for three servants to care for Sally so that Libby could enjoy society. Libby was wary as yet, as if unable to trust the turn of fortune, but sometimes she laughed in a way that hinted at the delightful child she'd once been. With God's grace, she would heal.

Both Sally and Libby were in Damaris's bedchamber on her wedding morning, ready to be her attendants.

Sally was dancing around in her fine yellow gown. Libby was shy in the company of the Malloren women. Lady Thalia and Lady Arradale were present, along with Lord Bryght Malloren's wife, Portia, and the Countess of Walgrave, who had been Lady Elfled Malloren.

Damaris's new family had made her wonderfully welcome, especially by treating Fitz almost as a family member, too.

Fitz.

They had talked so much over the past weeks, and though Damaris had been impatient at times to be wed, she'd appreciated the time to learn about each other more deeply. They'd even visited Cleeve Court, where Fitz had taken her around, recalling his past.

It was a solid house, though neglected, and they'd set in hand the plan to make it into an asylum for the insane. The kindly Dr. Erasmus had agreed to supervise it.

Hugh Fitzroger would never be happy in confinement, but there was no choice, for he continued to rave and threaten violence to all he saw as offending him. Lady Leyden seemed to find some sort of comfort in caring for him despite his ingratitude. Damaris could only pray for God's blessings on them both.

They hadn't visited Worksop yet, but they would, to sell the house and retrieve the few things Damaris wanted to bring into her new life. And to exorcise ghosts, she thought, for that life did seem like another one, a former one.

Here and now, all was laughter and teasing as her ladies assisted her to put on her gown, made for this occasion of Autumn Sunset silk and embroidered with a linked-ring design in tiny golden beads.

For contrast with her famous rubies and emeralds, she wore pearls that she had purchased for herself. Today she would wear nothing that came directly from her parents except, in a way, her wedding ring. She had given Fitz her mother's ring and asked him to have it remade, but with exactly the same words engraved inside: YOURS UNTIL DEATH. The words had also been engraved inside the cameo ring she'd given him. Together they would wipe away the past.

At the moment she wore only the betrothal ring he'd given her. It had caused considerable amusement. As she had enough precious stones, he'd commissioned a ring similar to the cameo she'd given him, but with a sailing ship carved upon it in exquisite detail—a ship flying the pirates' symbol, the skull and crossbones. It was perfect.

Fitz.

She suppressed a smile as people fussed with her hair, pinning pale gold roses into the complex weave of plaits. She could hardly wait to see him again—to pledge to be his and he hers forever. To seize her prize.

To let down her hair . . .

"You're smirking," Genova whispered.

Damaris laughed aloud and broke free of fussing hands to twirl around with Sally. "I'm going to float away soon. Isn't it time yet?"

Everyone laughed, but Diana slipped away to make sure all was in readiness in the grand ballroom of Malloren House. Damaris stood there jiggling simply because she couldn't stay still.

Then Diana returned. "All's ready. Their Majesties are here." She came over and kissed Damaris's cheek. "I can only wish you as much happiness as I have."

Lady Thalia fluttered over to hug Damaris. "So beautiful, my dear! And he's almost as good a man as my Richard. I shall cry during the ceremony, because I will be very happy and just a little sad, but you're not to mind me."

They all went out to where Damaris's brother, Mark, waited to escort her downstairs. She'd pondered this, for Rothgar could have performed the duty as suitably, but she wanted to break down all the barriers. Over the past weeks she and Mark had come to know each other quite well.

They might never be close, for they had little in common. His likeness to their father was all on the outside, whereas hers was more internal. He had been born and raised by a silly, indolent woman, whereas she had been shaped by sterner steel. She truly admired his amiability and lack of greed, but found him somewhat weak, too.

All this was as it might be with a full brother, however, so they would make do. She smiled as she took his arm and headed downstairs.

At last.

She paused at the door to the ballroom, which had been made into an arch of golden blossoms. A thousand candles lit the room, shooting fire from jewels and gold. She couldn't help grinning at the sight of Fitz, a shimmering figure in the cream-and-gold suit Ashart had worn for Christmas Day at Rothgar Abbey. They'd bought it off him, diamond buttons and all. Neither of them cared if anyone recognized it, for it was completely perfect for Fitz, especially with his blond hair unpowdered.

She walked toward him, needing to use all her willpower to do so slowly and steadily. She made herself turn her head a little to acknowledge the smiles of those nearby. So many people had become acquaintances and even friends during the winter season. She paused to curtsy deeply to the king and queen.

Then she had eyes only for Fitz. "My golden Galahad," she said softly as he took her hand, her heart pounding with pure bliss.

He raised her hand and kissed it. "I'd call you my ruby except that you're masquerading as a sunset. Say, rather, sunrise. You are my sun, Damaris. The light of my life. My new and everlasting day."

Tears prickled, but they were a sign of a happiness almost past bearing. "As you are mine, my love. My all, my everything. Oh, my, what need have we of vows after this?"

"We'd better make them all the same. Their Majesties await."

Startled by the reminder, Damaris cast an apologetic look at the king and queen, but both were smiling. Everyone was.

They plighted their troth in the traditional way and accepted the applause of their guests. Then music struck up, and they danced the minuet *à deux,* alone on the floor. Every touch, every look, spoke of love and desire, and Damaris grew weak with desire. How long must they perform this way before they were alone?

Not long after the dance the king and queen left. Then friends and family rescued them, bustling them away to their wedding-night chamber.

And there, at last, in urgency and in leisure, they plighted their troth and worshiped with their bodies, caressing with words and loving hands.

And later, much later, lying limp in Fitz's arms, kissing his beautiful clever hand and the ring she'd given him, Damaris said, "I'm glad you're a man of your word."

"What?" he asked, eyes heavy-lidded but smiling.

"You promised once to stand by me, and to make sure everything turned out as I wished." She wriggled up to kiss him. "I assure you, you have exceeded every expectation, my love, my champion, my perfect, handsome hero."

Dear Reader,

I hope you have enjoyed another book set in the Malloren world of the eighteenth century.

Readers often ask what the difference is between the Georgian and Regency periods. It's a very good question! Technically, the Georgian period is made up of the reigns of Kings George I, George II, George III, and George IV. However, for practical purposes it usually means the eighteenth century—1700 to 1799.

The "Regency" refers to the period from 1811 to 1820 during which the Prince of Wales was regent for his father, George III, who had gone mad. (This was almost certainly a disease called porphyria, but no one knew that then.) As the regent eventually became George IV, the Regency is part of the Georgian period, but it's treated as a distinct period, and generally thought of as 1800 to 1830 or so.

There are differences. Regency fashion put women in high-waisted, slender-skirted dresses, whereas Georgian dresses were shaped to the natural waist but with wide, hoop-supported skirts. Georgian gentlemen were peacocks in brilliant silks and flowing lace, which is one reason I love them. Regency gentlemen wore simpler clothing in more sober colors. Evening wear was almost universally black.

The Malloren world is the world of the early years of the reign of George III, and the time of true Georgian magnificence. It is also the world of great change and exploration in all areas. It was the Enlightenment, when all ideas were looked at afresh. This led to its being the time of the Agricultural and Industrial Revolutions. Change was seen as a good thing, and many members of the aristocracy were involved.

This didn't mean they were sober citizens. They saw no contradiction in someone being a glittering courtier, avid gambler, rakish wencher, scientist, agricultural innovator, and parliamentary orator. In fact, they'd think that a well-rounded gentleman.

I hope you found the idea about Prince Henry Stuart intriguing. It's all my own invention, of course, but I have long thought it sad that he died when he did. And, of course, the what-ifs of his not dying are fascinating.

If this is your first Malloren-world book, you may wish to read the others: *My Lady Notorious, Tempting Fortune, Something Wicked, Secrets of the Night, Devilish,* and *Winter Fire.* I also write novels set in the Regency and the Middle Ages.

For a complete listing of my books, please visit my Web site at www.jobev.com. While there, you can subscribe to my monthly e-mail list and be kept up-to-date about my new and reissued work. I think you'll find the background information to my books interesting, too.

If you prefer to write in the old-fashioned way, please do so, care of Margaret Ruley, The Rotrosen Agency, 318 East 51st Street, New York, NY 10022.

All best wishes, Jo

"Wickedly, wonderfully sensual and gloriously romantic."
—Mary Balogh

"A delicious...sensual delight."
—Teresa Medeiros

"One of romance's brightest and most dazzling stars."
—*Affaire de Coeur*

New York Times Bestselling Author
Jo Beverley

Available wherever books are sold or at www.penguin.com

S104/BeverleyList

Three romance classics in one volume from
New York Times bestselling author
JO BEVERLEY

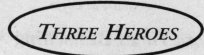

The Demon's Mistress
A wealthy widow hires a war-torn hero to pretend to
be her fiancé, but what will happen when he learns
the truth about the woman he has come to love?

The Dragon's Bride
The new Earl of Wyvern arrives at his fortress on the
cliffs of Devon to find a woman from his past
waiting for him—with a pistol in her hand.

The Devil's Heiress
No one needs Clarissa Graystone's fortune more than
Major George Hawkinville. Now he must ignore
the hunger in his heart as Clarissa boldly
steps into his trap.

0-451-21200-2

N598

New York Times bestselling author

Lisa Jackson

Impostress

Owing her sister a favor, Kiera of Lawenydd promises to pose as Elyn on her wedding day. The ruse is to last just one night, but the following morning, Elyn is nowhere to be found! Surely Kiera won't have to spend the rest of her life wedded to a man to whom she could never admit the depths of her deception—even as her desire for him grows impossible to resist.

0-451-20829-3

Available wherever books are sold or at
www.penguin.com

Penguin Group (USA) Inc. Online

What will you be reading tomorrow?

Tom Clancy, Patricia Cornwell, W.E.B. Griffin,
Nora Roberts, William Gibson, Robin Cook,
Brian Jacques, Catherine Coulter, Stephen King,
Dean Koontz, Ken Follett, Clive Cussler,
Eric Jerome Dickey, John Sandford,
Terry McMillan…

You'll find them all at
http://www.penguin.com

*Read excerpts and newsletters,
find tour schedules, and enter contests.*

Subscribe to Penguin Group (USA) Inc. Newsletters
and get an exclusive inside look
at exciting new titles and the authors you love
long before everyone else does.

PENGUIN GROUP (USA) INC. NEWS
http://www.penguin.com/news